PRAISE FOR JUDI FENNELL AND HER NOVELS:

"The opening . . . is one of the best hooks I've read. I don't know who could set it down after the first few pages . . . An excellent choice."   —Joey W. Hill, national bestselling author

"One of the most exciting and fun reads I have ever encountered."   —*Fresh Fiction*

"Phenomenally written novel . . . One of the best stories I have read this year, and I highly recommend it to anyone who loves a happy ending!"   —*Sizzling Hot Books*

"Will keep the reader enraptured."
                    —*Publishers Weekly* (starred review)

"I had a smile on my face and a sigh of contentment . . . lighthearted but full of emotion. The story stirred in me feelings of falling in love all over again. It was just downright enjoyable to read!"   —*That's What I'm Talking About*

"A light and breezy read for all . . . [Will] amuse the reader to the very last page. Well done, Judi Fennell!"
                    —*Night Owl Reviews*

"Rip-roaring fun from the very first page . . . This book is one for the keeper shelf."   —Kate Douglas, bestselling author

"A tale that shimmers, shines, sparkles, and sizzles."
                    —*Long and Short Reviews*

"Full of vivid imagination."   —*Seriously Reviewed*

"Sizzling sexual tension, plenty of humor, and a soupçon of suspense."   —*Booklist*

continued . . .

Titles by Judi Fennell

WHAT A WOMAN WANTS
WHAT A WOMAN NEEDS

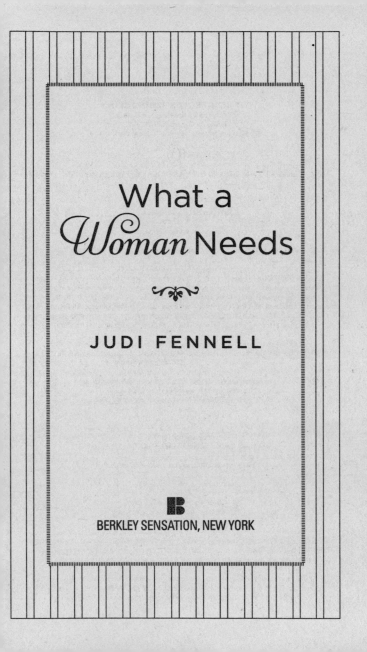

What a
Woman Needs

❧

JUDI FENNELL

BERKLEY SENSATION, NEW YORK

THE BERKLEY PUBLISHING GROUP
Published by the Penguin Group
Penguin Group (USA) LLC
375 Hudson Street, New York, New York 10014

USA • Canada • UK • Ireland • Australia • New Zealand • India • South Africa • China

penguin.com

A Penguin Random House Company

WHAT A WOMAN NEEDS

A Berkley Sensation Book / published by arrangement with the author

Berkley Sensation Books are published by The Berkley Publishing Group.
BERKLEY SENSATION® is a registered trademark of Penguin Group (USA) LLC.
The "B" design is a trademark of Penguin Group (USA) LLC.

For information, address: The Berkley Publishing Group,
a division of Penguin Group (USA) LLC,
375 Hudson Street, New York, New York 10014.

ISBN: 978-0-425-26830-8

PUBLISHING HISTORY
Berkley Sensation mass-market edition / June 2014

PRINTED IN THE UNITED STATES OF AMERICA

10 9 8 7 6 5 4 3 2 1

Cover art by Daniel O'Leary.
Cover design by Judith Lagerman.
Interior text design by Kristin del Rosario.

To my children, as always.

And to the man who's been an inspiration for this story, thank you.

Guys' Night . . . Plus One

❧❧❧

H E'D lost.

Bryan Manley stared at the cards on the table in front of him.

Straight flush. Jack high.

It beat his full house. It beat Liam's four queens and Sean's nine-high straight flush.

He'd lost.

To his *sister.*

The one who'd never played poker.

And she'd not only beaten him, but all *three* of them. Mary-Alice Catherine Manley had beaten the Manley men at their own game.

And now they were going to have to play hers.

Bryan cleared his throat, disgust burning the back of it. He, leading man, paparazzi fodder, starlet heartbreaker, and *People* magazine's Next Biggest Thing, was going to be someone's maid.

"I believe, dear brothers, you all need to be fitted for Manley Maids uniforms," Mac said as if it weren't the death knell on his image.

"I'm not wearing an apron." The words were out of his mouth before he'd even thought that far, but it just proved his instincts were right on. Every director he'd ever worked with had said so, and Bryan was damned glad for it right now.

An apron. Christ. The tabloids were going to have a field day with this. His agent? Not so much.

Interestingly, none of the brothers tried to talk Mac out of this ridiculous pay-up. They'd made their bets and lost fair and square.

But, Jesus. A maid.

"When do you want us to start, Mac?" Liam was the first to recover—if that's what it could be called.

"Whenever you can. I've got the business."

If Bryan didn't know Mac any better, he'd swear she was trying not to laugh. But that wouldn't be like Mac; she'd always idolized the three of them. Called them her knights in shining armor. Or football pads on occasion. But never this. Never an . . . an *apron*.

He'd swear it was a joke, but Mac had bet the only thing that could come anywhere close to what he and his brothers had bet: four weeks of cleaning service if she lost, four weeks of indentured servitude if she won. She wouldn't risk her business for a joke.

"I've got the time now. I'll get started first thing Monday." Sean stacked the poker chips. Meticulously, which was the only indication of Sean's emotions. He was pissed. At himself, probably. They'd gone against their instincts, all of them, and had let her play when she couldn't afford the stakes.

The fact that they were the ones paying was immaterial. They'd been protecting Mac, their baby sister, for pretty much all of her life since their parents had died and Gran had taken them in. They should have stuck to their No Girls rule for this game, but she'd wanted in so bad and they'd all always been pushovers for her that they'd let her.

And now she was going to be their boss.

A maid. God.

The one plus was it looked like Gran's cleaning lessons were going to pay off. Their grandmother had had her hands full with four young kids, and he and his brothers especially, had been pretty rowdy and messy.

He never would've thought he'd be grateful for those lessons. Hell, he even had Monica, his own maid from Mac's company, to keep his condo in shape just so he *wouldn't* have to dust off those cleaning lessons.

"Hey, can I do my place?" Kill two birds with one stone, so to speak, though the PETA people would probably take issue with that.

Mac frowned at him. "You'd put Monica out of a job to weasel out of the bet? Really?"

When she put it like that . . .

"I'm not weaseling out of anything." That's all he'd need the tabloids to pick up on. "You can count me in for Monday, too. I've got some time between projects and was looking for something to do anyhow." He'd hoped it would've had something to do with a certain actress, a beach, and a couple of Heinekens, but that wasn't going to happen now. At least he'd be out of the public eye for a while; maybe he could pull this off without anyone getting wind of it.

Yeah, and Gran was going to up and leave her new place for the mansion he'd been wanting to buy her, too.

Chapter One

❦

BETH Hamilton tripped over a big, yellow, hard-as-all-get-out toy truck, banged her shin on the coffee table, slipped on a page of shiny stickers, and landed butt-first in a basket of dirty laundry.

Again.

It'd be hysterical if it weren't so common.

She was constantly tripping over things. Constantly swerving one way to avoid an incoming wet dog or the twins chasing each other with lightsabers, only to end up on her butt anyway.

The sad part was, she had enough padding there that the falls didn't do a lot of damage to her body—not like the extra padding did to her self-esteem.

But then, what widowed mother of five could afford self-esteem? Especially when one of the five had attained teenager status, another was fast approaching, and the twins came up with daily nicknames for her from their favorite sci-fi movies—Princess Leia not being among them. No, she got stuck with names like Frodo, Chewy, and the ever-popular Voldemort. At least they hadn't gone for Barney. Yet.

Thank God for Maggie. The five-year-old still thought Mom could do anything.

If only she could.

The clock on the mantel chimed ten. Great. The cleaning service was going to be here any second and her house looked like a tornado had hit it. Tornado Hamilton. It came through on a daily basis. Sometimes twice just for kicks.

She needed help.

"Jason, did you finish straightening up your room?" She picked his remote-control helicopter off the hardwood floor where he'd crash-landed it, wincing at the nick the rotor blades had made. They'd probably done the same thing to her shin.

"Uh-huh." Jason muttered from somewhere beneath the mop of hair he called *cool*, but which she called a bowl cut. If she'd given him that hairstyle as a toddler, she'd never hear the end of it whenever she pulled out baby pictures, yet he'd actually *wanted* her to pay someone to do that to him. *Teenagers*.

"Your laundry is put away and the bed made?" Yes, she knew it was silly to clean up before the cleaning service arrived, but if the woman got a look at her house now, she'd either take off or double her fee. Maybe even triple it.

"Uh-huh."

Odds were Jason's *uh-huh* should be *nuh-uh*, but Beth had too much to do down here to run up the stairs to check out his story.

And Jason knew it, too.

Beth sighed. It'd been two years since Mike's death and while the kids had seemed to sprout right before her eyes, every day of those two years seemed to last longer than their allotted twenty-four hours.

What she wouldn't give for Prince Charming to ring her doorbell.

BRYAN ran his finger under the collar of the golf shirt and adjusted his hold on the bucket of cleaning products while he seriously contemplated not ringing the doorbell of Mrs. Beth Hamilton's home.

He was a freaking maid. A *maid*!

He checked over his shoulder. No one had seen him yet, unless the tabloids had sent out a slew of covert reporters—and the likelihood of that was on par with those alien abduction stories they wrote about. No, those people were like dogs with a bone and they traveled in packs. He'd never miss them.

Still, he tapped the rim of the baseball cap down another half inch. Not technically part of the Manley Maids mint green polyester nightmare of a uniform, but he didn't care. His face and build were recognizable enough; he needed some protection from prying eyes—

Like the ones staring at him from behind the sheer curtain on the sidelight beside the door.

Snagged.

Taking a deep breath and straightening his shoulders, Bryan bit the bullet and rang the bell.

Instantly a chorus of barks, shrieks, and a couple of "*Expelliarmus!*" spells erupted, followed by a nasty crash and some muttered cursing.

Then *she* opened the door.

For a moment, Bryan just stared.

Then his PR training kicked in and he ramped up the Charmer smile that was not only his signature look, but one that came naturally around beautiful women.

And *she* was stunning. From her artfully messy, wavy brown hair, to the curves just hinted at beneath the open neckline of the misbuttoned blouse, to the yoga pants that hugged shapely legs that went on forever, the woman was almost as tall as he was and built like a woman should be, rounded in all the right places with just enough to hold on to for the ride of a lifetime.

Maybe this wasn't going to be such a bad gig after all.

Then the kids hit the scene, heads popping out behind her like some dance number in a musical.

And they didn't *stop* popping. Three. Four. Five. She had her own basketball team.

Bryan reined in the smile. He didn't hit on married women, and he didn't hit on moms.

He especially didn't hit on married moms.

Of five.

"Who are you?" Kid number two, or maybe three, asked.

"Honestly, Kelsey, that's no way to greet someone." The woman rolled her gorgeous coffee-colored eyes as she flicked her finger under the girl's chin, then she wiped away her annoyed look and smiled at him.

This time his Charmer smile appeared of its own volition. Bryan couldn't help it. When she smiled, she was beyond stunning, and it made him glad he was a man—but annoyed she was married.

And a mom.

Of five.

"Can I help you?"

Let me count the ways. Bryan caught himself before he started spouting sonnets. "I'm here to clean your toilet."

Way to go, idiot. Brilliant opening line.

"I beg your pardon?"

She could beg for whatever she wanted, and he'd give her every single thing.

Bryan cleared his throat. "I'm a Manley Maid."

The shaggy kid snorted before he walked away, the picture of utter teenage disinterest.

Bryan rephrased his intro. "I mean, I'm Bryan. I work for Manley Maids. You hired us to clean for you?"

"*You're* the maid?" The little girl tugging on her mom's shirttails had no idea she was in danger of popping Mom's button and giving Bry a glimpse of something that, in any other circumstance, he'd be thrilled to see. And Bryan wasn't about to educate the kid.

But *she* was married.

And a mom.

Of five.

The other teenager lost interest and the younger two—twins from the look of them—took their crooked wands back into the den, leaving him and Mrs. Beth Hamilton alone with a preschooler.

Where was *Mr.* Beth Hamilton?

Bryan put his game face on. He'd dated dozens of beautiful women. Had slept with a lot of them. Beautiful women were a dime a dozen in his world.

But he wasn't in his world anymore. He was in Mac's and Mrs. Beth Hamilton's, and he better play the part before she either cited him for sexual harassment or failure to deliver. Either one would do more damage to his public image than being caught in a maid's outfit would.

He'd like to see her in a maid's outfit—

"Yes, I am the maid." He tapped the little girl's nose. "Do you need something cleaned?"

Big brown eyes blinked up at him. Solemn and serious. "Uh-huh. My castle. Mrs. Beecham made a mess."

Bryan looked toward Mrs. Beth Hamilton for translation.

"Our cat likes to take naps in Maggie's dollhouse and tends to leave enough fur to weave a rug, but we haven't read Rapunzel yet, so that's not happening."

Rapunzel. Wasn't she the one with the hair and the tower—an image Bryan did not need as he looked at Mrs. Beth Hamilton's shoulder-length, windblown hair.

He liked it like that, not fake, photo-shoot windblown hair. Mrs. Hamilton had come by her messy hair naturally and there was something about that kind of unselfconsciousness and abandon that just screamed *sexy* to Bryan.

To Mr. Beth Hamilton, too, if the guy had an ounce of red blood in his veins and, considering there were five little Hamiltons running around, apparently he did. And unfortunately for Bryan, that guy had every right to fantasize about everything Bryan did not.

It was going to be a long four weeks.

Chapter Two

❧❧

OKAY, maybe a woman *could* be Cinderella twice in one lifetime because Prince Charming had definitely walked through her door.

Prince *Bryan Manley* Charming, local boy turned Hollywood heartthrob. And he'd just walked through her door to clean her toilets?

Beth pinched herself. This was insane. It had to be a gag. Was someone punking him? But shouldn't she be in on the joke if they were?

She waved him in and looked around outside. No cameras. But they had to be there.

She stuck a hand up to her hair. Figures. The one day she didn't take the time to do her hair was the day she was going to show up on national television. Again.

She ran a hand down the front of her shirt and found a wet spot that she hoped was just Sherman's wet snout mark and not a stain. Knowing the dog, however, she wouldn't be surprised if it was both.

She looked down and groaned. Her shirt wasn't buttoned properly. God, she was a mess. Looked like her friends were right; she *did* need help around the house.

Well, of *course* she did—of the permanent kind—but this splurge the girls had gone in on to hire a housekeeper seemed to be just the thing in the interim.

Especially since they'd somehow finagled *Bryan Manley* for the job.

"Aren't maids thupposed to be girls?" Maggie slurped around her thumb. Beth had tried to break her of the habit before Mike's accident, but afterward . . . well, it'd just seemed cruel. The little girl needed whatever comfort she could get.

Brian hunkered down to Maggie's level. "Boys can be maids, too. Just like girls can be doctors and lawyers and even truck drivers."

"Or pilots. My daddy was a pilot and he told me I can be one when I grow up."

Beth winced at the past tense in that sentence. And at the thought of Maggie dying like Mike had. To this day, the thought of getting on a plane gave her an anxiety attack.

"You definitely can be a pilot when you grow up. Or how about an astronaut?" Bryan stood up and Beth caught his quick glance to her left hand.

She knew what he'd see: nothing. Her ring mark was finally gone. She'd taken it off on the two-year anniversary of the crash, finally facing the fact that Mike wasn't coming back and nothing would be the same again. None of the kids had commented on it, though she'd caught Kelsey looking at her empty finger more than once.

She sighed, preparing herself for the questions. *Divorced?* was usually their first question, accompanied by a commiserating smile that wavered when she answered, *Widowed,* and completely disappeared when she added in the bit about five kids. No surprise there wasn't a new ring on her finger.

"I guess," Maggie said, her thumb migrating to her belt loop. That was the quickest Beth had ever seen her daughter lose the comfort mechanism around someone new. "But the moon's kinda boring. All gray and rocky and stuff. I wanna be a teacher. Like my mommy."

A wet hand slid into Beth's. The trust that small gesture implied never failed to humble her.

"What do you teach?" Bryan asked as he stood up, and there was no doubt in her mind what had made this guy a movie star.

Wavy chestnut hair just begging for her fingers to run through it and gorgeous green eyes that made her forget her hair was a mess, or that she had a stain and a cockeyed shirt, or that there were five children, a dog, and two hamsters running around the place—oh, crap. The hamsters were still in their rolling balls somewhere around here. If Sherman got wind of them . . .

Beth lost her smile really fast. "I'm sorry. Will you excuse me?" She knelt down to whisper to Maggie about the hamsters.

Her daughter shrieked then ran away, which sent Sherman howling after her.

Those hamsters would be lucky to make it until dinner—and not *be* dinner.

She brushed a hank of hair back off her forehead. So much for having a movie star in her house. He was probably wondering what he'd gotten himself into. "I'm sorry. Trying to ward off a catastrophe." Number seven for the day. A new low. But the day wasn't over yet. "I'm Beth Hamilton."

She held out her hand and had to keep from swooning when he shook it. Charisma radiated off this guy like smoke from a campfire on a cool crisp night. Though there was nothing cool about his touch. It lit a fire under Beth's skin that she'd almost forgotten existed.

She yanked her hand away. She might have removed her wedding band, but she wasn't ready for *that* yet. Of course, could she really be blamed? He was, after all, *Bryan Manley.* The next Sexiest Man Alive if the magazine covers bearing his photo in the supermarket checkout lines were any indication.

"I'm Bryan, uh, Man—"

"I know who you are." Who didn't? "My question is, what are you doing here?"

He held up a bucket of cleaning supplies. "You hired a maid, right? I'm here to do your bidding."

Oh the smile that accompanied that statement. The man was a natural flirt.

"Are you sure you're up for this?"

He arched an eyebrow. She'd seen that look in his last movie right before the love interest had fallen for him. Beth had understood why the moment it'd happened on screen, but here, in the flesh . . .

Zero to full-out fantasy mode in under two seconds.

"Hey, it's like I told your daughter. Guys can clean just as good as women."

"Oh, I didn't mean it like that. I meant, are you sure you're up for *this*?" She swept a hand toward the family room.

Sherman had run through the clothesline again and dragged it in from outside. It was a favorite trick of his to jump up, grab hold of the lowest-hanging article, twist midair, and bring the whole thing floating down around him, then drag it all around the yard. Of *course* today would be the day he decided to drag it through the house for the first time.

Mike had wanted a Jack Russell terrier. She'd wanted a basset hound. But the dog had been his idea to give the kids for Christmas, and with all the energy the kids had, it'd seemed fitting at the time to give them a high-energy dog. Now? Notsomuch.

"Uh . . . Did you guys have a flood or something? Tornado?" Bryan Manley's sexy, flirty look turned perplexed real quick.

Beth smiled and walked over to the sofa to shove her panties behind a pillow. From now on, they were going in the dryer or hanging in her bathroom to dry. "Tornado Hamilton. It happens at least once a day here."

"Mom!" Mark came barreling into the room, his lightsaber leading the charge. "Tommy's cheating!"

"I am not!"

"Are too!"

"Am not!"

"Are too!"

"D2!" Bryan dodged the swinging blades and somehow managed to pluck them from their hands.

"Huh?" the twins asked in tandem as they often did.

"R2-D2." Brian set the plastic swords on the bookshelf behind him. "Don't tell me you guys are fighting with lightsabers and don't know who R2-D2 is."

"Of course we do," said Tommy. "He's Luke's servant."

"He is?" Bryan put a hand behind the boys' shoulders and led them away from the shelf. "I thought he was his friend."

"Well," said Mark, "he started out his servant but ended up as his friend."

"And why is that do you suppose?"

"'Cause Luke needed him lots of times and R2 came through for him," answered Tommy.

They weren't finishing each other's sentences yet, but the consecutive answers were a sign they were back on the same side and the bickering was over.

"Ah." Bryan kicked a pillow out of the way and one of the hamster balls rolled with it. Beth scooped it up and set it in the planter before Sherman got a whiff. "I bet you guys have that happen with you, huh? One of you gets in trouble and the other helps him out?"

"Tommy's always getting in trouble." Mark crossed his arms and nodded smugly.

So much for the end of the bickering.

"Am not."

"Are too."

"Am—"

"Guys. Hang on." Bryan took off his hat, cleared three T-shirts off the sofa, then steered the boys onto it. Then he handed Beth the semi-frozen, half-empty ice cream tub from the coffee table and sat on the edge across from them. Good thing the table was made of sturdy oak; she didn't want to have Bryan Manley sprawled all over her family room.

Her bedroom on the other hand—

Beth's mouth almost fell open. *What* was she thinking?

Well, okay, she knew what she was thinking, but the question was *why* was she thinking it? With all the dates her friends had set her up with over the last few months, she hadn't wanted to even think about *kissing* one of the men, much less have them sprawled across her—

Yes, there it was. That image. The one from the first movie she'd ever seen Bryan in, all slick and wet, coming out of the ocean with his camo shorts hanging below a killer set of abs.

She forced herself to pay attention to what he was telling her boys. What kind of mother was she to let an essential stranger work out her sons' daily midmorning argument while she drooled over him as he did it?

"It's much easier to look in front of you than behind you, so if you stay loyal to each other, you'll never have to watch your back because your brother will be doing it for you while you're doing it for him."

"Just like you and your brothers do," the boys said in tandem.

"Exactly." He ruffled their hair and Beth could see their

shoulders straighten. Their posture get a little taller. The smiles spread across their faces.

It'd been a while since anyone—any *man*—had talked with them like this. Mike's father hadn't dealt well with his son's death, electing to almost pretend it'd never happened, and her family . . . well, her stepfather wasn't exactly the role model she wanted her sons to emulate. Bryan's five minutes in her house showed her just how much the boys needed a man in their life.

Bryan met her gaze and winked. "So, guys, now that you're watching out for each other, you know who else you have to watch out for?"

"Our teacher?"

"Sherman?"

"Johnny Tyler," said Tommy. "He's a bully."

"No, Janey Weston. She's gross."

"Yeah, you're right. Janey's gross."

Bryan stood up, put his hands on the boys' heads, and swiveled them her way. "No, boys. You have to watch out for your sisters and your mom. It's a guy's job to take care of the women he loves."

Thank God Beth had something cold in her hand or she just might have melted on the spot.

S HE wasn't saying anything.

Bryan hoped that was a good thing, but in his experience, when a woman said nothing, it spoke louder than if she yelled at him. Or *Fine*'d him. He'd come to dread that word from a woman. Yet here he was, giving her boys life advice as if he had every right.

Where the hell was Mr. Beth Hamilton and why wasn't *Mrs. Beth Hamilton* wearing a ring?

"Yo, Beth, I—*whoa*." The shaggy-haired kid did a double take and skidded to a stop, his sneakers leaving skid marks on the hardwood floor.

God, now Bryan was even *sounding* like a maid.

"Hey, wait a minute. Aren't you—"

"Yeah, I am, and she's your *mom*, not *Beth*." Kid ought to be grateful he had someone around to call *Mom*.

"Bryan, it's okay—"

"No, it's not." Bryan ran a hand through his hair. Shit. He

should have stayed out of this. "Look, I'm sorry. It's none of my business, but I was raised to treat a woman—especially one's mom—with respect. I get teenage rebellion with the . . ." He waved at the kid's hair and three-sizes-too-big jeans that were barely staying on with the no-belt-or-hip thing happening. "It was an automatic response. Your kid, your rules."

Beth had the best smile. Soft and sweet, it wasn't all toothy, flashy, look-at-me, but held genuine happiness that reached her eyes—and reached out to him, landing somewhere in the middle of his stomach with a big ol' *thud*.

Holy hell. When's the last time that'd happened?

"Thank you, Bryan. Those are my rules as well." She looked at her son. "Was there something you wanted, Jason?"

"I uh . . ." Jason glanced at him through a gap in his shag. "Kev's gonna take me to the mall."

"I don't think so."

"Aw, Mom—"

"Jason, you're fourteen. You are not going to be parading around the mall with a bunch of guys. Security looks for kids your age. I don't need to get a phone call."

"You won't."

"That's right. I won't. Because you're not going. You're staying here to do your room."

"Aw, Mom!" Proving he *was* only fourteen, Jason stomped his foot. "Isn't that what *he's* here for?" The hair swung Bryan's way.

Bryan arched an eyebrow at the kid. "Sorry, but I didn't pull hazmat duty." He'd been a teenage boy once; he knew what was in the kid's room. He hadn't liked cleaning his own disgusting mess, no way was he doing this one's.

"Aren't you, like, a big movie star or something?" The kid swept the hair off his forehead. It fell right back. "What are you doing here?"

Bryan called on all the acting ability he'd developed over the years because he wasn't about to admit *how* he'd gotten here. His publicist would be so proud of him. "I'm helping out my sister. She owns Manley Maids and my brothers and I are lending a hand." An indentured one, but still . . .

"Just write her a check, dude. That outfit is lame."

Dude? Who said *dude* anymore? Last Bryan had heard, no one was remaking *Fast Times at Ridgemont High*. Pity because that sleeper had a huge cult following and he wouldn't mind loyal fans like that.

"It's a uniform. I'm required to wear it on the job." But he got what the kid was talking about. This thing was a disaster. Pants that looked as if they'd come from the seventies—the color of a pistachio and just as nutty. He couldn't believe Mac had found golf shirts in the same color. And the black utility shoes . . . Hell, he could tell Mac that a better way to improve her profile in this town, rather than having the three of them cleaning for her, was to lose the stupid uniform.

He smiled. Well, yeah, naked male house cleaners *would* go over pretty well.

"And some people don't want handouts. My sister, for one. She's building a business and I'm giving her a hand. Speaking of . . . any chance you want to give your mom one and get to work on your room? That way, I can actually clean it."

Bryan glanced at Beth out of the corner of his eye to make sure he wasn't overstepping his bounds.

She was looking at her son expectantly.

Jason sighed. Seriously, the kid ought to go into acting. "Fine."

Bryan liked that word even less from teenagers than from women.

"Mom, can Maddy come over? We want to, um, look over our schedules for next year." The older daughter swung her head out of what Bryan presumed was the kitchen, her words directed at her mom, but her gaze directed at him.

Oh hell. He'd seen that look before. At every event he did. Teenage puppy lust. That could be a problem.

"Class schedules, huh? That's definitely important to go over during summer vacation." Beth glanced at him with a twinkle in her eye. "Are you up for *that*?" she asked. "You had to know this would happen when you ventured out among your adoring public."

For the first time, Bryan didn't like that term. It was what he'd always wanted, what he'd aspired to—adoring fans could make a career—but coming from Beth . . . No. Definitely didn't like it.

Unfortunately, there was nothing he could do about it. There were certain necessities that went along with fame, and being accessible to the people who paid good, hard-earned money to see his work was one of them.

"It's no bother. Your house, your rules."

She cocked her head, losing a hint of the smile, that twinkle being replaced by something . . . Thoughtfulness? Admiration?

He wouldn't mind it being the latter.

Seriously. Where the *hell* was Mr. Beth Hamilton?

"Mom?" Her daughter switched her focus to Beth. Finally.

"Just Maddy," Beth answered. "I don't need a house full of teenagers today, Kels."

Kels—Kelsey—smiled and, whoa, Mr. Beth Hamilton was going to have issues when that one got older. She had the beginnings of the same sort of beauty her mother had.

And still he envied the guy.

"But Alyson's in our classes, too. She should be here."

Bryan coughed and turned away. Teenage girls . . . Maybe he didn't envy Mr. Beth Hamilton.

But then Kelsey was off with a dazzling smile and Beth turned a more reined-in one his direction. It had the same wattage and lit a slow burn inside him.

He ran a finger under the collar of the stupid shirt. Besides the fact that she was married—and a mom *of five*—he didn't *do* suburbia. The only reason he'd gotten roped into this gig was because of the monthly poker game with his brothers, the one that he made a hell of an effort to get to no matter where on the planet he was. If he could get off the set for a few days, he made it back for the game. With his star power rising, his agent said that time off might now be a negotiable item. But if future games ended up with him pulling maid duty, he was going to have to rethink that clause.

The poker game was the *only* reason he came back to town. It gave him a chance to see Gran, Mac, and his brothers, but he'd take the glitz and glamour of the South of France or LA or, hell, any location that didn't remind him of the hand-me-downs and the small run-down house where their grandmother raised them and that his sister still lived in. No, if it weren't for his family, he'd never come back to this town again.

Unless I had someone like Mrs. Beth Hamilton waiting for me.

Where the *hell* had that thought come from? She was married. And a mom. Of five. *Married.* He'd never hit on a married woman in his life and, gorgeous as she was, he wasn't going to start now.

And even if she *wasn't* married, beauty wasn't enough to get him to chuck the high life and his hard-earned success to wallow in the drudgery of mowing lawns and little league games with the occasional block party tossed in. God save him from suburbia.

"Are you sure you're all right with this?" Beth asked. "I could tell her no."

"Don't. Like I said, your house, your rules. I'm used to it. I'll sign a few autographs and that'll be it."

Beth arched an eyebrow at him. "You obviously don't know teenage girls."

"I do have a sister."

"Was she ever around a movie star before?"

"Well, no, but—"

"Exactly. I'll try to run interference, but you might want to consider a not-so-form-fitting outfit next time."

Damn if that slow burn didn't flare into a full-on raging inferno. She'd noticed his body.

He was damn proud of that body. Cost him five hours every freaking day of the last movie and a diet that left a lot to be desired. He'd lost some of the muscle and added some fat in the three weeks since it'd wrapped, so it was nice to know the body was still notice-worthy.

"This is kind of, you know, the uniform."

"Yeah, I know." She ran her eyes over him.

Where the *hell* was Mr. Beth Hamilton? Seriously, the guy needed to put in an appearance like pronto or Bryan couldn't be held accountable for jumping his wife. She was *that* hot.

"You do know boys, though, I have to say. Thank you for handling Mark and Tommy. Ever since . . ." She glanced toward the wall on the other side of the room. "Well, I appreciate you talking to them."

He followed that glance.

There, above the fireplace, was a picture. Of a man. In uniform. With a triangular wood-and-glass case on the shelf below it. An American flag was folded up inside.

All feeling left Bryan's body, draining out through his feet into a puddle, taking his stomach with him.

He knew what that was. What it meant.

It was Mr. Beth Hamilton's memorial.

Mrs. Beth Hamilton was a widow.

And Bryan was in a heap of trouble.

Chapter Three

❧⁕❧

BRYAN had never thought he'd be so happy for five kids as he was at this very moment.

Then five morphed to seven. And a crazy dog. Two hamsters. Some cat that the crazy dog was chasing through the house, one harried mom, and a neighbor asking for the proverbial cup of sugar amid a slew of phone calls where Beth kept saying she'd have to call them back.

Word had gotten out.

He was betting it was the daughter or her friends. One tweet and his anonymity had disappeared.

Bryan smiled at the measuring-cup-bearing neighbor while he hightailed it—with his bucket of cleaning supplies and an official Manley Maids broom (seriously? Mac had spent money to have *broom handles* imprinted with the Manley Maids logo?)—into the kitchen.

More chaos.

Maggie had decided to have a tea party.

Six dolls and stuffed animals were seated around the kitchen table, each with a place setting in front of it, with every snack she could drag off the bottom three shelves in the pantry set out before them—all of which the manic cat had charged through, sending most of it flying onto the floor in the most impressive arc of junk food he'd ever seen.

And guess who has to clean it up?

Bryan rolled his eyes, set down the bucket, and put the logo-ed broom to good use.

"Sherman's a bad dog." Maggie slid from her chair and stood next to him, a very thoughtful expression on her face as she looked at the pile of snacks he was amassing.

"Not bad. Just easily excited."

"Everything okay in here—oh no." Beth's gorgeous face made an appearance at the kitchen door.

And Bryan's stomach flipped right along with it.

Oh no was right. Talk about easily excitable . . . Bryan had come into this room to get away from the pull Beth had on him, so *of course* she'd followed him in. Ever since he'd sat down at that damn poker table with Mac his luck had evaporated.

"Maggie, what did I say about the snacks in the pantry?"

"That they're for guest-es. Those are my guest-es." The little girl's thumb went into her mouth and she took a step closer to Bryan, her tiny shoulder brushing up against his thigh.

Bryan's heart cracked just a bit.

He put his hand on that shoulder. "I think your mom means you need to ask her before you open them, Maggie. She has to plan what she's going to buy when she goes food shopping or she won't have enough when she needs it."

"Oh." The thumb-sucking got a little more manic. "Sorry, Mommy."

"It's okay, sweetheart, but Bryan's right. Ask me next time, okay?"

"I will." She pulled her thumb out and turned that sweet face his way. "Can I ask you? Do you go food shopping?"

Knowing that her father was gone, Bryan had a feeling he'd do whatever Maggie asked him to. "Sure. I can do that."

"'Kay. We're gonna need more snacks if Jason's buddies come over."

"Jason's buddies aren't coming over." Beth took the broom from him and squatted down to scoop the pile into the dustpan.

Bryan dropped to his knees beside her. "Here, let me."

"It's okay, I can do—"

Their hands met. Then their eyes. Bryan was seriously

considering putting their lips in touch with each other as well until Maggie poked her face between them.

"Yes they are. I heard him telling Kevin that a big movie star was here. They're all coming."

Beth slicked her tongue over her bottom lip. Quickly. But not so quickly that Bryan missed it.

She also glanced away. But not before he saw the flare of interest in her eyes.

How long had Mr. Beth Hamilton been gone?

And was he a dog for even wondering?

Speaking of which, the damn speckled bullet of a canine darted in from the hallway, made a beeline for the pantry that Beth managed to shut with the broom handle, then zipped over to the pile of scooped up snacks and started chowing down before Bryan had registered the thing was that close to him.

Of course he missed the dog when he lunged for it. The terrier managed to escape with a mouthful of treats and dragged the box of Goldfish Maggie had dropped.

Bryan slammed a foot onto the box with a thousand tiny crunches, but at least the dog let go. Right before it took off again.

Beth sighed and stood up, brushing her hands off on her thighs—which left her orange fingerprints right where he wouldn't mind his being.

He seriously needed to get laid. And not by Mrs. Beth Hamilton, no matter how much he wanted it.

"*Are* you a movie star, Bryan?" Maggie tugged on his ridiculous pants.

A curl had fallen onto her forehead. He brushed it back. "I'm an actor, Maggie. I work in films."

"Do you know Nemo? I like his movie."

"Nemo's a cartoon, runt." Jason schlumped into the kitchen. "Bryan here, he's bigger than that. He knows all the important people, don't you? Like Bradley Cooper and Spielberg, right? You get lots of hot chicks, too, I bet."

"Jason!" Beth's mouth dropped open as if she couldn't believe her little boy could know such things.

Bryan didn't have the heart to tell her all a fourteen-year-old boy *did* know. Or what he wanted to know. That's what dads were for.

And, like him, Jason didn't have one, either. Bryan knew *exactly* how Jason was feeling.

"Haven't met Spielberg." Cooper was another story, but not one he could leak to the media yet. And given how quickly word had gotten around about him being here, he figured the Twitterverse was alive and thriving in the Hamilton household, so he wasn't about to breathe a word to the teenagers. And as for the "hot chicks"—what was with this kid's vocabulary?— his grandmother had raised him to be a gentleman. He didn't kiss and tell. Besides, he hadn't gone out with all the women who were claiming he had. He let them say so, though, because it generated buzz. Helped both of their careers.

"So do you mind if, you know, I have some buddies over? They want to meet you."

Bryan nodded toward Beth. "That's a question you need to ask your mom. It's her house and I'm here on her dime. Not up to me."

Jason straightened and swung the roof of hair off his forehead. "Mom, any chance Kev and the guys could come over?"

Amazing how the kid's attitude changed when he wanted something from Beth.

But Beth wanted something from *him* if that desperate look in her eyes was anything to go by—and it wasn't what he wanted from her.

Bryan shrugged. "Up to you. Like I said, I'm used to it. Better to get it over with anyway."

"Is your room finished?"

"Aw, Mom—"

"You want something from Bryan and me, you need to give back. And it's in your best interests, Jase. You can't live in a mess like that."

Actually, yes, he could. Bryan remembered it well—well, for about half a day before Gran had put her foot down. The reverberation of his grandmother's will had been felt through the entire tiny house without her even raising her voice.

"Fine." Jason blew out an exasperated breath, dropped his head so the hair was covering his eyes, and shuffled back out the way he came. "They'll be here in a half hour."

"Then you better get moving." Beth swished the back of her son's hair as he walked out of the room.

"Can I invite some friends over? Kelsey's having some and now Kevin. And Mark has Tommy and I don't have anyone. Even Mrs. Beecham's gone because of Sherman."

Ah, the cat of the fabled dollhouse decorating; that's who Sherman had been chasing.

"Maggie, we don't need any more people in this house. And we'd have to invite their moms and I don't think Bryan's up for meeting more people. Can we hold off for another day? I can come to your tea party."

"No you can't. You're too busy. You're always too busy."

Guilt sliced through Beth faster than a hot knife through butter—but just as painful. It was true; she *was* always busy. Ever since Mike had died, she'd had to be both mother and father, and those were full-time jobs. Then there was her *actual* full-time job, and, hell, how was she supposed to do three full-time jobs *and* keep up with the house and the laundry and the yard and the animals and the food shopping and the bills and—

"Your mom's busy taking care of you and your brothers and sister, Maggie." Bryan took Maggie's hand and led her back to the kitchen table. He hiked her into her chair and righted the half-dozen tea cups Mrs. Beecham had run through. Then he poured out a small helping of the remaining Chex Mix onto each plate, and even plunked a tiara on his head just to distract Maggie from her loneliness.

Yes, Bryan was quite good at that.

Beth shook her head. She really had to get her thoughts back to reality. She didn't know why he was in this job, but she couldn't let it distract her. Life had to go on, and the time having a maid freed up could be put to so much better use than drooling over said maid.

But he *was* quite drool-worthy.

Had Kara known who she and the girls would be hiring when they'd contracted with the cleaning company? Everyone knew, of course, that Mary-Alice's brother was *the* Bryan Manley. There'd been a few sightings of him over the years since he'd made it big. She hadn't known him back when he'd been in high school, since she hadn't lived here then. Mike had moved them here after he'd left the Air Force to fly commercial planes, but she'd heard the stories. Star football player, Most Popular, good student, even the lead in the high school musical . . . The guy was golden.

And he was. From his bronzed muscles to his sun-kissed chestnut hair to the twinkle in his sparkling green eyes and the gleam of his gorgeous smile, the guy was the epitome of heart-throb. She'd have to be dead not to realize it.

She definitely wasn't. No, but Mike was—and for the first time since his death, she'd noticed a man.

It figured it'd have to be *this* man. Mr. Unattainable.

Who was here to clean her toilets.

There was some poetic justice in this world, apparently. Or at the very least, the universe had a sense of humor.

It'd be interesting to see if Bryan was still laughing when these four weeks were up.

Chapter Four

❧❦❧

TWELVE teenagers, their parents, and a few "drop-by" neighbors weren't too much of an intrusion as it turned out. Plus, Beth got to see a few people she hadn't seen since the funeral.

Had she really been busy for that long? Come to think about it, other than the monthly get-together her friends dragged her to at one of their homes, and the few disastrous dates they'd insisted she go on, the only times Beth had been out of the house were for school functions. Really, it was amazing she even knew who Bryan was, because she'd probably only seen one of his movies in the entire last two years.

But that one could get her through many lonely nights . . .

She shook off the image of him rising from that water like a god, sluicing his hair back off his forehead as the water rippled down his chest and abs. How his biceps had flexed and the shorts had hung low on his hips, the weight of the water dragging them down even further.

Bombs had been going off behind him, gunfire erupting all around him, but Beth's heart had tripled in speed solely because he'd been on that screen.

And now he was standing in front of her asking what more she wanted from him.

Let me count the ways . . .

"You're sure none of the bathrooms need cleaning? It *is* my job, you know. I actually came here to work."

"I know you did, and I thank you. But, really, I just did the bathrooms." Three days ago. But she didn't want anyone, least of all *the* Bryan Manley, seeing the havoc five kids and a menagerie could wreak on a bathroom. She'd clean those after the kids went to bed tonight. "You can get to them tomorrow. I can only imagine this isn't a normal day for you and you're bound to be tired."

He arched that one eyebrow that had the power to make masses of women swoon at once.

Geared toward just one woman, however, its effect was magnified. Beth had to poke her fingernail into her hamstring to remind herself where she was. And what her name was. But not what his was.

"But I barely got through anything today," he said, hiking the bucket of cleaning tools in his hand. Which caused his biceps to do that nice flexing thing she was so fond of. "And you do know that I can do other things besides clean, right? If there's something you need fixed . . . Handyman stuff."

Don't get her started on what he could be handy with . . .

"Trust me. It'll all be here tomorrow. Pretty much just as you found it today."

"Like *Groundhog Day*?" His smile was as potent as his flexing muscles.

"Yes, just like *Groundhog Day*." It figured his reference point would be a movie. Thankfully, that one hadn't been released in the past two years, so she actually knew what he was talking about. The only reason she even knew any of the current singing stars was because of Kelsey and Jason's love of their iPods and the portable speakers Mike's parents had bought them for Christmas.

Mike's parents. Oh, crud. The kids were supposed to spend one of the upcoming weekends with them at their shore house. They'd wanted a week, but Beth wasn't ready to give the kids up for that long. Sure, the kids were a lot of work and, yes, she wouldn't mind the break from the responsibility, but the truth was, she needed them just as much as they needed her. A weekend apart was all any of them could manage right now. She'd been both dreading it and looking forward to it since Donna had asked. She'd invited Beth, but they both knew Donna and John wanted and needed the time alone with their grandkids without their daughter-in-law around. Celebrate Mike's life instead of the constant reminder that he was gone with his widow hanging around. Beth got it and, really, she was fine with it, but no matter how much she tried to convince herself that she was looking forward to the peace and solitude of that weekend, it was a lie. It'd just give her more time to think about Mike being gone.

"Bryan!" Maggie came running out of the laundry room dragging a sock on her sneakers' Velcro closures, and threw herself into his legs. "You're coming back, aren't you? Tomorrow, right? You promised!"

Bryan, God love him, didn't hesitate, prying Maggie's little arms off and hunkering down to look her in the eye. "Of course I'm coming back. I told you I would. I'm just going to my house now. Work is done for the day."

"But we're not done. We live here. We can't go anywhere. Why can't you stay here? You could be my daddy now."

Silence.

Even the grandfather clock seemed to stop ticking.

Or maybe that was just because everything in Beth's body had gone numb.

Numb was good. Numb meant she couldn't feel pain.

Wrong.

It seared through her like a bolt of lightning. Her daughter wanted a father. God knew, Beth wanted her to have one. It wasn't fair that Maggie didn't have one. Wasn't goddamned fair.

She'd said that a lot in the past two years. But no one had promised her fair. Mike had often said that; that life wasn't fair. It'd been her mantra during the months after his death. And now . . .

"You'll always have your dad, Maggie." Bryan ran a hand over her hair. "I lost my dad when I was little, too, you know. You miss him being able to give you hugs and talk to you, but he'll always be with you right here." He touched Maggie's heart and Beth's throat closed up.

She had to look away, blinking like mad to keep from crying. She'd done so much crying. Too much.

"You'll never forget him and he'll love you forever. You just have to remember that when you get lonely, okay?"

Maggie scrunched her little face that was so much like Mike's it always took Beth's breath away. "That's what Grandma said, too. But he used to toss me in the air and now no one does. Mommy's not strong enough since I growed."

"Ah, well, that's easily fixed."

Bryan stood up, hiked Maggie up under her arms, and tossed her above his head.

Beth had never heard a sound so sweet as Maggie's laughing shriek.

"Do it again!"

Well, maybe that was just as sweet.

Bryan did it again. And again. And again.

He did it so much that tears of laughter were running down Maggie's little cheeks.

Tears of a whole different kind were running down hers.

"Aw, don't cry, Mommy. Bryan won't hurt me."

Beth knew that. She also knew he just might break *her* heart if she let him.

He glanced over with a worried expression. "Beth?"

She bit her lip and shook her head, clearing her throat to get the words out. "I'm fine. It's fine. Go right on—" She waved her hands and ran into the kitchen, mumbling something about dinner.

There was no dinner to see to. She hated cooking. Hated the planning and the preparing and the cleanup and who liked what and who had what practice and, oh God, she was going to fall apart again.

Beth gripped the edges of the countertop by her sink and sucked in a couple of ragged breaths. She should be over this by now. Or, at the very least, have a better handle on it, but the word *daddy* had the power to set her back eight hundred and eighty three days in one fell swoop.

It wasn't fair.

"It's not fair. I know." Bryan echoed her thoughts as he walked into her kitchen.

Beth glanced over her shoulder at him. It also wasn't fair how composed and put together and perfect he looked as she stood here, hunched over with bloodshot eyes she was sure, trying to catch her breath and still her racing heart while putting on a brave front for the kids.

"You don't have to be so brave." He was behind her now. "The kids will be okay. I know. I've been there."

That's right. She remembered something about him being raised by his grandmother. But he'd only carried *his* loneliness. She was carrying the kids' and hers. It was too much to bear. Too big of a burden. These past two years . . . She'd *gotten through* them; she hadn't *lived* them.

"Beth." Bryan's hands skimmed up her arms. He squeezed her shoulders gently. "It's okay to break down once in a while."

"No it's not. I can't." Her voice came out a hoarse whisper, but at least it came out.

He put some pressure on her shoulders and the next thing she knew, she was in his arms. Surrounded by him, his arms wrapping around her, safe and tight and blocking out the crushing pain in her soul. And when he pressed her face into his shoulder, when he gave her the permission to lean against him, it was almost her undoing.

She hadn't been held like this . . . since Mike. And she'd been carrying the burden ever since. The lone parent. The lone source of income. The only thing standing between her children and destitution or not having a family. Instability. She had to hang on. Every single day. There'd never been a respite and, oh God, it was hard. So hard to bear all the responsibility.

"Maggie's okay, Beth. She's going to be okay. All of you are." His words were soothing and so were the soft strokes against her hair.

Beth drew in a ragged breath and clamped her eyes shut, allowing herself to feel the warmth. To accept his comfort. If only for a few short moments, she needed this. Simple human contact and compassion. So easily taken for granted and so very much missed when it was ripped away by the fickle nasty whim of fate. Or sheer winds on an icy runway.

"It's okay, Beth. It's okay."

No it wasn't, but she wasn't going to argue with him. For this moment, now, here, she was going to take this from him.

She clutched the sides of his shirt, not quite willing to wrap her own arms around him, but she hung on. She buried her face into his shoulder, inhaling the warmth and scent of him. It'd been too long since she'd smelled that masculine scent. Too long since she'd felt strong arms around her, the tickle of his arm hair on her skin, the taut hardness of his abs against hers, the breadth of his shoulders harboring her from all the pain.

God, he felt good. So good. *Too* good.

Beth inhaled. One last time. That was all she needed. Just a moment more. A moment to compose herself. To settle her world back into its rightful order. Bryan didn't belong in that order and she couldn't forget it. He was being kind. Compassionate. Anything else she turned it into would just be foolish. But she'd always be grateful to him for this moment.

Another deep breath and she pulled back. "Thank you."

She cleared her throat and sniffed, thankful she hadn't gone all blubbery on him. It was one thing to allow a guy to comfort you, another to turn into a dishrag while he was doing so. Especially since the guy—for all she'd seen of him on screen and heard about him around town—was essentially a stranger.

But this stranger slid a hand beneath her hair and cupped her cheek, tilting her face to look into his. "It's okay, Beth. I can't imagine what you're going through, but I do understand what Maggie is. She needs her mom to be there for her and you're doing a great job. She's always going to miss him, but as long as she knows you love her and are here for her, she'll be okay. But don't forget to allow yourself to grieve, too. To feel the pain. You don't have to be a rock all the time."

He was right, she knew that, but the reality was that she could only be so strong and if she let her guard down, it might not come back up.

She licked her lips and swallowed, trying to rein in her careening emotions. "Thank you. For this. For . . . that. Tossing her. I didn't know she missed it so much."

"And you're not supposed to. You do other things for her. Don't forget that."

She worked a smile onto her face. Probably not her best, but then she wasn't exactly *at* her best right now. Probably had blotchy red cheeks and eyes brimming with tears and, hell, her nose was probably running. "I won't. Thank you."

He looked at her a little longer, his green eyes searching hers, his fingers tightening just a bit on her scalp, then he took a quick breath and let her go. "You'll be okay."

She would. The question was, when?

* * *

BRYAN didn't know how he managed to get out of there without embarrassing himself. He'd been *this* close to offering her comfort of another sort but sanity had reared its head and saved them both the awkwardness of that. Jesus. What was *wrong* with him? Okay, so she wasn't married, but still. A mother. Of five. Suburbia. And harboring a boatload of emotions for her dead husband that, even if she *was* ready to move on, would have him triple-thinking it even if he *was* interested in starting something with her. Which he wasn't. Not really. Sure, his body was all set to go, but Beth Hamilton wasn't made for a casual fling. Her kids certainly weren't and Bryan had been in their position. Knew what they were going through. The man who came into Beth Hamilton's life had better be not only prepared to take on five kids, but ready, willing, and able to do so. *He* was able, but the ready and willing parts? Not quite.

So he walked out of her kitchen, met all the kids' friends, finished his job for the day, and left the domesticity behind. He ruffled Mark's hair on his way out, gave the high sign to Tommy, returned Jason's nod, and gave Kelsey the Manley smile that would make her the envy of all her friends, his good deed for the day.

Beth stood at the front door with Maggie on her hip, waving as he pulled out of the driveway. Okay, so maybe the nod to Kelsey was his *third* good deed of the day.

Those deeds felt good. Not that that was why he'd done them. He'd heard the pain in Maggie's voice and it'd reached into his soul and twisted. He hadn't had anyone to toss him in the air. Hadn't had anyone to show him how to make a tree fort or mow the lawn or fix the bathroom sink when he'd leaned on it a little too hard. Life was tough enough; without a dad, it was even tougher.

Get off it already, Manley. You are not the kids' father.

Yeah, he knew it. Prided himself on not being *anyone's* father. Not until he was good and ready. And that meant a bank account hefty enough to cover any eventuality and a woman who'd be on board with his crazy lifestyle.

Chapter Five

❧❧

"WHERE'D you learn to do that?" Tommy asked for the sixth time since Bryan had arrived.

"I bet it's from a movie," said Mark. "I bet you were a supersecret agent who pretended to be a maid so he could learn the bad guy's plans, right?"

Bryan grabbed the wrench to turn the nut on the sink drain. "Right now I'm fixing the plumbing, guys, not cleaning." Yeah, it was semantics, but the meaning was important to him. He didn't want the guys to think this was a maid's work. It was plumbing, completely different.

Yeah, his masculinity was driving that sentiment. Sue him. Thankfully, Beth had taken him up on his handyman offer. He had to tell Mac—it'd be that extra *something* to set her company apart from her competition.

"Can you hand me the bowl? There might be some water in this trap and I don't want to end up wearing it."

They handed him a pink bowl. Covered in pictures of little white kittens.

So much for his masculinity.

Luckily for his ego, he managed a clean separation of the trap from the wall pipe with minimal leakage, directed the boys to hand him the new trap, and showed them how to replace it. Little fingers couldn't close the PVC nut tightly enough, so he made a few last-minute adjustments after they extricated themselves from the tight confines of the cabinet, the boys none the wiser that they hadn't done it all.

"What are you going to teach *me*, Bryan?" Maggie stood in front of him as he sat up from the uncomfortable position of lying partly in the cabinet and the bottom half of him on the kitchen floor.

His back hurt like a son-of-a-bi— "What do you want to learn, Maggie?"

"Mommy says girls should know how to change a tire. Can you show me? 'Cause she doesn't know how."

"Maggie, Bryan isn't here to do everything. I'll have Grandpa show you how to do it," *Mommy* said.

Maggie wrinkled her nose. "Grandpa smells funny," she whispered to Bryan. "And he's not our real grandpa, so I don't see why you can't show me." Maggie tapped his nose, then spun around to face her mother. "No thank you, Mommy. I want Bryan to do it."

Bryan got to his feet, wincing at the twinge in his back. Those stunts in Sri Lanka had pushed him almost beyond his limits and he was paying for it now. "It's okay, Beth. I don't mind. And if you don't know, I could show you, too. You're right; it's something everyone should know, not just guys."

"Can *we* learn?" asked Tommy.

"I already know how." Mark crossed his arms.

"Do not."

"Do too."

"Do not."

"Do t—"

"Guys." Bryan stepped between them. "Ten minutes. Driveway. Tire-changing lesson. Anyone who wants to learn, be there. Or don't call me when you get a flat. You'll have had your chance."

He strode out of the kitchen, flicking Beth on the chin as he passed. "That means you, too, cupcake."

"Cupcake? Did he call you cupcake, Mommy? That's silly." Maggie giggled.

Bryan wasn't giggling. He'd said it to be flippant, but, yeah,

Beth was as sweet and tempting as a cupcake. He wouldn't mind licking icing off her, either.

He took a deep breath and headed for Jason's room. Nothing like teenage-boy grunge to put his hormones on hold.

BETH reached for the kitchen chair once Bryan walked past her and sank into it. *Cupcake.* She ought to be offended. Disgusted. But all she could think of was Bryan licking icing off of her, one long, slow lick at a time.

"You feeling okay, Mommy?" asked Tommy.

"Yeah, you look kinda funny."

That's because she was having a hot flash and she didn't mean the menopause kind. Hell no. Bryan Manley could set her hormones buzzing with one glance, start them boiling with a word, and incite an inferno with a touch so insignificant that it shouldn't even be called insignificant.

"I'm fine, guys." Though that term was relative. "Why don't you go round up Kelsey and Jason? They could both use this lesson as well, since they'll be driving in a few years."

Wow. Thank God she was already sitting because that thought would have knocked her legs out from under her. Jason driving. He'd have to cut his hair first or he'd never pass the vision test. They frowned upon a kid having to look sideways and up from beneath his hair to drive.

Her baby driving. Wasn't it just yesterday that she'd brought that squalling bundle of energy home from the hospital? She and Mike had sat on the sofa with Jason between them and stared at each other, petrified out of their minds. What had they been thinking? They'd practically been kids themselves, yet there they were with the infant they'd created.

It hadn't gone too badly. It'd been chaos at first, a little more when Kelsey had come along, but by the time the twins were born, they'd found their rhythm. They were a good team. So when Maggie, the "oops," had arrived, she'd fit in seamlessly. Then fate had struck.

Beth inhaled and shoved the nightmare aside. The family counselor she took the kids to every few weeks—and who she saw on a few others—said not to dwell on *what ifs*. That *what ifs* got you nowhere. This was their reality and living in La-La Land would only do more damage than good.

Still, it was nice when she was alone to imagine what could have been. If Mike hadn't picked up that flight. If the weather had held off even a few more minutes. If they hadn't been late leaving the gate. There were a whole bunch of variables that had put him on the tarmac at that moment and any one of them could have changed the outcome, but the reality was, none had. Everything had conspired to put Mike and his passengers and crew at the wrong place at the wrong time, and she and the kids had to deal with it.

Still, life really sucked sometimes.

THE six of them gathered round Bryan's truck in her driveway, paying attention as he showed them where the jack was, how to set it up, how to remove the lug nuts and change out the tire. The twins wanted to climb in the tire well to see the truck's "guts," but Bryan yanked them out by their waistbands before they could.

"You could knock out the jack, guys, and the truck will fall on top of you. Remember, safety first. And never change the tire next to oncoming traffic. It's not worth the risk." He looked at Kelsey. "What do you do if that happens?"

Beth had to bite her lip to keep from laughing at Kelsey's rapt expression. She doubted her daughter had understood a word of what Bryan had said. Since he'd arrived, Bryan's movies had shown up on the DVR schedule to be recorded and there'd been a flurry of googling on the family room laptop. Beth knew who'd done that.

"Um, call someone?"

"Exactly. Who?"

Kelsey twiddled her hair and looked up at Bryan from under her lashes. "You?" She held out her cell phone.

Beth wanted to groan. Bryan Manley was *not* the guy for Kelsey to practice her feminine wiles on.

Beth on the other hand . . .

Bryan, bless him, chuckled softly, took Kelsey's phone, and programmed something into it. "No. You call your mom. She'll call a roadside assistance company." He held up the phone.

"This says ICE. In Case of Emergency. Emergency responders look for this in your phone, so you want to make sure you have your mom listed as your contact." He handed the phone back. "Any questions? Jason?"

Jason shook his mop. Beth wished he'd cut it, but she kept her mouth shut. There were fights she needed to have with her son and there were ones she didn't. His hair fell under the *Didn't* category, but that didn't mean she couldn't hope.

"No, I'm good."

"Glad to hear it." Bryan flipped the tire iron over. "Your turn."

Jason's face turned white beneath the mop. "My . . . my what?"

"Your turn. You're going to change the tire."

"But . . ."

The twins started giggling and imitating Jason's stutter—

Until Bryan put a hand on their heads and tilted them back to look at him. "And when he's done, you guys are going to do it."

"But we don't know how," said Tommy.

"That's what we were learning, dufus," said Mark.

"Good," said Bryan. "Then Mark, you can show Tommy how to do it when Jason's finished."

Kelsey, wisely, kept her mouth shut.

But Bryan wasn't kidding. He made each one of them—all six of them—change a tire. Even Maggie, but that was more to make her feel a part of the crew as much as the rest of them. She did look awfully cute sitting on Bryan's knee as she helped him crank the lug nuts with the tire iron.

And after six reviews, Beth was no longer surprised that she knew what a lug nut and tire iron were.

"Okay, then." Bryan set Maggie on her feet and stood up. "Anyone have any questions?"

"Yeah," said Tommy. "Can we learn how to change the oil, too?"

Kelsey and Jason groaned and Mark cuffed his twin on the back of the head. "You're a dufus."

"Am not."

"Are too."

"Am not."

"Are too."

Bryan shook his head and laughed, leaving the two of them

there to duke it out verbally, and held out a hand toward the house for Beth to precede him. "I hope that was okay with you."

"The lesson? Why wouldn't it be?"

"I don't want to overstep my bounds, but since all the kids were here, I figured it was as good a time as any for them to learn. They'll probably forget, but it might come back to them should they ever need it."

"I don't have a problem with it. It was a good idea. Thank you. Not that I ever want to change a tire. I do have roadside assistance on my insurance, but it can't hurt to know what to do just in case. And the kids really appreciated it, I think."

"They will if they're ever stuck. It gives them some comfort in knowing they can handle a flat tire if they need to. Make them feel more confident about going places."

"I'm not sure that's such a good thing with teenagers, but I know what you mean."

He meant that they felt out of control. That, with Mike's death, their world had been tossed upside down and flattened—just like Mike's plane.

Beth sucked in a breath as she stumbled up the last step into the foyer, the image searing across her brain. She'd tried not to see what had happened to the plane, but the media had broadcast it for what seemed to be twenty-four-seven, nonstop for days. Weeks even. She hadn't been able to go anywhere without seeing the inferno that had been her husband's last moments on earth. The really sad thing was, the kids had seen it, too.

And then there'd been the reporters. There'd been an investigation into the crash. Possible pilot error. Mike's career had come under intense scrutiny and, while she'd known there was nothing to work against him, it had still scared the hell out of her. She didn't need his name smeared when she was trying to hold the family together and deal with the fallout. The press had only compounded it to the point where the kids had been frightened to go outside for fear of having microphones stuck in their face. They'd become recluses in their own home with people staying away so that they, too, wouldn't be barraged by everyone looking for the story.

It'd taken the National Transportation Safety Bureau and the FAA entirely too long to clear his name and by then, the damage had been done. The kids were wary, scared. Withdrawn.

Jason hid behind his hair. Kelsey by laughing a little too loud. The twins had had each other, but they'd grown apart, no longer finishing each other's sentences. And Maggie had sucked her thumb. All coping mechanisms, but how *had* they coped? It was a question Beth was still working on.

"You okay? You're awfully quiet." Bryan held open the door for her.

"Me? I'm fine." As fine as could be.

"Fine, huh?" He chuckled.

"Yes. What's wrong with being fine?" It was what the counselor—and she—wanted for them. To be fine.

Beth didn't think she'd ever be fine again—oh. Now she got his chuckle.

She chuckled, too. "I mean, yes. I'm good. Thank you for teaching all of us. We appreciate it."

"My pleasure."

No, really, it was hers. If he kept smiling at her like that, she'd be way more than fine and good.

Chapter Six

THERE was something about a man cleaning a toilet.
    Or maybe it was just *Bryan Manley* cleaning her toilet,
but he had the best butt Beth had ever seen. And that was no
disrespect to her husband. She and Mike had joked about it
because Mike had been butt-challenged, though he'd had other
good points to make up for it.

Beth sighed and leaned against the doorframe, crossing a
foot over the other. The fact that she was referring to Mike in
the past tense was reason enough to not list what those points
were. She didn't need more waterworks after the plumbing
incident this morning.

"Is there something you need?" Bryan asked over his shoulder, sitting back on his heels from the on-all-fours stance in
front of the toilet that really shouldn't have been sexy but was.

Beth straightened and tugged the hem of her shirt down. "I
was wondering if you would like something to eat."

Seriously? *That's* what she went with?

Though . . . actually . . . it *was* lunchtime so, it was as good
an excuse as any.

"No, I'm good," Brian said, returning to his toilet-cleaning
pose.

She ought to leave. She'd asked the question, he'd turned her down, he had work to do. And she had no business hanging around Bryan Manley.

Of course that didn't stop her from staying.

"Where did you learn how to clean? I didn't think movie stars needed to know how to do toilets."

"My grandmother." He tossed the used paper towels into the trash can, then pulled a pristine cleaning brush out from his supply kit—and aimed it at her. "I wasn't always a movie star, you know."

"Oh. I hadn't thought about that. I guess you had an apartment or something? Had to pull your weight with your roommates?" She didn't dare ask if any of those roommates were female. It was none of her business.

And if she kept saying that, she might remember it.

"Actually, I didn't." He swirled the brush around the bowl with the cleaning solution and flushed it. "I lived at home until I moved to LA. My grandmother made us all clean. Every Saturday morning. We rotated the bathrooms. I got really good at it."

He peeled the latex gloves off his hands and tossed them into the trash. "Which means I can tell when someone has cleaned before me. You did it last night, didn't you?"

Beth could feel the blush blaze over her skin. "This place was, well, gross. You didn't need to see that."

"But that's why I'm here. Why hire me if you aren't going to use me?"

Don't answer that, don't answer that, don't answer that.

"*I* didn't hire you. My friends did." There. That was a safe answer. And it let him know where she stood on the subject. She was perfectly capable of taking care of her own home—or she would be once this initial push was over. Once Bryan left, the house would be in perfect shape and, hopefully, the kids would help her take better care of it than they had for the last two years.

"Your friends?" Bryan took a step toward her and Beth had to look up at him.

"They thought I could use a break. Relax a little." This was new for her. She was five-ten. Rarely did she have to look up at a guy. Even Mike had only been an inch taller.

She stuck her hands into her back pockets, then yanked them out because that movement stretched her shirt too tightly across her chest and she didn't want him to think she was coming on to him. It was one thing to fantasize about Bryan in *that way*; it was another to actually go for it.

Besides, who was she to even *imagine* she'd have a shot with him? He had movie stars and models at his beck and call; he didn't need a frumpy mom of five with a manic dog and a deranged cat.

Both of whom careened down the stairs just then.

Beth winced, waiting for the crash or screech, or the "Stop it, Sherman!" that inevitably followed Sherman's chases after Mrs. Beecham. She was listening for it so much that she almost missed Bryan's comment.

"It's got to be tough without your husband around."

She wouldn't have minded missing that one.

Beth forced a laugh. It was either that or cry and she was not going to do that. Not anymore. She'd cried enough and not a single tear had brought Mike back. "We're coping."

Bryan looked at the top of her head. His gaze traveled over her face slowly. Beth's breath hitched for the moment or two that he raised his hand hesitantly to brush a piece of hair off her face.

When his fingers grazed her cheek, she stopped breathing altogether.

This hadn't happened in, well . . . Not since she'd met Mike. In college.

"I'm glad I can lend a hand," he said softly, his green eyes searching for something in hers.

She didn't know what he was looking for, wasn't sure she wanted to know, and definitely knew she didn't have to breathe ever again if he'd stay right where he was.

What was she thinking?

That was the thing; she *wasn't* thinking. Her body was on autopilot here. It remembered what to do around a hot guy even if her brain didn't. And it didn't. She'd never even looked at another man. Mike had been everything to her.

So who was this Bryan Manley to have crept under her defenses so much and so quickly that she was imagining him creeping under other things—namely the covers of her bed?

Now she felt the blush blaze through her entire body. She hoped to God he didn't know it.

His eyes flared—just a second, but it was enough.

He knew.

And he wasn't stepping back.

Beth needed to breathe. Desperately. Metaphorically and physically, and she didn't care in what order. He needed to move away. Take even one step back. Give her some space.

Except . . . she could back away, too. She was the one in the doorway. All it'd take would be two simple steps and she'd be beyond his reach in the hallway. Away from these crazy thoughts and feelings.

He was, after all, *the* Bryan Manley. Heartthrob and ladies' man. She was just Beth from the suburbs. Soccer mom, helper with the school play, PTA rep. Teacher. *Not* movie star material and definitely not model material. Merely someone who was tied to this house and this town with five pairs of very visible roots.

She took a step back. Away from temptation. From madness. From what-in-the-hell-was-she-thinking?

From *what if* . . .

BRYAN let her go.

He didn't want to, but, seriously, what right did he have to do what he'd done? She ought to smack him across the face. He'd gotten too close too fast. Too familiar. And he wasn't even sure he *wanted* to get familiar with Mrs. Beth Hamilton.

The widow.

With five kids.

Bryan took a deep breath. "Well, I'm glad I can help out."

Not quite the way he'd like to if he had the choice, but then, he didn't. And shouldn't. And couldn't. And . . . Thank God she'd stepped back.

"It, um . . ." She absently re-tucked the hair that he'd tucked. "It's gotten, well, not easier, but more normal. Time helps. Some. I'm just sorry you have to clean up after them. I'm sure your sister has other jobs that would've been easier. Did you lose a bet or something?"

Bryan forced a laugh to cover up how close she'd gotten to the truth. "Hey, well, you know, this is what they pay me the big bucks for." He grabbed the toolkit of cleaning supplies.

Mac ought to get those logo-ed. And the toilet brush handle, too. It'd come in handy if he accidentally left one behind.

And he was babbling in his head, trying to cover the very visceral reaction he had to Mrs. Beth Hamilton.

He wanted to buy out her perfume manufacturer's entire supply. Or, better yet, invest in the company, because that scent—just one little whiff—turned him on faster than he'd been turned on in a long while.

And if she wasn't wearing perfume . . . well then, his trouble level had just gotten a whole lot higher.

"Mommy, can Bryan clean my room next?" Maggie, thank God, poked her curly little head out from the room next door, pulling the thumb from her mouth with a loud *pop*! She sucked that thumb a lot, he'd noticed yesterday. When she was thinking about something or considering him or watching TV or taking a nap, her thumb was never far away. He would've thought that, by her age, she'd have outgrown it. Perhaps most kids whose father hadn't died would have. He couldn't begrudge Maggie that small comfort.

What did Beth do for comfort?

Bryan gripped the toolbox harder and turned away, looking for something to occupy his other hand. And his mind. Because he didn't need to be worrying about Beth's comfort. He had to worry about her toilets. Yes, that was it. Toilets. Nothing sexy about a toilet. Or dust. Or baseboards. Or return registers. Or stovetops. All items guaranteed to require his full attention.

"Sure, Mags. Bryan can do your room next." Beth raised perfectly arched eyebrows that he'd bet had never seen a makeup artist in their life.

Since when had he noticed a woman's *eyebrows*?

"Sure, Maggie. I'll be right there." No way was he going to brush by Beth. She had to leave first.

Thankfully, she figured that out and moved out of his way.

Bryan took a deep breath, hiked the toolbox, and tried to burn the image from his brain of Beth's perfectly shaped backside as she walked down the hall.

Chapter Seven

✦❧✦

BRYAN groaned as his alarm went off the next morning. It was only day three of the twenty he was slated to spend at Beth's house and already it was too much. He'd cleaned Maggie's room from the top of the princess canopy draping over her bed, to the fluffy pink chair that had more cat hair than fabric on it, to the dozens of costumes spilling from her closet. She'd assured him that her room had been clean the day before, but she'd had a "wardrobe malfunction" last night and had to find something else to wear to bed.

Given the new sheets on her bed, Bryan had an idea of what she was talking about, but didn't let on that he did. She might only be five, but she knew enough to be embarrassed by bed-wetting.

Was that a residual from the trauma she must have gone through when she'd lost her father?

Then the twins had come in just as he'd finished up, arguing yet again who was the best lightsaber fighter, and he'd been roped into refereeing. Lunch had been an event, reminding him of when he and his brothers had been kids. He'd laughed at the surreptitious dog-feeding going on under the table, the cat perched on the room divider keeping a wary eye on the dog and any scraps that fell to the floor, the constant banter between the twins with Maggie's voice chiming in every so often, and Beth wiping bread crumbs off her nose—and smearing peanut butter on it in its place.

He'd jumped up to help her clean up, but she'd shooed him away, telling him to enjoy his lunch.

That was the problem; he'd enjoyed it a little too much. He'd spent last night hard and aching and chastising himself the entire time. Beth was off-limits. He couldn't care how pretty she was or how amazing she was to take care of those kids and keep her house and work at her teaching job. Granted it was summer vacation and the house was dirty enough that her friends had hired him, so she wasn't handling it as well as she obviously had been able to do before her husband's death, but still. Beth was holding it together when he could tell how much she'd loved the guy.

Something twinged inside him. What would it be like to have someone care about him that much? To be there every morning and every night? To share the little things of life with: making coffee, doing the crossword puzzle, watching the dog chase rabbits in the backyard first thing in the morning?

Watching the sun rise from the king-sized bed upstairs in her bedroom . . .

He groaned again and it had nothing to do with the early morning. Sure, he was used to getting up for early calls, but once the film wrapped, he liked to sleep in.

He swung his feet off the bed just as his phone rang.

He scrubbed a hand through his hair. Didn't recognize the number, but it was local. Hell, he hoped it wasn't a reporter. "Manley."

"Bryan?" Beth. Out of breath.

Every cell in his body went on high alert. "Beth? What's wrong?" All sorts of catastrophes were running through his head. Had one of the twins skewered the other with an impromptu dangerous sword? Had Jason taken the car out? Had Maggie choked on something?

Already he was yanking on a pair of running shorts—fuck the stupid uniform. He didn't need to spend the day in the ER in that concoction, plus the shorts were easier to pull on one-handed.

"It's Sherman. I have to take him to the vet."

Sherman. The dog. Bryan's adrenaline took a nosedive as the immediate threat to Beth and the kids dissipated. But then the worry in her voice registered. "What happened?"

"I . . ." Her voice broke. "He got himself tangled in the clothesline and I don't know . . . He's not . . . I don't know how long he was without oxygen."

Oh God. The kids would be devastated. "Did you give him mouth-to-mouth?" Even as he said it, he knew it sounded ridiculous.

Beth didn't laugh. "Yeah. And he's breathing again. Coming around, too, but, I don't know. I think I should take him in just to be sure. The rope marks around his neck are pretty bad."

"I'll be right there."

"You don't have to hurry. I just wanted to tell you I won't be here and I'll leave a key under the mat. I know it's cliché, but it's the easiest place and I've got to get the kids to their friends' houses so I can do this. I just wanted to know why we wouldn't be there."

"Which vet do you see?"

"Dr. Bingham on Harvest."

"I'll meet you there."

"That's not necess—"

"I want to, Beth." Because if the dog's prognosis wasn't good, she was going to need someone with her. He'd seen how much she cared about that dog. And he knew how much the kids did. Beth would hurt for herself *and* for them if something happened to the mutt.

"Oh, but Bryan, that's not necessary."

"Time's wasting, Beth. Get in the car and head over. I'll meet you there."

A N hour later, Beth was very glad Bryan had insisted on coming.

Maggie, who was the only one of her kids who hadn't had any friends home this morning and had to come, was a mess. She wasn't even talking for the furious thumb-sucking she was doing, and she was pacing just like Mike used to—just like she had when the police had shown up that day with the news about Mike's plane.

And just like then, Beth had tried to pull her daughter into her arms, but Maggie wouldn't take the comfort—also like Mike. He'd dealt with things in his own time and his own space and Maggie was just like him, right down to the curly black hair.

Sometimes genetics could be a real pain in the ass when she had the spitting image of the man she'd lost staring back at her from across the kitchen table every morning.

Still, Beth's fingers itched to reach out to Maggie and draw her into the circle of her arms, and she was just about to do that when Bryan returned from the reception desk where he'd asked for an update on Sherman and swung Maggie into his arms. "Hey, Mags. The vet said Sherman's going to be all right." He looked over at Beth and nodded.

She exhaled. He was telling the truth. Not sugarcoating it to make it easier to take.

"Can we take him home? I wanna leave this place."

"Not today. They're going to keep him overnight for observation just to be sure. But they said he's up and drinking water, and we can come get him tomorrow."

"But who's he gonna sleep with tonight?" Her thumb went back in her mouth.

Bryan gently pulled it out and kissed the back of her hand.

Beth's stomach thudded. Women the world over would *kill* to have him do that to their hands. And she was one of them.

She was a rotten mother, being jealous of her own daughter. The daughter whose world had been turned upside down with the death of her father and now the danger to her dog. Yet here Beth was, wanting what had so generously been given to her daughter.

Maggie giggled. "That tickles. Your beard is all scratchy."

Bryan put her palm on his cheek. "That's what happens when I don't have time to shave in the morning."

Now Beth's tummy fluttered. She missed watching Mike shave. Missed having a man in her life for those things that were so, well, dare she say it? Manly.

Bryan Manley . . .

Oh God. She had it bad. Just like half the women in America. And millions more across the globe.

She'd laugh if this situation were funny, for the fact that she had a movie star in the vet's office for a silly dog who liked to chase underwear. You couldn't *write* a story like this.

"So, what do you say we go grab breakfast?" Bryan asked Maggie. "I could use some pancakes, how about you? With lots of ice cream and whipped topping?"

Maggie giggled again. "That's dessert, silly."

"It is?" Bryan hiked her again in his arms, her curls bouncing around her head. "In my world, that's breakfast. And I've missed mine. So what do you say?"

"Mommy, too?"

They both looked at her, the smiles on their faces interestingly similar. Which shouldn't be, since they weren't related, but . . . were.

"Mommy?" Bryan asked with his tongue firmly planted in his cheek. "Wanna join us?"

She ought to be asking him that question.

Beth shot to her feet. "Uh, yeah, sure." *Sure* for breakfast. Him joining them—?

No. No way. Forget about it. Bad idea.

Well, actually, it was a good idea. It was just pointless to consider because he was, after all, *Bryan Manley, Movie Star.*

THE point was driven home—with nails pounded into the coffin of *what ifs*—the moment they stepped into the diner for those pancakes he was so eager to eat.

Everyone stared. And waved. And called out as if he were a returning hero. Though, actually, he was. The town called him one of their own. He'd been born and raised here, with just enough return visits to make it legit. They loved their Hollywood heartthrob.

It was evident in all the smiles. In the wistful glances of the teenage girls—and some of their moms. And the jealous ones from other women. Beth had never felt the glare of animosity so much as she did then, as if they were wondering who *she*, an outsider whose husband had come under suspicion, was to merit dining with *the* Bryan Manley.

Stop it! Stop thinking like that! Mike was proven innocent, and the onus is on them to acknowledge that, not for you to convince them of it. Be friendly. Smile.

"What do you think about this booth, Beth?" Bryan put his hand on her back.

Her smile suddenly came naturally. "It's fine."

They chuckled at that word.

She stopped chuckling when he slid in across from her and his leg brushed up against hers. His bare, manly, hairy leg against her equally bare, smooth, newly shaven one. (Yes, she'd shaved that morning when she'd gotten up, and no, it hadn't had anything to do with the fact that Bryan would be spending the day at her home, and why was she defending herself to her conscience?)

"You okay?" He tilted his head slightly, his concern zipping along her nerve endings right into her heart.

Why did he have to be so perfect? Sure, it helped in his line of work, but wouldn't physical perfection be enough? Did he have to be so incredibly nice and thoughtful and caring? Able to win over small, hurt five-year-olds with one kiss to the back of the hand?

Come to think of it, that would work with tall, middle-aged women by the boatload.

"Um, yes, I'm fi— Good. I mean."

His laughter broke the tension, and Beth finally let herself relax. He was still a guy. Another human being. All the trappings of Hollywood didn't define him. They were just window dressing.

Though what a nice window it was.

The waitress—or actually it was Claire, the owner—came over to take their order. "Hey, Bry. Haven't seen you in a long time." Insinuation dripped like maple syrup off every word.

"Claire. How are you? How's Roddy?"

Claire's left hand disappeared inside her apron. "Don't know. Moved upstate with his new girlfriend."

Okay, then. Single and letting Bryan know it. Yes, jealousy simmered just below Beth's skin. Jealousy she had no business feeling.

"Oh, man, I'm sorry to hear that."

Claire shrugged. "I'm not. He was drinking me out of house and home. That's what happens when you don't have enough drive to go after what you want outta life. Not that you know anything about that from what I can see." She glanced at Beth. "Aren't you that pilot's wife?"

Beth couldn't help the cringe. That's what she'd become: *that pilot's wife*. It hurt. Denigrated their marriage and Mike's reputation and never let her forget a minute of the scandal that had surrounded his death.

"This is Beth Hamilton," said Bryan, his eyes narrowing as he looked at her.

Beth shook her head slightly. Now wasn't the time.

"Did you know my daddy?" Maggie's thumb popped out and she leaned forward on her elbows. "My daddy was a pilot."

"Yes, sweetie, I know." Claire did, thank God, give Maggie a sweet smile.

Some of Beth's animosity faded. At least the woman was kind to her daughter. That went a long way toward Beth giving her the benefit of the doubt. Maybe Claire didn't know the effect *that pilot's wife* had on her. Maybe she hadn't meant anything by it.

"And this little urchin is Maggie." Bryan ruffled her curls. "And she wants a big stack of pancakes covered in vanilla ice cream, whipped cream, chocolate fudge, chocolate chips, and a bright red cherry on top."

Maggie's eyes widened and she yanked her head around to look at him in awe. "I do?"

Bryan tweaked her nose. "Sure you do. And you're going to share them with me."

"Do I have to?"

Bryan patted the seat beside him and just like that, Maggie sat. No begging. No pleading. Not even a word to tell her what to do, something Beth hadn't been able to manage with her headstrong (just like her father) daughter.

"Yes, you do. Or you'll end up with a tummy ache and we'll have to take you to the doctor's instead of bringing Sherman home from his."

"Oh. I don't wanna do that." Maggie nodded solemnly.

"I know. Besides, it'll be fun sharing with me. We can have dueling spoons."

"What's that?"

He tapped her nose this time. "You'll see." He looked at Beth. "And what are you having, Beth?"

*You with a big extra helping of hot fudge that I can lick off
every inch—*

"Um, just a glass of orange juice for me, thanks."

"What? You're not eating?" Bryan *tsk-tsked*. "That won't
do. Breakfast is the most important meal of the day." He looked
at Claire. "Beth will have some of our pancakes. Better bring
extra."

"Oh, but Bry—"

"And two cherries for her." He smiled that dazzling million-
watt smile at Claire, who looked dazed as she walked away to
bring *the* Bryan Manley his meal.

The smile had enough wattage that it resonated with Beth
as well. "You're going to have to eat most of it, you know. My
system can't take all that sugar."

"True. You're sweet enough as it is."

Okay, where'd her tongue go? She must have swallowed it.
Or it'd dried up at his comment.

He thought she was *sweet*? In what manner? Sweet as in a
"That chick is so freakin' sweet!" sort of way that sent her
hormones into a tailspin and her *what if* mechanism into high
gear? Or an "Awww, aren't you sweet?" meaning that would
completely suck, but would at least get her off this vacillating
do-I-or-don't-I-allow-myself-to-be-attracted-to-him seesaw.

"Mommy's not sweet, she's a prickly pear. That's what
Daddy used to say."

Maggie giggled while Beth's mouth dropped open that her
daughter remembered that. She'd been three when Mike had
been killed; how could she possibly remember that?

Mike had said it out of affection—they'd gone to Mexico
on their honeymoon and sampled the fruit. He'd said she was
just like it: a tough exterior with a sweet heart inside. It'd been
his term of endearment for her ever since.

Her heart twisted as she remembered that. So hard to believe
he was gone. But at least Maggie had good memories of him;
Beth had been worried she'd have no memories at all.

"A prickly pear, huh?" Bryan thrummed his fingers on the
tabletop. "I'm thinking more along the lines of a star fruit.
Sweet and being pulled in five directions."

Beth laughed at that. "Definitely feeling that pull. More so
as they get older."

"I don't know how you do it. Five kids would do me in."

She shrugged. "You do what you have to. And they're great kids. Really."

"Not Jason. He's moody." Maggie wrinkled her nose. "And his room smells like socks."

"All teenage boys' rooms smell like socks, Mags." Bryan put his arm around her and leaned in. "It's what makes boys grow so tall. They want to get away from their feet."

Maggie giggled again and Beth wanted to kiss Bryan for making her do so. Well, she wanted to kiss Bryan for other reasons, but this one, too.

Wait. She wanted to *what*?

She was still mulling that over when Claire returned with their food.

"Holy cow!" Maggie stood on the vinyl booth seat. "That's a mountain of pancakes."

It certainly was. There must have been a dozen buttermilk pancakes and a gallon of ice cream, and a whole canister of the whipped topping.

"Well, we have to keep up with those Hollywood folks, don't we?" Claire said, her gaze firmly planted on Bryan.

His shoulders, Beth thought. Or maybe his chest. Good thing he was sitting down with a table over his lap, because Beth was sure Claire would be staring *that* down as well.

She blushed when Bryan raised an eyebrow at her. Oh God. She didn't need him knowing what she was thinking. Or that she was jealous of Claire looking at him. She had no reason— no *right*—to feel jealous. Bryan was single. Unattached. And she . . . well, she was unattached at the companion-for-life level, but five kids were an anchor no man she'd dated had wanted to weigh in.

Which, really, was fine with her. She had more important things to fill her time than looking for a substitute father for her kids—namely, be a mom to her kids. That, plus everything else she had to do solo in life, was where she had to put her focus.

Other people stopped by their table once Claire had broken the ice, some asking for autographs, others for photos. Bryan graciously spoke to each person. Made them all feel as if they had his undivided attention, yet still managed to not exclude her and Maggie. He introduced them to people he'd known growing up—even garnered an invitation or two for Beth to join him at a party or get-together they invited him to. She wouldn't go, of course. Bryan was here to clean her house, not *play* house.

That idea, however, didn't go away, no matter how much she wished it would.

Chapter Eight

❧

"MOMMY, is Bryan coming to play today?" Maggie hopped onto the foot of Beth's bed the following morning, her T-shirt on backward and her sneakers on the wrong feet, but her smile was so bright and sunny, Beth didn't have the heart to tell her so.

She also didn't have the heart to tell her that Bryan wasn't here to be their friend. Though maybe she should; Maggie was becoming a little too attached to their temporary help.

Beth winced. Bryan was anything *but* "the help." The day before yesterday, he'd been the plumber and the mechanic. Yesterday he'd been the handyman when they'd gotten home from the diner. All the little things Mike had planned to get to that he never had had become glaringly obvious to Beth over the two years he'd been gone. The crooked cabinet doors on the laundry room cabinets, the shredded rug edges from when Sherman had been a puppy that'd started to spread from the constant tromping-on from five pairs of scuffling sneakers. Then there was the loose railing on the stairs to the basement.

Bryan had started with that last one first. Said it was a safety issue, which it was. She'd been meaning to get to it, but by the time she got home from work, made dinner, supervised home-work and baths, then set out clothing and lunch items for the next day, the last thing she'd wanted to do was household main-tenance. She usually saved that for the weekends, but Jason had joined the football team this year and Kelsey had made cheerleading, and fall weekends had turned into tailgating extravaganzas—minus the booze. It'd been fun, and she'd loved cheering her kids on, but the time-suck was amazing. Single-parenting was definitely *not* for the faint-of-heart.

"I have a tea party all set up in my room. Do you think he likes girl-may or darling tea?" Maggie scrunched her little face and tapped her lips as if Earl Grey and Darjeeling tea decisions would decide the fate of the free world.

"You'll have to ask him, Mags, but I'm not so sure Bryan likes tea. He didn't have any at breakfast yesterday."

But he *had* eaten most of Maggie's pancakes—a good thing because Beth hadn't relished the idea of a five-year-old's upset tummy. But if she'd said anything to Maggie about eating too much, she would've been the bad guy. She was tired of being the bad guy, so it was great that Bryan had figured out how to solve both problems by eating the bulk of them. And lord knew, he could hide those thousand or so calories a lot better than she could.

Though, not if he wanted that washboard he'd had in his last movie.

Beth thrust aside thoughts of his last movie, otherwise she'd have to admit that she'd watched it last night on her iPad, cour-tesy of her online movie subscription, and had almost had the first non-self-induced orgasm in two years.

She climbed out of bed and busied herself making it to cool down the flush that suffused her body as images of her dreams kept popping up in her head. Just like something else had kept popping up on Bry—

"Are Mark and Tommy awake yet?" she asked Maggie, yanking her robe on over her T-shirt to cover her hardened nipples. It was senseless to ask if Jason and Kelsey were up; teenagers didn't get up before the crack of two p.m. during the summer unless they were working. And even then it was a chore to get them moving. Beth hated to admit it, and felt like a bad mother for taking advantage of it, but it was a lot easier to let the two of them sleep most of the day while she dealt with the three younger ones' schedules. She'd managed to set up car-pools most of the time so that she only had one day of running everyone around. Nothing else got done that day, but that was okay. She enjoyed the time she spent with the kids and their friends. Life went by too fast to miss those precious moments.

Plus, Kelsey had had friends over last night. Beth had let the paltry excuse for a reason pass—Kelsey wanted to show Bryan off to a new set of friends, and while Beth wasn't in favor of it, her daughter did deserve to have sleepovers. The Bryan-ogling was going to happen; might as well get it over with.

"Tommy took Sherman out." Maggie hopped off the bed, dragging the comforter with her. That was Maggie, one disaster after another. And she was totally oblivious to all of it, which explained how she could live in the heap she called a room.

Beth never quite reached the same level of acceptance as her daughter.

She sighed and tossed the comforter back onto the bed. Maggie did have a point—why bother to make the bed when you were going to climb right back into it that night?

And maybe someone else would climb in, too . . .

Beth picked up a pillow off the floor and tossed it on the chair beside her bed. Great. Bad enough she was having erotic dreams about the guy, now her subconscious was inviting him into the room?

"Mom!" Mark hollered up from downstairs in the tone that could set Beth's mothering instinct on red alert in one second.

"Coming!" She patted Maggie's thigh. "Come on, sweetie. Tommy's in trouble."

"How do you know that, Mommy? From your third eye?"

Beth bit her lip. The kids had bought that story for as long as they'd believed in Santa. She'd miss the day Maggie grew up. "Yes, sweetie. So let's hurry."

She shoved her feet into her sneakers. Sherman's trip to the vet had left him with an overactive digestion problem—probably still recovering from the shock—and she wasn't about to run into the backyard without shoes on.

She did a double take as she passed Maggie's room.

"Maggie?" She leaned against the doorframe and poked her head farther into the room.

"Yes, Mommy?" Maggie poked her head around the door-frame under hers.

"Your room."

"Yes, Mommy. It is."

"It's neat."

"That's 'cause you painted it, remember?"

"No, I mean, it's all cleaned up."

"That's 'cause Bryan did it."

"Yes, but that was yesterday." *Neat* didn't stick to Maggie. It slithered off and shriveled up in a corner within ten minutes of making an appearance.

"Yes," said Maggie so matter-of-factly, Beth had to remember that this was *Maggie* she was talking about. Tornado Maggie. Messy Maggie as Jason called her out of Mom's earshot—or so he thought. Maggie didn't know the meaning of the word *neat* unless it meant *cool.*

"Is something wrong, Mommy?"

Maggie's erstwhile little face was turned up at hers with a smile so big Beth curbed her gut reaction—namely to ask if Maggie was feeling well.

"It looks very nice."

"Thank you, Mommy. Bryan said little girls who take care of their rooms grow into very successful women. You must have had a really clean room when you were little, right, Mommy?"

Chalk up one more reason Beth wanted to kiss Bryan Manley.

ANOTHER one was added to the list when she got to the backyard and saw Bryan removing the slat in the wood fence that was pinning Sherman in place, Tommy on one side, Mark on the other, both ready to grab the hyperactive dog the minute he was free.

"This end of the hammer is used for removing nails. See this V here?" Bryan slid the curved end of the hammer along the wood and pried out a nail. "Be careful with it once you remove it. Rusty nails mean a trip to the ER."

"Yeah, you have to get a big shot. Nick Miller had to do that when he stepped on one on the playground."

Beth winced, remembering when that'd happened. The blood had scared the kids, and then one had shared the big needle myth, which set Nick and the rest of the kids off. It would be a birthday party Nick would never forget, but unfortunately not for good reasons. It was part of the reason her younger three were so terrified of needles.

"Like anything else, guys, you learn how to do it properly and you reduce your risk of injury." Bryan pried out the other nail. "Now both of you hold on to Sherman 'cause he's going to want to run when I lift this board off him."

"I have his collar," Mark said from the other side.

"I have his tail," said Tommy trying to grab the stub that constituted Sherman's wagging appendage.

"You can't hold him by his tail," said Mark scathingly. Amazing how the two minutes separating their births gave Mark the big-brother mentality.

"Can too."

"Cannot."

"Can—"

"Guys, both of you hold on. He's going to want to get away. Ready?"

"Yeah," they said in unison, a sound so sweet to Beth's ears. Hadn't been so much when they'd wailed in unison as infants, but this . . . definitely.

"One." Bryan pried the board away from the one next to it with that curved end of the hammer. "Two." He slid his fingers beneath it and set the hammer down, then grabbed the other side. "Three." He pulled the board back just enough that Sherman could wiggle through, right onto Mark, who, thankfully, didn't let go of his collar.

"Told you I could get him!"

"I helped!" Tommy was off and running toward the gate to get to the other side of the fence.

"That's right, Tom. You did. Now hold on to him, guys." Bryan set the board back in place, grabbed two new nails, and hammered them in.

"Bryan! You did it!" Maggie ran across the yard and flung her arms around his neck as she leapt onto his back. "You saved Sherman! Again!"

Again? *Again*? Beth admitted to a twinge of hurt. *She* was the one who'd found Sherman and untangled him from the clothesline. *She* was the one who'd puffed into his snout and carried him to the car. *She* was the one who'd been terrified she'd have to break the news to her kids that someone else they loved had died. Yet Bryan was the one getting the hugs?

"Your mom saved Sherman the other day, Maggie. Not me."

Well, now he *did* deserve a hug for being so darn chivalrous.

Beth reached the two of them as he peeled her daughter's arms from around his neck and stood up.

Her steps faltered. She'd forgotten how tall he was. How he filled out that shirt.

That's because he wasn't wearing a shirt in your dream last night, sweetie.

How observant he was . . . His left eyebrow arched as she blushed yet again.

"Thank you." She tried to keep the huskiness out of her voice.

"No problem. The dog managed to wedge himself in there pretty good."

"Not for Sherman. Well, I mean, yes, for that but also for . . ." She glanced down at Maggie and cupped her daughter's chin. "Why don't you go help your brothers bring Sherman back home where he belongs?"

"Okay, Mommy."

Beth gnawed on her bottom lip for a second as she watched Maggie skip off, then looked up at Bryan. "I meant for what you just said to Maggie. That I saved Sherman. I know it shouldn't be a big deal, but—"

"Hey, you don't have to explain. Or thank me." He touched her arm in a companionable sort of way—until electricity shot up her arm. His, too, if his reaction was anything to go by because he yanked his hand away so quickly it was awkward.

"I—"

"I'm—"

"What were you—"

"You first."

Awkward reigned supreme.

Of course Bryan would be the one to break it. "I'm sorry. I shouldn't have—"

"No. It's fine. It's just . . . I'm not used to—"

"Oh right. I hadn't thought about that."

She was lying through her teeth. She didn't react that way to anyone else touching her. Hell, she hadn't reacted that way to the few kisses she'd received on those dates that hadn't worked out and they'd been a hell of a lot more sexual than a mere brush of his fingers. "No, it's not that. It's just . . ." Geez, what was she supposed to say that wouldn't embarrass them both?

"Beth, I—"

And there he went with the touching thing again. Granted, this time it was her shoulder, but still . . . same reaction. Only this time neither one pulled away.

But she should. She shouldn't be contemplating what she was contemplating.

But he looked as if he was contemplating it, too.

This was crazy. Insane. Foolish. It could go nowhere. And they were in her backyard where anyone could see them.

Including Jason and Kelsey if they looked out their windows.

"Sherman!" Maggie squealed from the other side of the fence.

Maggie. Oh God. And Tommy. And Mark. They couldn't see her and Bryan this close.

"Sherman, no!" This from Mark, accompanied by another squeal from Maggie and a word out of Tommy's mouth Beth hadn't realized he even knew.

"I need to see what's going on." Yeah, it was an excuse, but it was valid. Amazing that *Sherman* was her savior.

"I'll go with you."

Bryan grabbed her hand and they ran around the gate, all the while Beth was desperately trying not to notice the fire blazing along her nerve endings from her palm up through her arm and searing all throughout her body at the thought of what could have been.

Then she saw Sherman. Nothing like a good dose of dog-rolling-in-compost to cool one's sizzling nerve endings.

"Oh, Sherman, no!" all four of the Hamiltons said in unison.

"Oh, Sherman, yes," growled Bryan as he directed the kids to form a circle around the dog. "Come on, guys, get ready to grab him when he bolts."

Bryan shifted his weight back and forth, ready to pounce, and oh, what it did to his butt. And Beth wasn't looking away.

Then he lunged and the physical perfection that was Bryan was nothing compared to him coming to her rescue yet again—even when he slipped, taking a header onto the pile.

And it was that and the fact that he managed to keep hold of her squiggling pet that sent his knight-in-shining-banana-peel status up a whole bunch of notches.

Chapter Nine

❧

BRYAN used the fluffy pink towel Maggie had insisted on lending him before he'd headed into the shower, and tried hard not to look around Beth's bathroom when he finished. To imagine her in here, showering. Wet. Covered in suds.

Or not.

Okay, he wasn't doing very well on that front.

He scrubbed his head with the towel. Ah, that smelled like her. Not perfume, just an inexpensive bottle of shampoo, but combined with her natural scent . . . Bam! Got him right in the midsection.

As had that almost-kiss earlier.

He should have done it—well, no, he shouldn't have. There was too much baggage. His included. But, damn, he'd wanted to. Especially when he'd been within one tiny step of tasting her. Of holding her in his arms and discovering all the sweetness he knew was inside of Beth. Of feeling her against him, how her body would match the contours of his, how she'd fit into his arms. There'd be fireworks. He knew it. He didn't know how he knew; he just did. He hadn't felt fireworks in, well, years. Even with all the beautiful women he'd dated, he knew

Beth would eclipse all of them if he only had the chance to take her in his arms and kiss her.

But he didn't and he'd better suck that up and deal with it, not stand here mooning over something that would just complicate things. He wrapped the towel around his hips and looked for something to put on. Sadly, he doubted his uniform was out of the laundry yet, but he couldn't very well go walking around her house in a towel. He wasn't stupid; he worked hard at keeping his body in this shape and knew what it looked like. Knew the effect it had on women, and while he was glad of it around Beth, Kelsey . . . not so much.

Beth's robe was hanging on the back of the door. Of course it was pink.

He shrugged. Real men could wear pink, and hell, he was already in this fluffy towel with a cat's face on the edge; a pink robe was almost an afterthought.

Too bad it was too small.

Bryan pulled the one sleeve off. He'd gotten it up to his bicep. Beth might be the perfect height for him, but she wasn't built like him. And thank God for that.

He shrugged and opened the bathroom door. *Don't look at her bed.*

Uh, yeah. That didn't work.

The bed had the covers pulled up but not tucked in. The pillows were on the chair beside it. She'd gotten up in a hurry to rescue Sherman. Had she been wearing those short shorts she'd shown up in outside to bed? Or did she sleep in the nude? She hadn't been wearing a bra—that much he knew for certain and it'd tortured him throughout his shower.

He readjusted the towel. Yeah, that was pointless. A towel was not going to hide his growing erection.

Which meant that, *of course*, that was the moment her bedroom door opened and Beth stood there with clothing in her hands.

Which she dropped.

Bryan bent down to pick them up, almost smacking into her.

"I, uh . . ." Beth did that adorable hair-behind-the-ear move and the really hot lip-licking thing she had no idea would affect him as it did. *He* didn't know it'd affect him as it did—like a wave of lava rushing over his head and shooting straight to his groin. Good God, he wanted her.

Reason enough to back away. Which he did.

Of course the towel fell off when he did so.

Bryan scrambled to catch the thing somewhere by his knees, blushing for the first time in his life at his nudity.

"Oh. Shit. Sorry." The damn towel had shrunk two sizes in two seconds, and it was twisted around on itself so that if that pitifully narrow thing actually covered him, he'd turn in his man card.

Beth's blush matched the robe perfectly.

"Oh, geez. Here." She thrust out a piece of the clothing. Bryan snatched it from her and plastered it over his groin. Great. Nothing like standing in front of her holding his junk with his ass hanging out the window behind him.

He prayed there weren't any reporters out there. This picture would go viral in an instant.

Beth stood up and tried to avert her eyes—but he caught the quick glance to his nether regions.

Which caused said nether regions to get mighty interested.

Great. Nothing like holding your *erect* junk in front of the woman who'd made it that way.

Thank God, she turned around. "Those are, uh, were Mike's. He wasn't as, um, tall as you, but they should still fit. Until your uniform's dry."

"Thanks."

"I'll just leave you to . . . get dressed."

He didn't want her to go.

Thankfully, some shred of common sense prevented him from blurting that out, and he waited until she closed the door behind her before he moved.

He wasn't sure how he felt about wearing her husband's clothes.

Dead husband's.

Right. That distinction was important. He didn't hit on married women. Widows, on the other hand . . .

No, he didn't hit on widows, either. Hell, he didn't hit on anyone. He didn't have to. They all hit on him. But he hadn't taken up any married woman's invitation and so far, none of his lovers had been widows.

Beth could be the first.

He yanked on the shorts. Maybe wearing her dead husband's

clothes *was* a good idea; it'd keep him from making an ass out of himself around her. Seriously, he was not going to start something with Beth. She had too much going on in her life to handle a casual fling, and a casual fling was all Bryan was able to do at this point in his life. Especially with a mom from surburbia.

A little tap sounded from the door. "Bryan?"

He whipped the T-shirt over his head. "Hang on, Maggie. I'll be right there."

He gathered up the towel and hung it in the bathroom to dry, then opened the door to find Maggie standing there with a hopeful expression on her face.

Just like Kelsey's and her three friends' behind her. How many groups of friends did this kid have?

"Hi, Bryan." Kelsey gave him a flirty little tilted-head smile that would be devastating to twelve-year-old boys. Beth was going to have her hands full in a few more years.

The kid needs a dad.

Bryan sucked in a breath. He needed to go clean a toilet or something. Get his mind off that asinine notion.

"We were wondering if you'd, you know, take some pictures with us?" Kelsey asked.

"Yeah, it'd totally make everyone jealous," said one of the girls.

"And my mom, too. She thinks you're hot."

Bryan worked hard to plaster a smile to his face. This conversation had to be inappropriate on so many levels.

"Sure, girls, but let's take this downstairs, okay?" The bedroom was *not* the place to do a photo shoot. His agent would have a coronary.

The girls giggled and moved toward the stairs en masse in that odd way teenage girls did. Maggie rolled her eyes and shook her head as she reached for his hand. "Raquel's weird. All she talks about is boys." Maggie's sigh spoke volumes on her thoughts about the subject. "Boys are annoying."

Bryan's lips twitched. Ah, the blunt honesty of a child.

"Well, 'cept you," Maggie said, stopping at the top of the stairs. She patted his hand with her free one. "You're not annoying. You're nice."

His heart melted right then. He was surprised it wasn't sliding down the stairs, her words touched him so much. Because she meant them. Kids her age were brutally honest—and that truth could hurt or warm the heart.

He hiked her into his arms and rested his forehead against hers for a few seconds. "Thanks, Maggie. I think you're pretty special, too."

She patted his cheeks and gave him a kiss on the nose. "Now we're special buddies. That's what my daddy used to do with me before he died."

Bryan's heart melted the rest of the way and he could only nod. Hell, he even had to blink a few times just so she wouldn't see him tear up.

He carried her down the stairs, making his steps a little extra bouncy so her squeals of delight would wipe away the heavy emotion she'd tucked inside him. They could both use her laughter.

Kelsey was waiting not so patiently in the family room, trying to act all grown up and cool around her friends. How he remembered those days. It was tough growing up with one parent, and with the way her father had died . . .

He'd done his research after that first night. Read all the press coverage. Saw the suspicion that Mike Hamilton had been under in the days after his death. It couldn't have been easy for Beth, trying to deal with his death *and* taking care of her kids *and* handling the press coverage. The press could be ruthless, especially if they smelled a story. And they had. He'd found himself getting angry as he'd read the speculation that, in the end, had turned out to be pointless. Mike had been cleared of any wrongdoing and his record remained untarnished—as it should be.

Bryan hoisted Maggie onto the sofa and walked over beside Kelsey. Her shoulders went back. Her head went a little higher.

Then he put his arm around her. Her *cool* quotient grew exponentially; he could see it in her friends' awed looks. Good. If he could do this for her, putting on an apron was worth it.

"Okay, girls, I've got a few minutes to do this. Who's taking the pictures?"

"Oh, uh, right." Kelsey's face fell.

"I can!" Maggie raised her hand, her little face so full of hope Bryan was halfway into a wince because he knew what was coming when Kelsey shook her head.

"No way, Mags. I'll get Mom."

His wince turned into a smile he couldn't contain.

He tried to tamp it down when Beth showed up, wiping her hands on a dishtowel, looking so June Cleaver it ought to make him run in the opposite direction, but didn't.

She stopped short when she saw him, and the look she gave him was *far* from June Cleaver.

He had to talk himself out of his body's natural response. *Teenage girls* became his mantra. Nothing better to kill the effect Beth had on him.

The photo op went from "a few minutes" to a good half hour as the girls warmed up to him and stopped being star struck.

Then their moms showed up.

Beth answered the door when he was finishing up with the last photo and she walked back into the living room with an apologetic look on her face. "Um, Bryan? The moms were wondering if they could, well . . ."

"Sure. No problem. But why don't we go outside, ladies?" He did like meeting his fans and he knew as well as anyone that his looks were the draw. He had no illusions about that, and he worked on his looks for just that reason. They'd gotten him noticed, but he had to work at his craft to keep the jobs coming in. He didn't want to be a pretty boy joke when all was said and done. Which was why he was trying to segue out of action hero roles. No one won an Oscar for those. It was solid acting that came from portraying emotionally complex characters that got the Best Actor awards, and that was something Bryan had had his eye on since his first SAG role.

He posed on the deck for enough pictures to fill a magazine for an entire year, answered a ton of questions, and fielded a few not-so-covert invitations with his usual noncommittal good humor, all the while very aware that Beth was hovering in the background, glancing his way every so often.

She hadn't forgotten about the almost-kiss. Good. Well, maybe that was good. He *had* almost overstepped the boundaries and that would so not be good. For either of them.

No shit, Sherlock. Does she look like the type who goes around kissing random guys?

Jealousy churned in his gut, which surprised him because he'd never been the jealous type. Call it arrogance, but if a woman wanted someone else, he wasn't about to beg. The reality was, he had them lined up.

But with Beth . . . He didn't get it. She was everything he *didn't* need at this point in his life, just when his career was posed to go to that next level. His agent was counting on a new romantic lead role to give him an all-roles credibility. To be able to play emotional as well as action roles. He was going to be seen as a jack-of-all-trades and make it really big.

The last thing he needed was to pine away for a mom of five in middle-class America. This was his time to shine. To make his mark. Not be tied down with roots so deep he'd never be free.

Tied down? Tied down? What the hell are you saying, Manley?

He didn't know and he didn't want to know. Bryan plastered a big, charming, movie star smile on his face and looked at the last mom of the bunch. He swung her into his arms in a classic romantic pose, knowing it'd hit the Twitterverse within minutes and start the speculation about his upcoming film. It was all about the publicity. And always would be.

BETH couldn't help feeling a twinge of jealousy as Lori wrapped her arms around Bryan's neck and hung on. Beth wanted to be the one there. Which was silly. Ridiculous. She actually had a date tonight and Bryan was only posing for a photo op, not sweeping Lori off her feet to ride into the sunset with a happily ever after. Bryan wasn't cut out for this world. This life. He was made for bigger and better things. The glitz and glamour of Hollywood. Weeks in the south of France at film festivals. Award shows and red carpets and interviews . . .

Interviews. Remember that, Beth. Publicity. PR.

God, how she'd hated interviews. Everyone had wanted to talk to her when Mike's career had come under suspicion. She'd had to speak out then. Had to defend him. He was a good man, and a great pilot. He'd never put his passengers, his career, his *life* in jeopardy. That wasn't Mike, and that's what she'd told everyone. But still, they'd looked at every aspect of his career while the official investigation had gone on. Mike had been tried in the press. They'd never delivered a verdict because, Beth had surmised, they'd found out that Mike's image was so squeaky clean there was no story to be found.

But with Bryan . . .

No, she didn't need that kind of scrutiny in her life again, and while she had to admit that she definitely felt an attraction to Bryan, it could go nowhere. She wouldn't let it. She wasn't some on-set fling. She had five kids she had to set the example for. Five kids who depended on her for everything. She couldn't afford to lose herself in the hyperactivity that was Bryan's life, and she couldn't let herself get distracted by *what ifs* that would never come true.

So she buried her grimace when Lori squealed and tossed her head back, showing off the three-grand boob job, and sucked it up as if it meant nothing. Because, really, it could— *should*—mean nothing.

"Well, ladies, I'm sorry to cut this short, but I'm actually here to do a job. Beth's friends are paying for this, and I want to make sure she gets her money's worth."

Beth wouldn't mind getting it in another form of payment—

She had a date. Tonight. With a doctor. She had to put Bryan out of her mind.

She backed into the gas grill with a *clang.* "Oh. Sorry," she said when they all looked at her—a first since they'd arrived because they'd only had eyes for Bryan.

Bryan chose to take the distraction and, with Maggie trailing after him, headed to the outside stairwell toward the basement. Darn. She hadn't had a chance to get on the kids about straightening it up and God only knew what food they'd left down there.

"Come on, Beth," Julia, the wife of Mark and Tommy's soccer coach, asked once they watched him descend the stairs—and Julia didn't even *have* a daughter here with Kelsey. "He's not really *cleaning,* is he? It's just a cover, right?"

"Yeah, please tell us they're shooting a movie here or something? Magazine spread?"

"Hey, he can spread—"

"Mikayla!" Debbie Johnson slapped "Trash Mouth" Mikayla McCarty—who came by her name honestly if not classily—across the arm. "The girls might hear you."

"I'm hoping *he* might hear me."

Beth looked at the five of them, all soccer and PTA moms like herself, their eyes wide with anticipation, hopeful smiles on their faces.

Was this what they'd all become? Gossip-seeking teenagers in women's bodies, talking about a man they thought they knew from his public persona, but really didn't? Salivating over him? Turning him into a piece of meat? Was this what he lived with on a daily basis? Posing for pictures with strangers who liked the packaging but had no idea of the man inside it?

"Sorry to disappoint, ladies, but, yes, Bryan's here to clean." She adjusted the grill cover, then headed toward the French doors back into the kitchen. "I'll have Kelsey bring the girls around front to meet you."

She walked through the tornado of breakfast dishes Kelsey had served her friends on, grimacing when she thought of Bryan seeing this. He'd just made her kitchen spick-and-span yesterday; now it looked like a bomb had gone off. Tornado Hamilton had struck again.

She kicked her oldest's sneakers out of the path just as the TV came to life. Ah, good. Jason was up. "Jase!"

"Yeah?" His Cousin-Itt head rose off the sofa.

"Seriously? You're tired? Didn't you just get twelve hours?"

"Uh, not really, Mom. I was up playing *Call of Duty* with the guys."

She hated that game. Blood and death and destruction. It couldn't be healthy. She'd talked to the counselor about it, but the guy said to let him play. It was a social outlet for Jason, a way to connect with friends who didn't know about the family tragedy. It gave Jason the chance to escape the memories. A place and time where he didn't have to remember them and he could just be a kid.

But it didn't mean she had to like it or let him use it as an excuse to not do his share around the house. "Well, peel your tired self off the sofa and grab all the trash bags. It has to go out today."

"Aw, man, Mom. Why do I have to do it? Isn't that why we have Mr. Big Shot here?"

"I don't like your tone, Jason. And, no, that's not why Bryan's here. He's here to clean, not be your personal pick-up boy." She wasn't going to think about him being *her* personal whatever boy. "You might be finished with school for the summer, but this isn't a vacation. The man has other things to do in his life than pick up after you. And so do I." She flung one of his stinky socks at him. She hadn't had any brothers growing up. Just an older sister who was more like a babysitter than a sister. Being an "oops" wasn't fun when there were twelve years separating her from her only sibling.

"Aw, Mom, can't it wait 'til a commercial?"

"We have a DVR, Jase. Pause the show and get it done." There were some things to be said for technology.

Especially when Jason froze the screen on the next commercial—a photo of Bryan coming out of that lake with the bombs bursting behind him and nothing but a pair of low-slung cargo pants threatening to have a wardrobe malfunction.

"Hey, look who it is." Jason swung his mop of hair to the side, clearing his eyes. "Dude sure looks different in a maid's costume." He snorted.

"Jason, what exactly do you have against Bryan? You've been snarly since he got here."

He immediately hung his head and stared at his fingernails. "Dunno. It's just weird. A guy cleaning our house. What's he get out of hanging in some random family's house? Where's his man card?"

Man card? Her fourteen-year-old son was talking about *man cards*? She didn't know how to handle this. She wasn't a guy. Guys knew about this stuff. That's why she'd chosen a male therapist, hoping he could provide that male influence she wasn't capable of. But *man card*? What was she supposed to say to that?

"He gets paid, Jase. It's his job."

"Come on, Mom. Smell the coffee. The dude makes a zillion dollars a minute. No way he needs the money working here. So what's his angle?"

"He's helping out his sister. It's her business."

Jason shrugged. "If it were me, I'd write a check and be done with it. He can't *like* cleaning up after us. So what's the deal?" Now Jason looked at her. Intently. He even shoved his hair off his forehead. "Why *you*, Mom? Why'd he pick *you* to clean for?"

Her? Jason was making this about *her*? Had he seen what'd almost happened between her and Bryan after Sherman's fence escapade?

"Jason Michael Hamilton. I don't like what you're insinuating and I don't want to hear another word about this. Bryan is working for his sister, and Mrs. Leopold and Mrs. Harte were the ones who decided I needed a maid. They're paying for this. It has nothing to do with Bryan. I don't know why he's working for his sister, but that's not our business. The fact is, he's here, he's working, and that's the end of it. But he is not your personal slave, so round up all the trash and then tackle your room. It's getting to be a health hazard in there. Have I made myself clear on this?"

The hair went flopping into his eyes again as he mumbled something.

"I didn't hear that."

"Yes, ma'am."

She winced at the "ma'am." Nothing like aging twenty years with that term, but it was the biggest show of respect she could hope for, so she let it pass. He headed up the stairs to the disaster zone that was his bedroom.

Beth exhaled when he rounded the corner and she heard his heavy tread *schlumping* up the steps. God, what had he been insinuating? Did he really think Bryan was here for something other than what he'd been hired for?

Or was he *hoping* it?

She didn't know where that thought came from, but it resonated with her. Jason had had to grow up quickly in the two years since Mike's death. Two years, during which Jason had hit puberty, the most difficult phase of his life. All while dealing with his father's horrific death . . .

He didn't want to be the man of the house. She hadn't wanted that, either, but Jason had taken some things on himself. Not the trash—that one, she'd thrust on him because chores were chores and she needed the help. But the sense of responsibility he felt at times, the looking out for the other kids, the money he was socking away in the zipper in his beanbag chair that he thought she didn't know about . . . And the damn knowledge on his face every time he saw her with the checkbook, or on her last nerve with Tommy and Mark, or digging Sherman out from under the front porch . . . All things her husband should be worrying about, not her fourteen-year-old son. But the universe didn't see it that way. Which would be why she was, once more, going on a date she had no interest in going on.

"He's doing okay, you know."

Beth looked up, startled, to find Bryan in the doorway, back-lit by the sun—the perfect highlight to that crazy-ass physique of his that she had no business noticing but would have to be dead not to.

"I . . . I'm sorry. What?"

Bryan flipped a dust rag over his shoulder and sauntered into the room. Oh, he didn't do it on purpose, but the man was so naturally sexy that the swagger just happened. And made her drool, all the while wondering, in vivid Technicolor glory, how it would feel to be smashed up against that body, with his arms around her and his lips on hers and God! What was *wrong* with her? Bryan could be nothing to her. She was as bad as Lori and Mikayla and the rest of the moms.

"Jason," Bryan said, oblivious to the direction her thoughts were twirling. "His surliness is part of being fourteen, but he'll outgrow it. He's a good kid. Messy, but he did go up without giving you any lip."

He went to sit on the arm of the sofa, but Beth squiggled sideways so he could sit on the sofa itself. *Next* to her.

"And guess what?" He winked at her.

Winked at her. No wonder millions of women swooned whenever he was on screen.

"Beth?"

Oh God. He caught her fantasizing about him. "Uh, what?" That ought to cover whatever it was he'd asked her.

"I caught him taking socks out of his drawer this morning and tossing them around his room."

That blew away the fog Bryan had blown in over her normal rational thought processes. "What? Why would he do that? He spent all that time cleaning it up."

Bryan smiled and it was killer. "Exactly. He cleaned it up because you made him, but he wants to have control over his room. His environment. His world. He's had so little that that tiny act of messing up his room gives him pleasure. Gives him that sense of control he needs. It's a good manifestation. Better than other ways he could act out to take control of his life."

"I thought you were an actor, not a shrink."

A strange look crossed Bryan's face, and he glanced away. Oh, it was brief, but enough that Beth realized she'd struck a nerve.

"I, uh . . . I . . . saw someone for a while. A therapist. To, you know, sort a few things out. Learned all about needing to be in control."

"Your parents." The words were out before she could stop them. Thankfully, though, he didn't clam up or storm off.

Instead, he exhaled and nodded. "Yeah. It was rough."

"I can imagine. I'm sorry."

"Nothing for you to be sorry for."

"Well, for you to come into my home and see the same sort of thing you must have lived through."

"Beth."

He put his hand on her knee. It was a light touch. Completely asexual she was sure. Or at least that was probably how he intended it, but it so wasn't to her. A spark shot up her leg, through her stomach, taking every ounce of breath from her lungs, and lodging it all in her throat. Just like it had when he'd almost kissed her.

"I just wanted to tell you that, from what I can see, and having lived through something similar, your kids are doing fine. Sure, they're carrying the loss—that won't ever go away—but they're being normal kids. *You're* the one who sees that their father is gone every minute of every day. And I get that, I do. But they don't. There are times they actually forget. Or when the memories are good, not painful."

He then told her that Maggie had shared Mike's special hug with him, and Beth was floored. Not only that Maggie had shown Bryan that, but she'd smiled when she had.

"You're not just saying that to make me feel better."

He chuckled. "Trust me, if my brothers heard you say that, they'd tell you in no uncertain terms that I don't say things to make people feel better. That I'm brutally honest. To a fault at times." Now his fingers squeezed her knee just before leaving it. "No, if anything, I'd tell you the worst of it. But the truth is, kids *are* resilient. They only had however many years with Mike. You had so many more. It's harder for you to make the adjustment because he'd been in your life for so long. In your plans for the future. You've lost all that."

"Are you trying to make me feel *better*?" She was opting for humor. Because anything else would make her cry. Including the thought that Bryan Manley was trying to comfort her.

Her world had shifted so much these last two years, and here
it was shifting yet again.

It took a sharp turn to Uh-Oh-ville when he smiled sheep-
ishly. "Guess I'm not doing that great of a job, huh?"

He was doing so much more than he knew.

Stop it, Beth! her subconscious yelled. *This means nothing.
He means nothing. He's used to making women feel special.
It's his job. It's what's made him so successful. Stop reading
things into it that you want to be there. Because they aren't
and you're only going to end up getting hurt.*

Hurt. Right. Pain. Pain sucked. Pain was bad. She didn't
need any more pain.

She took a deep breath and stood, trying not to notice how
cold her knee suddenly felt without his big, strong hand upon it.

"Beth, what's wrong?" Bryan grabbed her hand.

She yanked it away. Or, at least, she tried. He didn't let go.

His gaze didn't let go of hers, either. Not the whole, long,
slow time it took for him to stand up beside her, his gaze level
with hers, then rising as he reached his full height. She'd forgotten he was so tall.

He reached for her other hand and brought their joined
hands between them, resting her knuckles against his chest.

His very firm, well-defined, muscular chest.

"Beth, if this is about what almost happened in the backyar—"

"Could we not talk about that?" She tried to surreptitiously tug
her hands free, but that was a lesson in futility. And humility.

"Obviously we need to or it's going to not only stay between
us but grow and become a huge problem."

"No it's not. Really. I've already forgotten about it." The
way her fingers were intertwined with his constituted being
crossed, right?

"You're lying."

Obviously not.

"I . . ."

"Don't, Beth." He took another step closer, though Beth
didn't know how that was possible, given that she was already
smushed up against him. "Don't deny it. You might not like it,
but don't deny it."

Problem was, she *did* like it. That was *why* she wanted to
deny it.

But then she made the mistake of tearing her gaze from his and looking at his mouth. At those lips that she'd imagined against hers and, all of a sudden, it was as if sunlight burst into the house through every nook and cranny and every window and door. Bright, blinding light, surrounding her and Bryan until there was nothing here but him. Towering above her, making her feel so small. And delicate. As if she needed protecting. As if he were the one who would do that for her.

It'd been too long since she hadn't had to be the one in control. On top of everything. Able to balance it all and not crumble under the pressure. Yet with Bryan here, holding her hands, his eyes so intense as he focused on her, his fingers clasping hers so tightly that for a moment, for one shining brief moment, she could let her burdens slide off and know that he would carry them on those incredibly broad strong shoulders.

She wanted to kiss him. Wanted to lean into him and press her palms against his chest, flattening them between them, the backs of his hands crushing against her breasts. It'd been so long since she'd had a man's hands on her and even longer for them being on her breasts and, oh God, she missed it. And for that reason, alone, she needed to stop this fantasizing now.

"Bryan."

"Beth."

Her name was soft. Breathy. As if he'd just woken up in her bed, his hair tousled, the remnants of a night of lovemaking clinging to his skin like she wanted, all warm and sated and sexy as hell, and where the *hell* was she coming up with this stuff?

"Bryan, I can't. We can't." She was lying. She was perfectly capable, and God (and she) knew *he* definitely was. Those pants left nothing to the imagination. "I have kids."

"I know."

"I'm a mom."

"I get it."

"I'm—"

"You. You're you." Bryan undid their hands and ran a knuckle down her breastbone, his gaze following it the whole way until it reached her shirt and he couldn't go any farther. Not without her permission.

She wanted to give it to him.

But didn't.

"I have kids I have to set an example for."

"I know."

"They can't see me kissing you."

"I know."

"They wouldn't understand."

"Do *you*?"

The question was soft, but it spoke volumes. No, she didn't understand. She didn't get how or why *the* Bryan Manley was in her home, picking up after her children and the dog and the hamsters and . . . *her*. Now he was picking up after her, only with her it wasn't something tangible like her underwear or her laundry or the checkbook or a frying pan. Bryan was picking up the pieces her life had shattered into. Unknowingly, perhaps, because how could he know or *want* to know what she'd been through in the last two years that now defined who she was in the future? And why would he even be interested in doing it? She wasn't blind; she had a backside that had spread a little more than she would have liked. Okay, a *lot* more. And she was a mom. Of sullen teenagers, hyperactive twins, and a dog that beat out the Energizer Bunny. How and why would *the* Bryan Manley find her attractive enough to want to kiss her?

"No. I don't understand."

His gaze searched her face. He ran a hand over her hair, his fingers remaining a little too long, fiddling with the ends, testing the weight of it as he slid his hand beneath it to cup her cheek.

His thumb stroked her lips and it took every ounce of self-preservation in her to not kiss it. To not open just enough to take it inside.

His hand slid down her throat, his thumb now resting on her thrumming pulse point.

"This is crazy," he half whispered.

Beth stiffened. She wished he'd kept it to himself. He didn't have to confirm her worst suspicions.

She took a step back, but Bryan didn't let go. "Don't run away, Beth." This was definitely a whisper.

"You said it yourself: This is crazy."

He never took his gaze from hers, but his thumb found her bottom lip perfectly, and stroked it. "What I'm feeling for you is crazy. What I want to do with you is crazy." His thumb brushed her cheek so softly, but it lit a zillion fires under her skin. "I want to toss you over my shoulder and storm up those stairs and kick open your bedroom door and stay there for at least a week."

Her knees gave out. Literally.

Luckily the sofa was right there, because she managed to park her butt on it instead of melting onto the floor, but the sentiment behind those words . . . The blatant carnality of that mental image . . . The look in his eyes as he refused to release her gaze . . . Beth couldn't believe the fire his words ignited was even more of a scorcher than the one his thumb had flared to life on her skin.

"I'm sorry."

He didn't look very sorry.

"I shouldn't have said that."

"You're right. You shouldn't."

Not unless you can back it up.

What the *hell* was wrong with her?

Nothing, sweetie. You're a normal, red-blooded American woman who's been on her own for two years. You're craving a connection and good ol' Bry here is one big powerful one. Go for it, babe. Enjoy.

It wasn't Mike's voice in her head, but she could almost image it could be. He'd want her to move on. Be happy. Be loved. Wanted.

But with *Bryan Manley*? And wasn't that a lesson in futility anyhow? Sure, he'd said he wanted her, but for a *week*. No matter how good that week was, she needed a man who wanted her for a lifetime. And maybe this guy tonight would be that guy. Why jeopardize that for a fantasy?

Summoning what small amount of mental fortitude she had somewhere inside her, Beth took a deep breath, willed her knees to function properly, and stood back up. She even managed to tug her hand free. "You're right. This *is* crazy. I'm not that woman, Bryan. I'm a mom. I have kids. I can't lock myself in a room for a week and forget the outside world. It must be nice to live in your world where you can, but out here on Acorn Lane, I have carpools and soccer practice and piano recitals and a day job." She squeezed his hand and she felt an answering squeeze in her chest. She was doing the right thing. "I appreciate you saying those things, but it's probably best if I don't go down that route, even in my dreams. You'll be gone, back to your glamorous life in a few weeks, and I'll still be here. With the carpools, and the swimming lessons and—"

"Mom!" A giant stuffed animal wobbled into the room.

"And Chewbacca." She dropped Bryan's hand, took another deep breath, and slammed that door shut. For good. "Maggie, give your brothers back their toy." Mike had bought a four-foot-high stuffed animal replica when the boys had been two, and they still cherished that thing to this day. Which might have something to do with the fact that Mike had given it to them, but which Beth banked more on the fact that it was big enough to lie on when they watched TV.

"But Mrs. Beecham needs a date."

Bryan arched an eyebrow at her. "The cat dates?"

Beth rolled her eyes before she strode away to head off the next Tornado Hamilton as the boys would chase Maggie through the house, the giant stuffed animal knocking things off every wall and table when Maggie ran by. "Welcome to my world. Chaos central."

BRYAN was liking Beth's world, strange as it might seem. He was thoroughly enjoying watching the boys race after Maggie with their capes flying out behind them, the Storm-trooper helmet flying off—okay, it wasn't pretty what it did to that crystal thing. And then the crazy-ass dog joined in the chase and—

He plucked Chewbacca out of Maggie's hands as she almost tackled him, while she burrowed her face against his thigh and squealed, "Bryan! Save me!"

The thing was, he had the ability to do so. All he'd have to do was marry their mom.

Chapter Ten

❧

BRYAN couldn't get out of Beth's house fast enough.
Marry their mom.

All afternoon, he'd seen the kids imprinted in every room in that house. On every wall. Pictures, drawings, trophies, ribbons . . . He hadn't really noticed how every room in Beth's home was a trophy case of sorts to her children and her family.

And Mike. Let us not forget Mike.

The thing was, Bryan wanted to. Wanted to pretend he had the right to do for Maggie what she'd asked. When she'd come running in to him, it'd been like Mac all over again. The nights she'd come into their room, scared and shaking from her dreams. She'd crawled into bed with him the most and he'd been the one to soothe her fears. He and Mac shared a special bond. Maybe it was because Sean and Liam looked so much alike. Thought alike. They were leaner than he was, quarterback material to his linebacker. They were both in the real estate business, had always had a bond that, while not excluding Bryan, let him know that he wasn't quite the same as them. If he hadn't had Mac, it would have bothered him.

So when Maggie had asked him to rescue her, it thrust him right back to the past, and all he'd wanted to do was wrap his arms around her and keep her safe from the world and whatever was after her.

Even the fact that her pursuers had been Tommy and Mark hadn't dampened that almost primordial instinct to shove her behind him and face her pursuers dead-on.

But Maggie wasn't Mac and he wasn't ten anymore. And then there was Beth.

Yeah, he definitely wasn't ten.

Marry their mom.

So he'd scooped the twins up under his arms and deposited them outside in the shed, with orders to take everything out so they could clean it out. It'd been a good plan, but unfortunately, he hadn't realized how much time it'd take the boys to unload it (next to none, given that they made it a competition) and then *re*load it (three hours to be finished up tomorrow). It'd taken Beth's call to dinner for him to realize what time it was and remember the fact that he had a date that night.

One he didn't want to go on.

Surprising, because the woman was someone he'd dated in high school. She'd been hinting last time he was home that they ought to reconnect, and he'd given her a call the day of the poker game. Unfortunately, he couldn't bail on her now just because he found spending a chaotic dinner with a woman and her five overactive kids more appealing.

So, he hightailed it home for a quick shower and change, not wanting to show up on the date in uniform.

He was doubly glad he'd done so when he saw Beth walk into the restaurant forty-five minutes after he and Amber had ordered. Which was about forty minutes after he'd figured out that there'd been a reason he and Amber hadn't gone out for very long back in the day.

He'd been contemplating ways to end the date early when Beth had walked in wearing a light green dress that made her hair seem shinier—and her curves curvier—and Bryan's blood had surged just at seeing her.

It'd surged some more when the guy she was with had rested his hand against the small of her back as they'd walked through the restaurant. Then he'd slid it across her shoulders beneath her hair and, even from where he was sitting, Bryan could see

Beth tense up. He had half a mind to go teach that guy a thing or two about how to treat a woman.

". . . So would you be interested, do you think?"

Bryan caught the tail end of Amber's question and the hopeful smile on her face, thankfully, before he'd made some noncommittal commitment that could have gotten him in trouble. What had she been talking about?

"Um . . ."

"Oh, you don't have to give me an answer now." Amber rested her hand on his forearm. "We have some time. Cassidy rents the beach house for the first three weeks of summer, but after that, we could have it if we wanted."

Cassidy. Cassidy Davenport. Town socialite. Father was a bigwig in the real estate market. Bryan knew exactly what beach house Amber was talking about; it'd made an issue of Architectural Digest with its innovative design and that secluded hot tub on the roof that was pretty much a private oasis.

Definitely *not* going there with Amber.

With Beth on the other hand . . .

Speaking of hands, the guy she was with had his draped across the back of her chair and seemed to be playing with her fingers with his other. His body language was loud and clear: *I'm getting lucky tonight.*

If only the self-important schmuck knew who he was with. Beth wasn't like that. She wouldn't be all over this guy, and she certainly couldn't be enjoying his almost claustrophobic posturing.

"Bryan?"

Darn. Amber needed an answer.

Bryan reluctantly tore his gaze from Octopus Guy and focused it on his own date. "I'm sorry, what did you say?"

She curled her top lip in between her teeth for a second. Bryan willed himself not to react. It wasn't Amber's fault that her lip nibbling wasn't sexy like Beth's was, and she couldn't help that she wasn't the woman he wanted to be with right now.

Or that that woman was sitting twenty feet away, fending off the mauling of a professional mauler. He ought to go rescue her.

But he couldn't. He had no right. An almost-kiss and an unfinished discussion about that almost-kiss didn't give him that right.

The hand sliding to her knee, however, was a different story.

"I'm sorry, Amber, but there's something I have to take care of." He stood and placed some money onto the table. "There's enough here for the bill." He didn't compound the insult by saying he'd call. He wouldn't. Ever.

"Oh, but . . . but . . ."

It wasn't well done of him to leave her sputtering, but Octopus Guy's hand was making a foray up Beth's thigh and Bryan couldn't understand how the guy didn't get the hint when Beth stiffened. He'd have to be dead not to notice.

And if that hand went any higher, he just might be.

"Beth?" Bryan put his best audition-quality *surprise* into his voice. "I thought that was you." He slid into the chair across from her and the Mauler. "You didn't tell me you were coming here tonight when I left your house earlier."

Take that, asshole. I've been in her house. Naked in her shower, too.

If it wouldn't reflect badly on Beth, he would've said it.

"Oh. Bryan. Hi."

He couldn't tell if it was relief or surprise in her voice, but he was going with relief. Beth wasn't the type to want to be mauled.

Kind of what you wanted to do to her earlier?

Hell, now he *couldn't* get up from the table. Not without making it very clear that he had the same thing on his mind that Octopus did.

"Um, Bryan, this is, um . . ." She tucked some of her hair behind her ear. "He's, um—"

"Rob Linders. *Doctor* Rob Linders." Octopus Guy didn't offer to shake hands. Good thing or Bryan might just have broken it. Then where would the *good doctor* be?

Bryan, at most, glanced at the guy, more concerned with how uncomfortable Beth was. Oh hell. Was it because he'd shown up?

Damn. He hadn't thought about that when he'd gone Caveman. Maybe she *had* enjoyed the good doctor touching her. Maybe her reaction was simply because she wasn't used to it.

"So you guys come here a lot?" Yeah, he was fishing, but, hell, he had to know.

Why?

He'd answer *that* question later.

"Um." She glanced at the doctor. "No. This is the first time. Our first, um, date."

She was nervously licking her lips so much that Bryan wanted to do it for her. After all, he almost had earlier.

"First date?" Now he did glance at Octopus Guy. "Oh, sorry. Didn't mean to interrupt." Yes he did. And give the guy a hell of a lot to think about. "Well then, I guess I'll be going. After all, have to be in your bedroom first thing tomorrow. Linders." He now made a point of shaking the guy's hand—so it'd be off Beth—and turned on every ounce of the famed Manley charisma. Let the guy deal with *that* while wondering what the hell he'd be doing in Beth's bedroom.

Suck on that, asshole, he thought as he strode out of the restaurant.

Beth's date ended six and a half minutes later. The prick actually left her in there. Alone.

Good.

Bryan waited around the corner of the restaurant as the *good doctor's* car pulled away from the curb. Beth didn't come out, though Amber did. Too bad she hadn't come out the same time as Linders; they could have gotten together and that would have put to rest two of Bryan's problems.

He'd examine why they were issues later. Right now, he was wondering where Beth was.

He gave her another four minutes and thirty-four seconds before he headed back inside.

She was there, at the table where he'd just left her, sipping a glass of wine, looking so ethereally beautiful in the candlelight and the backdrop of the lit waterfall, it was as if some director had staged the shot perfectly. Her natural grace as she sat there, poised, sipping delicately on her wineglass that caught the sparkling light from the water and reflected it onto her serene face, made Bryan's breath take a hike. She was simply . . . stunning.

He should walk away. Just forget about those ideas zooming around in his head, and leave her alone. Nothing good could come of going back to that table and sharing a romantic dinner with her. Nothing.

Yet that's just what he did.

"Hey, I didn't mean to ruin your date." He slid back onto the chair he'd vacated eleven minutes ago.

She arched her eyebrows and took another sip of his wine.

"Okay, so maybe I did. But the guy was getting gropey."

She swirled the glass around and studied the wine for a moment. "Thank you."

"I—what?" He sat back.

She set her glass down and folded her hands together on the table in front of her, looking like a cool ice princess that he wanted to thaw. "I said 'thank you.' He *was* getting gropey and I'm out of practice fending it off. One of my friends set us up, and well . . . you know. They were hoping it'd work out, but, honestly? He was making me claustrophobic."

"That's what I thought, too."

"What are you doing here?"

"Oh. I, uh . . ." Shit. He didn't want to admit he'd had a date. Of course, she'd been on one, so she couldn't take offense to that. Not that he even had the right to *ask* her to take offense. He was a big boy; he could date if he wanted.

And so could she.

"I had a date."

Her composure slipped just a notch.

Good.

"A date?"

He winced. "Well, it was sort of a dinner with someone from high school, but she was . . . I'm just not interested, you know?"

She sighed and picked up her wineglass again. "Yeah. I know."

"You weren't, either?" For some silly reason, his stomach got butterflies in it. Which made no sense, but then, a lot of what he was doing tonight made no sense in his Grand Plan for his life. But somehow he couldn't seem to stop himself from going down this path. "Guy's a doctor. Good catch."

She chuckled. "He certainly thought so."

Bryan shared that laugh. "Ah. Into his degree, was he?"

Beth shrugged. "Comes with the territory, I guess. I know

Mike's job always came up at some point in the conversation. I'm sure yours must, too."

"Well, yeah, it does. That's because most people know who I am. Kind of inevitable."

"You're pretty good-natured about all the fame. I couldn't tell if you were bored or not with all the moms, getting your picture taken."

"Hey, the minute I get bored with that is the minute I should quit. Every one of those women and girls today, and Jason's friends the other day . . . They're all paying customers. They spend hard-earned money to see my movies and allow me to do the job that I love. If I can't take the time to do something as simple as pose for pictures with them, then I don't deserve to be in this business."

"How do you handle it? Always being on? Always having people look at you and stare at you and think they know you by what they see in the media?"

Bryan picked up an untouched fork. "It goes with the territory. I knew what I was getting into when I signed up for this job. Was *hoping* I'd have to deal with it because that means you've made it. If you look at it that way, as job security, it's not so bad. As long as I can still have a private dinner with a beautiful woman on occasion, I'm good."

She looked even more beautiful when she blushed. "I'm sure you get to do that all the time."

That was the problem; most people would assume the same thing. But this dinner with Beth wasn't like dinner with any of the other beautiful celebrities he'd dated. Not by a long shot. And they hadn't even *had* dinner yet.

He reached for her hand, intertwining their fingers. He liked touching her like that. "No, Beth, I don't." He signaled the waiter for menus. Neither of them had had the chance to eat, and he didn't want her having whatever Octopus Guy had ordered. She seemed surprised and twirled her wineglass around a little more. Funny, he'd never really noticed a woman's hands before. Not unless they were on his body.

Oh hell, now he could actually support the table with the party in his pants just *thinking* about Beth's hands being on him.

What was it about her that affected him like this?

"Do the kids know you're on a date?"

Oh, great. Way to go, idiot, bringing up the doctor again. Kill the moment, why don't you?

But then she smiled a little half-smile and Bryan's temperature notched up a few degrees. No moment-killing going on.

"I told them I'm out with a friend. I don't want them to get attached to anyone unless I know it's going to be permanent. They've had enough upheaval in their lives and it's not fair to them to parade guys in and out of their lives."

"There's a parade?" The words left his mouth before he could stop them. Hell, before he could *think* them. He hadn't thought; he'd just reacted. In this instance, that probably wasn't the best course of action. It was no business of his who Beth decided to date, or how many.

You really believe that shit you're telling yourself?

Bryan waved the waiter over and ordered for the both of them. No, he didn't believe it and he was starting not to care that he didn't believe it. He was starting to care, period.

"No parade. But I've been on a few dates. Nice guys but not with that, you know, spark."

Yeah, he knew.

He took another swig of the drink. At this rate, he might need another.

"So tell me about your job, Beth. You never did get the chance the other day before we got sidetracked." By the way she'd looked in her misbuttoned shirt, with her hair all windblown and finger-combed while the dog and kids had careened through her house. He needed something mundane to get his mind off the image of how sexy she'd been, standing there while the chaos had whirled around her—and how beautiful she looked right this minute in a dress that brought out the color of her eyes and hinted at the perfection beneath it. Perfection he wanted to hold against him tightly while he kissed her.

He *was* going to kiss her. Maybe not tonight, but he was going to. He couldn't *not*.

But then she told him about her job and Bryan realized there was nothing mundane about it at all. Beth was a special education teacher for the elementary school. With the stories she told him of her kids—her school kids, but she said it with the same affection and caring that she had when she spoke about her own kids—Bryan realized that Mrs. Beth Hamilton had just gotten even more special in his eyes.

He also realized that he was falling for her.

WAS Bryan coming on to her?

Beth stared at those gorgeous green eyes, the ones staring so intently into hers, and she had to search around for her breath.

Was he talking about her? Did he mean he hadn't had dinner with other beautiful women before? Of course he had. Was he flirting with her or . . . or could he actually *mean* what he was saying?

And if so, how did she feel about that?

She reached for her wine again and raised it shakily to her lips while Bryan stroked her fingers with this thumb.

"I'm sorry. I'm making you nervous."

"No. That is . . . Well . . ." She took another sip. She didn't know how to do this. Didn't know what the protocol was. What she was supposed to say. How she should act.

Bryan took the wine glass from her and set it down. "Beth."

She mustered some courage and blinked at him, her throat still too constricted to allow her to utter anything.

"I think you're very beautiful."

Her stomach hollowed out. Bryan Manley had a way of delivering a line that was like no other.

And it *was* a line. It couldn't *not* be. After all, she had five kids who'd altered her figure. A dog that ran her ragged, and a house that was a disaster zone on a good day. She never had time to even *try* to look beautiful, let alone actually look it.

"And I know this is probably totally inappropriate, but I want to kiss you."

There went the rest of her breath. And all the feeling in her body except for the tendrils of want spiraling out from where his skin touched hers.

"Not here, of course. We don't need that making national news." He laughed and, oh, what it did to his face. His gorgeous, beautiful, movie-star-handsome face. "Not that I will, either. Well, unless you tell me I can."

He was giving her an out. It made sense to take it. After all, this wasn't some romance novel where the suburban housewife ended up with the Sexiest Man Alive and lived happily ever after. Not with five kids, the dog, and the disaster zone. Still, her constricted throat wouldn't let her say anything.

Yeah, that's it. Blame the poor constricted throat.

She licked her lips.

"God, Beth. Don't do that." Bryan's voice was hoarse. Strained. Low and sexy and it growled along her nerve endings like a match to gunpowder. "Not unless I can do it, too."

Her stomach fluttered. No, actually, it rippled. In a totally good way.

Beth licked her lips again—and resurrected the essence of her femininity that'd lain dormant these past two years among the mothballs of her soul. "If you want the right to claim me, Bryan, then claim that right. Don't ask for it. Kiss me like you want to. If I pull away, at least you won't have any regrets for trying. But if I don't . . . well"—she shrugged—"who knows?"

Chapter Eleven

❦

BRYAN almost swallowed his tongue. He hadn't known she'd had it in her.

From the look on her face, she hadn't, either. Was that a good thing?

He didn't care. She'd just given him permission—well, she'd said he shouldn't ask for permission.

"I'm suddenly not very hungry. At least, not for dinner." He ran his thumb over the back of her hand, because he could and because it was so damn smooth and sexy and he needed to touch her to keep from leaping across this table and kissing her right here and right now.

He wasn't going to be able to restrain himself for long, though.

"That's a shame. Because I am." Beth picked up the wineglass again and touched her lips to the rim. "Very hungry."

Holy hell. Who *was* this woman and what had she done with Beth? *His* Beth. Not that he was complaining—it was nice to see this sexy, flirty side of her—but Beth as a mom was incredibly sexy to him.

Where the hell was their waiter?

A hint of a smile slid across Beth's lips—like his tongue

wanted to do. Then she took a sip of the wine and Bryan's pants got extremely uncomfortable when he caught a glimpse of her tongue flicking out to catch the remnant of a drop on the rim.

She was torturing him. And enjoying it.

Two could play that game.

He slid his fingers from hers. Her self-confident look shifted for a second before she recovered.

Then her eyes flared when he brushed her leg with the toe of his shoe.

"Bryan!" she half squeaked.

It was his turn to pick up his water glass and take his sweet time taking a drink, all the while never breaking eye—or toe-to-leg—contact.

"What?"

"I . . . it's . . . Nothing." She sipped her wine a bit unsteadily.

Bryan leaned forward and took the glass from her, then handed her a water glass. "Careful, Beth. You're going to need to keep your wits about you."

So he could completely fry them the minute he got her out of this restaurant.

No. Not the *minute*. He wasn't going to jump on her like a teenager as soon as they hit the pavement. This would be their first kiss. It had to be special. Memorable. He wanted her never to forget it.

She's not the fling type, Manley. Remember that.

Yeah, he knew it. But a kiss didn't mean a fling. He didn't have to take it any further than a kiss.

But then she slid her toe beneath his pant leg and, holy hell, she'd taken off her shoe.

Bryan sputtered the water he'd just sipped and grabbed for a napkin. "Beth! You can't do that here!"

Her self-satisfied look was back. "But you just did."

"Yeah, but that was different. I kept my shoe on."

"I didn't want to do any damage with the heels."

Did she *have* to point out that she was wearing heels? Was there a guy *alive* who didn't like heels on women? Heels made a woman's legs longer, shapelier, usually put her within perfect kissing distance, and gave him fantasies about all the ways he'd like to remove them. Or *not* remove them. Just Beth and her heels, and, oh hell, he was going to be able to lift the table without using his hands.

He pulled his legs back beneath his chair. There was only so much torture a man could take. And he hadn't expected to get any from Beth. Showed what he knew.

He wouldn't mind getting to know so many more things about Beth.

Which he did over the inordinately long time it took the waiter to bring their meal, and then the extra-long time it took Beth to eat it. He could have slurped it down in under six seconds, but his "throw you over my shoulder" comment earlier was as Caveman as he wanted to be with her. And if he were honest with himself, he was enjoying her deliberateness. She took her time with each scallop, savoring every bite, and Bryan found his gaze glued to her lips.

The thing was, Beth had left all her teasing to that one brush of her foot against his leg. The food had shown up and whatever sultry sex kitten thing she'd been trying on him had vanished at her true, unabashed enjoyment of the meal. He could watch her eat for days.

A week preferably. In her room. In bed. Just like he'd suggested before. Naked.

He shifted uncomfortably again. He had to get his reactions under control or he wouldn't get anywhere near kissing her because he wouldn't be able to leave this table.

"So why *are* you helping out your sister?" she asked him. "This can't be something you *wanted* to do. Is it research for a role?"

He grasped onto that explanation with both hands. Beat explaining that Mac had outplayed all of them.

"Mac needed help and I figured, why not? I had some time to kill."

"And then you'll go back to the glamorous life? Yachting to Monaco and driving a Porsche down Rodeo Drive?"

"Have you ever been on Rodeo Drive? I try to stay far away from that tourist mecca. But Monaco? Yeah, it's sweet. A nice perk to the job."

She asked him about what he did then, but not the way most people did. *They* wanted to hear names of people he met, money items, inside gossip. With Beth, it was as if she were asking how his day at the office was, and she was genuinely interested in his answers from a personal standpoint, not a sensational one. It was nice. New and nice.

Shit. He was getting in over his head here and he still had three more weeks to go. Was he going to be satisfied with merely kissing Beth tonight?

Bryan shook his head. He knew himself. But he also knew Beth. If tonight's kiss-to-come was all she allowed, he'd be happy with that.

If she allowed it at all.

B ETH picked at her rice pilaf. She wasn't very hungry—her stomach had been in knots since Bryan had sat down across from her and Rob. Well, truthfully, it'd been in knots when Rob had gotten touchy-feely. But for Bryan to then show up . . .

He looked utterly delicious in the cream polo shirt and khaki pants with a brown jacket hanging off his shoulders as if it'd been custom tailored. Which it probably had been. The guy was incredibly attractive, and the clothes, while not making the man—because, really, Bryan was his own man—they certainly made that man look spectacular.

And he wanted to kiss her.

Her stomach fluttered again at the thought and it was all she could do to take another bite of the rice. It was a stall tactic. She hadn't tasted one morsel of the scallops. Couldn't tell if the wine was sweet or dry. Only knew what the asparagus tasted like because that taste never changed. Because the moment he'd said he wanted to kiss her, Beth could think of nothing else.

Bryan wasn't talking a mere peck on the cheek or a quick meeting of the lips she'd done so far on her dates. No, there would be no chaste peck-and-go with Bryan.

What if she'd forgotten how? What if she didn't measure up to the movie stars he kissed on a daily basis? What if she was lacking in that department? After all, she hadn't really kissed anyone but Mike in years.

"Do you want dessert?" Bryan asked her.

It would be another way to stall off the inevitable—but *why* was she stalling? She wanted to know what it was like to kiss him, too. She'd hardly been able to keep her eyes off his lips all throughout dinner.

Then say no and let's get the heck out of here!

"Thanks, but no. The meal was filling enough."

Liar! The butterflies are filling your stomach.

She mentally *shushed* her conscience and patted her lips with her napkin, then sat it on the table beside her plate.

The waiter appeared in a second with their bill and Bryan handed him some cash before Beth had had time to blink as if the two of them had choreographed it. "Bryan, you don't have to—"

"I want to." He reached for her hand again, his fingertips brushing over her knuckles. "Come on. Let's get out of here."

Beth got a little shiver at the urgency in his voice. At the command that was still a question and one she still wasn't sure she was capable of answering.

"Did you drive?" he asked as they left the restaurant, the night sounds and twinkling lights scattered throughout the trees setting the scene for romance immediately.

"N . . ." Beth cleared her throat. "No. Rob did. He's my neighbor Anne Marie's cousin."

Bryan reached for her hand. "Good, because now I have the pleasure of seeing you home."

He led her to his pickup truck and held the door for her. Beth felt a thrill rush through her when her dress hiked up her thigh and his breath caught. Not bad for a mom of five. With a movie star no less.

She watched him walk around the front of the truck. Bryan wasn't just a movie star, though. He was Maggie's confidant, the twins' buddy, Jason's hero, and Kelsey's . . . well, Kelsey's crush.

And Beth's.

There. She admitted it. She was crushing on him every bit as much as her daughter was, but on a whole different level. One that knew what could happen between a man and a woman, and she was curious to see what happened between *them*.

Bryan didn't say anything during the ride, just flicked on the radio to a soft rock station, his hand firm and steady on the stick shift as he switched gears, and again, Beth got a shiver at the way he handled the truck. She could only imagine how he'd handle her.

And, oh, how she wanted to be handled.

He pulled into the parking lot at the township park, stopping by the path leading to the gazebo. He shut off the engine and rested his forearm on the steering wheel, staring straight ahead.

Beth was staring at his profile. The man was simply breathtaking.

"Would you like to take a walk?" He turned those gorgeous eyes her way and Beth's breath got stuck somewhere between her heart and her throat and she could only nod.

He brushed his fingertips across her cheek briefly, his gaze shifting right to her lips, and goose bumps shivered across her skin.

"Stay here," he whispered, then slid out of his seat and strode around to her side.

He opened the door and Beth felt as if she floated out of the car, his hand helping her down. Then he tucked her arm beneath his, pulling her close so that her shoulder brushed his bicep, his scent tickling her senses. She couldn't name the cologne, but she could definitely name the Bryan Manley part of it; she'd learned his scent so well from her home. It lingered on the towels he'd folded and the one he'd hung up after his shower in her bathroom, and on Mike's clothes that she was, at some point, going to wash. And on her pink robe . . .

She could smell Bryan all over her house. Even in Maggie's hair when she'd kissed her good-night last night.

This wasn't good. He was becoming too much a part of her life. Too much of her focus. Yet she was powerless to stop it.

He led her up the steps to a gazebo decorated with hanging baskets of red geraniums and twinkling Christmas lights along the railing.

Bryan stopped in the center and stood in front of her, never once letting go of her hand. If anything, he intertwined their fingers tighter. Held on to her more securely. Took a step closer and raised his other hand to cup her cheek, then drew his thumb across her lower lip.

The butterflies in Beth's stomach went fluttering so fast they were stealing her breath.

"I want to kiss you, Beth." He nuzzled her nose with his.

She licked her lips, her eyes drawn to his. "You don't need to ask."

It was all the permission he needed. His thumb drifted away as his lips descended onto hers and, oh God, it was amazing. His lips on hers, teasing, tasting, sliding across hers with such promise, Beth had to gasp to get air going in.

Dear lord, the man could kiss.

His arms slid around her, pressing her against him, and the kiss wasn't just a kiss any longer. It was a full-out event. Beth had to slide her arms up his back and grab his shoulders—his incredibly strong shoulders—and his arms tightened around her. His tongue delved into her mouth, sending her nerve endings to *tremble,* and he stole every ounce of air from her lungs. But Beth didn't care because if he just kept kissing her, if he just kept holding her and pressing against her and wanting her, she could go on like this forever.

And the kiss did go on. As she'd thought, this was no quick nibble. Bryan was tasting every part of her lips, exploring every inch of her mouth, his breath hot and heavy against her cheek, his arms strong and supportive around her, his hands—dear God, his hands . . . She had a thing for a man's hands and Bryan's were strong and big and capable and oh so sensitive when he swirled his fingertips over her back, igniting another whole round of flames beneath her skin.

This couldn't be happening. She couldn't be standing here, beneath the gazebo with its hanging flowers and soft lights and the pond gurgling in the background, a practical fairyland, kissing *the* Bryan Manley.

No. Not *the* Bryan Manley. Bryan Manley.

Bryan.

She was standing here, running her palms across the broad back and shoulders of Bryan, the guy who was here to clean her home, but who'd slid inside it and given it new life. All in less than a week.

Beth stiffened. Less than a week. She couldn't feel something this strong for someone in less than a week. It was crazy. It was stupid. And the fact that it was *the* Bryan Manley, movie star, was unbelievable. At some point she was going to have to wake up from this dream and deal with reality.

Then he slanted his head the other direction and Beth realized that reality had shifted a few degrees to the left.

Bryan ran his hand down her spine, stopping just above the curve in her back that led to her backside. God, she wanted him to touch her there. To cup her and squeeze and pull her against him so there was no doubt how he was feeling.

But Bryan didn't. As a matter of fact, he gentled the kiss, pulling back just a bit so there was a sliver of air between them.

Beth shivered.

"Cold?" Bryan whispered against her lips.

She shook her head—because she was too filled with desire to be able to reply coherently.

He stroked his knuckles down her cheek, his gaze boring into hers. "You're right. You're so hot I forgot myself. I shouldn't have taken advantage of you like this, Beth. All I can say is that I wanted to kiss you so badly that I couldn't help myself. I've been wondering about this. Imagining it, fantasizing about it ever since I first laid eyes on you. And when I found out you were widowed . . ."

He drew in a shuddering breath and leaned his forehead against hers. "I couldn't think about anything else. I had to have you in my arms. Had to know what kissing you was like."

Beth licked her lips and felt a thrill run through her when his breath caught. "And now that you do?"

Bryan caught her bottom lip between his teeth, then ran the tip of his tongue along it. "Now I want to know more."

For a moment—okay, maybe two . . . or seven—Beth saw that image. Them, in her bed. The lights low, maybe some candles, soft music playing, and Bryan above her, staring down so intently into her eyes as he stroked the hair from her face, telling her in minute detail everything he wanted to do to her . . .

Beth clenched her thighs against the ache there that was, well, not surprising exactly because she knew what was what, but it'd been so long that she'd sometimes wondered if she'd still remember how.

She remembered.

Bryan caught the movement and tugged her hips into him. "Hey. Where you going? I won't bite." He slid his hand low on her back and rounded it over the curve of her backside, pressing her into him. "Not unless you want me to, of course."

He wanted her. There was no question of that and no way Beth would ever forget what *that* meant. Bryan wanted her and, God help her, Beth wanted him. Here. Now. She didn't care. Didn't care that it was a public park. That it was against the ordinances. That her name would be in all the local papers on the police blotter if they were caught. That it was wide open and anyone could walk by . . . It didn't matter. Bryan would be hers.

"Beth . . ." His breath was hot on her neck. "You are driving me wild, do you know that?"

She could only nod because, really, there was no air going in. Especially when he nibbled on her neck like that.

"God help me, you're a beautiful woman." He cupped her jaw with his other hand and nuzzled her ear, sending fireworks rocketing through her. Her knees were threatening to give out, so Beth hung on as if her life depended on it. Somehow, she had a feeling it did.

That was the moment reality came crashing back with a vengeance. She was nuts. *This* was nuts. He was Bryan Manley. He was a movie star. He wasn't a settle-down-in-the-burbs kind of guy and she was not about to live his lifestyle.

Not that he'd even asked her to.

Right. There was that.

Beth let go of the hair at the base of his neck she hadn't been aware she was threading her fingers through.

She un-arched her back so her breasts—her aching breasts— were no longer plastered up against that magnificent chest. So her pelvis was no longer in contact with that glorious rise beneath his pants that promised heaven, but only for a very limited time.

She had kids to think about. A heart to protect. Bryan Manley wasn't what she needed in her life.

"What's wrong?" He pulled back and tilted her chin up with one finger. "Where'd you go?"

She glanced away, but then sucked in a breath—finally!— and looked back at him. "I can't do this, Bryan."

Something flashed across his face. Disappointment? That was a surprise. It wasn't as if she were the only woman in town. Hell, several of the moms had already made it abundantly clear that they were more than open to the possibility. No, she had to be reading things into it that weren't there because even if Bryan did want her, it was only to scratch this very pleasant, very *hot,* very complicated, itch.

G OD, he was an ass. Kissing her in public like this when he had zero intention of staying around. He was so used to the LA lifestyle that he'd forgotten that he shouldn't do this, especially knowing that Beth wasn't a casual type of woman.

He let go of her cheek. Her smooth, soft cheek that tasted so good, his fingertips brushing that hollow beneath her ear. That sexy spot that smelled like her and drove him wild.

He resisted the urge to brush his fingers across her lips. That would just be cruel—to him. He knew what those lips tasted like. Knew their shape and their texture and their softness. Knew how they parted when he wanted to slide his tongue between them, and how her bottom one felt between his teeth. Beth had been designed for him in every way but for the fact that she was tied to the very thing he never wanted to be tied to.

So he let her go with a deep sigh and set her from him. "I better take you home."

And leave her there.

Alone.

Chapter Twelve

❦

SHE had to get out of the house before Bryan showed up. It was Beth's first thought when she opened her eyes the next morning. The morning after.

God, she'd *wanted* him. In the carnal sense. The biblical sense. Every sense she possessed. But then she'd have to give him up.

She'd done that before, and it sucked. Losing Mike had been devastating. She couldn't do that again. And she had a feeling losing Bryan could be just as damaging.

Still . . . wouldn't it be better to have the memories?

Beth clutched her pillow to her abdomen and rolled over, squeezing her legs together as she did so. She ached. She wanted. Hell, she was even getting wet just *thinking* about what could have been.

She couldn't be here today. Couldn't see him in her home, bending over, reaching up, moving around as if he had every right and not want him. Because she did. Here, in the privacy of her own bedroom—her lonely bedroom—she could admit that she wanted to know what it was like. Even if only for a few days.

That scared her. She'd be opening herself up to too much.

And her kids . . . her kids already liked him. If she took their relationship to a new level, would the kids pick up on it? And what would happen when he left?

Beth sat up and tugged her T-shirt down over her aching thighs. Yes, she definitely was *not* going to be here today. Maybe spending time with five I-don't-wanna-go-shopping kids was just the thing she needed to get her mind off one incredibly hot movie star.

BRYAN didn't want to get out of bed. It had nothing to do with that stupid job, and everything to do with the wet dream he'd just had about Beth. Yeah, him. A wet dream. He hadn't had one of those since he'd been fifteen. But Beth . . . God he wanted her. And his subconscious had let him have her.

He reached for the tissues and cleaned up. He was in a shitload of trouble if she could do this to him in a week. He still had three more to go and they couldn't go by soon enough. In the meantime, he'd have to do *something* to keep his mind off her.

Going to her home and cleaning her bedroom was *not* it.

He wanted her so much it scared him. How had this woman with five children commandeered his thoughts so completely? How had she suddenly become the first thing he thought of when he woke up and the last thing he thought about before he went to sleep? And every minute in between?

Kissing her had only made it worse. Now he *knew* what it was like to hold her in his arms. To taste her and feel her and inhale her. Want her. Because he did. So damn much it scared him.

She made him question things he'd never thought he'd question. Things he'd made up his mind about years ago. But one tousled-haired, green-eyed smile and he was reevaluating everything. And he didn't want to face her, see her, hear her, *want* her while he was doing that—because Beth could make him forget his own name, never mind his heretofore firmly held principles.

Only the thought of Mac giving him hell got him out of his bed, into the shower, and into that hideous uniform that was getting too tight in the crotch every time he thought about Beth.

He took a huge breath as he stood on her front porch, willing himself to ring the doorbell in a way he hadn't had to when he'd walked into this sentence on his first day. Then, it'd been dread. Now . . . Now it was fright. The thought of caring for her. Of wanting her. Of trying to make something work between them while still maintaining his career and industry status.

Jason answered the door. "Dude. Mom's shopping."

"Jason." Bryan peeled the Manley Maids cap off his head, sending off a quick *thank you* to the goddess of shopping. "Did you finish your room? I plan to give each room a thorough cleaning today." Work up a good sweat and keep his mind and body busy enough so if he did see her, he'd be too tired to respond.

He hoped that idea worked. Hell, she was out and he *still* wanted her.

"Doesn't it bother you that you're cleaning other people's houses?" Jason asked. "That you're doing what they should?"

There was a reason for his question, but Bryan wasn't sure what it was. But Jason wanted something, and his hair and pants and sullen attitude screamed of a need for attention, so Bryan subjugated his pride to see if he could help Beth's son out.

"Nothing wrong with an honest day's work. Besides, your mom's friends paid for me to be here. No different than a plumber or electrician."

"Yeah, but they don't wear something like that." Jason flipped the hair off his forehead, so Bryan got a glimpse of the same green eyes Beth had.

"Clothes don't make the man, Jason. Actions do. Your word does. I promised my sister I'd help her out. I agreed to take on this contract, therefore, I'm here."

"But just for a certain time, right? A month?"

"Yeah, a month."

"Blows."

"It's all what you make of it." Bryan nodded for Jason to sit in the chair in the family room, then he sat on the sofa across from it, forcing Jason to look at him. The conversation was a start, but if he was going to get through to this kid, if he was going to have the opportunity to do some good here by showing Jason the reality of life so he'd help his mom instead of creating more mess every day, then he had to engage him.

"I don't like cleaning, Jason. But it needs to be done and once you do it, you feel good that you've taken pride in your house or your car or your room or your locker, and owned it. When you own something, be it a thing or your action, you care for it. And by doing that, you care for *you*. For who you are, how you present yourself to the world."

"You trying to get me to cut my hair? Mom doesn't, you know."

Bryan scrubbed his own. "Your hair is your hair. That's between you and your mom and I don't know why you even brought it up. I haven't said a thing about cutting it."

"You thought it, though."

"What I think doesn't matter. It's what *you* think that does." No way was he going to get in a discussion about hair. Time would extract its own revenge when Jason looked back on the pictures from now. "I'm just saying you need to take pride in your room and this house. Not for just your mom, but for you, too."

"Dude, I couldn't care less about this house."

"Really? What if you had to move?"

Jason's head shot up. "We have to move? Mom said we don't. That the life insurance covered it. That we're fine."

Shit. He hadn't meant to worry the kid or bring up anything to do with his dad's death. He was blowing this. "If your mom said that, then she means it. I'm just saying, this is your home. Your mom's working really hard to keep it that way, and you could give her a hand by keeping your room neat and picking up some more around the place. I'm only going to be here a month. After that, it'll be on you guys to keep the place in shape. You might not want to create more mess. And you might be able to get more privileges if you actually do some of the work."

"No clue what you're talking about." Jason went back to sulking, crossed his arms, and plunked his feet on the coffee table—knocking a pile of magazines onto the floor. And didn't move to pick them up.

Bryan arched an eyebrow.

With an award-winning sigh, Jason dragged his lanky body up off the cushions enough to retrieve the pile. He plopped them down on the table in another mess.

Bryan just stared at him.

With another sigh that could probably be heard in the next county, Jason restacked the magazines, then glared at Bryan.

"Not too tough to do." Bryan nodded at the stack.

"I guess."

"Good." Bryan stood up. "Then how about you tackle the room? Just think how happy your mom will be when she gets home."

Never mind how happy *Bryan* would be when Beth got home.

B UT Bryan wasn't there when Beth got home, and Beth had mixed emotions about that.

She couldn't get that kiss out of her mind. Which went with her *being* out of her mind. Bryan Manley was out of her sphere. Her realm. And it'd been driven home to her today at the stores.

There'd been the stares. The whispers. It'd started like a light breeze across a meadow when she'd walked in, but as she went through the aisles, she could feel the breeze picking up steam, the metaphor for a storm brewing disappointingly accurate. By the time they were halfway through the grocery store, she knew she wasn't going to outrun the winds of gossip by the time she reached the last aisle.

Sure enough, there'd been people hanging in the aisle, just waiting for her. The questions about Bryan . . .

No, she didn't know what his favorite color was, and no she didn't know how tall he was (just the right height for kissing) or how broad his shoulders were (broad enough to wrap her up and blow her mind) or what his next movie was going to be or if he was dating anyone or why he'd come back to town . . . The questions went on and on, as if she were his publicist.

Someone had even asked her that and it'd been on the tip of her tongue to tell them that, no, she wasn't his publicist; she was the woman he'd been kissing last night at the Palmer Park gazebo, but that would only bring on more questions and the kids were already overwhelmed by this round.

The kids. Hell. She'd had to get them out of there quickly. She could see the same bug-eyed look on Kelsey's face that she'd worn when one reporter—a seemingly gracious, caring young woman, had spoken softly to Kelsey up until the scene had gone live, then grilled a ten-year-old about what it was like to lose her father.

Beth had seen red and almost shoved the woman away. Instead, she'd ended the interview and hustled Kelsey back to the car. She did the same thing in the grocery store.

So now, here they were, all at home, the specter of Mike's death hanging over them, and Beth was dreading opening the front door. She couldn't face Bryan. She just couldn't. She had to hold it together for the kids, make them dinner, and pretend that everything was as it should be.

She took a deep breath and unlocked her front door, praying Jason hadn't managed to turn the order Bryan had brought to her home into yet one more tornado.

She wasn't holding out much hope.

Except when she opened the door, she stared at the family room in amazement. The room was spotless. It was straightened. Even the bookshelf was in order. And the magazines. Mike had been military and even *he* couldn't have stacked them any straighter.

Dragging the four younger kids and six bags of groceries into the kitchen, she got another shock. The cat flap was on the back door, the drain board was nowhere to be seen, the leaky faucet wasn't leaking, every fingerprint was gone from the stainless steel fridge, *and* the artwork was lined up nice and neat with a magnet on every corner, the kitchen floor spotless enough to eat off of, and the three missing cabinet knobs had been found and replaced.

Unless Jason's body had been taken over by aliens, Bryan had done this.

"Mark, pick up those marshmallows, please," she said as her son dropped the half-eaten bag they'd bought at the supermarket onto the table—only to miss and have them scatter onto the floor, Bryan's hard work undone in two seconds.

"But Mom, Sherman will eat them."

That's what she was afraid of.

And, of course, on cue, Sherman came racing into the room and vacuumed up several of the treats before she could get to him. And then he started wheezing. Great. Another trip to the vet.

Luckily, she stroked his throat and got the marshmallows down. Mark and Tommy got a stern lecture on the hazards of feeding Sherman things that dogs shouldn't eat, and they all put away the groceries and other items so that the kitchen and their rooms looked exactly as Bryan had left them.

Beth walked into her room with the bag of toiletries and wasn't surprised to see that Bryan had been there. He'd said he would and he had.

That shouldn't surprise her—and it didn't, not really—but he'd been in her room. Moving her things to dust. Seeing where she slept. Bathed.

Her thighs tingled at the intimacy that implied. Sure, he'd had cleaning products in hand, but after that kiss . . . She'd been the one to end it. Her sense of self-preservation had kicked in and she'd wanted to kick herself. But the kids came first. They had to and Bryan's lifestyle wasn't what she wanted for them. *If* she'd even had a chance at it. Kissing did not a commitment make, and Bryan had such an amazing career, she couldn't ever see him giving it up for this. Real life.

"Hey, Mom."

Though real life had just shifted ninety degrees to the right. Jason's hair was . . . *gelled back?* "Jason?" She could actually see his face, but she still wasn't sure it was him.

"Yeah, I, uh, straightened up the basement and was wondering if I could have some of the guys over for gamer night?"

He'd attempted these all-nighters before and they usually fizzled out about three in the morning. They'd sleep 'til noon, then head home with a late morning pancake breakfast in them that Jason had always helped her prepare. If that was the price of all the work Jason did *and* the new hair, Beth was all for it.

Kelsey, of course, then had to have *her* friends over, and Mark and Tommy had to have *their* friends over, so Maggie did, too, and, well, at least obsessing about keeping the dozen and a half kids in her home separated by gender and age kept her from obsessing about Bryan all night.

At least until the phone calls started.

Chapter Thirteen

❦

BRIGHT and early—too damn early—the next morning, Beth was fielding phone calls. She shouldn't have been surprised, given the circus in the grocery store, but that didn't mean she had to like it.

And after the fifteenth call, she'd had enough. She called all the sleepover kids' parents, gave them her cell number, then unplugged the house phone.

That only escalated things. By noon, the news vans were parked on her street.

Beth called all the parents back and let them know what was about to descend upon her home and suggested they pick up their kids in front of the neighbor's house behind her, then called her neighbor to warn her about the teens crossing her yard, rounded all the kids up, and instructed Jason and Kelsey to lead them out the back while she went to the front porch as if this were some covert operation. Her neighbor, Jillian, would keep the kids there until the coast was clear.

In theory, it would work. In reality, Beth was a mass of shaking nerves. She didn't want to talk to these people. It was no one's business what Bryan was doing at her house. There was no reason this should make news, and while it wasn't the scandal that Mike's death had been, it didn't make it any less invasive.

She did, at least, manage to button her blouse correctly and make sure she was wearing makeup and clothing with no stains, but that didn't make her feel any better. Microphones were shoved in her face and questions shouted at her as if this were a national emergency that everyone needed the answers to immediately.

"Does Bryan really clean or is he doing this for a movie role?"

"Is this a publicity stunt?"

"How were you chosen?"

"What do your kids think of you having a man in the house again?"

That was the question that made her freeze. The one that shut her down. And almost made her cry.

"Bryan is *not* the man in my house and even if he were, that's none of your damn business. Can't you people leave me alone? Leave him alone? Why does it matter what he's doing in his time off? He's helping out his sister and that helps me. It has nothing to do with what happened to my . . . my husband or my life and I want you to leave my kids out of this and get off my property. Now."

She didn't wait for the questions to stop because, of course, they didn't. Those people were out there doing their jobs, having no real grasp of what that job was doing to her.

She closed the door behind her and leaned against it, her head thudding on the hard wood. *I won't lose it, I won't lose it, I won't lose it.*

She kept repeating it until her stomach settled, her breathing returned to normal, and the burning behind her eyes stopped.

Then her cell phone rang. She didn't recognize the number, so she didn't answer it. The call went through to voice mail but before she could listen, it rang again. Then she got a text.

Beth, it's Bryan. Please pick up. Let me know you're okay.

Bryan? Bryan was calling her? How'd he get her number? *Why'd* he get her number? And how did he know what was going on?

"Are you okay?" He didn't even give her time to say hello when she answered his call.

"I am."

"Did they leave?"

"I don't know. I don't want to look."

He cursed inventively. "You should *not* have to deal with this. I told Mac I didn't want this happening. I'm really sorry, Beth. I should have just given them a sound bite and been done with it. I should've realized I couldn't get away with it. Anonymity doesn't go with the territory. I'm really sorry."

Beth had to shake her head to clear it. What was he apologizing for? "This isn't your fault, Bryan. You didn't send them here."

"I might as well have. Anything I do these days makes the news and I should have seen this coming. I'm sorry. I didn't mean to drag you and the kids into it again. How are they?"

"The kids? They're fine. They're at my neighbor's house. I got them out before the questions started."

"And you? How are you?"

"I'm . . . fine." She was lying. Her knees were wobbly, her stomach was still queasy, and a cold sweat was dampening the back of her neck.

"Look, I know I have no right to ask you this, but if you want to tell them I'm holding a news conference at three today at the Manley Maids' office, that'll get them off your case. They just want some info. I'll give it to them."

She sucked in a shaky breath. She didn't know if she could face them again. Didn't want to open the door to that pack of wolves.

"Beth? Did you hear me, honey?" His voice was so soft and low just like it'd been last night when he'd said he'd wanted to kiss her.

Oh God, what if someone had seen him kiss her and taken a picture and now *that* would be plastered all over the news along with the story that he was cleaning her house? She could just hear the headlines now about *playing* house with her. Oh God. She couldn't do this. Not again. She couldn't live through this circus again. Couldn't face the stares and the looks and the pointing fingers and the questions—always with the questions as if they had the right to delve into her life, her most personal thoughts there for public edification.

"Beth, are you with me, honey?"

Through a fog of panic, she heard Bryan's voice.

"Beth, please answer me." There was an edge to his voice now. One she could totally relate to.

"I'm here." Just the act of saying those words, of acknowledging him, of communicating with someone who wasn't trying to suck out her soul, helped Beth calm down.

"Good. I'll fix this, sweetheart. I promise. You won't have to worry about reporters again. I promise. I'll have Mac assign someone else to you for the rest of the month and you won't have to deal with this or see me again."

"No." The word was out before she thought about it.

"What?" He sounded just as surprised as she was. "But if I'm not there, they won't bother you."

"You can't run out on the kids. You can't teach them to cower." Even though that was what she was doing right this very minute—at least they weren't witnessing it. "I can't let the press dictate my life. My kids' lives. They like you, Bryan. My kids like having you around. Do you know Jason has done something to his hair? I can see his face because of something you said. I've tried for two years to get through to him and I couldn't. You can't walk away from them now because of this."

Okay, she was laying a lot at Bryan's feet, but she'd do whatever she needed to for her kids. Maggie had shown him that special hug thing she'd had with Mike. Tommy and Mark were finishing each other's sentences again. Kelsey was enjoying the prestige at school, and Jason . . . She hadn't seen her son's face full-on since before the funeral. She'd deal with the aftermath of Bryan leaving when his month was done, but for now, he couldn't *not* be here. What would that teach the kids about dealing with problems? That you walk away?

"But Beth, if I'm there, it'll only continue."

"So you give them what they want at your press conference. You're the story, not us. But after that, we want you to come back."

BRYAN wanted to come back, too, but Beth didn't have a clue what could happen. Sure, *he* was the draw, but a beautiful widow of an airline pilot with five kids and him in the house? Cleaning? The story was perfect for the tabloids *and* the legitimate press. The perfect romantic storyline with the movie star and the housewife. His agent had seen the possibility the minute he'd told him what he was going to be doing for Mac, which was why Bryan wanted to keep a low profile. *Especially* after he'd read about Mike's death. He should have pulled out then. Should have told Mac to find someone else before the kids had gotten attached.

Attached.

Oh hell.

They weren't the only ones. And it was the worst and best feeling in the world. He liked her kids and he'd be lying if he said that he wasn't the tiniest bit proud that what he'd said to Jason had caused him to not only clean up, but do something about that hair. He'd heard in Beth's voice how happy it'd made her. That one little thing and he'd had a hand in it.

Hell, he ought to have Mac get someone else just *because* of that little hitch in Beth's voice.

But he wouldn't. He didn't want anyone else in here, seeing Beth's bedroom or Maggie's stuffed animals or the twins' figurine collection, or telling Kelsey she looked nice and seeing her big, beautiful beaming smile that was so like her mother's, or helping Jason grow into a man.

Helping Jason—? Holy *hell*. When had the Hamilton family crawled beneath the armor he wore around his heart?

This was so not what he needed in his head as he went out to face the media that afternoon. He prayed his thoughts weren't plastered all over his face.

"So, Bryan," asked one of the reporters, "does this mean you're backing out of *The Pause Button*?"

The romantic comedy had been generating buzz even before the script had been finalized, every actor in Hollywood vying for the leads. When he'd won the role, his agent had sent him a case of Dom. At some point he'd drink it—when the film had wrapped and he felt good about his performance.

"No, I'll be on schedule for shooting. This cleaning gig is temporary. My sister, Mary-Alice Manley's cleaning business, Manley Maids, is booming and she needed help. Since my brothers and I have the same reference for what constitutes a clean house—our grandmother—Mac had a ready-made crew for the new jobs."

"You mean that you clean your own home?" asked another reporter.

"Not now, obviously. I'm never there. As a matter of fact, I'm also a Manley Maids' customer."

Another reporter shoved his mic in Bryan's face as he elbowed his way through the others. "So why *this* house? Was it because of the beautiful widow?"

Bryan glared at the kid reporter. Even a few of the veterans moaned. They might smell a story, but they'd never get the real one if they pissed off their target, and it didn't take a brain surgeon to see Bryan wasn't happy with the question.

"I'm here to do a job for my *sister*. That's the only play that went into any of this." He didn't deny that Beth was beautiful—he'd never do that, because she was—but he had to put an end to the speculation here and now. He wasn't about to bring any more publicity to her doorstep. He'd watched the news bites from when her husband had died, had seen the panic on her face, had heard it in her voice earlier; she didn't need that nightmare again.

He fielded a few more questions, threw in a couple of plugs for Manley Maids, mentioned the movie, and prayed that the scandal that'd been brewing had resolved itself.

Luckily, he'd had the forethought to wear the hideous uniform and agreed to pose for pictures afterward. Mac couldn't get better publicity than that. Give them what they wanted and hopefully they'd leave Beth and the kids alone.

Just like he'd volunteered to do.

But she *hadn't* wanted him to leave. And not for herself, but for her kids. He would've argued with her, but when she'd brought it up as being in the best interests of her children, he couldn't. What kind of man would he be if he left at the first sign she needed help?

Not the kind of man he prided himself on being.

Chapter Fourteen

❧

"MOM is going to be so mad at you, Mags."

"No she's not. I'm making this for Bryan. Mommy likes Bryan."

Bryan was about to walk into Beth's kitchen when Maggie's words stopped him. What was Maggie making? Why would Beth be mad? And just how much *did* Beth like him that *Maggie* had picked up on it?

And why did it matter? As that reporter had reminded him yesterday, filming was due to start in three weeks and he had to be there. This little sojourn into suburbia was only temporary.

"Well duh, Mom likes him. Every woman likes him." Kelsey sounded much older than twelve.

"Like you, Kels?"

Bryan could picture Maggie sticking her tongue out at her sister, and it made him smile. How well he remembered teasing his brothers.

"Don't be a dork. I'm too young to like him."

"Then why do you act all silly when he's around?"

Bryan wanted to sigh. He'd been dealing with teenage girl crushes his whole life, but he'd never been more bothered by one than he was at this moment. Kelsey couldn't have a crush on him. He didn't want to hurt her. Especially since *his* crush was definitely on her mother.

"I don't act silly. At least I don't go making some stupid collage thing that's got glue all over the table that he's never going to hang up anywhere anyway."

"He will, too. Bryan likes me. He'll 'ppreciate the picture."

He certainly would. Right after he got over choking on the emotion clogging his throat. He'd hang whatever it was on the door to his dressing room on every set he would ever be on.

"Mom's not going to appreciate the glue, Mags. You're gonna get in trouble."

"Am not."

"Are too."

"Am not."

This was where he had to step in. It was one thing for the boys to disagree; as twins they had a bond that would be stronger than the damage their words could inflict, but the seven years separating Kelsey and Maggie would take a lot longer to heal and Bryan didn't want to be the reason for discord between the sisters.

"Hey, girls." Bryan tilted the brim of his cap at them and got the giggles he'd hoped for from Maggie. He got the sigh and shy smile from Kelsey he'd been hoping *not* to get.

"Whatcha doing, Maggie?"

Kelsey was right. There was enough glitter glue on the table to decorate Rodeo Drive. In pink.

He hid his smile. He'd take a ton of ribbing on set when he hung whatever it was up, but he didn't care.

"I'm making you a picture, Bryan. To remember us by."

Now his throat did close up. Then he looked at the picture and it threatened to choke him. There were the five kids—Jason with the new hairstyle—with a beaming Beth behind them, her arms outstretched over the five of them.

The symbolism was rife in that drawing and it was all Bryan could do to talk. "That's a great picture, Maggie. I'll be honored to have it."

Kelsey sighed.

"But Kelsey's right. We need to get this cleaned up before the glue dries on the table." He had a feeling it was too late. He picked up a glitter glue stick and read the fine print. At least it was water soluble. "Kelsey, could you fill a bucket with warm water?" It'd give her something constructive to do and snap her out of the teenybopper phase she was reveling in at the moment.

"Sure, Bryan. Anything else?"

He bit his lip at the hero worship in her eyes. "If you can find a sponge with a scrubber thing on the back, that'll help."

"I think we have some in the pantry."

"Great. Thanks." He looked at Maggie. "Come on, Maggie. Let's get this cleaned up before it dries. You want to be able to use it again."

"Mommy says you're going on location. What's that mean?"

"It means I'm going to go to the place where we're filming the movie."

"I thought movies got made in Hollywood?"

"Not all. Sometimes it's easier and less expensive to go to a location, like the seashore or the mountains or a city than to build it in Hollywood."

"Do you have telephones there?"

"Sure. It'll be as if we were filming here in town."

"With all the people and all the cameras just like when Daddy died?"

He sucked in a breath. He'd heard the panic in Beth's voice at the cameras, so he hadn't expected Maggie to be so nonchalant about it, but then, she'd only been three. Maybe it hadn't made as big an impression.

"I told your mom I was sorry about that. I didn't think people would care that I was here."

Maggie shrugged. "Well, *I'm* glad you're here. You make me and Mommy smile. But Kelsey . . . she's just acting weird. Maybe you could get her to stop being weird."

"Maggie!" Kelsey banged the bucket on the counter, sloshing water over the side, and sent a stricken look at Bryan right before she ran out of the kitchen. "I hate you!"

"Stay here, Maggie, and start cleaning up. I'll be right back." He had to nip this in the bud before Kelsey let it grow to gargantuan proportions.

Of *course* she'd run to her room. Great.

Bryan heard her crying on the other side of her door and took a deep breath before knocking.

"Go away, runt."

"It's me, Kelsey."

There was silence. Then a sniffle. Then a hiccup. Feet dragging across the floor, then the lock turning.

A distraught face appeared in the crack in her door. "Maggie doesn't know what she's talking about."

"Can we talk, Kelsey?"

She closed her eyes, then swung the door open. "I guess."

"Let's go sit on the porch."

She nibbled her lip and preceded him down the stairs and out to the wooden rockers, hanging her head so her hair covered her face.

"About what Maggie said—"

"She's a dork."

"She's your sister and little sisters like to tease. Trust me, I know. I've got one."

There was the hint of a smile.

"I don't think you're acting weird. What you're feeling is normal for a girl your age. And I'm flattered. But I'm too old for you."

Her face was blazing, but she was definitely Beth's daughter, facing him down with the same grit. "Yeah, I know. Plus, all the moms like you."

He refrained from pointing out that the moms *were* his age.

"So do you like my mom?"

He hadn't seen that one coming. "Uh, well, yeah. Your mom's a nice woman. And with what she's been through, with what you've all been through, your mom's a special lady."

"Yeah, but do you *like* like her?"

How had this conversation veered down the path he hadn't wanted it to go? He'd thought approaching Kelsey's feelings would be the delicate part . . . "I like your mom a lot, Kelsey. But I'm not going to be here long. I have a movie coming up in a few weeks and I'll be gone for months. Then there will be more. My career takes me all over the world. I can't be here. And your mom deserves someone who'll be around. Who'll be there for her."

"Oh."

And he better remember this. Because for a while there in the kitchen with Maggie, and the other night in the gazebo, he'd let his mind wander. Imagine. Pretend.

His *professional* life was all pretend; he didn't need that in his *real* life. And the reality was, no matter how much he was attracted to her, no matter how much he was enjoying being with her and her family, Beth was a reality he couldn't have.

BETH stepped away from the front door. She shouldn't be listening in, but when she'd seen the two of them head out there, she'd been about to ask what was going on until Kelsey's body language had kept her back. And then she'd heard what Bryan had said. He'd dealt with Kelsey's crush beautifully.

And what he'd said about her . . .

He was right. Every word was right—he was going away. He couldn't stay here and she had to remember that.

But he liked her. She was "a special lady." A tingle had run through her when he'd said that. A tingle she hadn't felt in years—until the night in the gazebo.

Bryan was leaving. He wasn't hanging around. Tingles didn't matter when it came to that. Her kids needed stability and so did she. Bryan's lifestyle wasn't good for any of them.

Chapter Fifteen

❧❦❧

BRYAN packed up the Manley Maids' cleaning kit, and gave the kitchen one final survey. Maggie's glue had been a nightmare, and the glitter all over the floor hadn't been fun, but the two of them had worked hard to get it all up while the picture she'd made him had dried on the countertop. He'd weighted the corners down so they wouldn't curl and insisted Maggie sign her name when it was dry.

She'd beamed at him when she'd done it, and Bryan knew he'd always treasure the crooked, pink concoction. Maggie Hamilton was going to be a hard one to forget. All of the Hamiltons would be. Just like Tommy and Mark when they came barreling through the kitchen again, dragging a mud-caked rope with them and leaving muddy footprints from the back door through the kitchen, and if he hadn't been standing in the doorway to the family room—the gateway to the rest of the house—those footprints would have continued onward.

"Halt!" He thrust out his arm. "Who goes there, soldiers?"

The boys looked at each other, confused for a moment, then big smiles crossed their faces, and they snapped to attention.

"It is I, Sir Markus. I've come to tell the queen that her royal dog has escaped."

"Dog?" Tommy rolled his eyes. "It's Her Majesty's *prisoner* who's escaped. He's running through the neighbor's garden."

Sherman. Again.

Bryan set the cleaning toolbox on the counter. "Lead on, men."

It was an afternoon of torture. He'd been in great shape for the last film, hadn't thought he'd been too out of it now, but chasing after an Energizer Bunny dog and two young boys showed him just how wrong he was.

The damn dog had learned a few tricks since the fence escapade, and it took Sir Markus's and Sir Thomas's "army" of friends to round him up.

Bryan and the dozen ten-year-olds finally surrounded Sherman at a neighbor's pool, advancing on him, tightening the circle. Unfortunately, at the center of that circle was the pool itself and Bryan had a feeling this wasn't going to end well.

Especially when Sir Thomas decided to lead the charge of the lightsaber brigade.

Seven kids went into the water. One dog came out.

And scampered away with a quick shake, a yip, and too much spring in his step.

Bryan fished the boys out, wrung out T-shirts and shorts, gave them a quick lesson on poolside warfare for the next time, then led them out the back gate after the damn dog.

The damn dog was having a field day. Literally. There was a field at the edge of the neighborhood, but it was the last bastion of safety before the busy road.

"Okay, guys, here's the deal." Bryan called the boys into a huddle. "Tommy, Johnny, Kevin, and Kyle: you guys flank to the right."

"What's a flank?" Kyle asked.

"You're going to go around to the right." Bryan pointed to a dogwood. "See that tree? I want you to go behind it and come up to that stump. Then walk in quietly, drawing closer together as you come in. You other boys circle in from the other side. We're going to trap Sherman between us just like we did the last time."

Mark told the others about the compost pile incident— complete with Bryan's header into it. "Bryan saved the day *and* the dog. It was awesome!"

Okay, so he'd own the compost-pile header if the boys thought it was awesome.

The subsequent shower and seeing Beth afterward had been pretty awesome, too.

Bryan glanced at Sherman. The dog was on his haunches, tongue lolling out the left side of his mouth, that grin-like curve to his snout mocking them. "Okay, guys, walk slowly to your positions."

Sherman shifted when the boys fanned out, eyebrows quirking. Bryan hadn't even realized dogs *had* eyebrows.

The dog looked back and forth between the two groups of kids. Each time Sherman turned his head, Bryan slid forward a few steps. At one point, Sherman glanced in his direction, so Bryan froze.

The dog shifted nervously. Bryan looked at the boys out of the corner of his eyes. They were almost in place to start moving forward. If he kept Sherman focused on him, the boys could get close enough to tighten the circle so the dog wouldn't have a chance of escape.

Tommy waved his arm. Mark did shortly thereafter, too.

Bryan nodded and the boys walked in slowly.

Sherman got to his feet. Shit.

Bryan fanned out his arms, trying to make himself look bigger. Animals responded to bigger threats by cowering.

Of course *this* damn dog didn't.

Sherman, practically dancing on his tiptoes, turned in a circle, his little stub of a tail going rigid when he saw the boys. Bryan used the opportunity to take a few more steps forward.

The dog looked over its shoulder—which gave Tommy and Mark the chance to advance.

Bryan wanted to tell them how proud he was of them for figuring out the tactic, but he didn't want to spook Sherman any more than he already was.

He took another step when Sherman looked back at the boys. Then another. He was within three feet of the dog when one of the kids stumbled.

It was all the reason Sherman needed to bolt.

Luckily, he made the mistake of trying to run past Bryan, and Bryan dove onto him.

And landed in a pile of rabbit pellets.

At least it wasn't deer or horse, but still . . . This damn dog had caused him to need a shower twice.

"We got him! Great job, Bryan!" Mark called out, the boys all high-fiving each other in their great team effort as Bryan held the squirming, smelly Jack Russell as his prize.

He tucked the dog under his arm and hooked his thumb into the collar so the menace wouldn't try some twisting movement and escape again.

The group marched back to the house, Roman legion style. Beth had rounded up the girls—who were now speaking to each other, it appeared—and held out a tray of cookies. "Conquering heroes must be rewarded. Thank you, men."

They descended on the cookies as one would expect a horde of hungry ten-year-olds to do. Good thing Bryan didn't want any; chasing after Sherman showed him he better lay off the sweets.

Especially Beth.

"And what do I get, m'lady?" So much for that. She looked so darn cute "bestowing" the cookies upon the boys and he was, after all, holding the prize pooch.

Kelsey looked at her mother. Damn. He really shouldn't have asked that question around her daughter after that conversation on the porch. Especially when Beth blushed.

"I, um, could make more?"

Kelsey rolled her eyes. "Mo-om." She took Sherman from Bryan. "You have to give the knight a kiss. Don't you know anything?"

Oh, Beth knew all about kissing. Bryan could attest to that. And getting one from her here, in front of all these witnesses was *not* the best idea.

But Kelsey wasn't going to give up. Not with that pointed look at Bryan.

So he reached for Beth's hand, went to one knee, and gave her the quickest, most chaste kiss he could manage—despite wanting to tug her down and roll on the grass all night long, kissing her until the sun came up tomorrow.

Instead, he got his head back into reality, stood up quickly, then bowed to both Maggie and Kelsey. "And now, my ladies, if you'll excuse me, I have a job to finish." Those muddy foot-prints weren't going to clean themselves.

"Hold on, Bryan." Beth tapped her sons on the shoulder. "Boys, there's a mess in the kitchen with your names on it. How about if you two march yourselves inside and take care of it? That's not Bryan's job."

The boys stuffed their cookies into their mouths and did what she asked.

Bryan raised his eyebrows at Beth. "No arguments?"

She shrugged. "What can I say? They're conquering heroes. They saved Sherman."

Maggie tugged on the hem of Beth's shirt—which pulled the scoop neckline down low enough for Bryan to get a glimpse of cleavage.

Fifteen seconds more of torture.

"Mommy, *Bryan* saved Sherman. He jumped on top of him. Kyle told me."

Bryan chucked her under the chin. "No, Maggie. It was a team effort. Everyone did their part. I just happened to be there when Sherman ran. We *all* saved Sherman."

Maggie crossed her arms. "Nuh-uh. You did. Kyle said so. You're just being modish."

The look Beth sent him said she wanted to hug him. He hoped it was for more reasons than giving her sons the credit.

"Kelsey," she said, breaking the look between them that had gone on a heartbeat too long to be proper, "please take Sherman into the laundry room. He needs a bath."

"So does Bryan." Maggie pinched her nose. "Pee-ewww."

Which was how, once more, Bryan found himself naked in Beth's bathroom.

This time he took his time. Last time, he'd been so uncom-fortable at the intimacy, but now, after having her in his arms, after the effect she had on him . . . he wanted any intimacy he could get. The gazebo had only whetted his curiosity.

He shouldn't have kissed her. Shouldn't have tortured him-self that way. Just like he shouldn't be torturing himself now, imagining her in here with him, lathering the soap all over her body, rubbing against her under the water as it beaded on her skin, lifting her foot to hook it around the back of his thigh, pressing her breasts and nipples against his chest, and, oh hell, he was going to come in her shower if he didn't stop this train of thought.

He lowered the water temperature and decided *not* to linger. The pink towel Maggie had insisted he use yet again helped defuse the situation, and by the time he could open the door to her bedroom, he had himself under control.

Except now he was staring at her bed.

The images returned full force and so did his erection. God, he wanted her. Wanted to lay her down on that bed and kiss her from her gorgeous eyes to that pert nose and sexy-as-hell lips. Down to her chin, then trail his tongue beneath it, down her throat, tickling the hollow of her collarbone before feasting on her breasts. He wanted his hands on them, his lips, his tongue, taking her into his mouth and driving her crazy with desire.

She'd been in the moment with him in that gazebo. She'd wanted him. She'd been smart to not let it go too far—for both their sakes—because he'd wanted her badly. She couldn't *not* have known that.

He tightened the pink towel around his waist, hoping for some relief to the pressure, but the friction of the cotton across the sensitive head only made him ache more. He wanted Beth and he was starting to worry that he might not be strong enough to withstand the temptation.

Bryan shook his head. That was ridiculous. He had thousands of women—gorgeous, sexy model types—throwing themselves at him. He could have whomever he wanted.

But he only wanted Beth.

He whipped the towel off, half hoping for the sting of a sharp end to catch him in the thigh and pull his focus off the fact that his dick was hard and throbbing and wanting to be buried deep inside her. Beth. Widowed mom. Of five.

For the first time, that thought wasn't scaring the shit out of him.

He grabbed his boxers off the bed and snapped the waistband tight on his abs, hoping the sting would deflect what he was feeling. Nope. Nothing. Still hard as a rock. He grabbed the shorts then. Her *husband's* shorts.

He took his time stepping into them, imagining Mike doing

the same thing. After he'd made love to Beth. *That* ought to cool him down.

It didn't. It only made him want her more.

He was losing his mind. Being here was getting to him. He needed a break. Neutral ground. Something else to focus on.

He shoved his arm into the T-shirt—also Mike's—and dialed Sean on his cell.

"Hey, Bry, what's up?"

His dick, but if he said so, Sean would never let him hear the end of it. And *not* hearing about it was exactly the reason he was calling his brother in the first place. "You need anything done at that estate of yours? I have some time to kill and wouldn't mind the workout."

"You're volunteering to help? Free of charge or were you expecting me to pay you? I can't afford movie star rates these days."

That was Sean, always getting a dig in somewhere. His brothers *were* happy for his success, but it was too easy for them to poke fun at his lavish, unsuburban lifestyle.

"Consider it sweat equity."

He'd already invested a chunk of change to be a partner on the estate his brother was planning to turn into an exclusive resort. Liam was in on it, too, and as soon as the will was probated, the property would be Sean's. Then the real work would begin. Right now, Sean had gotten lucky enough to be assigned there by Mac, so it worked out all the way around. Especially if it got Bryan out of Beth's home for a few hours and gave him some breathing space.

Chapter Sixteen

❧❧❧

 THINK you should bring him to happy hour."

"Oooh, great idea, Jenna. That way we could all meet him."

Beth raised her eyebrows at her two friends who were acting more like Kelsey's contemporaries than grown women. Jenna and Kara wanted to ogle Bryan. They were both happily married, but it was no secret that Bryan Manley was on each one's Hall Pass List.

Their poor husbands. When the Hall Pass List had come up in conversation, the guys had gone along in good fun, but now, when the number one guy on each one's list was actually in town and in her house . . .

"He's not a trophy to be displayed, Kar." She watched Mark run down the soccer field and winced when he got clipped on the ankle. By his brother. It figured. The two of them *were* literally two peas in the same pod.

"Then, sweetheart, you haven't been watching him enough. What do you do when he's bent over fluffing your pillows? Walk away?"

The blush blazed over Beth's face and she dug into her knapsack for the boys' extra water bottles she always packed on the off chance that they'd go through the other one. "He's not a piece of meat."

Jenna didn't even make a pretense of watching the game. But then, her son Ben was on the bench at the moment. "Honey, he's a prime specimen of beefcake and you can't tell me you haven't noticed. That blush you've got going on is speaking volumes, even if you're not."

"Fine. Yes, he's a good-looking guy. I get it. But he's not here to be ogled, and you two aren't paying him to be here after hours, so, no, I'm not going to invite him to happy hour."

It was a tradition in the summer. Every Friday night someone hosted a party. They called it happy hour among themselves— called it family hour for the kids because, really, it wasn't a good idea to teach kids that happy hours were a normal occurrence. Plus, the school would have a conniption when the teachers read the kids' summer journals.

"Come on, Beth. At least ask him. What's the worst he could do, say no?"

No, the worst would be if he said yes. Bryan had been out of her house at four o'clock on the dot the last two days. He showed up right at eight, took his hour lunch—down to the minute—and then left the moment he could. Actually, she'd told him he could leave earlier if he had things to do, but he'd only looked at her and said he'd work until four.

She didn't know what'd happened. Why he'd gone from that knight-in-shining-pistachio-green-uniform to this . . . polite stranger. But for whatever reason, he'd decided to keep her and the kids at arm's length. For herself, she was fine with that because she'd been thinking about him way too much, but the kids missed the camaraderie they'd shared. And she'd missed hearing the laughter.

The ref blew the whistle and Mark stormed off the field, his face as red as hers, but in anger. She was about to climb down the bleachers when his coach, Mr. Weston, put his arm around him and led him back to the bench, talking to him the whole time.

Beth's heart ached. The kids needed a father. Mike would have known the right thing to say to Mark. Things the coach was probably saying, but would they mean as much coming from his friend Eric's father instead of his own?

Once more, the wave of sadness that'd encompassed her after Mike's death threatened to wash over her. The support group said the feeling would subside over the years, but would never truly go away. That the *what ifs* would always be hovering in the back of her mind.

She hated those scenarios. She couldn't live in *what if*; she was in the here and now. As were her kids. So whatever words of wisdom Mark needed, she was realistic enough to know that the coach would have to be the one to give them to him.

Then she saw Bryan striding toward the field from the other side of the park. Still in his green uniform, the man was *still* a sight to behold, and those butterflies he'd ignited in her stomach in the gazebo woke up and paid attention, wings fluttering in her belly in anticipation.

But he didn't head for her. For a moment, the butterflies' wings drooped, but when he headed toward the bench, shook hands with the coach, then hunkered down in front of Mark and talked to him, the butterflies went nuts.

"And you think *that* isn't a prize? What are you, blind?" Jenna fanned herself. "Seriously, Beth, can you not see *that*?"

That was the problem. She could and did see him. And it was getting harder to look away the longer he was around.

So she didn't. She watched him with her son. The game went on around them, kids came and went on the bench, whistles blew, the crowd cheered or groaned, and Jenna was saying something to her every now and then, but Beth only had eyes and ears and every other sense focused on what was happening on that bench in front of her.

Mark's slumped shoulders gradually eased. His back got a little straighter, his nods a little stronger. Then he re-tied his shoes and stood up, dancing from foot to foot, tugging on the coach's shirt to get his attention.

Bryan stepped over the bench at one point and faded back a few feet to the edge of the track that surrounded the infield. He stuck his hands in his front pockets—which did very nice things to the backside of his pants, also something that was hard to look away from—and nodded when Mark looked back at him.

Mark finally got the coach's attention, and they had a quick heart-to-heart. Mr. Weston glanced at Bryan, then nodded to Mark. Then into the game went her son.

Tears pricked the backs of Beth's eyes. For that moment alone, Bryan was her Prince Charming.

"Oh my God. He's heading this way!" Kara forced the words between her teeth. "Quick! Jenna! Do you have any gum?" She put her hand in front of her mouth and breathed.

"Seriously? You think you have a *shot* at kissing Bryan Manley now? Here? With Beth sitting next to us?"

This time Beth didn't blush. This time she let Jenna's words sink in. Rolled them around on her tongue to savor them.

If only . . .

No. She shook her head. *If onlys* were just as bad as *what ifs*.

"Hey." Bryan climbed the bleachers, those pants hugging some powerful thighs and the shirt stretched across a mighty fine set of shoulders. All things she'd noticed about him the first time she'd seen him on screen, but now, seeing him here in the flesh . . . And that just added to the problem.

"What was going on with Mark?"

Her friends parted like the Red Sea, giving him the perfect chance to sit next to her.

Lucky for her, he took it. Or maybe not so lucky because one of those firm thighs was now pressed against hers and the scent of his day's exertion was wafting around her, lingering on her tongue, daring her to taste him.

God how she wanted to.

But she wouldn't. She had impressionable children to consider. And moms eyeing her with envy.

And a telephoto lens aimed at them from the bleachers on the opposite side of the field.

Son of a bitch.

"He had a few choice words for his brother for clipping him in the ankle. Coach wanted to nip that in the bud before it escalated."

She wanted to nip something else in the bud, but was afraid that if she told him, it'd generate even more publicity that she didn't want. "So what did you say to him?"

Bryan shrugged. "That Tommy clipped him by accident and he's family. You do *not* insult or disrespect your family. You don't do it to anyone, but especially not the ones who will always be here for you."

"Aw, that's so sweet." Kara stuck her hand out. "Kara Leopold. I'm a friend of Beth's. And this is Jenna Harte."

"Nice to meet you." Jenna didn't miss the chance to touch him, either, and it surprised Beth how much she didn't like it. "Our sons play soccer with the twins."

"Ben and Nick." Kara brushed some hair behind her ear and cocked her head just a tad, with a soft smile to her lips Beth had never seen before.

Oh, puhleaze. Really? The woman was happily married to her high school sweetheart, yet one smile—okay it *was* a devastatingly handsome one—from Bryan and she conveniently forgot that she was head over heels for the man she'd known since fourth grade?

"Nice to meet you, ladies." Bryan was an expert at extricating himself from sticky situations—female situations; she'd seen that firsthand with Kelsey—and he put the experience to work now. "The guys and I had a conversation just this morning about having your brother's back, so when I saw Tommy's face, I was a bit surprised."

"Tommy's face?" Beth couldn't hide *her* surprise.

Bryan nodded. "I saw the play and Mark's reaction to it, though I couldn't hear what they said. But then Tommy looked as if he was going to cry. With what we'd talked about this morning, well . . ." He kneaded the back of his neck. "I hope I didn't overstep my bounds, Beth, but given the conversation, I thought I could add a little more to the coach's speech."

Beth didn't know which to cry at first. That she was such an incompetent mother that she hadn't noticed Tommy's pain, or that Bryan had the words of wisdom for her boys she never would. She just hoped the photographer hadn't snapped that shot.

What was she going to do about that photographer? Much as she'd like to, she couldn't just pretend he wasn't there. That never made them go away.

"No . . . no. It's fine. I appreciate you taking time from your schedule to do this."

"No problem. They asked me to come."

They had? News to Beth. The boys weren't as enthused

about soccer now that Mike wasn't their coach. She'd had to bribe them with the ice cream parlor afterward and a big speech about not letting their teammates down before they'd put on their uniforms for every game. Knowing Bryan would be here would explain why they hadn't given her a hard time today. Her family was becoming a little *too* attached to Bryan Manley.

As was Kara, who'd sidled a little closer and turned her body just enough that Beth could almost swear she was thrusting out her chest—already an impressive size thanks to her husband's anniversary gift for their twentieth. Not something Beth would have wanted, but Kara had been pleased with them.

Now, watching her trying to get Bryan's attention and the overt interest she was showing, Beth had to wonder if the boobs had been an attempt at saving the marriage rather than enhancing it.

"Maggie!" Beth called over to the sandbox where Maggie was working on a miniature sand castle with her third bottle of water. Beth had learned to bring at least six because Maggie had found her medium in wet sand. Beth swore her youngest was going to become an artist someday. Possibly a sculptor.

"What, Mommy?"

"Bryan's here. Want to show him what you're making?"

Yes, it was wrong to use her daughter to distract Bryan and get him out of the photographer's line of sight, but nothing she could do would distract Kara. Beth had a feeling that if Kara's husband walked up here buck naked it wouldn't distract her. Another reason to get Bryan off that guy's telephoto map.

Maggie popped up out of the sand, destroying the castle in the process, before taking off to race across the grass toward the bleachers. "Bryyyyyyaaaaaaaaaaaaannnnnnnnnnnnnnnn!"

Darn, Beth had been hoping to get Bryan down there and away from not only the photographer but also Jenna and Kara's temptation. *Not* that he was looking at all tempted. Tempting, yes. Tempted by them, no.

Then he looked at *her* and Beth was half tempted herself.

"You sure you don't mind that I'm here?" he asked. "I know this is your time with the kids, but since the boys asked . . ."

"I don't mind at all. It's nice for them to have someone else cheer them on." He thought she wanted this time alone with her kids? Didn't he realize she had so much time with the kids that game time was for *her*? For the chance to interact with other parents while the kids were occupied and happy? There'd been so much sadness in their lives these past two years that being outside at the games, around friends, was a blessing.

"Bryan! You came!" Maggie climbed up the bleachers on all fours, looking like a scampering little monkey, then launched herself into Bryan's unsuspecting arms.

The hug rocked him back so that he caught Maggie with one hand and braced himself with the other on the bleacher behind her and for a moment—a brief, tiny, moment of *what if*—Beth imagined that it'd gone around her and that he had the right to do so. That she had the right to expect and accept it.

Desire slammed into her gut so hard and fast it stole her breath. Good lord, she wanted that. Wanted Bryan to put his arm around her. To be hers. To *want* to be hers and stake his claim in front of everyone.

Including the photographer who was sure to be taking loads of shots of Bryan and . . . Maggie.

Oh hell no. She was not going to permit those photos to be published anywhere. Her daughter had a right to privacy, and Beth would be damned if she'd let some money-grubbing paparazzo take that away from her.

She stood up. "Bryan, can you keep an eye on Maggie? I'll be right back." She was so done with this crap.

W HOA, there, kiddo! You almost knocked me off my seat." Bryan straightened up and settled Maggie on his knee, trying to get his wind back as he watched her mom climb down the bleachers. Well, to be truthful, her mother's backside as it swished down those bleachers had a hand in stealing his breath, but Maggie had done the rest of the job with a knee to his gut.

"You came, Bryan! Just like you said you would."

Her smile finished the wind-stealing job. "Well, sure I did. Why say it if you're not going to do it?"

Maggie kissed his cheek, removing the residual air from his lungs. "Jason said you wouldn't. That you were too busy to come. I told him he was wrong and now you showed him."

He ran a surprisingly shaky hand over her hair. "I always stand by my word, Maggie. You can count on that."

Oh God, what was he doing? He shouldn't be here, telling her she could count on him, or dispensing fatherly advice to Mark or compassion to Tommy. Holding Maggie in his arms and on his knee, happy as shit to have her there. And being close to Beth . . .

One of her friends had a hungry look in her eyes, and the other was starstruck, but he only had eyes for Beth. He'd seen her sitting in the stands the moment he'd gotten out of his car in the parking lot. Like a beacon, the sun had shone on her hair and it'd called to him. He'd seen her smile light up her face and it was as if she'd bewitched him; he'd half floated across the grass to get to her.

He would have floated all the way up the bleachers if not for the ref's whistle and Tommy and Mark's words. Their argument had pulled him out of the fog he'd been in ever since the boys had asked him to come today when all he'd been able to think about was being with Beth and her family.

The stands around them erupted in cheers, and Bryan dragged his gaze off Beth as she walked on the track to watch the boys high-fiving another kid who was walking around with the soccer ball tucked proudly under his arm.

"Oh, look, Mrs. Harte! Ben made the goal!"

The woman—Jenna?—finally stopped staring at him and started cheering. "Go, Benny!"

Her son looked up and shook his head.

"Crud. I forgot he doesn't like that name," his mom muttered.

"Most boys outgrow their nicknames before their moms do. My grandmother still calls me—" Bryan shut his mouth. *That* was personal. He didn't need it bandied about in the media. Besides being embarrassing, his grandmother would be hurt if people made fun of her nickname for him. And "Baby Bry-Bry" wasn't something he wanted to be known by. Only Gran could call him that and get away with it.

He had to admit he liked when she did. Usually it was when

he had her wrapped in a big hug and she'd whisper it in his ear. "You're my favorite, Baby Bry-Bry."

He knew it wasn't true, that she called each one of them her favorite, but it'd always made him feel special. Wanted. Loved. He'd needed that in the years after their parents had been killed.

"What'd she call you, Bryan?" Maggie tugged on his collar.

"A special nickname just for me. It's private, Maggie."

"I don't have a private nickname. Kelsey calls me Mags. Jason calls me runt."

"Older brothers can be annoying. I know, I have two."

"I have three brothers. Tommy and Mark don't call me names, only Jason. And Kelsey. But that was only 'cause she was 'barrassed because she didn't want you to know she likes you."

He could see the interest perk up in the women. Great. Kelsey wouldn't appreciate this gossip getting around any more than she'd appreciated Maggie's glee-filled disclosure.

"You shouldn't have told me, Maggie. You knew it'd hurt her."

Maggie's lips twisted and she stopped patting his arm. "I guess."

"Did you apologize to her?"

"No."

"I think you should when we get home."

Maggie's face lit up with a smile exactly like her mother's and it was one more reason for the air in his lungs to take a hike.

"*Are* you coming home with me? I thought you didn't want to live with us?" Maggie's voice raised an octave and a few decibels. The two women's interest suddenly was no longer on the game.

Great. *Beth* didn't need this kind of gossip getting around. "Just like some people go to an office, or a restaurant, or stores to work—"

"Or an airplane."

"Or an airplane. Just like they all go to work, I go to your house to work. I don't live there."

"But you could. We need a daddy. Grandma said so the last time she and Grandpa came to visit."

Out of the mouths of babes. And grandparents.

Though, if he were honest with himself, he had to say that he kind of liked the idea.

And that thought seared across his brain, jump-started his nervous system, and buried itself somewhere in his chest cavity. Right near his heart.

Chapter Seventeen

❧

GIVE me the camera."

"Back off, lady." *Click, click.*

The asshole didn't even stop taking pictures. Beth had a feeling he'd taken them during her entire walk across the park.

"That is my child in those pictures and I won't allow you to sell those photographs."

"Her face will be blurred. That's the way we do it with minors."

"And mine?"

"Look, lady. Bryan Manley is big news. You're big news. The two of you together could pay my rent for a year."

"Rent? This is about your *rent*?" Beth wanted to rip the camera from this guy's hands, but she'd get in more trouble for that than allowing pictures of her to surface. She didn't need a mug shot on top of that. "We're talking about my *family*. My privacy. My life. How can you justify your rent for my family? Haven't you people done enough damage? Do you know what it's like to have to calm my children down when the cameras won't stop? Answer their questions about why people won't leave them alone? And now you're going to thrust me into the spotlight again?"

"Then you shouldn't be hanging out with a movie star. Kinda goes with the territory, ya know?"

"I'm not *hanging out* with him. He works for the cleaning service. He's doing a job. Leave him alone."

"Seem awful protective of someone who's working for you. Like you got something to hide."

She fisted her hands, trying desperately not to rip his face off. Forget about the camera. She took a deep breath and counted to ten, knowing it'd do no good. Not when he threatened her family.

She tried another tactic. "What's your name?"

"No way, lady. I'm not telling you that. I don't need to be sued."

"Then who are you going to sell these pictures to?"

"Again, not telling you. I don't need you making any threatening moves before I get paid. Once they're theirs, sue all you want. I'm in the clear."

"Not if you touch me you're not." In a move even she wouldn't have expected, Beth ripped her own shirt sleeve and messed up her hair. "One word. One shout from me and this is over. Don't make me do it." She had her hands on the waistband of her shorts.

"Jesus, lady, you're crazy."

"No, I'm a mother protecting her children. I'll do whatever I need to in order to save them from the hell you're about to put them through. Give me the memory card."

"No way." He took a step back, thankfully not taking any more pictures.

Beth tugged her shorts and the button popped free. She took a step toward him. "One more step and I start yelling."

The guy looked hesitant. Good. Let him wonder if she was serious. *She* wasn't wondering; she'd do whatever it took to get those pictures and protect her family.

She opened her shorts a little more. "You willing to risk it? I've got nothing to lose that you're not going to lose for me with those pictures."

The guy looked around as if he was expecting someone to jump out of the trees around them.

Beth took a deep breath, surprisingly calm for what she was about to do. She opened her mouth to scream.

"Don't." The photographer choked on the word. "I can't risk it. My career will be over on the suspicion alone. My wife . . . she'll leave."

"Is it worth it? Paying your rent this way? For all you'll lose?" Beth kept one hand on her shorts and held out the other. "Give me the memory card."

The guy looked like he was ready to bolt.

"Don't do it, Steve."

He looked at her, his eyes wide.

"Steve McAllister. It's on your camera bag. I can ID you."

"Shit. Motherfucking shit."

"Give me the memory card, Steve." She wanted to keep saying his name; let him know she knew it.

"Fuck." He looked at the back of the camera. Then at her. Then at the trees behind them.

"Give me the card, Steve, or I scream. Now." She ruffled her hand through her hair for good measure. "You willing to risk everything?"

"Fuck no, lady." He opened the camera and took out the card. "Keep your fucking pictures. Your privacy's toast anyway. Everyone knows who you are. Who your kids are. Who your husband was. You'll never get any peace."

She didn't rise to his bait. She just took the memory card and stuck it inside her bra. Now if he went after it, she really would have something to pin on him.

"If I see you again, I'll tell your wife you came on to me for a story. I'll make her believe me; don't think I won't."

She had the satisfaction of watching him blanch. Good. Now he knew what it was like to have his family and his personal life threatened.

SHE was surprisingly calm as she headed back to the bleachers. She'd worked on her hair, zipped up her pants, but the button was gone and the rip in her shirt was going to be attributed to getting stuck on a tree branch.

"Mommy!" Maggie scrambled off Bryan's lap and bounded down the bleachers to her. "Can Bryan come to the ice cream parlor with us? Can he?"

"Okay, sweetheart." Why not? She was looking her worst,

feeling grumpy, and her clothes were ripped. Absolutely the best time to be seen out and about with Bryan Manley, who managed to look scrumptious in a uniform that ought to suck his masculinity right out of him.

"Beth? Are you okay?" Bryan walked down after Maggie, concern etched all over his handsome face. And curiosity etched all over Kara and Jenna's. "Where'd you go?"

"I thought I saw the Dynert's dog." Poor Muffy had been missing for over a week. Beth felt bad about using the Dynert's loss, but she would do anything to protect her family. And that, right now, included Bryan. He didn't need to know about the photographer.

"Was it, Mommy? Is Muffy coming home?"

She cupped Maggie's chin, sad to have to tell her daughter yet more bad news. "No, honey, it wasn't Muffy. I think it was a fox." A sly, cunning one that she'd outwitted, thank God.

"Oh." Maggie's bottom lip quivered. "I miss Muffy. I wish she hadn't left, too."

Oh hell. Beth felt about six inches tall. She shouldn't have used the dog as an excuse, but it was all she could come up with. And even then, she wasn't sure Bryan completely believed her.

She tugged her shirt down over her missing button. Maggie's solemn face tugged at Beth's heart. "We can go looking for her tomorrow if you want."

"Yes. I'd like that."

She patted Maggie on the back. "Okay, then. How about we round up the boys and head out for ice cream?"

"That match isn't over yet," said Bryan.

Yes, Bryan saw way too much and the look he was giving her said he had questions.

"Oh. Right." She glanced at the field. Both boys were sitting out right now, so at least she wasn't missing their playing time. But she couldn't have risked having the photographer get away with those photos, so if she'd missed them playing for a fraction of one game, she missed it.

More cheers erupted around them while they headed back to the stands and within ten minutes the game was over, the twins' team had won, and the younger three kids were shouting their ice cream orders at her.

"Hang on, guys, I'm not the waitress. Tell her when we get there."

"Are you coming with us, Bryan?" Mark circled his shin guards on the end of one finger.

Beth grabbed them to keep them from flying away. That hard plastic could be painful.

"Yes, Bryan is coming. And I'm sure he'll order something fabulous, too." She grabbed the gym bag and stuffed both boys' shin guards inside.

"Can I ride with you, Bryan?" Tommy asked, running to Bryan's side without waiting for an answer.

"Me, too!" Mark, of course, joined in.

"Well, I don't kn—"

"It's fine with me, Beth."

"Can I come?" Maggie asked.

"But Maggie, Mom needs kids with her," said Mark.

"Jason and Kelsey can go with her. They don't talk anyway so Mom can have her piece of quiet."

Bryan ruffled Maggie's hair. "Maybe your mom *wants* to talk. Maybe you should go with her."

"But I want to go with you!"

Bryan looked at Beth. "Is that okay with you?"

It was so okay it was almost scary. No, scratch that. It was downright scary. Her kids had glommed onto him like nobody's business and if she'd *wanted* this to happen, it wouldn't have.

Question was, *did* she want it to now that it had?

THE love fest only continued at Buster's Ice Cream Shoppe, with the younger ones clamoring to sit next to him. Beth had had to play referee, since there were only two places beside Bryan, convincing Tommy and Mark to switch off every half hour while the other one sat across from him. This, luckily, kept Kelsey out of the rotation, but her oldest daughter sat at the corner where she couldn't miss looking at Bryan.

It was an odd thing to feel jealous of your own kids, but Beth did. Bryan was so natural with them, laughing and cracking jokes. He even got Jason to open up about where he'd gotten his hair cut: his girlfriend's mom.

He had a girlfriend? Beth almost fainted at that news. How had she missed her eldest child reaching that milestone?

God, she felt like such a failure as a parent at times, especially now, watching them all with Bryan. He had a natural affinity for kids and it extended to more than just her kids. She'd watched him when the game had ended and all the kids had wanted to shake his hand. Bryan Manley was someone in this town and they all wanted a piece of him.

As did she.

There, she admitted it. It was hard not to. Bryan was starting to fill most of her thoughts during the day. She woke up thinking about him and went to bed thinking about him—aching for him. Got to watch him work around her home all day. He'd even begun clipping the hedge beneath her kitchen window. She'd argued that it wasn't part of his job description, but he'd countered with, "Mac says to always make sure the customer is satisfied. So that's what I'm doing."

She knew other ways he could satisfy this client . . .

Beth gasped and shoved a big, cold spoonful of dessert into her mouth. The end of this month couldn't come quick enough.

Because if she kept thinking about things like him satisfying her, she would, too.

Chapter Eighteen

❧

BRYAN showed up early for work the next morning.
And he knew exactly why he'd done it.

These early morning hours were precious in Beth's home. Usually he used them to redo what he'd done the day before that the kids had undone, but today there was the mess the boys had left as they'd tramped through after the ice cream parlor. If he'd driven them home, he could have done it then, or at least supervised them to *not* leave a trail behind.

They really needed a father.

He dropped the mop into the water bucket. He was out of his flipping mind to be thinking what he was thinking. Yes, sure, they needed a dad but they did not need *him* to be that dad. He wasn't cut out to be a dad.

Yet last night . . . God, it'd been so nice. So fun. Him, Beth, the kids, all chatting at the ice cream parlor. Teasing each other, reliving the highlights from the game. Even discussing the ankle-clipping incident. It'd all been so nice. So normal. Like that time with his brothers and Mac and Gran—

Bryan's breath hitched. He'd forgotten when Gran had brought them to Papa Gino's market. A general store with a deli counter, a butcher shop, and a soda fountain. They'd had root beer floats and sat in one of the booths, a treat for "paying folk" as Gran had said. She hadn't had a lot of money, so those floats had been special.

Bryan could still feel what it was like to be sitting at that table and have the waitress look at him with a kind smile and ask him what he wanted. Liam and Sean had known instantly, but he and Mac had had too many choices to decide so easily. Gran had just smiled and patted his arm and told the server they'd have to think about it some more.

Ah, the patience she'd had in taking on four scared, sad children. Sure she loved them, but it couldn't have been easy. Widowed without more than her old home to her name, Gran had somehow made do. She'd saved them from the foster system and for that he'd always be grateful. It's why he was paying the extra it cost at her retirement community for the apartment she'd wanted. No one knew, not Liam or Sean, not Mac, and especially not Gran. The arrangement was between him and the director and he'd bought the unit outright so all Gran had to do was pay for her care. He would have arranged that for her, too, but Gran did have her pride. He knew all about pride.

He swept the mop over the cleat marks on the hardwood and took care of Sherman's muddy paw prints as well. Even the dog was starting to grow on him.

He sloshed the mop back into the bucket. Two and a half more weeks. How was he going to survive without falling for all of them?

His cell phone rang, thank God, pulling his head back to reality.

It was his agent.

"Hey, Don, what's up?"

"I got a call that they're starting the shoot early if they can get enough people on set. You up for it?"

He would be, but that'd mean breaking his commitment to Mac. It'd also mean leaving Beth and the kids. He *couldn't* do that.

"I'm committed to this job, Don. Can't really back out. Is that going to be a problem?"

Uh, hell yeah. You're putting your career on hold to clean?

"The widow, huh? Anything happening there that I need to know about? I've seen some rumblings in the press."

"You know how the press is. Any story they can find. There's nothing here."

Liar.

"Pity. It'd make for good press. You sure you don't want to start something?"

"You did not just ask me that." He was surprised. Sure, he knew people planted stories to generate interest to make themselves more marketable, but he'd never done that. Don knew it, too. They'd discussed it. He'd make it in his career on his own merits or he wouldn't make it, but no way would he ever lie to get ahead.

"Sorry." Don didn't sound very sorry. Not that Bryan could blame him, but it was the seedy side of this business. Casting couches were another. Whoever said they didn't still exist in this day and age hadn't been around the block enough.

"So I'll tell PJ you're out for the early shoot, right?"

Bryan smiled. This was why Don was such a good agent; he wanted clarification on every point from both the studios and his own clientele. His career was in good hands with Don.

"No go, Don."

"All right, then. Two weeks from Friday you'll be on set."

Seventeen days in total. That was all he had left with Beth and the kids. "Yeah, that's it. I'll be there then."

Even if he didn't want to be.

"Bryyyyyaaaannnnn!" Maggie ran across the kitchen floor, her arms outstretched and a smile so big it covered almost her whole face. God, he'd miss this. Miss her. Miss her hero worship of him—but not from his movies or what he did for a living. Maggie loved him because of who he was.

Maggie loved him.

Shit. She did.

Look at that face. Those bright eyes. The smile that stretched from ear to ear. She'd wanted him to move in. To be her father.

And he was going to leave her.

It wasn't his fault that she needed a dad. He was here to clean. So he helped out a bit. Had taken to her. Liked her inquisitiveness. Her questions. Her tea parties and her messy drawings. Why did that have to make her love him? Why couldn't she just enjoy the time and the attention and it'd be no big deal?

Because she was five, she missed her father, and she'd found a substitute right in her very own home, that's why, moron.

"Will you make me a peanut butter and applesauce sandwich?" She blinked her big brown eyes at him.

Some day she was going to be a heartbreaker. He just hoped to hell that his wasn't broken when he left because *hers* was.

He needed to pull away. Not be so involved in the kids' lives. He had to create that distance so they wouldn't be upset when he left. Hell, this wasn't supposed to have happened. He was supposed to have come in, cleaned the house, and gotten out. Live his life away from Mac's company.

But he'd signed on for extra projects—he was doing the mudroom closets today—to help out "the widow."

Beth.

Mother of five.

Widowed mother of five.

Sexy widowed mother of five.

Who could drive him insane with just one look.

And with a kiss . . . have him thinking things he'd never thought he'd think.

"You want a sandwich for breakfast?"

"Yep. Daddy liked sandwiches for breakfast. I miss that."

Another knife to the heart. He could *not* be Maggie's dad.

He was going to make her that sandwich, though. "You're sure you want applesauce on your sandwich? Not apple butter?"

"Apple *butter*?" Maggie scrunched up her face. "Butter comes from cows, not apples."

Okay, then. Applesauce it was. He wasn't about to get into a discussion on butter-making because he had a feeling he'd lose to Maggie's convictions.

He propped the mop in the bucket and let her lead him by the hand back to the kitchen. So much for detachment.

Maggie had already started to make her sandwich. The evidence dripped from the countertops, down the cabinets. Sherman was in an orgy of pleasure, running between the cabinets to lick the different ingredients.

Bryan hoped to hell that peanut butter didn't make dogs sick. Though it'd serve the mutt right if he got an upset stomach.

"First order of business, we're putting Sherman outside." He scooped up the dog and looked for his leash. He found it lodged behind the potato bin.

Once Sherman was out, barking and pulling against the leash, Bryan closed the back door to muffle the sound, then grabbed a set of sponges from the pantry. "Come on, Maggie. Let's clean up the mess before we make another one."

"Well that's silly. We should just keep making the same one so we only have to clean it up once."

Words of wisdom from a five-year-old.

"Did you ever have peanut butter and applesauce when you were little, Bryan?"

He tried to remember back—because he'd tried so hard in the interim years to forget. "Not applesauce, no. But I did have peanut butter and banana." Both of which were staples from the welfare system.

His gut twinged. He'd vowed to never eat peanut butter again once he'd had a job, yet now he was going to do just that.

Surprisingly, the applesauce was good with the peanut butter. It also smeared across Maggie's face every time she took a bite and dripped onto her plate, once with such a big drip that it splashed applesauce onto her chin.

Maggie's eyes sparkled with laughter as she giggled and wiped it off. "Kelsey says I'm a messy eater."

"I think you eat messy food."

She cocked her head sideways with a look on her face that stole his breath because it looked so much like her mother. "I think you're right. I like messy things. Glitter glue, applesauce, peanut butter, my room. Well, except for Mrs. Beecham. I don't like her messes. But I like her. She's cuddly."

Bryan had gotten more than a few glimpses of the Maine Coon cat. Cuddly was a good word for it. So was messy. The cat shed enough fur to knit a winter blanket from. That's what he'd found himself cleaning up the most of, especially in the corners of the dining room on the hardwood floor. Forget dust bunnies, the cat shed dust *kitties*. It'd watched him clean up its fur once. Sat there licking its front paw as it washed its whiskers, complete boredom in its stance. Cats were peculiar that way. But he was even coming to like the damn thing almost as much as he liked Sherman.

Wait. When the hell had he ever decided he liked the dog?

Bryan shook his head. Dogs, cats, kids . . . they were all going to cease to be important once his contracted date was up.

And would you be interested in buying a bridge in Brooklyn while you're at it, Manley?

"Will you help us look for Muffy, Bryan? Mommy and I are going out in a little bit to search. You're so good at finding Sherman, I bet you can find Muffy."

No pressure . . . Bryan didn't even think about trying to get out of it. The truth was he *wanted* to help them find the missing dog, though he wasn't so sure he believed Beth's story yesterday. There'd been a gleam in her eye and a purpose to her stride that hadn't seemed like a lost-dog finding attitude, but when he'd asked her about it, she'd stuck to her story.

He wanted to know what the truth was and why she was hiding it, so for that alone he'd go with them.

To be around Beth . . . well, that went without saying.

And speaking of the devil—er, angel—Beth ran into the kitchen at that instant, and came to an abrupt stop when she saw him.

"Bryan! What are you doing here?"

"He works here, Mommy," Maggie, in all her five-year-old wisdom, answered. "And he's going to help us find Muffy."

Great. Beth had counted on being able to have Maggie home in a half hour by saying she must have been mistaken. But with Bryan . . . He wasn't going to buy that so easily.

After the soccer game, he'd looked at the tear on her shirt and the missing button and her hair. He'd smoothed it down and it'd been a major lesson in keeping her composure that she hadn't melted in to him and told him the truth.

Especially after she'd looked at the pictures last night. If she ever saw Mr. Steve McAllister again, it'd be too soon. His pictures had made it look as if there was something between them. He'd captured her, Maggie, and Bryan laughing, with Maggie on Bryan's lap. She hadn't even remembered that Bryan had put a hand on her knee, but Steve McAllister had captured that moment for all posterity.

She'd kept the memory card instead of destroying it. Stuck it in her safe where no one but her would ever be able to see those photos. Should the need ever arise, that was.

Or should she *want* to relive these surprising days in the lonely years to come.

"Uh, sure, that's great if he wants to come. Another set of eyes is always good." Though it would be torture on her acting skills to keep up the pretense. He was the actor of the bunch, not her. She couldn't even lie about Santa effectively. Mike had been the one to keep that myth going for their kids. When he'd died and Maggie had been so into Santa and the Easter Bunny, and the stork . . . Christmas had been tough these last two years.

The next hour rivaled Christmas for toughness.

"Are you sure you saw something over here?" Bryan asked for the umpteenth time, moving branches around.

Beth nodded. Oh, yeah, she'd definitely seen something, but it'd been much higher than the knee-high branches Bryan was searching through. Mr. Steve McAllister was at least six feet tall and so was his tripod. Too bad he hadn't used the camera— the very big, very expensive camera—to find a lost dog instead of stealing someone's privacy and well-being.

"I don't see anything. Especially not a hole for a fox's den." He let the branches fall back into place. "You're *certain* this was the spot?"

"Yes, but that doesn't mean the fox lives here. He could have been wandering around."

"Not in the day. Foxes are nocturnal."

Crud. She knew that. She also knew that Maggie *didn't* know that. "Maybe it was rabid?"

"And you went after a rabid animal?"

He had her there. She'd never have done that. "I thought it was Muffy."

He arched that eyebrow at her again, but didn't say anything. It was a good thing she hadn't picked acting as a career choice.

Beth let them wander for another hour, knowing full well they weren't on Muffy's trail, but she didn't want to freak her kids out or make Bryan feel guilty about the paparazzi any more than he already did.

"Hey, aren't you Bryan Manley?" A kid on a skateboard popped a wheelie to stop beside them.

"I am." Bryan stopped walking to talk to the kid. Beth admired that about him, that he hadn't forgotten where he came from or didn't forget to appreciate that fans were why he could do what he did.

"Any chance I can get you to sign my board?"

"You have a marker?"

"Yeah." The kid pulled out a marker—Beth had no idea why he'd be carrying one—and thanked Bryan for signing it before riding away.

"Why do people want you to sign things, Bryan?" Maggie tugged on his shirt.

He picked her up and settled her on his hip. "It shows people that they met me."

"Why do they want to meet you?"

"I guess they like my movies and it makes them feel like they're a part of it when they meet me."

Um . . . no. At least, that wasn't why Kelsey's friends and their moms wanted to meet him. But Beth was thankful he didn't share that info with Maggie. She'd learn soon enough. And when she learned that Bryan had held her in his arms . . .

"Hey, can I get a picture of you two?" She pulled out her cell. This was a memory for Maggie, not a publicity shot.

"Yay, Mommy!" Maggie wrapped her little arms around Bryan's neck and rested her head against his cheek.

The image on Bryan's face was priceless. Stunned and happy all in one.

Beth felt a lump rise in her throat. He was holding her daughter so tightly, one hand on her back, the other arm holding her against his waist, and the smile on Maggie's face . . .

Beth worked a smile past the lump. "That's great, Maggie. It's a good picture of both of you." Not that either could take a bad picture.

"Let me see!" Maggie kicked her legs.

Luckily, Bryan's reflexes kicked in so he avoided some, ah, damage.

Beth hid a smile as she showed them the photo.

"Oh cool! Maybe you can sign this for me, Bryan?" Maggie wrapped her arms around his neck again and gave him a kiss on the cheek. "Please?"

Bryan averted his eyes from Beth's. Then he cleared his throat. "Uh, yeah. Of course, Maggie." He gave her a final squeeze, then set her down. "How about we give it another few minutes to find Muffy and then head home? Your mom can print it out."

"Nah, let's go home now. Muffy's not going to go this way. She doesn't like the McNulty's dog, Bruiser. He's a bully."

Bull*dog*, but it was close enough. Beth grabbed Maggie's hand. "Okay, kiddo, let's head home."

Maggie reached for Bryan's. "Come on, Bryan. You have to walk with us."

Bryan was lucky not to be stumbling back. Too much emotion was clogging his chest, making breathing difficult. The moment he'd held Maggie in his arms and she'd wrapped hers around his neck . . . The look on Beth's face, then that photo . . .

He was never going to make it through the rest of the time without doing something he'd probably live to regret.

But, hell, if he didn't do something, he'd live to regret that as well.

Thankfully, Liam called to say their friend Jared had scored some last-minute baseball tickets, so the four of them had plans for the evening. He even left Beth's house early, though Maggie begged him to stay for dinner, but that was too much temptation. His brothers would never let him live it down if he blew them off for a five-year-old. Well, and her mother. But still . . .

But despite the fact that he was out with his best friends in the world, not to mention the thirty thousand other people in the stadium, it turned out to be a pretty lonely night when all he could think about were the six people he'd left behind.

Chapter Nineteen

❦

"OH no, Sherman, not again!"

Bryan winced when he heard Kelsey's whine.

Beth came flying out of the kitchen. "What'd he do now?"

Bryan peeked around the corner from the mudroom. This room was going to take him all day to clean; the Hamilton children had taken the name to heart. Plus, there was a tear in the vinyl flooring that was going to require some work to fix. Beth needed a handyman more than she needed a cleaning service. He was definitely going to talk to Mac about adding the service.

"He dragged my underwear through the Templetons' backyard."

The laundry line. Again. That made four times since he'd been here. No wonder they had so much laundry, the dog was making more work.

That was it; he was building Beth a freestanding clothesline that the dog couldn't get to.

"Hey, Jason. Want to come with me? I need to head to the hardware store."

"Not really." The kid was flat on his back on the sofa with a handheld in his hands, thumbs punching feverishly.

"Dude." Bryan tugged the game from his hands. "It wasn't really a question. Let's go."

"Aw, man. Do I hafta?" Jason swung his long, gangly legs off the sofa and looked at his mom. "I got stuff to do today, Be—Mom."

Beth raised her eyebrows. "What kind of stuff?"

"Uh, you know. Stuff. School stuff." Jason put a smile on the end of it as if he'd thought Beth would believe him.

"You can do that after you go with Bryan. I'm sure he wouldn't have asked you unless it was important."

It wasn't a question, and Bryan appreciated the support.

He tapped Jason on the shoulder. "Come on. Let's get going. The quicker we go, the quicker we can come back so you can get to your stuff." Stuff both he and Beth knew didn't exist. Jason could help him when they got back. It'd be good for the kid to learn about tools and building things. Mike had a nice array of power tools in the garage.

Beth couldn't help but watch her son leave with Bryan. Couldn't help imagining how real this could be. What it would have been like if Mike were still alive. He would have taken Jason there and shown him things, taught him to mow the lawn, fix the mower, maybe even use some of the tools he'd collected over the years. Although . . . *she* was pretty handy with a drill; she could show him—all of them—how to fix things.

Funny, but she hadn't really given that a thought until now. It'd been a constant struggle to make sure their mental health was okay with all of this, and to keep being their mom. Being their dad was a whole other element and it was becoming a more important one than she'd realized. If she needed any reminders, that tire-changing lesson had drilled it into her. Jason wasn't getting any younger. Two more years and he'd be driving. Then Kelsey two years after that. Look what had happened in the last two years. Those seven hundred and thirty days weren't as long as she'd like.

"Mommy, why do you look like that?" Maggie poked her head up from the coffee table where she was drawing yet again. The therapist had said to give Maggie a tablet and crayons, since she'd been too young to write when Mike had died. That tablet had become her daughter's constant companion and it turned out that Maggie had some real talent in that area. Beth had removed the frightening images she'd drawn right after the accident once the pictures had started to change into pleasant things. Butterflies, flowers, Sherman, Mrs. Beecham—another addition the counselor had suggested and whom Maggie had named after her preschool teacher.

"Look like what, honey?"

"Like you want to go with Bryan and Jason?"

Beth snapped out of whatever fog she'd been in. Maggie had picked up on *that*? Things were getting a little too much out of hand. No, not *things*. Her *emotions*. She had to distance herself from Bryan. Had to make the kids do so, too. Mike's departure hadn't been his choice; Bryan's would be. A necessary one since he had a career to get back to, but the kids wouldn't see it that way. He was here only for a brief moment in their lives; she had a feeling they didn't get that. So when he left, it'd be one more person they cared about leaving them.

BRYAN could feel the noose tightening. The kids were getting to him. Jason had grumbled the entire ride to the hardware store, mostly about the company logo magnet on the truck and how *uncool* it was. Bryan told him *cool* was in the behavior of the person, not the trappings, and zoomed the truck into a parking spot in an impressive move one of the stunt guys had taught him on his last film. That had gotten Jason's attention and opened the door to what they were doing at the hardware store.

"You're sure Sherman's not going to be able to get to this?" he asked as he helped Bryan haul the lumber to the truck.

"I'm fairly certain."

"Then why are you doing it if you're not totally sure? That dog is a monster."

Bryan had to agree with Jason on that one, but didn't voice it. "I think we can come up with something to outwit a dog." He crossed his fingers.

"I dunno." Jason picked up the roll of nylon rope. "I'll bet the mutt chews through this in a day."

"You're on." Not that teaching a fourteen-year-old to gamble was a good thing, but it'd keep him engaged in the project once they were finished building it. "So you're going to help me build this, right?"

Jason swished his nonexistent roof of hair out of his face and looked surprised to find it missing. Or maybe the surprise was because of what Bryan had just asked him. "Me? Build? I don't know how."

"Good." Bryan clasped him on the shoulder. "Then you'll have no bad habits I have to unteach you. You'll be learning the right way to do it from the get-go."

"Why are you doing this? It's not in your job description."

"Because Sherman creates more work for everyone. A little extra effort now will save a ton of work later on."

"But it's not in your job description."

"Sometimes, Jase, it's not about what you're supposed to do. Sometimes it's about what's the right thing to do. And the right thing here is to prevent the dog from doing what he keeps doing. It'll make everyone's life easier."

Jason looked out the window and mumbled something.

"What? I didn't hear you."

For a second, Bryan wasn't sure Jason had heard him—or wasn't planning to answer. But then he turned his head and looked at Bryan. "I said, it'd be nice for Mom if life got easier. She's been stressed out since Dad died."

Bryan sucked in a breath and prayed for the right words. "Then it's a good thing we're doing this. Every little bit we can all do to make her life easier will be a help."

"Yeah. That's why I did my room. You were right."

There was a moment. A teenager telling him he was right. Bryan ought to record this moment for posterity.

But . . . why? He was leaving, remember? Jason would have more of these moments with the next man in Beth's life.

Bryan didn't want there to be another man in her life— which was ridiculous since he couldn't be.

Yeah, it made no sense, but then, a lot of these past two weeks didn't.

Or maybe it did and he just refused to listen . . .

"BUT, Jason, I want to mix the cement. Bryan said I could." Mark stuck his tongue out at his older brother.

Jason held the trowel over his head. "You're too little, Mark. You don't have enough arm strength. It has to be done thoroughly and quickly, and you can't."

Bryan took the trowel from Jason and knelt down by the posthole. "It'll be a moot point if we don't get this mixed and the post in, guys. So let's work together, okay?" He wiped the sweat from his forehead onto his shoulder. The backyard had a lot of shale below the surface, so he'd had to make another trip to the hardware store for some quick-set cement. Of course Maggie had wanted to mix it, then the twins had joined in, and all of a sudden, cement mixing had become a family affair.

And he was smack dab in the middle of it. Wouldn't his brothers be laughing their asses off if they could see him now? And considering he had dinner with them and Gran tonight, he didn't need to give them any clue what was going on here.

What is *going on here, Manley?*

He didn't want to analyze it too closely.

"Okay, guys, let's tie up the post." He'd rigged four lines to the post and gave each of the older kids, Kelsey included, a rope with a stake on the end. "Maggie, you watch the level to make sure that water bubble stays in the middle, okay?"

"Aye, aye, captain." Maggie saluted him. For some reason, she equated the dry cement with the beach and had been making nautical references all afternoon.

Whatever worked.

Bryan held the post straight while the kids worked the stakes into the ground. He'd shown Jason how to adjust the ropes so once they were in, he could go around and shore them up.

"Okay, everyone, while that sets, we're going to build the clothesline. You guys ready to help out?"

"Yeah!"

"Cool!"

"Sure."

"Whatever." The last was from Kelsey, who wasn't as eager as the boys but who, nevertheless, had chosen construction over helping her mom prepare lunch.

Speaking of which, every so often, Beth would step out onto the deck in her pink shorts and flowing white top, her feet bare, and her hair its natural state of windblown, and Bryan would have to find his breath yet again because she kept stealing it.

Thankfully, the whirr of the miter saw was enough to get his body's reaction under control—nothing like having a spinning steel blade with nasty teeth at groin height.

He measured out the angle, matched it to the drawing he'd made, and set it up for Tommy to make the cut. "Now, remember, Tom, take it slow. You don't want to drive the blade down too fast, or the wood will splinter and we don't need that." He lowered Tommy's safety goggles in place. "Remember, safety first."

"I know. Mom always says that."

Of course she did because Beth was a great mom.

Each kid got a turn to work the saw and the drill, but by the time they were on their second screws, the novelty had worn off. Only Maggie hung around to help him compile the frame and string the rope along it. They finished just as Beth carried a tray of sandwiches onto the patio.

"Lunch!" she called out.

Kids came running from all parts of the house. Some that didn't even belong to Beth.

"Kelsey, you and Amanda please bring the iced tea out here. Mark, you grab the cups. Tommy, the ice. Kevin, you can bring a big spoon, and, Jason, there are chips and fruit on the island."

"What about me, Mommy? I want to get something." Maggie tugged on Beth's shirt again.

And just like before, Bryan wasn't about to tell her to stop. Especially when the neckline dipped lower and the hint of cleavage she'd had going on was more than just a hint.

Not that he could have said anything anyway because his mouth had dried up. His throat, too, and his chest was constricting as blood flow headed south.

God Almighty, he was a dog. Her kids were here, for Christ's sake. Neighbor kids, too. It was inappropriate. It was stupid. It was just plain wrong.

But it didn't stop him from looking.

She had a pink bra on. Light pink, a shade darker than her skin, and Bryan's imagination went into overdrive. He wanted to peel that shirt off her, up over her head, then slide his palms down her arms and around her back, undoing her bra and slipping it off, revealing her to him in tiny tantalizing glimpses, brushing his fingertips gently over her skin, causing her to shiver. Then he'd cup her, his thumbs stroking her nipples, watching them harden as he lowered his head just as she said—

"Do you want something, Bryan?"

Thank God he looked up without telling her exactly what he wanted. Thank God he looked up before he just took it.

Her entire family was staring at him.

"Are you okay, Bryan? You look kinda weird." Tommy handed him a glass of something. "See? We told you it was too much work. That's why me and Mark took a break."

He gulped the drink. Iced tea. Good. He needed something to clear his head.

He finished the glass with a big *ahhhh,* then wiped his mouth with his forearm just for the boys.

Beth rolled her eyes and handed him a napkin. "I swear, you boys never outgrow that."

"You're right. It's too much fun." He used the napkin to prove he wasn't the heathen she'd think he was if she could read his thoughts.

"So when are we gonna put the top on the pole?" Mark asked, reaching across the table for the chips.

"Mark Joseph Hamilton, we do not reach across the table. Especially when we have guests."

"But Bryan's not a guest. He's—"

That stumped him. Stumped Bryan, too. What exactly was he? Not an employee—he didn't work for her. He worked for Mac. He could be an outside contractor, but he doubted the kids would know what that was.

"He's a member of the family!" Maggie popped up from under the picnic table, squashing the massive cat in her arms. "Just like Mrs. Beecham!"

The cat let out a long, bothered, *"Mrrrrooooowwwww,"* making all of them laugh.

Good thing, because Bryan was about to do anything but.

A member of the family. Was that how Maggie saw him? Was that how they all saw him? Well, the kids. Beth knew better. But what did she think of Maggie's declaration?

He risked a glance at her. *Stricken* was the word that came to mind.

Oh, great. She was horrified. Upset. Not on board with the idea. Then again, he wasn't, either. But the kids . . . This wasn't good for the kids. They couldn't think that about him.

He'd known letting himself get reeled in wasn't a good idea,

but he'd been able to handle it. The kids on the other hand . . .
He had to do something about this.

B RYAN finished early.
    Beth ought to be thankful about it. And she was. Sort of.
They needed to talk. What Maggie had said at lunch . . .

She couldn't get the idea out of her head. And it was a bad
idea. Bad for her kids to think it. Bad for her to *want* it. Bad
because Bryan had looked as if someone had stuck a hot poker
up his—

Out of the mouth of a five-year-old, and there was nothing Beth could do to undo it. And she *needed* to do something about it. Maggie had been distracted by Mrs. Beecham,
and then Kelsey had wisely kept her occupied so she was out
of Bryan's hair, but her statement still hung over them.

A member of the family.

She'd never thought there'd be another man she'd even consider having in Mike's home. In Mike's bed. But Bryan, with
his sexy good looks and the amazing way he kissed, and most
of all the way he was with her kids—and with her, if the truth
be told—he'd wiggled in under her defenses and made her want
Maggie's description to be true.

He'd said something about tackling the garage, and off he'd
gone. Hadn't even asked Jason to help, which they had discussed earlier. She'd been undecided as to whether to press the
issue at the moment, but Jason had suddenly decided to keep
his younger brothers entertained. Never getting that kind of
attention from him, they'd lapped it up and the three of them
were off devising a Quidditch field. Kelsey, too, had suddenly
become interested in braiding Maggie's hair, and the two of
them had disappeared upstairs for the rest of the afternoon.
Beth was almost afraid to see the mess in her bathroom once
she heard the tub go on, but the mess that was hovering over
the picnic table was enough for one day.

Her cell phone rang as she closed the front door after Bryan
left. Silly her, her heart started pounding, thinking it was him.
Though why he'd be calling her when he hadn't spoken two
words to her all afternoon was a mystery.

It was Kara Leopold, sadly. No, *gladly*. No sense wishing for what couldn't—and shouldn't—be. "Hey, Kar, what's up?"

"Tomorrow night. You *have* to bring him. My nephew is coming. He wants to break into acting and if he could just talk to Bryan, he might have a shot."

"Kar, I haven't even asked him to come." And wouldn't now. "He might be busy." Oh, he was busy. Whether he knew it or not.

"You are kidding me! You haven't asked him? Why? Are you trying to keep him all to yourself? You don't want anyone else around him?"

Beth held the phone from her ear and looked at it in surprise. Yes, that was Kara's name on her caller ID, but the woman on the phone? Beth didn't know who she was. "Are you crazy? Do you even hear yourself? I am not keeping Bryan Manley all to myself and I am *not* going to ask him to the happy hour so you can grill him about getting Dylan into the business. The man's on a break from all that. He's cleaning my house, for Pete's sake."

"And your pipes? Is he cleaning those?"

Beth's mouth fell open and she shook her head. "I don't like what you're insinuating. *You* chose him for this job, not me. I had no say in the matter. Matter of fact, I distinctly remember you *and* Jenna both saying that if I refused your gift, you'd never speak to me again." Right about now, that sounded pretty good.

"I just think it's pretty selfish of you to keep him in your home all day and not let any of us hang out with him."

"He's not here to make friends, Kar. Here's here to work, remember?"

"Yeah, well all work and no play makes Bryan a very bored guy. Bring him."

No way in hell. She'd seen glimpses of the female feeding frenzies Bryan instilled; she wasn't inflicting her friends on him. Who knows, the rest of them might end up as crazed as Kara and she'd end up with no friends. And no Bryan.

A member of the family

No. She wasn't going to end up with that, either. And that was how it should be.

Chapter Twenty

❧❀❧

"YOU look awful pretty in green, Bryan. Matches your eyes."
    Bryan clenched his fists as he waited in the living room in Gran's new assisted living facility. Sean loved needling him and while, most of the time, he could give as good as he got, tonight was *not* the night. "Don't push it, Scene." There. Let Sean stew on his old nickname. Always pissed him off when they were kids and, right now, Bryan wouldn't mind someone picking a fight with him. He needed to work off this . . . this . . .

This what? Anger? No, he wasn't angry. Terror? Yeah, that might be it.

Frustration?

Hell yes. He was definitely frustrated.

And the damn uniform wasn't helping any.

He picked up a copy of *People* and thumbed through it, but pictures of hot women in barely there dresses weren't helping, either. None were as beautiful as Beth.

He tossed the magazine onto the table. "Seriously. How does Mac expect us to call ourselves *Manley Maids* when we're wearing the most *un*-manly pants in the history of work uniforms? See? Now *that's* a work uniform."

It was the PR shot from his last movie, where he'd had

bombs bursting behind him, a gun in each hand, and a woman clinging to each arm. Bikini-clad women. Back in the days when he *wasn't* frustrated.

"Hey, I'm up for giving Mac the money for new uniforms." Liam slapped Sean on the shoulder when he arrived. "I feel like a frickin' girl in those clothes."

"We could sing like one, too," said Sean, adjusting himself. "Who the hell designed them?"

"I did."

Oh shit. Gran.

"I take it there's a problem?"

"I'm sorry, Gran," said Sean. "We didn't know—"

"I realize that, Sean. I know you boys would never deliberately hurt me." She touched Bryan's arm and he bent down to kiss her cheek, trying to undo some of the damage their comments must have done.

"The uniform's fine, Gran," he whispered. He'd put up with this thing if it meant not hurting her.

She raised an eyebrow at him, skepticism etched across her face. "So you boys tell me what needs to be done and I'll work on another design."

Bryan recognized that look. She was determined to fix it. And if one of them didn't give her any direction, God only knew which direction she'd go.

He took a deep breath and took the plunge. At least he might get something good for the three of them if he spoke up now. "They're a bit, uh, tight, Gran."

"Tight, how?" Gran asked as if the answer wasn't going to embarrass the hell out of all of them as she led them down the hall to a private dining area like the dame of the manor.

"You know, Gran, *tight*." Bryan nodded to the residents they passed. Here, he was just Catherine Manley's grandson and he liked that he could be just that. The bright lights were great, but sometimes, it was nice just to be him.

Liam held the door open for their grandmother and they followed her in like ducklings. Bryan hid his smile. His brothers used to call him the ugly one. That picture in *People* told a different story, and if his face and his body were the tickets to never having to worry about putting food on his table again, so be it.

"Sean, you bring the chicken over to the table. Liam, the potatoes. And Bryan, you can pour the wine. But not those Hollywood-sized drinks you're used to. I don't want any of you boys getting drunk."

"Yes, ma'am." He rolled his eyes. *Hollywood-sized* drinks. He'd tried to bring her out to the west coast a few times to show her it wasn't the Sodom and Gomorrah she thought, but Gran wouldn't hear of it. *She wasn't getting on a plane at her age and she could see Bryan better on TV than with hordes of people shoving microphones in his face.*

He had her argument down pat because she'd said the same thing every time he'd broached the subject. Gran was content here in this little burg, a feeling he'd never understood.

Then an image of Beth and the kids at the soccer game flashed into his brain and for a moment—a moment as quick as that flash—he considered it.

No. No way. He'd worked too hard to get out. To move beyond. To move up. He wasn't coming back here for his grandmother, let alone a widow with five kids.

Five kids who needed a dad.

A widow who needed a man in her life.

Jesus H. Christ. He wasn't that man and he could put the damn thought out of his head. He had a film to start. Another one in the can. Promo tours. Awards ceremonies. Endorsements to consider. Things were finally happening; now was *not* the time to chuck it all for soccer games and finger painting.

"Don't you roll your eyes at me, young man. You might think you know everything because you're a big movie star, but I can still take my switch to your behind if you get too big for your britches."

"That's what I'm trying to tell you, Gran." Bryan set her wine in front of her. "I *am* too big for those britches."

"Bryan Matthew Manley, there's no reason to be crude."

Sean choked on his wine and Liam looked like he was going to as well.

Bryan just wanted to be sick. "I . . . I didn't mean . . ." He had *not* meant anything of the sort; she was his *grandmother,* for God's sake!—

And to add insult to injury, Sean took a picture of him with his cell.

"What the hell was that for?" Bryan was still trying to process Gran going with sexual innuendo.

"Insurance. Against poverty." Sean sat down. "I'm sure some magazine would pay big bucks for that look on your pretty-boy face."

"Sean Patrick Manley, you stop teasing your brother," said Gran as if she hadn't just been talking about . . . *that*. "Hand me that phone."

"Aw, Gran—"

"The phone." She wiggled her fingers.

Bryan got no small measure of satisfaction when Gran deleted the photo. He even had to hide the chuckle when she deleted the rest of Sean's photos—accidentally of course, but still . . . it served him right.

What *didn't* serve him right were the complications going on with his current project that some of those pictures related to—a project that had a lot of Bryan's money tied up.

"What kind of complications?"

Sean winced. "Merriweather threw a slight wrench into the plans. She's giving her granddaughter the chance to inherit the estate."

"Son of a bitch." Bry tossed his napkin onto the table. The estate was supposed to be Sean's flagship property and the first of the Manley Brothers' projects. They lost this and there wouldn't be a second project.

"Language, Bryan." Gran took a bite of chicken, those two words admonition enough. She'd always been able to get their attention with just a word or a look. They'd all been too worried over losing her to health problems to want to upset her.

"Sorry." Bry put his napkin back on his lap. "What are you going to do, Sean?"

His brother swiped a hand across his mouth. "As I see it, I've got three options. One, make sure Livvy fails and the sale can proceed as planned. Two, I was going to ask you guys if you wanted to cover the difference. For commensurate ROI, of course."

"So you'd be the minor partner, then?" Liam asked.

Sean nodded. "Obviously not what I wanted when I planned this, but we can work out the terms and I'll gradually buy you out. If you can float the money, that's my second option. The third would be to bring in outside investors, but that'll dilute everyone's take."

"That option's out." Liam rubbed his chin. "This is supposed to be a Manley Brothers project. We bring someone else in, we lose that edge, both in calling the shots and the publicity."

"But you have Bryan," said Gran. "He's the best publicity you could ask for."

Bryan shook his head. Three weeks ago, he might have said yes. Now? He was not going to be responsible—well, any more than he already was—for bringing the spotlight on Beth and her kids. And that's just what would happen if he got publicly involved in a local business. "No go, Gran. I'm the silent partner. I don't have the background these two do for this business. We start plastering my face all over this and it'll become a circus. The media's great until it isn't. Sean's got what I can afford." Not to mention, he wasn't about to involve Beth and the kids any more than they already were.

"So how are your assignments coming, boys?" Gran asked.

"How's it going?" Bryan choked on the words before he thought about the consequences of saying them. Consequences he quickly tried to mitigate when Gran looked at him sharply. "I seriously have no idea why people procreate. You ought to see these five kids. I get the place all clean and nice, and by the time I've finished the last room, I have to start all over again. It's like each kid is their own tornado. Inversely proportional to their size, too. That little one . . . *whew*. She can create a mess of epic proportions."

"She's hurting, Bryan. Acting out. Have patience," said Gran. "Her father was the pilot of that plane crash a few years ago. Sad."

So much sadder than anyone had realized. And given what'd happened to *his* parents, Bryan was in the perfect position to empathize, hence his *issues*.

He cut a slice of bread. "I know *exactly* what she's feeling, Gran."

"I know you do."

Gran squeezed his hand and for a moment, he was back in the church the day of the funeral when she'd done the same thing before he'd broken down completely.

And just like then, she changed the subject. "Liam? How's Cassidy?"

Liam shook his head. "She's Cassidy."

"Now, Liam, don't judge her by what everyone says about her."

That she was a spoiled socialite without one iota of a clue how to live a normal life since her rich father paid for everything. Airhead Central.

The thing was, it'd be easier to deal with Cassidy Davenport and her cluelessness than Beth and her down-to-earth-ness. Her realness. And the kids . . . God, the kids. The fact that he knew what they were going through . . . Why'd Mac had to give him *this* assignment? Why couldn't he have gotten some old woman with fifty years' worth of cobwebs and dust bunnies to deal with? Or, hell, even Cassidy. He'd take Cassidy any day over wanting Beth so much that his chest hurt when he thought about it.

And he was thinking about it a lot. Missed half the dinner conversation thinking about wanting Beth. Christ. He was a mess. He took a swig of his wine. He really needed to get out while he could. "So what do you think about switching, Sean?"

Sean shook his head. "I'm sorry, what'd you say?"

"Your assignment. She must be a babe if you haven't even told us word one about her. I'm thinking I might have to check her out if you're not calling dibs on her. Maybe we can switch jobs." As soon as he said it, he knew he wouldn't do it. Sean might not be in movies, but he was a good-looking guy. And local. Beth and the kids could get attached to Sean as much as they'd get attached to him.

"You have your own client to deal with."

Gran drilled him with her gaze. People called her eyes slate blue; Bryan called them steel. His grandmother was made of stern stuff and she didn't miss a trick. It'd made it tough to get away with shit when he'd been a kid and it looked like things hadn't changed much in the intervening years. "And she's quite lovely if I remember correctly from the newspaper."

The newspapers hadn't done Beth justice. "Yeah, she's hot, but she's got five kids. Nothing destroys a woman's attractiveness faster than a bunch of kids hanging around." He was lying. Beth could have ten kids and it wouldn't change how he felt about her, so who was he trying to convince?

His brothers. Because if they had even an inkling of the

struggle he was facing when it came to Beth and her family, he'd never hear the end of it.

"Ahem." Gran drilled him with her eyes. Her hard, cold, steel blue eyes.

Why?

Oh shit. Gran had raised four kids and he'd just made that stupid remark. . . "I'm, uh, sorry, Gran. I, uh—"

Gran lifted her hand. "I raised you better than that, Bryan Matthew. That woman has a lot to offer someone, and those children are blessings. You should be so lucky to have her even *think* about going out with you. With comments like that, you don't deserve her."

He knew that. He didn't deserve her. And more importantly, she deserved better.

So then why, a few hours later when he'd survived the dinner with eagle-eyed Gran, did he jump at the chance to spend Friday night with her when her friend Kara called to invite him to the neighborhood happy hour?

Because he was obviously a glutton for punishment.

Chapter Twenty-one

❧❧❧

HE was definitely a glutton for punishment; he spent the entire next day working on the closets in Beth's bedrooms. She'd left him a list of things to do—he refused to call it a Honey-Do list because that would imply he was her honey and he did *not* need those implications—and the most pressing seemed to be the loose clothes racks. He hadn't counted on what, exactly, he'd be touching.

Or maybe he had.

There he was, shoulder to shoulder—and cheek to cheek—with her dresses, removing them, draping them over his arms, feeling the silky fabric slide against his skin, imagining it doing the same to hers. Imaging *her* sliding against him. Replaying the kiss in the gazebo over and over until his *dick* could have held all the clothes up. And her perfume . . . It lingered in the air of her closet, surrounding him, taunting him with something he had no right to want.

Thank God she was gone for the day. At least when he was walking around with a boner big enough to hang clothes on, no one was there to witness it.

"Dude, please tell me you're not into ladies' clothing."

Except for Jason.

Shit. He'd forgotten that Jason was old enough not to go on every excursion Beth took.

Ah, well. Nothing deflated a boner quicker than the kid of the woman he had that boner for.

"I'm fixing your mom's closet."

"Actually, that's my dad's."

Double shit. Boner gone; empathy ratcheting up six zillion degrees.

Silence. Jason glaring at him, daring him to say something. So he did.

"Then maybe you ought to help me fix it."

Jason blinked. Fast. A few times. He looked away briefly, too. But then he sucked it up, choked back the tears that Bryan could tell were brimming just below the surface, and nodded.

It was enough.

BETH stared at the price tag. Again. She couldn't even say how long she'd been staring at it or even what the price *was* because her mind was a million miles away. Well, four point two miles to be exact. That was exactly how far her front door was from this store. She drove here hundreds of times a year, but that wasn't why she knew it was four point two miles from her home. No, that she knew because she'd watched the mileage tick up as she drove farther from her home this morning. Before Bryan had arrived.

She hadn't wanted to be there. Well, that wasn't quite true. She'd wanted nothing *more* than to be there, which was what was wrong. Bryan. Was. Leaving. She had to get it through the thick, charisma-induced fog that'd filtered into her brain cavity the day he'd shown up.

"Mommy, are you gonna get that one or not 'cause I'm gettin' bored." Maggie plopped her chin in her hand and looked up at Beth with Mike's eyes.

Beth dropped the price tag and shook her head. "It's not exactly what I want." Because what she wanted couldn't be bought off a rack.

Two more weeks. The maid service had been the perfect gift, but the more Bryan worked around her house, the more he fixed her home aesthetically, the more he did it emotionally. Mentally. Spiritually.

It was nice having a man around her house. Nice seeing his broad shoulders reaching places she couldn't, doing things she didn't have time to do. Setting her home to rights. As if a sweep of testosterone was all they needed to put the house back to the way it was before Mike had taken off that morning.

Except that testosterone couldn't be Bryan's. Maybe she should go out and start trying to find someone. Someone for her. Maybe that's what this was all about. The raw, blatant, knock-her-socks-off appeal of Bryan's sexuality had woken her up. Made her want again. Made her ache again, and she'd forgotten what that was like. Forgotten what it was like to yearn for someone. To want to be physically and emotionally close to someone. No, Bryan couldn't be that man, but he sure as hell was the best wake-up call there was. She owed it to her kids to find someone. To make the house a home again. And she owed it to herself to love and be loved. To find that companionship the whim of Mother Nature had ripped from her.

Happy hour tonight. There were several single guys in the area. Many of her friends invited their friends. Maybe she'd come out of her shell a bit and actually talk to some of them with an eye toward dating instead of hiding behind her widowhood. Maybe it was finally time to live again.

"Can we get hot dogs, Mom? Please?" asked Tommy.

"Yeah, I want mustard on mine. And kraut," said Mark.

"You don't like kraut."

"Yes I do."

"No you don't."

"I do too."

"You do not."

"Do too."

"Do not."

"Dorks!" Kelsey plopped a hand on the twins' heads and swiveled them around to look at her. "Remember what Bryan said? You have to watch each other's backs. You can't do that if you're fighting, so knock it off. You don't like sauerkraut, Mark. You said it tastes like seasick worms and we don't need you puking on the ride home." Kelsey glanced up and shook her head at Beth.

Remember what Bryan said . . . Great. Now her children were quoting him. Living by his rules. By the example he'd set.

She was never going to be able to replace him in her life.

Then she showed up at happy hour and realized that, for tonight at least, she wasn't going to have to.

Chapter Twenty-two

❧

"DID you *see* who's here?"

"Oh my God, it's Bryan Manley!"

"Bryan *Manley* is here!"

"A *movie star* is on Kara's *patio*!"

"I'm going to have an orgasm right this minute!"

Beth could relate to every comment. Especially that last one, though it was just wrong that it came from Jason's math teacher. It was weird enough seeing Mrs. Shuman in her robe getting her newspaper on Sunday mornings in their neighborhood, but now this?

Someone sidled up next to her and slid an arm around her waist. "Beth! I'm so glad you decided to share him."

Beth looked at the woman next to her. Bethany Cavanaugh. She lived four doors down, drove a Jag, and was single. Beth had spoken to her maybe six times in all the years the woman had lived here and now they were buddies? "I, uh—"

"Oh, it wasn't Beth." Kara slipped through the crowd with a sly smile on her face and handed Beth a glass of wine. "I invited him."

"How'd you get his number?" Bethany asked the question Beth would've asked if she could speak.

"I have my ways." Kara took smug to a whole new level.

Of course she did. And of course she'd use them to get him here. Beth should have seen that one coming. But what the hell did it mean? Kara was married. Happily, or at least Beth would have thought so, but then, you never could tell what went on in other people's marriages. She sipped the wine.

"Well, aren't you the hostess with the mostest?" Bethany sidled up to Kara.

Beth suddenly felt the need to take a shower.

Even more so—and in a totally different way—when Bryan looked up at that moment and caught her staring.

She wanted to shower with *him*. To get all sweaty and then soapy with him. Slide up against him in her sheets, then in the shower and, hell, maybe even on the bathroom rug.

"So you *didn't* know he was coming?" smirked Bethany. Though their names were similar, Beth was *plain Beth* while Bethany was as sleek and sexy as her Jag. "Honey, *I'd* sure know if he was *coming*."

Oh, the innuendo. Beth so did not need it.

Bethany, apparently, did. She left her new *bestie* Kara to saunter over to Bryan.

Beth felt a slight moment of gratification to see Bryan glance at Bethany, take in her breezy summer dress that had slits in all the right places, then look back to *her* with a slight smile hovering on his lips that said he'd seen this before.

Was it wrong that it made her happy to know Bryan saw through the woman?

True to his graciousness and charm, however, when Bethany planted herself in front of him and held out her hand for him to take—back of it up as if she expected him to kiss it—Bryan did turn on the charm. Beth could have told him not to have bothered; Bethany was his for the taking, even if he wanted to run through his lines while she did him. It was almost laughable.

Almost.

"So how much longer do you get to enjoy him?" asked one of the other women.

"Has he done your drawers yet?"

"Cooked in your kitchen?"

"Changed your sheets?"

The innuendoes wouldn't stop, and while Beth could

appreciate the humor and good-natured teasing behind them, she was having a hard time holding on to her composure.

Then he appeared at her side. "Hey, Beth. Ladies."

He'd singled her out. The envy in the other women's eyes was almost palpable. Especially Bethany's when he leaned in to whisper in her ear. "Your friend Kara invited me tonight."

"So I heard."

"It was nice of her."

Nice had nothing to do with why Kara had invited him.

"Thank you for fixing the bars in my closets. They were accidents waiting to happen."

"Yeah, they were pretty loose. Jason helped me."

"Jason?"

"You know, your son? Used to have a mop on his head but now you can see his face? Surly kid."

God, the man was gorgeous when he teased her.

Focus on the conversation, not on his dimples.

She took a quick sip of her wine. "Oh. Him. Yeah, I think we've met. But the Jason I know had zero interest in helping me around the house."

"Well he suddenly became interested. He helped with the rest of the clothesline project, too." His fingers tapped her waist and Beth was suddenly interested in something also.

Well, no. That wasn't true. She'd been interested in *that* since she'd laid eyes on him on her front porch.

She shoved the thought aside, took another sip of wine, and dragged her brain back into their conversation. After all, they were talking about her *son* for Pete's sake. She ought to be able to keep lust-filled thoughts at bay while discussing her *child.* "He has a vested interest in the clothesline. He doesn't want his boxers showing up in the neighbor's hedges again."

Bryan's left eyebrow went up and, oh, was it a good look on him. "Again?"

Beth nodded. "Sherman's an equal-opportunity humiliator."

"Ah. That explains Jason's enthusiasm then when we finally erected it."

Did he have to use *that* word? It was all Beth could do not to glance at his groin.

Several of the women, however, weren't so circumspect, and Beth was amazed to see Bryan blush.

"So, are there any more like you in Mac's stable? If so, sign me up for a lifelong contract," one of the woman said, earning a nice round of chuckles.

"Sorry, ladies. My brothers and I are taken for the month, but I'm sure Mac will be hiring more guys since there's been a lot of interest."

No, *he* was what caused the interest. Mac Manley had known what she was doing when she'd put her brothers to work.

Just like Kara had known what she was doing when she'd invited him to the party. It went on longer than any of the other happy hours had lasted before, to the point where kids were starting to drop like flies and Kara's basement den became one big sleepover because none of the parents wanted to leave.

The thing was, Bryan charmed them all, not just the women. The men got over their initial animosity to talk about his movies and the stunts and what it was like to work with "hot babes," and all the stars he'd worked with. Bryan was amazing about deflecting a lot of the attention, though. When the conversation would go on for a while about his life, he'd turn it around and ask other people what they did or where they were going on vacation or how their kids were doing in sports or school or boy scouts . . . The man really knew how to work a crowd and make it seem genuine.

But then, Bryan *was* genuine. Beth liked that the most about him. Sure, he was nice to look at and he could kiss her right out of her clothes if he tried hard enough, but in the end, he was a genuinely nice guy. There were no airs, no look-at-me-I'm-better-than-you, no false modesty, just a genuineness and self-effacing honesty that made him all that much more attractive.

"So, Beth, why don't you bring Bryan along on Sunday?" Dena Reardon tucked the lone curl dangling from her updo behind her ear with a seductive tilt of her head.

Only in this crowd would an invite to an amusement park include a come-on.

"Sunday?" Bryan did his own head-tilting, but it was completely natural and devoid of invitation.

That didn't stop Beth from wanting to run her lips along his jaw and kiss her way down his throat and run her fingers through his hair—

"Um, we're going to Martinson's Amusement Park. The kids

have wanted to go since it opened in April, but with school it was too hard to schedule. I promised them we'd go at the beginning of summer and Sunday's the only day it works until August."

"I remember Martinson's." Bryan's face lit up in a smile. If he hadn't already been a movie star, that smile would seal the deal. "I could never get enough of that place growing up."

"You should come," said Dena, now twirling that lone curl. Seriously?

Then she touched the corner of her mouth with the tip of her tongue. "I'm bringing my boys. They're friends with Tommy and Mark."

"And Alex," interjected Beth. "You're bringing Alex, right?" Alex was Dena's husband. An important person to include.

Dena reluctantly dragged her gaze off Bryan. For about a minute. "Uh, yes. Of course Alex is coming. He loves to go on the rides with the boys. So, you should bring Bryan. That way Alex won't be the only man."

Nothing like being put on the spot. Both of them.

"Thanks for the invitation, Dena," he said and Beth smiled. Here was her out.

"I'll have to think about it."

He'd *think* about it? Not *I already have plans because why would I want to do suburbia and five kids, not to mention a mom who can't hold a candle to all the actresses I come in contact with on a daily basis*?

"You *should* take him, you know." Kara tugged Beth back against the stone wall when someone got between her and Bryan.

"He doesn't want to spend the day at the amusement park with my kids."

"No, I'm guessing he wants to spend the day at the amusement park with *you*, and your kids come along as a package deal."

Beth, apparently, was the only one grounded in reality around Bryan. "Not happening."

"Pity." Kara took a leisurely sip of her drink, but Beth wasn't fooled. Kara might be staring at her, but her peripheral vision was all over Bryan, and the calculating gleam in her eye said she wasn't about to put this matter to rest. "So . . . two more weeks, huh?"

Beth restrained herself from rolling her eyes. "Yup."

"You *cannot* let him go."

"Kara, I don't have any hold over him."

Kara *did* roll her eyes. "Oh, please. I see the way he looks at you."

"You're wrong."

"No, I'm not. He keeps glancing back as if he's making sure you're still here. You should have asked him to come here tonight with you. You should ask him to go with you on Sunday. Stake your claim so every woman here isn't trying to sink their claws into him."

"You, too?"

"Hey, if I thought I had a chance, who knows?" she continued while Beth tried to close her mouth. "But I'm married, but you . . . you *do* have a chance. And you're single. There's nothing to stop you from taking the opportunity, Beth. Hell, if not for yourself, do it for the rest of us."

"Don't you mean, do *him* for the rest of you?" The sarcasm just rolled off her tongue.

"Hell yes I do."

That sarcasm obviously rolled right off Kara's back.

"I mean, why not? You're young, single, and the man is drop-dead gorgeous. Oozes sex all over the place. This would truly be a case of taking one for the team because you know every woman here is going to go home tonight and imagine what it's like to be with him. Imagine what it's like to be you."

They hadn't wanted to be her two years ago. Some of them still didn't—well, right up until the moment Bryan Manley had crossed her threshold.

"I am not sleeping with him to fulfill everyone's fantasies."

"Oh, sweetheart, just fulfill your own. That'll be enough for the rest of us."

"How did we get on this conversation?" What had happened to her normal, everyday life? That wind shear had tossed more than Mike's plane around and Beth was still reeling from its effects, not the *least* of which was having Bryan Manley in her home.

"You still haven't gotten it, have you? Jess and I didn't hire Bryan to *clean* for you, Beth. We hired him for *you*. The minute I heard Mac say what she was planning and who she was planning to use, I knew we had to do this for you. Who is more perfect to break you out of your self-imposed widow's weeds than one of the Manley brothers? And Bryan of all of them!"

Beth stopped her wine glass on its way to her mouth. She could *not* have heard what she thought she'd heard. "You were trying to *set me up* with him?"

"Well, duh. If we were going to spend that kind of money to cheer you up, it certainly wasn't going to be for cleaning. Dust comes back after a few weeks; money down the drain. No, sweetie. We bought Bryan Manley for you."

Beth was going to be sick. Her friends had just turned one of the nicest guys into a gigolo. Or at least, they were hoping to.

"Are you out of your mind, Kara?" Beth pulled Kara aside and lowered her voice to a stage whisper. "That's prostitution."

"Only if you sleep with him." Kara smirked and waggled her eyebrows. "And even then, *you* aren't paying him. And we're paying whether he sleeps with you or not, so it's not as if he's getting paid specifically to have sex."

Beth glanced back at Bryan, hoping the smile she flashed him didn't say she was going to be sick, and all the while praying he—and everyone else—hadn't heard Kara. "Oh my God. Do you hear yourself? How can you think this is okay?"

"Oh come on, Beth. You can't tell me you haven't thought about what it'd be like. Hell, every woman in this place has had that thought. *You* actually have the chance to find out. You're the envy of every woman here. What's holding you back? He's certainly interested. You can't tell me you're not. Mike's been gone for two years. A woman has needs, and who better to meet those than the Sexiest Man Alive?"

Beth couldn't even speak. Couldn't say a word. It was . . . unbelievable. Amazing. Things like sex-for-hire went on in her neighborhood and her friends thought it was a good idea? She didn't know thcsc womcn.

And they sure as hell didn't know her if they thought she'd just have a casual fling with someone. And then *talk* about it?

"I have to go."

"Beth—"

"No, Kara, don't. I can't stay here. I'll get the kids and leave. We have to get up early anyway." She headed toward the driveway entrance to the basement so she could avoid the too-curious looks she was getting.

"But what about Bryan?"

What about him? She wasn't his keeper, and by the looks of him, he was enjoying himself. Why subject him to the ridiculousness of what her so-called friends had done? Let him live in ignorance because the knowledge was just so . . . so . . . tawdry.

There was a word. A bit old-fashioned but it was the right one. What Kara had done was so far below any standard that it was the only word that fit.

God, Bryan could never find out. The *tabloids* could never find out.

"Bryan will be at work on Monday just like he has been for the past two weeks. That's not going to change or there will be too many questions, but so help me, Kara, if you push this, if you say anything to anyone, our friendship is over. I can't believe you would put me—or Bryan—in this position and then *admit* to it. What has happened to your common sense? I have kids, Kar. Kids who don't need a parade of men through our front door and my bedroom."

"What about what *you* need, Beth? Two years is too long to be alone at your age. You're young. Vibrant. Sexy. You need a man in your life."

"In my *life* is a hell of a lot different than in my *bed*, Kar."

"No it's not. That's part of it."

"Part. Not the whole. And with Bryan, that's all there could be."

"Ah! So you admit there could be something."

Beth wanted to bang her head against the wall. Or Kara's head, actually. "This conversation is pointless. Just don't say anything to anyone, okay? It's not happening."

"That's a shame."

"*You* should be ashamed. What kind of woman do you think I am?"

"At the risk of being blamed for repeating myself, you're a normal, healthy, vibrant woman who needs to have some fun in her life."

Fun sounded good; heartache, not so much. "Your definition of fun is different than mine."

Kara shrugged and Beth could tell her argument was falling

on deaf ears. "All I'm saying is, live a little, Beth. Stop feeling guilty for being alive. Enjoy the moment."

HOLY hell, that was harsh. Bryan heard that sentence and wanted to rush in and slay Beth's dragon lady because who the hell said things like that to a widow who was still grieving?

Except she hadn't been grieving that night in the gazebo. That night, it'd been just them.

"Butt out of my life, Kara. This is none of your business."

"You're my friend, Beth. I hate to see you locking yourself away from the world."

"I have five kids to take care of, a job, and a house. I'm not locking myself away, even if I wanted to. I have responsibilities."

"And that's all you have. What happened to fun? To a girls' day at the spa? Have you used that gift certificate the women from church gave you?"

"I haven't had time."

"You haven't *made* time. And what about the lunch at the Bistro? Or the babysitting Courtney and her friends offered?"

"I am not going to run off to have a facial while some teenagers not much older than my own try to hold down the fort. The twins alone are a handful."

"And they would survive for two hours. But you don't give yourself that time, Beth. You're always on the go, doing for your kids. That's great, but sometimes you need to do something for you."

Bryan was getting the picture. Beth loved her kids, but Kara was right; she did need time for herself. To be Beth. Not Mom Beth, or Widow Beth, or Teacher Beth, but the woman beneath all of that because if she didn't nurture *her*, take care of *her*, there wouldn't be any of those other Beths to do everything that needed to be done. And if that woman was out for the count, all hell would break loose in the Hamilton household.

"I know it's hard, but you need to get out. Mike wouldn't want you to become a hermit."

Beth sucked in a harsh breath. "Do not bring Mike into this."

Her voice had a definite shakiness to it. Whether in anger or tears, Bryan wasn't sure he wanted to know. He wouldn't relish dealing with either one.

"You have no idea what Mike would or wouldn't have liked."

"Really? You're going to tell me that he'd be happy to see you withering away in your widowhood when there's a hot guy in your home who looks at you like he can't wait to scoop you up and cart you off somewhere?"

That's what Kara saw? Christ. He thought he'd kept his emotions better hidden than that.

"You're exaggerating, Kara."

She wasn't.

"No I'm not. The man wants you and you'd be un-American not to want him. What the hell are you waiting for?"

"You make him sound like someone there to do my bidding. He's a person, Kara. You can't force him to do something he doesn't want to do, just like you can't force me. So back off, will you? I'll move on in my life in my time, not yours."

Well, if he needed any further proof that a fling with Beth wasn't a good idea, that was it. Talk about ironic. For as long as he could remember, he'd had women throwing themselves at him whether he wanted something to do with them or not, yet the one woman he *did* want to have something to do with was the one who didn't want to.

Chapter Twenty-three

❧

"BRYAN, what are you doing here?" He was not the person Beth had expected to be ringing her front door at nine a.m. on a Saturday morning. Especially when she'd left the happy hour before him, so God only knew what time he'd gotten home.

And she didn't want to know. Maybe he was on his way home from some lucky housewife's bed.

Which was probably why she snarled at him.

"I've come to rescue you," he said with his most charming smile.

It might have worked, too, if she weren't imagining him climbing out of Mrs. Shuman's bed. Or Kara's. Or Bethany's.

She hefted Maggie higher on her hip. Her youngest had put on some weight. "I'm doing good on my own, thanks."

He cocked his head and, damn him, it was a good look on him. "You okay?"

No. "I'm fine. I just have a lot to do today. Sherman's decided trashcans are more fun than clotheslines and figured out how to wiggle into the kitchen cabinet to get to ours, and I have to get to the supermarket at some point today, and Kelsey's got an orthodontist appointment, and Jason wants to go to his friend's house."

"And I'm going to Carly's!" Maggie chimed in, her smile taking up most of her face.

"Yes, sweetie, you are. Somehow." She looked at Bryan. "So you can see, I'm going seven different directions at once."

He took Maggie from her. "Then it's a good thing I'm here."

"Why *are* you here?" It felt weird not to have Maggie in her arms, yet it didn't feel weird to see her in Bryan's. And *that* felt weird.

"I've decided you need a day off."

"I have all summer off."

"You have summer off from *work*. Not from being a parent."

"There *are* no days off from being a parent. Especially when . . ." She looked at him pointedly. She didn't want to bring up Mike in front of Maggie.

"Well, today *is* that day. You're going to go do some girly thing and I'm going to take the kids. We'll do all your errands and I'll drop Maggie and Jason off where they need to go."

"But Kelsey has to go to the orthodontist. You can't do that; only her parent can."

"I don't have to go today." Kelsey, thank God, showed up at the most opportune moment. "It's not like Dr. Taylor hasn't changed this appointment five times already."

"Three, Kelsey. Don't exaggerate."

"Whatever. All I'm saying is, don't let me stop you from having a girl's day. Bryan's right; you do need one. I can go to Maddy's."

"There, see?" Bryan flashed his famous smile and Beth could feel her resolve weakening. "Problem solved."

"Did Kara put you up to this?" Yet another angle by her well-intentioned-but-misguided friend?

"No. Why?"

It sucked that he was such a good actor because she couldn't tell whether he was lying or not. But then, she had no reason to suspect him and it was just paranoia at Kara's machinations fueling her suspicions. "No reason. And I appreciate the effort, but—"

"Go, Mommy."

"What?" Now her youngest was chiming in on the act?

Maggie nodded her head so furiously her curls bounced in Bryan's face. "You need to go to the hairdresser and look all pretty."

Great. So now she looked like crap. With Bryan Manley standing right in front of her. No wonder there was no hope of anything happening. Why bother with the mom from the 'burbs when he could have the most beautiful women in the world?

"Now, Maggie, your mom looks beautiful just the way she is. This is a day to make her *feel* good. Like a massage or a facial or something." Bryan kissed the top of Maggie's head and looked at Beth with the look that had launched his career, and the thing was it was completely natural on him. "Don't change a hair on your head, Beth. You don't need to."

A *thud* hit her midsection, filling her with warmth and those butterflies again. Why'd he have to be so darn nice?

"Go. Have a good time. I've got the kids. You take care of you."

She wanted to. She did. Then again, she wanted to stay here with him.

And that was the reason she went. A complete change of scenery would do her good.

FIVE hours later, *Bryan* was the one who needed a change of scenery. He'd been joking when he'd complained to his brothers and Gran about the havoc five kids could wreak, but now . . . Just Mark and Tommy were enough to put him over the edge.

He'd rescheduled the ortho appointment and dropped Jason, Kelsey, and Maggie off with their friends, then taken the twins food shopping with him. Of *course* he'd run into Sean, who was going to tease him mercilessly about being Mr. Mom, and then the boys had knocked down a tower of mac-n-cheese boxes while running down the aisles with pretend lightsabers, begging for soda the entire time.

Sean's client, Olivia Carolla, had been there, and for all that he and his brothers wanted her out of the picture, the woman had given the boys an experiment to try with the soda that she'd said would cure them of their soda cravings for good, so she couldn't be all bad. Just inconvenient for their plans.

So now he found himself in Beth's kitchen, pouring three glasses of cola—because he *knew* Maggie would want in on this experiment—and putting a hard-boiled egg in each.

"Now what?" Mark asked, plopping his chin in his palm.

"Yeah, now what?" Tommy did the same thing, only mirror image. They were fraternal twins, but some of the things they did were eerily similar.

"Now we wait. Ms. Carolla said that if we leave this alone, something will happen to the egg."

"What?" asked Tommy.

"Bryan doesn't know," said Mark.

"Does too."

"Does not."

"Does too."

"Guys." Bryan hunkered down next to them with his elbows on the counter. "It's okay not to know. That's why we're doing the experiment. We'll check it tomorrow and see what's happened."

"So we can't drink the soda, right?"

"Out of the cup? With the egg in it? No. Why would you want to?"

The boys got the same grin on their faces, glanced at each other and said in unison, "To see what happens."

He laughed. Couldn't stop actually. Especially when the boys started with the belly laughs and then it was open season on laughter. And then there was tickling—them on him.

Somehow Bryan ended up sitting on the floor with the two of them jumping on top of him, tickling him 'til he couldn't breathe.

He wiggled back on the kitchen floor and leaned against the dishwasher. "Guys, cut me a break, will ya? I'm an old guy."

"You're not old," said Tommy.

"You're well-seasoned," said Mark.

"What?" He chuckled. "Where'd you hear that?"

Tommy shrugged and sat next to him. "Grandpa. He always says that to Grandma when her 'thritis starts actin' up."

Mark sat by his other side. "What's 'thritis?"

God, he loved these kids. "It's nothing for you guys to worry about for a long time."

"Grandma's not gonna die, is she?"

"Is 'thritis gonna kill her?"

Oh wow. The mood turned somber and Bryan realized just how important his answer was going to be to the two of them. "No, guys. Arthritis is not going to kill Grandma."

"Yay!" they said together, high-fiving each other in front of him.

Great. Now when their grandmother *did* die they'll think he lied to them. "But you know that eventually she will. We all die."

"Yeah, our dad did," said Tommy.

"But he shouldn't have," said Mark. "Everyone says so."

"Yeah, they do." Tommy nodded sagely. "But that doesn't make him come back."

"That's 'cause he's in heaven," said Mark.

"Nuh uh, silly. He's in the ground."

"Well first he went in the ground, but then he went to heaven," said Mark as if they were discussing planting flowers or something.

But then it all changed when Mark added, "Right, Bryan? Dad went to heaven."

Shit shit shit. Bryan wasn't prepared for this. He didn't know Beth's religious beliefs. He didn't want to steer the kids down a path she wouldn't want, but he had to tell them something.

"Your dad will always be with you, guys. Right here." He tapped the boys on their hearts, and he felt his *thud*. Please God, let him say the right thing. "Always remember him as you knew him and know that he loved you very much. If he could have lived through the accident to be with you, he would have."

Of course Mike would have; that's what parents did. Bryan hoped the accident had happened fast and Mike hadn't had the chance to realize what was about to happen or worry about his family.

No need to worry, buddy. I've got them.

The thought just popped into his head and Bryan suddenly found himself staring through the kitchen doorway to that memorial above the fireplace.

What in God's name was he doing promising a dead guy something he had no business even thinking?

Chapter Twenty-four

❧❦❧

BETH pulled on her blouse and worked the buttons with boneless fingers. God, she hadn't had a massage in years. She'd forgotten how awesome they were.

She *wouldn't*, however, forget how awesome Bryan was for making this possible for her today.

"Is there anything else I can get you?" asked Molly, the receptionist as she handed her the bill.

Beth was half tempted to say "Bryan Manley," but she'd been through that with Kara last night.

But last night he'd been *Bryan Manley*. Today he was just Bryan. A man who was thoughtful enough to take on her five kids just so she could take a break.

Why?

That was the question she'd been asking herself all day. Sure, he was a nice guy, but this went above and beyond *nice*, and she was sure babysitting wasn't part of his Manley Maids' duties. He had to have other things to do on a Saturday. Especially when he'd be back at her place on Monday.

She was actually giddy at that thought.

Shaking her head, Beth took her change and rolled up a few

bills for her masseuse's tip and handed them back to Molly. "Can you get this to Hayley?"

Molly wouldn't take it. "She'd rather have Bryan Manley's autograph. We were talking about it."

Of course they were. So, too, Beth realized, were all the other women in the salon. With the cucumber slices on her eyes, the New Age music filtering through the earbuds they'd given her, and the sheer release of tension from her facial and massage, Beth hadn't been aware of the stares. She was now, though.

"I'll see what I can do." She didn't want to do it. She didn't want to ask him. But it was such a small thing and would mean so much to Hayley that Beth had to suck up her embarrassment. He'd do it; she knew he would. That wasn't the problem. The problem was, she didn't want to be just another groupie.

Yeah, but you are, so you might as well embrace it.

She'd rather embrace him. And not because of who he was professionally, but who he was personally. This day had been such a gift. A few precious hours when she didn't have to worry about the kids or stop what she was doing to take someone somewhere.

"I'll see what I can do," she said again, tucking the bills into her wallet.

If only Kara hadn't said what she'd said last night, Beth wouldn't feel so embarrassed to ask him. Heck, she'd hardly been able to talk to him last night after that revelation. God, if he ever found out or, worse, thought she'd been in on the plan, she'd never be able to look at him again. Here he was, being a regular human being, and her friends wanted to hire him out as their fantasy booty call. Where had her normal life gone?

"He seems like a really nice guy," said Molly.

The pumping for information wouldn't stop until Bryan was gone. And even then, Beth was sure the questions would continue for months. She pulled out her keys, jingling them so there was no mistaking that she was leaving and the font of town gossip would soon dry up. "He is. Very nice. Does a good job around the house, too."

"If he were in my house, I'd just have him sit there and look gorgeous."

Oh no she wouldn't. Molly would be angling for other

activities. As would half the women here, according to Kara. "Believe it or not, that would get old. Besides, it's not all about a person's looks."

Molly, in her early twenties, looked at Beth as if she was speaking a foreign language. To a twentysomething, she probably was. "Seriously? I don't believe it."

Beth shrugged and slipped her purse strap over her shoulder. "After you've been through what I've been through in the past two years, you realize it's the person inside who matters, not what they look like."

"Yeah, but how cool is it when the outside matches the inside?"

Hmmm. For a twentysomething, Molly did have pretty good insight.

It was something that stuck with Beth all the way home. And flared up again when she walked in to find Bryan and her three youngest huddled around her kitchen table, checking something out on an iPad.

"Ewww. That's gross."

"They're lying. That's not what's gonna happen."

"See? Mommy always says soda's bad for you. You keep drinking it, you're gonna look like the Bominable Snowman with no teeth." Maggie sat back in her chair and crossed her arms with a definitive nod of her head. "Right, Mommy?"

Three more pairs of eyes turned her way and for a second, it felt as if Bryan had every right to be there and she had every right to expect him to be.

"Uh, right about what?"

"A lady at the grocery store told Mark and Tommy that soda will eat your teeth. Is that true?"

She looked at Bryan for this one. "Eat your teeth?"

"Destroy the enamel." He held up the iPad with a really gross picture on it. "See?"

"Um, no thank you. I don't want to look at that." She walked over and nudged the iPad back onto the table, picture side down.

Bryan smiled at her and the next thing she knew, his arm was around her waist and she was sitting on his leg.

And they both looked startled at the same time.

"I—"

"Uh—"

"I should—" Beth stood up.

"Sorry." Bryan crossed his arms and buried his hands in the crooks. "I didn't mean to— Well, I shouldn't have touched— I don't know why I did that."

He didn't? Damn. She'd hoped it'd been the same reason she'd allowed it. Not that there'd been any conscious thought about it; it'd just happened. He'd pulled her onto him and she'd gone along. The most natural move in the world. She and Mike had done it thousands of times.

But Bryan isn't Mike.

Like she needed the reminder.

"Mommy, why do you look so funny?"

And now her face was flaming red. "Because I just had a massage and my face was in a hole in the table."

That led to more internet surfing so she could show them what a massage table looked like—*judicial* internet surfing because looking up "massage" might as well be akin to searching "porn." She finally had to step away from the iPad while Bryan did the search because some of the images were just too blatant for her to be looking at with Bryan Manley in her kitchen in front of her kids.

Mainly because she wouldn't mind *trying out* some of those images with Bryan Manley in the kitchen, but definitely *not* in front of her kids.

Luckily, the kids grew bored with the massage discussion, then showed her their egg experiments, then, of course, demanded to know what was for dinner. She was so tired of thinking about what was for dinner. Who'd eat what, what she had in the house, how long it'd been since they had that particular meal. If it were up to the kids, they'd have hotdogs and hamburgers every night—which was probably what she was going to go with tonight since it was easy.

"Why don't we go out to dinner? My treat?" Bryan shut down the iPad and stood up. "We can grab Kelsey and Jason on the way. What's everyone in the mood for? Beth?"

What she was in the mood for wasn't something for dinner. "Bryan, you don't have to do this."

"I know, but you've had a relaxing day. No need to have to come home and cook. Let's go out. It'll be fun."

"Yes! Let's go! I want tacos!"

"I want fish sticks!"

"I want ice cream!"

"You can't have ice cream for dinner," said Mark, flicking Maggie's curls.

"I can if I want to, can't I, Bryan?" Her daughter turned those baby browns on Bryan and Beth saw him visibly melt.

"You're going to have to ask your mom that one, Maggie."

"Great. Make me the bad guy," Beth muttered so only he could hear.

"Sorry. Not my intention," he whispered back.

"Uh-huh." Poor guy looked like a deer in the headlights, which was pretty funny when he'd done the talk show rounds and dealt with hundreds of reporters and crowded streets of fans, but he couldn't come up with an answer for a five-year-old about ice cream?

"We can have ice cream after dinner, Maggie." She brushed Maggie's curls off her face. "But first you have to eat something healthy."

"But you said ice cream is healthy, Mommy. It's made of milk. And strawberry ice cream has fruit in it."

Darn. She hated when she had her words thrown back in her face. Especially from a night when she hadn't felt like cooking and had given in to the idea of ice cream for dinner. "Only on special occasions, Maggie."

"Tonight's special. Bryan's with us."

Had Kara coached Maggie?

Bryan coughed. "Let's have the ice cream for dessert, okay?"

"Double scoop?"

Bryan looked at Beth.

She nodded.

"Okay, double scoop it is. Let's grab your brother and sister and get in the truck."

"In the van, silly. We can't all fit in your truck."

BRYAN never thought he'd see the day that he would be driving a minivan anyplace other than on a movie set, yet here he was doing it in his home town. But with Beth and the kids in with him it was funny how he didn't mind.

You are in a heap of trouble, Manley.

It was funny that he didn't mind *that*, either.

He didn't mind the minivan, he didn't mind the looks as they all walked in the restaurant. He didn't mind the waitress barely being able to take their order, and he really didn't mind the pea incident that drove Beth nuts. Apparently, the twins differed on their opinion of peas and Mark delighted in sneaking them into Tommy's mashed potatoes. Tommy then delighted in shoving them down Mark's shirt.

"Mark Joseph Hamilton, you switch places with Jason this instant," Beth stage-whispered across the table.

"But he started it."

"Did not."

"Did too."

"I don't care who started it, I want it ended. Move, young man. Now. Or you're going to be sitting out of a lot of rides tomorrow."

Testament to Beth's parenting skills (or threat), Mark *did* actually move. Even more impressive, Jason didn't groan about having to sit between Tommy and Maggie.

Not that Maggie was giving them any trouble. The "log cabin" she was building on her plate out of French fries was keeping her very well occupied.

"Can I still go on the Whirring Devil tomorrow since I moved my seat?" Mark asked in a contrite voice Bryan hadn't heard in the eleven days he'd been with the family.

"It's the Whirling Dervish and yes," answered his mother, managing to look amazingly beautiful in a simple white T-shirt and a pair of dangly pink earrings Maggie had proudly announced she'd asked Beth to wear since they were going out to dinner. Maggie had picked them out for Beth from her school Christmas bazaar last year.

"Cool. I'm gonna ride it all day."

"You'll get sick," said Jason, shoveling spaghetti in as if he were baling hay. "This guy John in my class, he did that. Said he can't go near the ride ever since. Makes him sick just to think about it."

"He got sick for real? Like right on the ride?" Tommy forgot about the land mines in his potatoes as Jason shared the teenage-boy-appropriate story while the girls kept saying

"Gross" and "Ew" and Beth told Jason to zip it at least three times. Not in those terms, but perhaps she should have because Jason had to get all the way through the story before he'd stop.

"So what rides are you gonna go on, Bryan?" asked Maggie, his champion in the Hamilton household. It warmed his heart how she always wanted to include him. A bad idea, he knew, since she was becoming too attached, but Bryan couldn't find it in himself to set her straight and tell her that what she was doing—what she was hoping—wasn't ever going to happen. He and Beth were not going to be together.

"You're coming to the park with us?" Jason perked up at that. "Cool. Everyone's gonna be talking about it."

Kelsey came out of her texting haze. "Really? You're coming? I have to text Maddy. She so needs to go to the park tomorrow." Back she went to her phone, but this time with a smile instead of a scowl on her face.

"Hang on, guys, I didn't say I was coming." *Beth* had to say he was coming. He'd go in an instant, but only if *she* wanted him to, not because her kids did.

"You hafta come!" Tommy shoveled a forkful of potatoes into his mouth and didn't even grimace on the pea Bryan saw at the end of it.

"Yeah, you need to ride the roller coasters with us. They're awesome!" said Mark. "Please, Mom? Can Bryan come? I'll pay for his ticket."

"I can, too!" said Tommy.

"Me, too. I have some money in my piggy bank," said Maggie.

Kelsey and Jason chimed in and Bryan almost choked on the last bit of his steak. The kids' generosity just about killed him.

"Well, Bryan, I guess that means you're invited to the park with us tomorrow." Beth said it with a smile, but he wasn't sure if the invitation was genuine or not.

Not that it mattered because the kids' cheers gave him no out. He was going or he'd have five very disappointed kids on his hands come Monday.

He took a sip of water to clear his throat. "I'd love to come, but on one condition."

"What?" the kids said in unison, looking at him with such hopeful eyes that he got choked up again.

He took another sip. "You all have to go on the Whirling Dervish with me."

"Maggie can't. She's too small."

"Then you'll have to do another ride with me, Maggie. Twice."

Maggie's frown turned into a grin just as he knew it would. "Okay. We can do the teacup ride. They go round in circles."

Beth half choked behind her napkin and her eyes were sparkling. "I hope you don't get motion sickness."

"Trust me. With some of the stunts I've done, the teacups will be nothing."

"If you say so."

So it was settled. He was going to the amusement park with them tomorrow. Then he'd start back again at Beth's house on Monday. Twelve days in a row with the Hamilton clan.

Something was telling Bryan this wasn't a good idea, but there was no way to back out now.

Besides, whatever was telling him to run, something else was equally vocal, compelling him to stay.

It was a no-brainer which one he'd listen to.

Chapter Twenty-five

❧❧❧

THIS was the best day Beth had had in the past two years. Her kids were smiling and laughing and chasing each other with such carefree exuberance and happiness that it was almost as if the plane crash had never happened.

Almost.

Because instead of Mike, their father, there was Bryan. Their housekeeper.

Beth giggled. He always looked awfully cute in the green pants and shirt his sister had chosen as uniforms, but he looked even better today in cargo shorts and a T-shirt. He readjusted his baseball cap—it, surprisingly, had kept the stares at bay because no one would expect *the* Bryan Manley to be hanging out at Martinson's with a passel of kids.

"Come on, slowpokes!" he hollered to Beth and Maggie and Kelsey at the back of the pack. "We're going to leave you in the dust."

"There's no dust, Mommy," said Maggie, looking very perplexed as she glanced around. "It's all pavement."

"It's a saying, Mags." Kelsey was still tweeting her friends continuously, but she'd promised Bryan that she wouldn't mention him being with them. It was killing her teenage daughter, but Beth was proud of her for resisting temptation.

It was probably only the thought of having her picture snapped while she had amusement-ride hair that stopped her, but Beth would take whatever did the trick. Today was just for them. A chance for Bryan to be just Bryan, Mac's brother, her kids' friend, and her . . . well, whatever he was. It was just nice to not have to worry about the reporters and the cameras and whether someone was recording something that could be taken out of context for a story. She didn't understand how he could live in such a fishbowl, but it was a good thing he could since it came with the territory.

And she definitely hadn't been upset when Dena had called to say her son had a fever and they couldn't join them, but maybe they could do it another time? Beth hadn't reminded Dena that there wouldn't be another time with Bryan once he left.

Bryan jogged back and scooped Maggie up in his arms. "Come on, Mags. You need to lead us."

"Yay! I like doing that. I did it in school once. I was the leader of the Halloween parade."

That'd been the last Halloween Mike had been alive. Obviously, they hadn't known it then, but God, how Beth remembered it now. They'd both been beside themselves with indulgent laughter and tears as Maggie, dressed in her favorite princess costume, had perfected the royal wave as she'd led her classmates around the parade route at preschool. Then she'd stopped right in front of them, curtsied, and blew them a kiss with, "I love you, Mommy and Daddy," loud enough for all the parents to hear. Even now, Beth's heart thudded at the memory. Sometimes God gave you gifts in ways you never expected, and it was those moments that always caught her off guard and made her appreciate them that much more.

Like now. Bryan had her daughter on his shoulders and her head was thrown back as she laughed her infectious belly laugh. It got the boys laughing, too, then filtered back to her and Kelsey. A moment in time she'd cherish forever; when a new man had come into her life and brought the laughter back.

"I wanna do the log flume!"

For about a minute.

"I want to do the rock wall!"

"No, the net climb!"

"The spider!"

"Ferris wheel!"

"Guys," said Bryan, commanding their attention with that one word in a way no one else could. "We'll be here all day. We've got time for all of it. So let's do what Maggie wants first, then take turns doing what everyone else does. Including your mom."

Bryan smiled at her and Beth felt her knees melt.

"So what do *you* want to do, Beth?"

He was asking her this and Beth, to her shame, went right for a bed and the two of them naked.

"Log flume." That was a no-brainer. She needed something to cool herself off.

Which was how she found herself walking behind Bryan again, this time with his shorts plastered to his backside, thoroughly enjoying the show and making no bones about it to herself. Being a slowpoke had its advantages.

The Ferris wheel came next so they could scope out the rest of the park—*and* because making Maggie wait would be torture for all of them.

Beth and Bryan rode in one car with Maggie and the twins, while Kelsey and Jason got their own car with a stern admonition to behave themselves from Bryan.

Beth hid her smile. Those two knew better than to do something stupid on a Ferris wheel. She had about another year and a half before Jason reverted back to stupid teenage boy stunts, but right now, fear continued to be his motivating factor. Still, Bryan looking out for her kids made the butterflies start fluttering again.

"Ooh, look at our van down there!" said Maggie, leaning a little too excitedly over the edge of their car. "It looks like one of Mark and Tommy's play cars."

Beth went to grab for her, but Bryan had a good grip on the waistband of her shorts.

"Where?" Tommy climbed onto the seat and Beth had to lunge to keep him from going over. "Thomas John Hamilton, sit down in your seat this instant."

"Aww, but Mom, then I won't be able to see our van."

"If you go sailing over the edge, you're *never* going to see it." Bryan tugged Tommy's leg. "Sit."

Not one word of protest left Tommy's lips. With her, he'd argue and rationalize his actions. She was sure he was going to be an attorney when he grew up.

"Yeah, Tommy, you're supposed to sit down in Ferris wheels," said his brother, smugly. "Don't you know anything?"

"I know that you're a dufus."

Maggie giggled, which didn't help matters.

"Am not."

"Are too."

"Guys."

And just like that, the boys shut up. Even Maggie stopped giggling at Bryan's tone. They were good kids and usually listened to her, even if it took a little more effort for her than Bryan had to make. But he was new to them. A novelty. His word carried more weight than hers, since they'd listened to her for so long. She'd forgotten how much easier it was with a partner to balance parenting duties.

A *thud* landed in her stomach. Parenting duties. That's exactly what this was like. Had been, since Bryan had shown up this morning. It'd been all about the kids. He'd spared her a quick smile—a quick, *devastating*, smile that had set all sorts of *what if* scenarios into action—then had started working on getting everyone ready and into the van for the park as if they'd done it a dozen times before. Beth was amazed—and worried. How quickly she—and they—had accepted it.

The ride ended with a plan in place for the rest of the morning's rides and then lunch. With five kids, someone was always hungry and usually it was Jason. Beth couldn't imagine the day when all three of the boys were teenagers. She'd have to get a second job just to feed them.

"I'm gonna get three hotdogs for lunch, too." Of course Mark would because Jason had just said he was going to, and Mark had taken to emulating his older brother since Mike's death. Before then, he'd been all about being just like Mike.

Mark needed a dad. As did Tommy. So did Jason.

And the girls . . . girls needed their father.

"Race you, Bryan!"

Kelsey was challenging Bryan to a race? Kelsey didn't run—it messed up her hair and made her sweat. She hated to sweat. The only reason she hadn't piled on the eyeliner and mascara she liked to wear—that she'd pilfered from someone because Beth wasn't a fan of twelve-year-olds in makeup—was the threat of raccoon eyes from the heat.

But apparently all that went by the wayside with Bryan around, and her daughter's long brown hair flew behind her like a horse's tail as she took off toward the Tilt-A-Whirl, long legs eating up the ground.

She was going to be gorgeous. All the signs were there and the interest in looking good for boys . . . Beth only had to watch her daughter look at Bryan to see that hormones had kicked in.

A girl should have a father to help her navigate the tricky world of hormonal teenage boys.

Stop it. You are not putting Bryan Manley in that role. He's leaving, remember? Has a life that doesn't include your five children. Or you. Get that through your head and you'll be a lot happier. Kara didn't know what the hell she was talking about.

She might have believed her subconscious if it hadn't added that last part. Kara had known *exactly* what she was doing, both in hiring Bryan specifically and in spilling her guts at the happy hour, thereby putting the idea in Beth's head. Well, making the idea *bigger* in Beth's head.

Shaking the thought *out* of her head, or at least into the far recesses, she hurried up to her kids and Bryan at the ride. She used to love this one as a kid.

"Mom, you have to ride with Bryan and Maggie or it'll be uneven from the weight."

"Are you saying I weigh what Bryan does?" She ruffled her hand through Kelsey's hair.

Kelsey pulled away. "Mom! My hair's going to get all messy."

"Duh, it already is." Maggie rolled her eyes with such a worldliness Beth was afraid to ask where it'd come from. "You were running."

"Bryan beat you, you know," said Jason, finally catching up to them with his distinctive lope he never changed for anyone or anything.

"Nuh-uh. I won. Right, Bryan?" Kelsey's hand went on Bryan's arm and the smile on her face was so genuine, Beth's breath caught . How natural it was for her daughter to touch him, to ask him a question, to have that camaraderie between them.

If only he wasn't going to leave. If only he could stay and have a normal life with them.

If onlys were as useless to let into her life as *what ifs*, so Beth slammed that mental door shut and focused on the fact that she was about to get onto a ride that would have her smashing up against the hottest man in the world. Was there a downside to this?

They climbed in and pulled the safety bar back. Beth was in the middle, Bryan to her right, and Maggie on her left to allow for the centrifugal force that would send them slamming into him.

Beth tried not to. She did, but the ride was too strong, and after the first time they were whipped around the cabin, her wrists straining from the death grip she had on the safety bar, Beth gave up. His shoulders were big and strong enough to take her weight. He'd known what he was signing up for when he'd gotten on the ride.

Maggie was squealing as the second slam hit them before they changed direction. Beth wrapped her arm around her youngest as the force sent her careening back into Bryan again.

His chest was just as strong as those shoulders. And, oh my, what his flexing muscles felt like against her back . . .

And then there was the arm he wrapped around her shoulders, plastering her to his side.

"Stay here." he said in her ear, the loud music and children's squeals making it seem like a whisper—complete with a skin-shivering breath across the back of her neck. "Hang on to Maggie and we'll just go with the flow."

She wanted to go with the flow all right.

"Relax, Beth. I'm not going to bite, I promise." He laughed when he said it, reminding her how he'd said it under the gazebo when he'd kissed her.

The ride spun them around again, and Bryan's other hand landed next to hers on the safety bar and, ohmygod, the skin shivers ratcheted up to quaking. And then he shifted his foot to brace himself in place, his calf brushing hers, and Beth couldn't stop some quivering.

Seriously? She quivered?

"You okay?" he said in her ear again, giving her yet *more* shivers.

Hell, she hated that Kara's idea had merit. She *should* just have a fling with him. She obviously had needs and Bryan could definitely meet them.

Could she do that? Have a fling?

Duh . . .

Okay, so physically she obviously could, but mentally? Emotionally? She'd never done that before. She was a commitment sort of person. What would it be like to just, for once, take the adventure and live a little?

"Beth?"

She looked at him over her shoulder and at that moment, the ride shifted, and somehow Beth's lips ended up on his.

Holy moly, it was amazing.

The hand he'd had on her shoulder keeping her against his side now became buried in her hair. Bryan didn't let her move (not that she was planning to) as he did some delicious skin-shivering, toe-curling moves with his lips on hers.

What might have started out because of centrifugal force was continuing thanks to the force of nature.

HE was kissing Beth.

He shouldn't.

He needed to stop.

This wasn't a good idea.

All of this ran through his mind, but Bryan didn't stop. Couldn't. This was . . .

It was Beth.

The ride shifted again, but Bryan refused to let it separate them. He flexed his fingers in her hair, keeping her head right where it was so he could keep her lips right where they were—right where he wanted them—and he grasped her other hand on the safety bar, the most physical contact he could get right now. He wanted more, but he'd take what he could get.

And, God, he wanted this. He wanted her. Wanted to taste her again, inhale the scent and taste that were all Beth. The ones that would keep him up nights when he left.

No, he wasn't going to think about leaving her. Not yet. Not now.

The ride shifted and, shit, separated them. Beth's startled gaze met his and he could see just how much the kiss had affected her, too. Her breathing was shallow and the grip she had on the safety bar beneath his fingers said a lot.

"Beth." He didn't know what to say, but he had to say something and her name was music to his ears. Such a simple yet beautiful name, it could be said on a sigh with such feeling, or ground out in a moment—or hour—of passion, or whispered softly with full emotion behind it. It was a perfect name, just like her.

Then she licked her lips and, holy hell, the rest of him wanted in on the action.

He had to laugh. Here he was, out in public on an amusement park ride, where the whole world could see, with her five-year-old daughter on the other side of her, and all Bryan could think of was turning Beth to face him, wiggling her out of her shorts, and settling her down on top of him. Now *that* would be one hell of a ride.

Thankfully, this ride came to an end before his hormones got the better of his judgment, and he brushed her cheek with the backs of his fingers, reluctant to stop touching her but knowing he had to. "Thank you."

She looked startled. "For what?"

He was glad to hear her voice was shaky. And breathy.

"For that kiss. I needed that."

She glanced at Maggie who, thankfully, was engrossed in the sights and sounds of what was going on around them, and not what was going on inside this ride. "*Needed*?"

Shit. He hadn't meant to go there. He brushed some hair out of her face as the safety bars clicked open on the ride. "Let's talk later."

TALK. Bryan wanted to talk.

That wasn't what Beth wanted to do. What was she supposed to say? *God, yes, can I jump your bones?*

How exactly did one give a guy the okay to get the ball rolling on something like this?

And *was* she committed to getting that ball rolling?

As she watched him swing Maggie onto his shoulders, then wave the twins over to walk beside him, asking each one how the ride was, thanking Jason and Kelsey for looking out for their brothers, Beth knew her answer was an unequivocal *yes*. She wanted Bryan, and if she could only have him for a night, she'd be foolish to not take the chance.

But she wasn't about to share any of it with anyone. Whatever they did together would be for her alone.

Chapter Twenty-six

❧

BRYAN couldn't remember a day when he'd had so much fun. Or was so exhausted. And he'd thought filming stunts was hard work? Nothing could compare to keeping track of five kids at an amusement park, feeding said brood, *and* refereeing the bickering over anything from lunch to what flavor of cotton candy to get to who was sitting where on the van ride home.

Thank God the three younger ones had fallen asleep and the older two had their earbuds in.

He glanced at Beth, her face illuminated by the dash and street lights. She was beautiful in a graceful, quiet sort of way. Calming. Soothing. Well, except when he touched her. And kissed her. And held her.

Or *thought* about doing any of those things. He wanted Beth with an intensity that defied logic, given that she should be everything he didn't want.

Yet was everything he did.

He reached for her hand. The older two were zoned out and no one else would notice.

Would she let him hold it?

She looked at him, startled, then glanced back and relaxed when she saw what he'd seen.

He squeezed her fingers gently. She looked at their hands, then back at him.

She ran her tongue over her lips.

God, what that did to him. He knew what her tongue felt like. Wanted to feel it again on his lips. Wanted to pull her close and press her soft, curvy body against him, and let her feel what she did to him.

You're gonna regret this, Manley.

Probably. But right now, he didn't care. Today had been perfect. What was more perfect than ending it with her in his arms?

He brought her hand to his lips and kissed the back of it. Beth's gorgeous chocolate eyes followed him the whole way, her lips parting with a soft O she probably wasn't even aware of.

But he was. He was aware of the quickened flutter in her throat and the way her eyes widened when he ran his thumb over the spot he'd just kissed before kissing it again.

They pulled up her driveway and Bryan reluctantly let go to maneuver the van into the garage.

Kelsey and Jason came out of their trances when the garage door went up and the light came on, but the three younger ones didn't budge.

"I'll carry them in if you can hold the doors."

Beth shook her head and caught Jason by the sleeve as he went to walk past her. "Jase, take Tommy. Bryan will carry Mark and I'll get Maggie. Kelsey, please hold the door for us."

She peeled the sweaty, grimy clothes off her sleeping children, pulled on T-shirts, then tucked them into bed before heading into the kitchen to thank Bryan before he left.

She so didn't want him to leave.

He handed her a glass of ice water when she walked in, then reached around her to turn off the kitchen light, so that only the moonlight filtering in through her greenhouse window above the kitchen sink and the sliders off the deck lit the room.

"Let's go out on the deck," he said, his voice so low she thought he'd hear the pounding of her heart over it.

Beth swallowed the sip of water she'd taken and preceded him onto the deck after he swept a hand forward for her to do so.

She watched him close the sliders behind him, allowing herself to enjoy every step he took until he was by her side.

She nervously sipped her water again, feeling Bryan's eyes on her the entire time.

He took the glass from her when she'd finished. "Still thirsty?"

She shook her head. If she'd tried to say anything, she'd be a liar, because suddenly her mouth had dried up and it was all she could do to get that last little bit down her throat.

"I had a great time today," he said, brushing a piece of hair from her forehead.

"Isn't that supposed to be my line?" Look at her, coherent enough to joke with him. She never would have thought.

"It's not a line."

Okay, there went her knees melting again. They were going to do this. They were really going to do this.

What, exactly, *this* constituted remained to be seen, but Beth was more than ready to find out.

"I had a great time with you and your kids today, Beth. A better time than I can remember having in a long while." He took a step closer and the butterflies in Beth's stomach put in another appearance.

"You're just saying that. You can't tell me that being at a local amusement park outranks the Academy Awards."

"It does if I'm not up for an award. And even then . . . that's just the trappings of my profession. What we did today . . . that was real. What life's about."

Beth's heart skipped a beat. What life was about? Where was he going with this? Movie stars didn't commute to Hollywood from suburbia.

She licked her lips again. Couldn't help it; they were so dry.

His gaze zeroed in on her mouth and the butterflies turned into dragonflies. Or better yet, just dragons because her insides were on fire, a bundle of twisting writhing threads of want and need and if *he* didn't do *something* she was going to have to.

"Beth—"

"Bryan—"

They both did something. They leaned in and their lips met and it was as if they'd never left the amusement park. Beth's stomach took the same twists and turns it had on the roller coasters and her body felt as if she were on the Tilt-A-Whirl again, only this time Bryan was smashed up against all of her and his arms were around her properly and she could run her hands all over his strong, sculpted back, dipping down to his waistline, the temptation to feel how perfect his butt was almost shocking her out of the moment.

Almost.

"God, Beth, I want you," he murmured somewhere between her jaw and the hollow beneath her ear, his words tickling her skin while their meaning sent shivers throughout the rest of her.

This was it. The moment. Yes or no?

"Bryan—"

"I know. I get it. I'm leaving and you're not that woman, but please, can I just kiss you and hold you a bit? I don't have much time left and"—he planted another knee-melting kiss on her lips—"I want to know you, Beth. Want to explore what's between us, even if it's only through holding you and kissing you. I'll never forget you, Beth Hamilton. You are one special lady."

She was one *melting* lady. His desire, his respect, his control, the way he was with her kids . . . and her . . . She could fall in love with Bryan very easily.

"Yes, Bryan," she said on a whisper before leaning in to kiss him. Yes to everything he wanted, and so much more that she did. She wrapped her arms around his neck and pressed her aching breasts against his chest, his thin cotton T-shirt doing nothing to hide the perfection that was beneath it. God, she wanted this. Wanted him.

He grabbed her butt and pulled her against him.

He wanted her, too.

How was this going to happen? The logistics were a bit tricky since her room was beyond the others up the stairs. They'd have to pass all the kids' rooms and she couldn't set that sort of example for them.

Doomed before they even got started.

He leaned back against the deck railing and pulled her between his legs. There was no mistaking how much he wanted her and Beth couldn't help the surge of pride that she'd done this to him. Her. Mother of five and he still wanted her.

It's not as if he wants to marry you; he's a man and you're a woman. Not that big of a deal.

Except it was to her. So she wasn't going to let doubts or insecurities ruin this.

She tangled her fingers in his hair, loving the texture and the curls and the fact that she was kissing a new man and thoroughly enjoying every second of it and couldn't get enough of doing it. The at-her-door fumbling on those other dates . . . Those were nothing compared to this.

He released her mouth and trailed his lips along her jaw, kissing every inch, then down along her throat. She tossed her head back, giving him better access, as every spot he touched made her see stars. God, the things this man's touch did to her.

"You taste so sweet," he whispered.

The night breeze brushed over her heated skin but that wasn't the reason for the chills that suddenly enveloped her. No, she was placing the blame firmly at Bryan's fingertips—literally, because he'd wrapped his arms around her so tightly that his fingers brushed the sides of her breasts, and, holy moly, what that did to her insides. And her outsides—her nipples were so tight they ached.

She moaned into the night air and it was enough to startle her into opening her eyes. Ohmygod. The full moon lit up her deck like a stage light, right where she was making out with Bryan Manley. Was she out of her mind? Anyone could see.

Even Jason and Kelsey if they looked out the window.

"Bryan . . ." She pulled her fingers from his hair and braced them against his biceps. "Someone might see."

He took one last kiss on her collarbone, and nuzzled the skin just below it, making her nipples tingle all over again before he lifted his head.

"I guess," he sighed. "But, God, Beth, I've wanted to do that all day. And so much more."

"We can't."

"I know."

"It's, well, it's not smart."

"I know."

"And we couldn't, that is, my room, it's beyond the kids'."

"Oh, trust me. I know exactly where your room is."

Her body heated at the thought of him in there, touching her things. Holding them, setting them back in place. Seeing the most intimate part of her house, where she slept and dreamed and ached about him.

She'd been alone for so long.

"The tree fort." The words were out of her mouth before she'd even thought of them.

"The what?"

She couldn't back down now. She'd said it and, frankly, the idea of making love to Bryan in the tree fort—where no one would ever know, where it'd be just them—held huge appeal.

"The tree fort." She nodded at the big oak at the back corner of her yard. "We could go there."

Bryan smiled that devastating smile and kissed the tip of her nose before he put some space between them. "As tempting as that idea sounds, and as much as you make me feel like a teenager, Beth, I am not about to make love to you in a tree fort. I have a lot more class than that and you deserve so much better."

Forget class; she wanted him so badly she'd consider this deck if it had a roof so her kids wouldn't accidentally see. The hell with the neighbors. They could all eat their hearts out.

Ohmygod, who was this woman? Exhibitionism? What was the man capable of driving her to?

He drew the backs of his fingers down her cheek, then ran the pad of his thumb over her lips. "Plus, it's not the right time now. I have to leave for the set soon, and you, well, you have all this to handle. You're not a one-night woman and I'm not about to make you compromise your principles. You don't need that or me to complicate your life."

"But what if I want you to complicate my life?" Again, who was this woman, and thank God she'd shown up.

"Ah, Beth, you tempt me to do just that." He kissed her quickly—not nearly long enough. "But I couldn't live with myself."

And he wouldn't be living with her. That was unsaid but hanging between them.

She ought to be glad he was so thoughtful. Glad that he respected her and her kids enough to not take her up on her offer. But that didn't mean it didn't suck.

He leaned his forehead against hers. "Thank you for an

amazing day. I'll never forget it. And I'll never forget this." He nudged her nose so he could look her in the eye. "I'll never forget you."

WALKING away from Beth was the hardest thing he'd ever had to do. He left her on her deck, leaning against the railing, her hair messed from his fingers, her lips swollen from his kisses, her nipples clearly outlined beneath her T-shirt, and he'd felt the dampness between her thighs when he'd pressed his knee between them. Heard her sigh when he'd run his tongue along her throat.

And that tree fort idea . . .

He shook his head as he got into the truck, adjusting himself so he could sit comfortably in the bucket seats, but he had a feeling he'd never sit comfortably around Beth again. He wanted her. Badly. And she'd wanted him. Had offered him *the tree fort* of all places. For a second he'd considered it, but then . . . no. What he'd said was true. Sure, it'd slake the passion for the moment, but making love to Beth was a moment to treasure, not one to hurriedly get through in the kids' tree fort. If he ever took Beth to bed, it'd be with all the romantic bells and whistles: champagne, rose petals, soft music, and a bed big enough that they could enjoy themselves in so many ways because once he got her into bed, he'd never want to get out of it.

He pulled out of the driveway and saw Beth in her room, her silhouette illuminated by the tiny strand of lights she had in the silk tree in her sitting room. She was watching him drive away, when all he wanted to do was be up there with her.

He shifted gears, glad for the distraction. He wanted Beth, but he couldn't have her. For all that the tabloids called him a playboy, this nobleness was going to kill him.

Chapter Twenty-seven

❧

"HEY, isn't this the movie you're doing, Bryan?" Kelsey shoved the newspaper in Bryan's face the minute he walked through the front door the next morning.

His eyes met Beth's before he took the paper.

Beth went back to cleaning up the dog toys that Sherman had, yet again, managed to drag all over the house. The dog hadn't figured out that he was actually supposed to play with the toys, not the basket, and make them all play fifty-two pickup. At least it was better than the clothesline, but still . . . The dog was more work than the kids.

"It says the actress shut down the set for a few days. Does this mean you don't have to go?"

Bryan took the paper and removed his baseball cap. Jason took it from him and hung it on the key hook by the door, then looked over his arm to read the article.

"Hmmm." Bryan skimmed the rest, then opened the paper to the next page. "My agent hasn't called, so as far as I know, I'm still good to go."

"What happened?" Beth asked with the sick feeling in her stomach. She didn't want him to go and she didn't want to talk about his movie and she *really* didn't want to talk about the actress he was going to be working with. And probably kissing. He kissed gorgeous women in all of his movies.

And in his private life, too, don't forget that.

As if she could.

She glanced at the mantle. At Mike's picture. He'd want her to be happy; they'd talked about it in that what-would-you-do sort of way married couples do, though, she'd assumed they'd been discussing the other *marrying* someone else, not hooking up for a night of passion.

God, she could so use one of those right now.

"It says the actress threw a hissy fit and destroyed the set." Kelsey looked a little too happy reciting the story.

Beth tossed Sherman's toys back into the basket. Of course one missed. "Kelsey . . ."

Bryan grabbed the runaway tennis ball. "The report says that Carina Dempsey took exception to the staging and wanted it changed." He skimmed some more, then folded the paper up and tucked it under his arm. "You can't believe everything you read, Kels."

"Yeah, I know." Kelsey flopped onto the sofa and crossed her arms with a sour look on her face.

Beth needed to nip the gossip-mongering in the bud now before it caused problems later on. Teenage girls could be vicious.

"Like when the reporters said Dad was drinking before the flight."

Beth would have been so much happier if Kelsey's attitude *had* been about gossip.

"Nuh-uh. They *speculated* that he had." Jason, obsessed with his father's reputation, had read every article Beth hadn't been able to keep from him. He'd learned the idea behind the concept of *speculated* within the first week and it'd been his mantra. It'd seemed like forever before the NTSB had released the results of the toxicology screen and vindicated Mike. "And they were wrong."

"So you mean she *didn't* trash the place?" The power of gossip took over.

Beth shook her head. Teenage girls . . .

"Hard to tell what's what," said Bryan. "I'll know more when I get there."

"When do you go?"

"I'm due on set in two weeks. I can go any time, so I might go out the weekend before. Get the trailer set up, learn the lay of the land, see who's there already. It's helpful to know who you're working with before you show up to shoot."

"You're going to shoot?" Mark, of course, *would* perk up at that. "A gun? Or a laser?" He brandished his lightsaber.

"I bet it's a machine gun," added Tommy, grabbing the water machine gun Mike's dad had bought them for their birthday. Crap. She needed to get that thing outside. There'd already been one water fight in the bathroom.

"No, a cannon."

"A tank!"

"Yeah, a tank would be cool!"

Nothing about Bryan leaving was cool. Beth bent down to hide the feelings that thought evoked and found at least eight socks under the sofa that Sherman must have misappropriated. She was going to change his name to Sock Monster, and just call him Monster for short. It was fitting.

And *of course* the aptly renamed monster nailed her in the back of her thighs, making her take a header into the sofa, hitting, *of course*, the wood frame, and for a moment she saw stars. Unfortunately, they weren't the kind she'd seen with Bryan last night.

"Sherman!" Tommy went running to rescue the menace who'd bounced off and went sliding across the hardwood floor.

"Mommy!" Maggie came running to Beth's aid, brushing the hair out of Beth's face. "Are you okay, Mommy? Do you have to go to the hospital?"

Maggie had an irrational fear of hospitals. People went there to die in her experience.

"No, sweetie, I'm fine." Beth rubbed the bump and sat on the couch.

Bryan knelt down in front of her and, oh, the image that presented.

Man, she must have really hit her head hard.

"Here. Let me take a look at that." He brushed the hair off her head. "You've got an egg."

"An egg? Why does Mommy have an egg on her head? You didn't take it from our 'speriment, did you, Mommy?"

"The experiment!" Tommy jumped off the back of the sofa, machine gun in hand.

"My egg!" Mark ran after him.

After a second of indecision, Maggie ran into the kitchen, too.

"Well, I guess that lets me know where I stand on the level of importance around here."

Bryan smiled and it made her head hurt a lot less. He brushed her cheek with the backs of his fingers. "They made sure you were okay, then they went after the, and I quote, coolest experiment in the world. If I ever see Sean's client again, I'm going to have to thank her." He touched the lump again. "In the meantime, let's get some ice on that."

"Great. Just what I need. A goose egg on my forehead."

He held out his hand to help her stand. "The good news is, it's beneath your hair line. And blue is a good color on you."

She nudged him with her shoulder, inordinately pleased that he'd noticed what color looked good on her, and annoyed with herself for being pleased.

The doorbell rang just as they made it to the kitchen to see three very intent children studying the eggs in the cups.

"I'll get it," said Bryan. "You go see what Louis Pasteur, Madame Curie, and Pavlov are up to in there," said Bryan as he headed to the front door as if he belonged here.

But he didn't. And he couldn't. So she turned her attention to the kids who *did* live there, who *were* the focus of her life and the reason she couldn't go chasing Bryan down on movie sets.

She did, however, go chase him down a few minutes later, when he hadn't returned, to see what the hold-up was.

She should have known. There was a pack of hungry jackals, er, reporters on her front porch.

"I have no comment on that," Bryan was saying. "I'm not there so I don't know what's going on."

"Do you plan to fly out sooner than scheduled?"

"As you can see, I have prior commitments." Bryan nodded his head toward her house. "I'll be on set when I'm due. As to the rest, I can't comment. Now, if you wouldn't mind leaving so this family can have their privacy back, I'd appreciate it."

"Do you expect Carina to get fired?"

"There have been other reports from other sets she's ruined when she wasn't happy."

"Word is they're looking to replace her."

"Would you continue with the film if she's replaced?"

The questions didn't let up, but Bryan deflected them. Beth had to admire his professionalism and ethics for not throwing the actress under the bus even though *she'd* heard the same things about Carina, who was known for on-set theatrics. Frankly, Beth was always of the opinion that the woman did it on purpose to keep her name in the papers. As they said in Hollywood, there was no such thing as bad publicity. In suburbia, however, it was a whole other story. Beth could do with never having her name mentioned in the paper ever again.

Which meant, *of course,* a reporter decided to drag her in the conversation.

"Mrs. Hamilton, would you care to comment on Bryan's services in your home?"

Oh, the sniggers *that* question got from the assembled crowd—and oh, the anger it got from Bryan. "Beth is *not* involved in this. Leave her out of it."

"But surely your sister would like the publicity for Manley Maids? We just need a quote from your *client*."

Yeah, the reporter was going deep with the innuendo. Beth wanted to be sick.

Bryan just got madder. "My sister wouldn't appreciate the innuendo."

He was close to losing his professional cool and that would not be good for his image—or her reputation because the minute he started defending her, people would think he had a right to, which meant there would have to be something between them and that'd open another whole can of worms.

"Mac runs a professional service and comments like yours have no place in it. Press conference is over, folks." He turned around and entered her house without a backward glance—but with a definitive slam to the door. "Sorry about that."

"It's not your fault."

"Well, technically, it is. If I weren't here, you wouldn't have to deal with them."

"You're only here for a few more days. I'm sure I can put

up with it 'til then." It was a small price to pay to have him around because at least there was an end in sight.

Wait. Was that supposed to be a good thing?

"I'm glad *you* can."

"Um, okay?"

Bryan looked behind him out the front door, then steered her into the study, away from the prying eyes of the press still on her porch.

He shut the door. Then he put his hand behind her neck and pulled her into another knee-melting kiss.

Five minutes later—or maybe thirty—he finally let her go. And, man, did she have a hard time letting him.

"I'm sorry," he said as his lips left hers. "I shouldn't have done that."

"Kiss me?"

"Yeah."

"Because? I mean, you did it last night, too, and I wasn't complaining, if you remember."

"I do. And that's the problem."

"It's a problem that I don't ask you to stop kissing me?"

"Yes. Because if you did, I would stop. And then I wouldn't think about what else I want to do with you."

"What *else*?"

He arched an eyebrow at her. "Come on, Beth. You've had five kids. Presumably they weren't immaculate conceptions."

She blushed. "Of course not."

"Then you know what I'm talking about."

"Well, yes, but . . . But you're leaving."

"Exactly. And it's wreaking havoc with my control. I can't have you; you're not that kind of woman, but it doesn't stop me from wanting you. And when I talk about leaving, about not seeing you again, walking out of your life so someone else can walk into it, well, it's not what I want."

"What *do* you want, Bryan?" God, she could hope for so much . . .

"That's just it, Beth. I want *you*. But I don't want this."

"This?" Her kids? Her life? Her world? God, that hurt. He gave her everything in one sentence and ripped it away in the next.

"I have a career that's starting to take off. I can't walk away from it now. I've worked too hard to get where I am."

"I'm not asking you to walk away from it."

"I know. But I'm thinking about it."

God, so was she. But if she'd ever thought there could be some compromise to their differing lifestyles, that media event on her front porch had put an end to it. Her kids didn't deserve that upheaval. And she didn't deserve the heartache. "Then perhaps you should leave now, Bryan. Make the break easier."

For a moment, he looked pained. But he was a good actor, able to call up emotions at will, and she saw him do it. Saw him suck it up, tuck it away, and pull out his professional side.

He raked the hand that wasn't still behind her neck through his hair. "Yes, perhaps that'd be for the best. You're right; your family doesn't need this intrusion. You all have lived through enough. My career and all that goes with it are my choice, and it's not fair to thrust it on you. I'm sorry, Beth. For so many things."

For what could have been . . .

"I'll just go say good-bye to the kids and—"

"I'd rather you didn't."

"What?"

She took a deep breath, knowing she was doing the right thing, but also knowing they would be hurt that he didn't say good-bye. But better a clean break than one drawn out with tears and promises of what could never be. "They don't need the separation messiness. Just go. I'll tell them you got called to the set and that you had to leave. If you stay and make a production out of leaving, they'll put more importance on it than there should be. After a week or so, they'll move on."

BRYAN didn't think his insides could have been ripped apart any more after she'd asked him to leave, but telling him the kids would move on . . . That did it.

As an actor, he knew the power of words, but as a man, he'd never been faced with the true feelings they evoked.

He choked back that emotion, blinked a few times because, yeah, it hurt, then pulled *stoic* out of his repertoire. "You're right, of course." He flexed his fingers behind her neck, surprised to find he was still touching her there. He'd been kissing her not two minutes ago, his fingers buried in those silky curls he wanted spread out on a pillow beneath them, and now he had to let her go.

He exhaled and dropped his hand. "I wish you all the best, Beth."

"You, too, Bryan." Her voice was husky and if she hadn't been the one to ask him to leave, he'd swear she was choked up about it.

"Well . . ." He cleared the huskiness out of his own throat. "I guess I'll get my hat and go. Mac can come by for any supplies I left."

"Yes. That's fine."

"Good-bye."

"Good-bye, Bryan. Best of luck with your movie."

The damn romantic comedy that he didn't feel one ounce of happiness about making right now because he would be portraying on screen what he might possibly just have given up in real life.

Chapter Twenty-eight

✦❧

THE kids were disappointed. Well, Kelsey was devastated, certain that her newfound popularity would take a Twitter nosedive. Jason, too, seemed subdued, morphing back into the sulky teenage boy mien he'd lost in the last two weeks.

The twins kept saying, "When Bryan comes back," and Maggie had set up a special place on her desk to make a list of everything that happened in her days so she could remember to tell Bryan when he returned to clean out her dollhouse from Mrs. Beecham's fur.

Beth didn't have the heart to tell her that wasn't going to happen. They would all figure it out eventually, hopefully when the excitement of him being here had faded. She didn't want to destroy their dreams.

But, God, *her* dreams. Every single one was of Bryan. She woke up the next day with an ache between her thighs that hadn't been there even when he *had* been.

She should have slept with him. Should have made him take her up on that tree fort offer. Should have made the memories that would carry her through the next few weeks—months maybe—until she got over him. Damn it; she hated that Kara had been right.

The phone rang, thankfully giving her the distraction she needed—until she heard who it was.

"Hello, Mrs. Hamilton. This is Mac Manley. I understand you terminated my brother's position and I wanted to find out what the problem was. I'd like to fix it if I can."

The only problem was that he was too sexy for her own good. "There wasn't any problem. It's just that he's done everything that needed to be done, and well, he has that movie coming up—"

"Which he wasn't slated to start for another week and a half. Did he do something? Ruin something?"

Only her for another man.

Snap out of it!

Beth shook her head to clear it because Mac couldn't see her do it. "No. Bryan was a great worker. He went above and beyond, but, well, he was finished. I don't have anything more to keep him busy, and it seemed foolish to waste his time by making up things for him to do. I figured he'd be better off on his movie set."

Mac sighed on the other end of the phone. "I could send someone else out. Free of charge of course. I'll refund the balance of what was paid."

"That's not necessary, really. Bryan did the work in good faith. I was the one who let him go. Keep the money. And, no, I don't want anyone else."

She had a feeling she never would, either.

Okay, Beth, really. Snap out of it! You are not going to waste the rest of your life pining for this guy. He's moved on; you need to as well.

"I certainly am not going to keep the money if Manley Maids didn't earn it," said Mac. "I will be returning it."

"Why don't you donate it, then? To the library or the school or something. Someone else who can use your services but can't afford to pay for them. Really, it's not necessary. Bryan did a great job; it's just that it's over now."

Something she'd be reminding herself for many nights to come.

WHAT did you do?"

"Mac—"

"So help me, Bryan, what did you do?"

"Mac—"

"You leave me some bullshit message and I have to call my own client to find out what happened. And *she* wouldn't tell me anything. Did you pull some of your Rico Suave crap and make her fall in love with you, then brush her off like yesterday's starlet?"

"Mac—"

"Four weeks, Bry! *Four* weeks! That's all I asked. That was our bet, remember? And you couldn't even do that? Seriously, what is the *matter* with you? Do you have to run after everything in a skirt? I thought a woman with five kids would be enough of a deterrent, but, noooo. Not my brother, the stud. Has to put a notch in every bed post, I guess. I can't believe—"

"Hold the hell on, Mary-Alice Catherine Manley!" Bryan's blood pressure rose along with his voice and he dropped the boxers he'd been trying to shove into the duffel bag. His car was going to be here in less than five minutes. He did *not* have time for this. "I am not some Neanderthal who has to make a conquest wherever he goes and you know it. Don't say that shit to me! I was nothing but circumspect around Beth and her kids."

Well, except when he was kissing her. Then he'd been horny as hell. But so had Beth, so he doubted she'd ratted him out to his sister for that.

He picked up the boxers and shoved them into the duffel, then zipped it—and *of course* the damn teeth caught on them. Wedging the phone between his ear and his shoulder, he tried to yank the cloth free. "Beth had issues with the media coverage that comes with the Bryan Manley package and I can't blame her. After what she and her kids have been through . . . Why the hell did you send me there?" Something Mac had said came back to him. "Fuck. You sent me to her *because* she had five kids? Because you know that's the *last* thing I want in my life and you're so worried about me hitting on your clients that you had to send me to the one you thought I wouldn't want?"

He was insulted. He'd never given Mac any reason to mistrust his professionalism or his word. And he'd *given* her his word he'd be professional while working for her—granted, he'd meant in how he cleaned the homes because he had, after all, tried to get out of this damn bet, but seriously? She thought he'd hit on her clients?

"Oh don't turn this around on me, Bryan Matthew. I did it for you. I mean, no one's going to think you'd be interested in a widow with kids, least of all her. It was the safest assignment I could come up with. Can you imagine if another client had had her sights set on you? You'd be changing sheets and light bulbs and dresser drawers in her bedroom and wondering how you were going to get out of there at the end of the day. I did you a favor."

He wasn't going to tell her exactly how much of a favor she *had* done him. Well, *would have* done for him if this thing with Beth could go somewhere. But it couldn't. And Beth, smart lady, had known that enough to ask him to leave.

He looked around for the folder with his script in it. He was going to have to bone up on his lines because he hadn't been as diligent as he normally was about memorizing them, since he'd been so busy with Beth and the kids. "I didn't do anything, Mac, but I'll pay for the rest of the month."

"She won't let me return the money. She told me to donate it."

Ah. There was the file on top of the island in his kitchen among half a dozen bills he better pay before he left. Shit, he didn't have time. He stuck those inside the file. "Pick out a victim's group. I'll double whatever you donate."

"You're a prince, Bry."

"Yeah, yeah, that's what they tell me." He tucked the file into the front flap of his laptop bag.

"I was being sarcastic. Far be it from me to build your ego any more than it already is."

It was an old mantra. Mac would never let him get a big head out of love.

"So we're good?" He looked around his house for anything he might have forgotten. Sadly, the place was woefully bereft of *things*. Just a high-def TV, a sound system to blow the roof off, and some paintings a decorator he'd hired had said to buy. He didn't even like impressionistic art, yet there it was on his walls. This place was about as homey as Maggie's dollhouse. Actually, the dollhouse was homier, given that Mrs. Beecham's fur gave it a lived-in feeling, whereas his place felt more like a way station. "You're going to get off my case now about doing something to piss her off?"

"You promise you didn't?"

"I promise." Pissing Beth off had never been his motive.

Turning her on, getting her hot and bothered, yeah. All the things Mac had specifically decided Beth wouldn't be interested in.

Mac hadn't been in that gazebo. And on the deck last night.

He swung the duffel bag straps over his shoulder as the limo pulled up out front. Nice perk, that. "I gotta go, Mac. Send someone else over to Beth. She deserves a break."

"Like I said, Bry, you're a prince."

"And now I get to go play one in the movies. I'm heading to the coast."

"You still owe me, bro."

"What?" He juggled the phone and his keys as he locked up.

"The bet. It was for four weeks and you're cutting out early."

"It's not enough that I'm paying for it? Double?" He dumped his keys in the duffel. Wouldn't be needing them for a while.

"You always renege on a bet?"

"I never do." He slung the straps over his shoulder, juggling the phone and his temper. "Fine. Next time I get a break between films, I'll do the remaining eight days."

"I'm going to hold you to that."

He nodded to the driver who opened the door, then slid into the back. "You do that."

"I will."

"Good."

"Fine."

"Bye, sis."

"Bye, big bro."

She hung up before him of course. Mac liked having the last word and she loved to tease him about being her big bro. He was the youngest of the three brothers and it never failed to bug the shit out of him when his brothers called him *the baby*. Well he'd shown them. The biggest name on the marquis for this movie was going to be his. He was finally on his way to the big time.

Too bad it felt more like being on his way merely to a job.

YOU let him get away?" Kara literally almost dropped the bottle of wine, which was a major sin in Kara-Land.

Beth took it from her and set it on the slate patio table. "I didn't *let* him do anything. He was finished, so he left."

"I'm not buying it." Jess threw her hands up. "No one, and I mean *no one,* lets Bryan Manley leave before his time is up. You had him in your home, in the palm of your hand if you wanted, and he was under contract to stay there, and you let him leave? Honestly, Beth, are you trying to sabotage your love life?"

Beth looked around for the bottle opener. Something to distract them from this conversation. Wine ought to do it. "There *is* no love life, guys. That's what I'm trying to tell you. Just because you put him in my home doesn't mean sparks are going to fly."

"Uh-huh." They both sat back and crossed their arms.

"You forget, we saw you at the happy hour. We saw *him* at the happy hour. The man couldn't take his eyes off you."

She'd felt them. At least, she'd hoped that'd been what it was, but realistically, she'd told herself it was just wishful thinking.

The *whole* thing with Bryan had been wishful thinking.

"Can we change the topic? I'm kind of sick of talking about him." That was because the reporters hadn't left. Funny that she and Bryan had agreed he'd leave to end the invasion, but that'd only started another round of interest. They'd been all over his duties in her home and why she had fired him.

So, of course, she'd had to defuse that rumor, and then there'd been the questions of how her kids were dealing with their newfound fame, given what'd happened two years ago, and it hadn't been pretty as she'd tried to shield the kids from the questions and comments while trying to get these people off her property and not show them how painful it was, because in her experience, the more emotional an issue, the more they buzzed around it like bees. If she made it out to be no big deal, they'd back off.

So Beth had had to suck it up and pretend that all the commotion on her yard wasn't turning her into a mass of nerves and smile sweetly and answer their questions with as noncommittal an answer as she possibly could. Hence, tonight's gathering at Kara's, with the kids in the pool and the game room, and her with a glass of wine in front of her, now that she'd pried out the cork and poured some for each of them.

"Okay, so what else do you want to talk about?" Kara picked up her glass and swirled it around like a sommelier. "The new clothesline in your backyard? Oh, wait. Bryan did that. How about your new sink in the kids' bathroom. Oh, wait. Bryan again. And what about the hole in the fence that got sealed—oops, Bryan again." She punctuated each sentence with a swirl of her wine. "Your trip to Martinson's Amusements? Oh, Bryan was there, wasn't he? And what about the doctor you had dinner with? You know, the one who was tossed out of the restaurant by none other than one Bryan-Manley-to-the-rescue. Gee, Beth, what else is there to talk about?"

Beth glared at Kara over the rim of her glass. "How about summer camps? How about where you're going on vacation? What about the sun room you're putting on, Jess? Who your kids got for teachers next year? There's a lot we can talk about and it doesn't have to revolve around Bryan."

"I just don't get it. Don't you want someone in your life?" Kara's wine was still swirling. "Don't you want to be wanted again, Beth? To have a companion?"

The hell with it. Beth downed her wine. Not that it was a lot, since she'd only poured a quarter of the glass, but still, it felt good to make the statement.

"Of course I do. But not with Bryan. Come on, guys, you know what kind of life he leads. I can't raise kids in that fishbowl. And who's to say I'd even get that chance? Bryan doesn't want to raise someone else's kids. And definitely not five of them."

"He looked awfully cozy with your kids any time I've seen him," said Jess.

"And he did show up at the soccer game when he didn't have to." More pointing with Kara's wine glass. It was a good thing Beth had only given her a little; it'd be sloshed over the side if there'd been more. "And then there's the trip to the amusement park. That was his day off yet he spent it with you guys. All six of you."

The arguments weren't anything Beth hadn't already thought of. But she'd been the one to hear him say that what she had, he didn't want. She knew the reality; why couldn't her friends get on board with the program? "He went because they *asked* him to. He's a nice guy; he wasn't going to say no if he didn't have to."

"Seriously? A big movie star like him has nothing better to do than spend a day at an amusement park because a kid *asked him to go*? He'd be at amusement parks every day if he did that. Your kids aren't the only ones who'd like to spend the day with a movie star."

"They didn't ask him *because* he's a movie star. They asked him because they like him."

"Exactly our point."

Kara sat back with a smug look on her face and raised her glass. "Your kids like him. He likes them. *You* like him and he likes *you*. What is wrong with this picture?"

Darn. She wished she hadn't finished her wine because she needed a few minutes to come up with an argument. It'd sounded good to her when she'd made it to herself. "Okay, so they all like each other. But that doesn't mean we're going to have a relationship. He's got a career that isn't conducive to raising kids, and I have kids who aren't conducive to jet-setting all over the globe. It'd never work."

"You won't know until you try." Kara had a Cheshire-cat grin going as she took a sip of her wine.

"You need two people to try to make a relationship work, Kar. He left the minute I suggested it. He even"—damn; she wished she still had some wine to make this next part palatable—"told me that what I had wasn't what he wanted."

"He did not say that."

"Yes he did."

"He didn't mean it the way you think he did." Jess leaned forward, twirling the stem of her glass between her hands.

"It doesn't matter *which* way he meant it; he left. He's on set. Doing his job. Living the life he wants. I can't begrudge him that. And I'm certainly not going to give him an ultimatum or anything."

Kara set her glass down with a *clink* on the slate. "Seems like you already did."

"What?"

"You told him it wouldn't work for you, so he left. Was there talk of a compromise? Did you ask if you could come out to the set? Lots of actors have families who show up on set. Don't they give them big trailers? I bet his could sleep all seven of you. Especially if the two of you are sharing a bed."

What Beth wouldn't give to share a bed with Bryan—except for her children's stability and sense of security. Those were non-negotiable. Her kids were everything to her. She'd have her time once they were all grown and on their own. Well-adjusted and thriving. Then it'd be her time.

Who knew? Maybe Bryan would still be free then.

Him? Seriously? Didn't you just spend two weeks with the guy? Someone's going to snatch him up the minute he even thinks about settling down. You lost your chance, babe.

"I think you should go to where he's filming." Kara refilled Beth's glass, and this time it wasn't merely a quarter of the glass.

"Are you trying to get me drunk?"

Kara handed her the glass. "Yes. Maybe that'll put some sense into you because sobriety isn't doing you any good."

Beth didn't touch it. "I'm not going to go to his movie set."

"Why not?"

"Because he didn't invite me. And there are the kids."

"So take them." She slid the glass closer to Beth.

"Oh, right. Like I'm going to descend upon his movie with five kids in tow."

Kara shrugged. "Why not? If you end up together, the kids will be on location with you anyway. Might as well start now."

"Bryan and I are not going to end up together."

"Well you won't if you don't *get* together. That has to happen first."

"I say you take the refund Mary-Alice offered," said Jess, "and buy airline tickets for you and the kids to go to San Francisco. Isn't that where they're filming? Make it a nice family vacation and see Bryan while you're out there. When's the last time you had a vacation?"

About three months before Mike's death. She hadn't been on a plane since and highly doubted she ever would again.

"The kids are going with Mike's parents this weekend." His mother had called this morning to remind her. Thank God Donna had, because with everything going on with Bryan in their lives, Beth had forgotten.

"So let me get this straight." Kara tapped her fingernail on the slate tabletop. "Your five children are going away for the weekend with their grandparents, and you sent, arguably, the world's hottest man away? You do get that you're going to be alone this weekend, right, Beth? I mean, the man can't have short-circuited your brain enough for you to not realize that. You could have him all to yourself for two whole days! What are you doing sitting here? You ought to be out buying sexy lingerie."

"Hey, I'm up for a shopping spree." Jess tossed back the rest of her wine. "I'll call us a cab."

"You will not." Beth slid her glass to the center of the table. None for her, thankyouverymuch. She didn't need anything clouding her judgment or she'd end up going along with this ridiculous idea. "I am not going to spend the weekend with Bryan. It can go nowhere, so what's the point?"

"Oh my God." Kara drank some of Beth's wine. "Seriously? A hot weekend of amazing sex when you've been celibate for two years? You don't see the benefit of that? It's not like you'd have to marry the guy. Just have a good time."

"Unless . . ." Jessica's eyes narrowed. "You *want* to marry the guy."

"Okay, you've had way too much to drink." Beth dumped the rest of the bottle over the deck railing into the flowerbed. "I've known him for two and a half weeks. I am *not* marrying Bryan Manley."

"Pity." Kara pulled another bottle out from the cooler. "He's just what you need, Beth. A great guy who likes your kids and liked you pretty well, too. And he certainly can keep you in the style to which you've become accustomed. I don't see a down side to it."

"Well, aside from the fact that we'd need his agreement, there's the public fishbowl aspect of his life. Don't you remember what it was like when Mike died? All the hounding by the press? The kids were terrified to leave the house. I couldn't do that to them again, even if Bryan was even *remotely* interested in a relationship. Which he's not."

"And you know this how?"

Oh hell. This was going down a path she didn't want to go with these women. They might be her two best friends, but some things were just too personal to be shared.

"You talked about this with him already, didn't you? You guys talked about having a relationship." Jess raised her glass for Kara to fill it with a smug grin on her face. "I knew it."

"He just said that he wants the glamour of his movie star

lifestyle. Suburbia doesn't offer the same glitz and glamour, I'm afraid. It's not going to happen, you guys, so can we drop this please?"

"Okay, fine, but that doesn't mean you can't have this weekend. Go. Fly out to where he's filming. Enjoy yourself. Then come back on Monday and go back to your regular life. Think of the great time you'll have and the memories you'll make. No one says you have to be a saint, Beth. You're a normal woman, with needs like the rest of us. Bryan can fulfill those."

She'd love to go. She would. Kara and Jess put up a good argument and if she didn't already like him so much, she just might do it. But the problem was, she *did* like him too much. If she went, she was worried that *like* would turn into more and she couldn't face that heartache.

No, in the interest of self-preservation and maturity, she was staying put.

Being a responsible adult sure did suck sometimes.

Chapter Twenty-nine

BRYAN got out of the limo at his trailer on the set. A new trailer. Gone was the standard issue, second-banana trailer. They'd gone all out for him.

He tipped the driver. Sure, he wasn't supposed to; the studio took care of that, but he hadn't forgotten how hard it was to make a buck and now that he had more than he needed, he liked to share the wealth.

"Hey, Bry. Good to see you!" One of the key grips, Josh, had worked with him on the last film.

"I didn't know you'd be doing this picture."

"Yeah, got a call last minute. Pretty cool, though not gonna be the rush the last one was, eh? No guns and explosives and hot babes in bikinis."

"Carina looks pretty good in a bikini." And he was pretty sure there were some bikini shots in this movie. Funny that he couldn't remember for sure even though he was working with one of the hottest actresses in the industry.

He'd rather see Beth in a bikini. Or *not* in a bikini.

Christ. He had to get her out of his head. That part of his life was O-V-E-R.

"Carina might look good on film, but between you and me,"

Josh leaned in to stage-whisper to him, "her shit attitude is making her real unattractive. Wardrobe is ready to quit, they're all so pissed about her wanting new costumes. The woman thinks a suburban housewife ought to be in ball gowns."

Beth had had a couple of nice gowns in her closet. Probably some fancy function she'd gone to with her husband.

He'd love to see her in one of those, the clingy fabric shimmering all over her curves. Beth was built like a woman ought to be and his fingers were just itching to roam all over her.

His cock had an itch, too.

Hell. He really needed to get over her.

"She's still on set, then? From what I read in the papers, I wasn't sure."

"Yeah, she's here. Not happy about it and PJ's not happy with her. Makes filming a real kick, you know?"

PJ, the director, had directed half a dozen rom-com hits and made Carina what she was today. With the two of them on this picture, Bryan had been assured of getting some buzz, but if Carina was going to make it difficult, the whole thing could be a disaster. Then he would have left Beth behind for nothing.

He yanked open the door to his trailer. "Thanks for the heads-up, Josh. I'm gonna catch a few winks before I venture out. Sounds like I'm going to need the energy to keep up with Carina."

"If she has anything to say about it, you're going to need that energy for a lot more where she's concerned. She's already warned every female in the crew to stay away from you."

Bryan paused on the third step up. "Are you kidding me?"

"Hey, man, what can I say? The woman wants you."

"Yeah, well I might not want her."

"Seriously? The woman's a babe. A pain in the ass, but what difference does that make if you're banging her?"

"I am not going to be banging Carina Dempsey." Bryan wanted to throw up at the thought.

Funny, in the past he might have looked forward to being with her, but now? He just wanted to get the scenes done and head back to his trailer. PJ had said he could play with the schedule when he learned Bryan was coming out early. Actually thanked him for doing so. Now Bryan knew why.

Josh kept regaling him with Carina's theatrics, but Bryan

only pretended to listen. He pulled out the file with the script in it to see which scenes they would be filming first. He hoped to God it wasn't one of the romantic ones. That was the last thing he'd need after wanting Beth so badly.

Maggie's drawing was in the file.

It sent him right back to that home. To the kitchen and the mess she'd made when she'd created it. To the way her little tongue had swiped the corner of her mouth as she'd worked so intently.

There were all five of the kids—Jason with his short hair—and Beth.

He sank onto the leather bench seat at the table and shoved the hair off his forehead a little harder than necessary. That would explain the wince and moisture in his eyes.

"You okay, Bry?" Josh asked mid-Carina disaster story. "Need anything? I think they stocked your fridge with some beer."

"No, I'm good." In a manner of speaking.

"Okay, man. Well, if you want, there's a poker game tonight in room two-thirty-two at the Holiday Inn. Been going five days straight now. I'm up a hundred and fifty. You're welcome in, if you want."

A poker game? That was what had gotten him into this mess; he was not about to play it again. God only knew what the next game would do to him.

Chapter Thirty

"ARE you sure you aren't going to come with us, Mommy?" Maggie hugged Mrs. Beecham one last time. Poor cat looked like she could use the break, too.

"Honey, I told you. This is for you guys and your grandparents. It's a special time. You won't even know I'm not there."

"I will, too. Grandpa snores and Grandma makes us drippy eggs. I don't like drippy eggs."

Poor Donna tried to get Maggie's over-well-done eggs just right, but Maggie was persnickety. Just past runny but not quite hardened. Mike had been the only one who could do them right—until the accident, then Beth had spent over three hours and six dozen eggs to perfect her daughter's favorite breakfast.

"Grandma tries, honey. And maybe you could try eating what she makes without complaining. If she could do it the way you like it, she would, but at least she's trying."

Maggie heaved a big five-year-old-understands-everything sigh. "I know." Mrs. Beecham got another squeeze. "Bye Mrs. B. Don't get lonely without me."

"She's got Sherman to keep her company," said Tommy,

ruffling the monster's ears—the action a Jack Russell terrier on switch.

Sherman started bouncing—literally—off the walls. He knew the kids were going away and he wasn't happy about it. That would leave him only the cat to annoy, and Mrs. Beecham had perfected the art of ignoring the dog whenever possible. It also left him Beth, a prospect neither was happy about.

"So can I get extensions, Mom?" asked Kelsey, suddenly going Valley Girl. Teenagers. Always trying to define themselves, which would explain this latest request by her eldest daughter. "They're like three-fifty each on the boards and I can get all different colors. Jenna says they're so cool and that everyone's getting them this summer."

"Three. You can have three. No more." She slid fifteen dollars into Kelsey's hand. "And I want the change."

"I have to tip them, you know."

"Okay, fine. But only three."

"What about a bellybutton piercing?"

Beth rolled her eyes. Always pushing the limit was Kelsey. "Out. Now. And don't come home with any more holes in your body than God put there."

"Ew, that's gross." Tommy made a gagging sound.

Mark, of course, had to tease Kelsey. "Kelsey's got holes in her body. Kelsey's got holes in her body," he sang.

Kelsey palmed the top of his head like a basketball. "I'll tell you who's going to have holes in his head if he doesn't shut up."

"Ooooh, Kelsey said shut up!" Maggie made a *tsk-tsk* motion with her fingers—which ensured that she'd drop Mrs. Beecham, who took off the minute she got a look at—and growl from—Sherman.

Thank God Donna and John showed up then. Grandparent chaos was much better than kids-chasing-after-dog-chasing-after-cat chaos, and Sherman would settle down once all the noise left.

"Hi, kids! You ready for a fun time at the beach?" John had a booming voice just like his son had had.

Beth's heart clenched at the thought of Mike never doing for their grandkids what John was able to do.

God, how was she going to survive grandparenthood alone? Beth shied away from imagining what it was like for her in-laws. She'd gone there during the funeral planning and it'd been too much. She hadn't been able to shoulder her sadness, her kids' sadness and their fear—her own, too—*and* empathize with Mike's parents. There just hadn't been enough strength within her and here, two years later, she still couldn't imagine what it must have been like for them to lose not only a child, but their *only* child. She'd never mind having so many kids. No matter how much work and stress and money, these kids were her everything and she never lost sight of that.

Not even when Kara and Jess had dangled a very tempting proposition in front of her last night.

She grabbed the closest duffel bag and hoisted it over her shoulder, glad for the change of focus. Bryan was off-limits for every reason she'd told Kara and Jess. "Come on, guys, let's get your bags out to the car."

"It's a truck, Mommy," Maggie stage-whispered. "Grandpa said it's his truck."

"It's an SUV, Mags." Jason swooped his little sister up in his arms, a first for him, and took the duffel from her without being asked.

Beth's throat tightened as Maggie squealed in delight, just like she used to do with Mike. As she'd done with Bryan. And now with Jason. Her family was rebuilding. Finding the laughter in everyday life. Returning to themselves. Two long years and finally, they could move forward.

"You're sure you don't want to come?" Donna asked as John corralled five excited kids out the front door.

"Thank you for asking, but this is your time with them. You don't need me around. Enjoy being grandparents. Spoil them." Beth kicked another of Sherman's toys under the sofa. Or actually, she thought that one might have been Tommy's. Maybe her home would actually stay presentable for longer than five minutes this weekend.

"Yes, that is a grandparent's prerogative."

"And they need it. With me, it's all about schedules and chores and summer reading." She fluffed a pillow on the sofa. First time she'd done that in two years. "They deserve a break."

"And so do you."

She fluffed another pillow. "I love my kids."

"We know you do, honey." Donna put her hand on Beth's arm. "But you're human like the rest of us. You need a break. You need to relax and be you. Just you."

Beth couldn't answer Donna because the insight was too overwhelming. She did need to be her. To find out who *her* was again. And maybe even redefine this new *her*.

She squeezed Donna's shoulders and kissed her cheek. "Thank you so much for doing this."

"Oh, it's our pleasure, Beth. We just wish we could do more, but with where we live, well, there are rules."

The beauty and the curse of a fifty-five-plus community was that grandkids couldn't stay for longer than a weekend. Given that Donna and John lived an hour and a half away, it wasn't really worth the effort to do those weekends on a regular basis, which was why this long weekend at the shore was so appreciated.

"I hope you have something special planned for this weekend." Donna fluffed a pillow and they smiled at each other. "I heard about that movie star who was working for you. Maybe something there . . ."

Yeah, it felt kind of weird to have her mother-in-law trying to play matchmaker.

"It's nothing like that, Donna. Besides, he's gone off to film his new movie. He was just helping out his sister. She owns the cleaning service."

"Oh. That's a shame. I mean, Michael wouldn't have wanted you to be alone. You need a partner in this, Beth. Raising five kids is hard enough for two parents, but for one . . ." Donna patted her arm. "John and I worry about you, dear. You'll always be our daughter-in-law, but we don't mind sharing if you find someone else to love you and the kids. We just wanted you to know that you have our blessing."

Beth couldn't respond. She could barely breathe, let alone speak. Instead, she enveloped her mother-in-law in a huge hug and fought back the tears. She'd be so blessed in her life if it weren't for that damn plane crash.

Donna patted her back, then straightened with all the brisk no-nonsense-ness she'd raised her son with. "So you have a nice relaxing weekend all by yourself. Be sure to pamper yourself, Beth. A massage, a facial. Take in a movie. Go out to eat. Treat yourself."

"Oh Mommy already did that," chirped Maggie from the door. "Bryan made her. Then he took the boys shopping so we could devolve eggs."

Donna raised an eyebrow at Beth.

"*Dissolve* eggs. They were doing an experiment about the effects of soda on egg shells to show how it affects teeth."

"Yeah and it was gross. I'm never gonna drink soda again 'cause I wanna keep my teeth. Is that why Grandpa doesn't have any? Did he drink lots of soda?"

John had removed his dentures in front of the kids once by accident. They hadn't been scared and begged him to take them out whenever they saw him.

"Why don't we go ask him that, Maggie?" Donna held out her hand and looked back over her shoulder at Beth when Maggie latched on. "We'll see you Sunday night, Beth. Do something special this weekend."

Kara had a good suggestion.

For a second, Beth considered it. Just grabbing the first plane to the west coast and visiting Bryan on his movie set.

It was a tempting thought.

One weekend just for her. No one to answer to or worry about or pick up from a friend's house or drop at an activity. She could think only about herself and what she wanted. What she needed. Because, as much as she hated to admit it, yeah, she did need Bryan. She needed that human touch. That physical contact. She'd never realized how important hugging was. How much she'd miss it. But with Mike's death, a whole new world of emptiness and loneliness had been opened to her, and these past two weeks, Bryan had filled some of those.

She was a grown woman. She could take this weekend for herself. No one would ever have to know. Just her and him and—

And the paparazzi. Already the news coverage of Bryan being on set had made even her local news. The press were still interested in what he did, where he went, who he went with.

So, as much as she wanted to go, she wouldn't. Besides the fact that Bryan had respected her wish and left, she'd have to get on a plane. That would be harder than being a casual sort of woman.

Chapter Thirty-one

✧❦✧

"CUT!"

Bryan took a deep breath and tried not to glare at Carina. She was purposely sabotaging the scene.

PJ walked out from behind the camera. "Carina, you cannot straddle Bryan. It's not in the script and Megan wouldn't do that."

"Megan's a little too reserved." Carina, not moving an inch from where she was plastered across his lap, pulled a lipstick from her back pocket and slathered it on her silicone-enhanced lips.

Bryan tried not to gag. He really hated the taste of lipstick. Women definitely wore it for themselves and not for men because no guy Bryan knew ever said anything about how great a woman's lipstick tasted after kissing her.

PJ ripped off his baseball cap and ran his arm across his forehead. Only eight thirty and already tempers were hot. "Megan is *supposed* to be reserved. That's part of why she and Mike don't jump into bed together right away."

"Well I think they should. It'd spice this picture up some." She gave Bryan the once-over.

God no. Bryan tried not to squirm. The fewer love scenes he had to do with Carina, the better.

He coughed to hide his laugh. Here he was with one of the most beautiful women on the planet in a job more than half the male population would kill for, and he was trying to find ways to *avoid* kissing her.

"Then we wouldn't have a movie."

Carina rolled her eyes, then stared pointedly at his mouth before sliding her leg across his lap, slowly, the invitation still in her eyes. "I think we'd have a better one."

"Well it'd be a different one, that's for sure." Bryan stood up and caught Carina's glance at his crotch. *Sorry, babe, but he's not reacting to you.* Probably the first time that'd ever happened to her.

PJ nodded at Bryan and blew out a big breath. "Okay, then. Let's take it from where Mike surprises Megan in the garden."

"What about Bryan doing that scene without a shirt?" Carina tugged the hem of his T-shirt. "That would really surprise Megan and maybe start her thinking about sex a little sooner. It takes a while to get to it in this storyline."

"Carina, let's do it the way it's written, okay?" PJ settled his hat back on his head and tugged the brim down. "We're building the sexual tension for the big payoff at the right moment. Anything sooner is going to dilute it."

Carina grimaced. "PJ probably hasn't gotten laid in years," she muttered. "What's he know about sexual tension?"

Bryan chose to ignore her. The thing was, he was feeling like *he* didn't know what it was because he was so not into Carina that she could be a guy for all he cared. Okay, so maybe he was exaggerating, but trying to muster some attraction for her was stretching his acting muscles in a way he hadn't anticipated. After all, who *wouldn't* want to make out with a beautiful woman?

Him, apparently, if the woman wasn't Beth.

Bryan kept his shirt on, literally and figuratively, worked through Carina's diva-ness, and they got the scene in the can for the day. Two hours longer than it should have taken them, but at least that one was done. Why had he agreed to do this again? Oh, right. Because working with Carina Dempsey in one of her signature rom-coms was supposed to be good for his career.

He was beginning to question why. Sure, she was Hollywood's hottest actress right now, but he wasn't exactly a slouch in the in-demand department. One film with her. That's all he was doing and then he'd live and die by his own merits. He just hoped he survived this movie because if this was what one scene could do to him, he wasn't looking forward to the rest.

He should have stayed at Beth's and finished out his four weeks. Or, hell, stayed at home and cleaned his own place to fulfill Mac's bet instead of coming here early. What the hell had he been thinking?

You were running. From Beth and the kids and all the ties.

Yeah, he had been. So what? He wasn't going to apologize for it or be made to feel guilty by his own freaking conscience, for God's sake. He *didn't* want that middle-class life and that was all Beth had to offer. It sucked, but it was what it was. At least he was honest with himself, and with her. Their lives were on different paths.

"Okay, let's go over blocking for the kitchen scene." PJ directed the camera crew to swing the cameras from a different angle. "Come on, Bryan, let's see how good you are in a kitchen."

He was damn good in a kitchen; just ask Beth.

Of course, he was also damn good in a gazebo and on a back porch, and he'd be absolutely perfect in a bedroom if he could ever get Beth there.

Carina's fingertips walked up his abdomen. "I'm *so* looking forward to doing some cooking in the kitchen with you, Bryan," she said in an almost purr.

He wasn't saying a word.

"Let's stick to the script for this one, 'kay, Carina? Then maybe we can wrap early."

"You want to hang out after? Grab a bite?" She pointedly ignored PJ—and she wasn't talking about food.

"Thanks, but I've got plans." Like getting right back on a plane. He'd walked out on Beth and the kids for this? What had he been thinking?

He hadn't. He'd been reacting. To Beth asking him to leave. To running from everything she represented, everything he didn't want in his life.

Except he wanted Beth.

He wanted her kids.

Shit. He was so fucked. And not the way Carina obviously wanted him to be as she walked around him, dragging her hand across his abdomen. *Low* on his abdomen.

"What can you possibly have to do that's more fun than hanging out with me?"

He wasn't about to remind Carina that they were within an hour's drive of San Francisco. Not exactly a hole-in-the-wall place. "Things."

She sucked in her bottom lip. Yeah, getting shot down was definitely a new experience for her. She dropped her hand—right down the front of him, but that would only confirm that he had zero interest in starting anything.

"Okay, then. Guess I'll find something else to do. And the rest of the time we're filming together."

"I think that's probably best." He just hoped she was professional enough not to let it cloud their working relationship. Even though she was riding the wave right now, one bomb could damage her marketability; she had to know that. He certainly had no intention of screwing up the film—nor screwing the film's female lead.

He needed to talk to PJ. The director had rearranged the shooting schedule when he'd shown up early; now Bryan knew why. Anything to keep from having to work one-on-one with Carina. Well, it couldn't be helped. Contractually, he wasn't scheduled for another week and he had things he had to sort out back home.

He was going back.

Chapter Thirty-two

❧❦❧

"LET me get this straight." Liam handed a slice of pizza to Bryan. "You came back here because of a woman yet you're here playing cards with us?"

Bryan took a bite of his favorite pizza. No matter how many cities he'd been in—Rome included—nothing compared to Vinny's Pizza around the corner from the house he'd grown up in. "Uh, yeah."

"And why did you do this stupid-ass thing?" asked Sean, dealing out the first hand of the night. "I mean, I know we're *bros-before-hos*, but if this chick was good enough to turn down Carina Dempsey for, then I say you ought to have your head examined for sitting here with us. I mean, we're good-looking but we totally bat for the same team you do."

"Not to mention, we're related."

"Yeah, there is that. That's kinda wrong."

"Kinda."

Bryan chuckled. He could always count on his brothers to keep him in line. Nothing like family to bring you back to yourself and not let you get away with shit. Like dropping Carina's name. There'd been a pair of raised eyebrows, but that was about it.

"So what *are* you doing sitting here?" Sean looked at his cards. "Ante up while you're at it."

"Sure." Bryan checked his cards. Fours were wild and he had two. With the seven showing, he had three of a kind. Not a bad hand to start out with.

It got better on the next two, as two more sevens showed up. Five of a kind.

So symbolic it was scary. He won the hand with them—his last two cards being a king and queen of hearts and he didn't need the universe to tell him twice.

He grabbed another piece of pizza, cashed in his chips, and called it an early night. He loved his brothers, but they were right. What *was* he doing here when the person he wanted to be with was a few miles away?

BETH turned off the TV. Seriously, she should *not* be sitting here in the dark with a glass of wine she'd been nursing for the past four hours watching a Bryan Manley movie marathon. Just call her a glutton for punishment.

She glanced at the last text the kids had sent. They'd been happily riding the boardwalk rides, though Maggie said they weren't as much fun without Bryan around.

A lot of things weren't as much fun without Bryan around.

She sighed and pulled herself off the sofa, dragging her T-shirt down over her thighs. So much for sexy lingerie. It was a good thing Bryan wasn't here for that reason alone.

And that was the only reason she could think of that she was glad he wasn't there.

She picked up the wine glass and the half-eaten bowl of popcorn. Some exciting night this was turning out to be . . .

She let Sherman out. Even the dog wasn't liking the quietness of the house. He'd taken to following her around like, well, a puppy—in a way he never had even when he'd *been* a puppy—and even Mrs. Beecham had deigned to curl up on the top of the sofa instead of in Maggie's dollhouse, as if she wanted to make sure there was *someone* still in the house.

Was this what it was going to be like when the kids all grew up and left?

Knock it off, Hamilton. You're still young enough to find

someone. When the kids get a little older, they'll be able to handle you dating.

Well she wasn't going to find anyone tonight and it was time to call it.

She set the bowl and glass in the sink and let Sherman back in, then put him in his crate. Without Jason to curl up with, the terrier would roam the house looking for his buddy. She'd spent one too many sleepless nights in the past until she'd figured out to put one of Jason's shirts in the crate and lock him in. Sherman slept like a baby then, and so could she.

"Night, Sherman. Pleasant dreams." She was talking to the dog about dreams. Maybe she should do something special tomorrow. Spend the whole day at the spa. Drive downtown and see a show. Something instead of spending her time moping around the house, looking at the walls, and conversing with the pets.

She turned off the kitchen light and was walking through the darkened family room to the front stairs when the doorbell rang.

She glanced at her cell phone. Ten forty-seven. Who was ringing her doorbell at quarter of eleven on a Friday night?

Kara, wanting to drag her out for a hot night on the town.

Beth headed to the door. It'd serve Kara right for her to answer the door dressed like this.

Only . . . it wasn't Kara.

Chapter Thirty-three

❧

B RYAN."

    "Hi, Beth."

It figured. She looked like hell and he looked . . . he looked as gorgeous as ever. Even travel weary in rumpled clothing, Bryan looked amazing.

"What are you doing here? I thought you were filming your movie?"

"I was. And now I'm back."

He hadn't moved off her front porch. Hadn't moved a muscle actually. His hands were in his pants pockets and his head was cocked a little to the right and his feet were firmly planted an inch from the threshold.

She, on the other hand, couldn't hold still. She was shifting her feet, wringing her hands then putting them on her hips, then behind her back, then crossing them in front of her . . . She couldn't find a comfortable position. "But . . . why?"

He took a deep breath. "Can I come in?"

"Oh, um, yeah. Sure." She stepped back, thankful that she'd turned off the lights. She didn't want him seeing her in this stupid old threadbare T-shirt she'd pulled from the bottom of her closet.

"The kids are in bed?"

"Oh. They're not here. My in-laws took them to the beach this weekend. They're gone until Sunday night."

"So you're alone?"

Beth's heart rate tripled. She was alone in a dark house, dressed in practically nothing, with Bryan Manley, the man she wanted more than anything, who, if what he'd said on her deck the other night was true, wanted her just as much. "Yes."

Bryan pulled his hands from his pockets and raked one of them through his hair. "Jesus, Beth. Did you have to say that?"

"You asked."

"I know. But that was because I didn't think the answer was going to be yes."

"I'm sorry, but I'm not following this discussion. Why are you here?"

"This. This is why I'm here."

It took him two steps and he had her in his arms. Another second and he was kissing her. Half a second after that, she'd recovered her wits enough to lose them all over again when the kiss went from *hello* to *hot* in the next breath.

God, she wanted this. Needed it. Needed him.

"Beth, tell me to stop," he groaned as he ran his hands over her back, down to her butt, then, ohthankyouJesus, under her T-shirt.

She shook her head, and sucked his bottom lip into her mouth. She wasn't telling him to stop. Not now. He shouldn't have come if he hadn't wanted this.

He pulled her up against him. Oh yeah, he wanted this.

"I want you, Beth. I know I said I shouldn't, but I do, and I can't stop thinking about you."

The words were incredible and so were his hands and his lips and the scent and taste of him and thank God he couldn't stop because she didn't know what she'd do if he did.

Beth wrapped her arms around his shoulders and pressed her aching breasts against him. God, she wanted him to touch her there. Needed him to. It'd been so incredibly long since she'd wanted someone's hands on her. And lips and tongue . . .

"Bryan, touch me. Please." She hadn't wanted to beg, but that *please* sure sounded like begging and, funny, she didn't care.

Bryan got it. He cupped the back of her head with both hands and brushed his nose against hers. "I will, Beth. I will. Among so many other things . . . if you'll let me?"

His green eyes danced between hers, looking for an answer. Beth wasn't quite sure of the question but she knew that whatever Bryan asked her to do tonight, she'd do. And tomorrow as well. Even Sunday, right up until the kids came home.

Now was *not* the time to think about the kids. It was time to think only about her and Bryan and what they could do for and to and with each other.

But Bryan stopped kissing her. "Beth. Sweetheart. I'm sorry. We shouldn't. I shouldn't have—"

"I don't want to hear it. You came here for a reason. What was it, Bryan?" She wasn't playing games. She, more than most, knew how quickly life could be gone. She wasn't going to waste one more minute of hers on *should be*s. It was time for *could be*, and she wanted a *could be* with Bryan.

She wrapped her fingers in his hair and tugged. "Tell me, Bryan. What had you leaving your movie set and coming back here? Tonight? At eleven o'clock? To your home town that's so far from the bright lights of Hollywood?"

He searched her eyes once more, then took a deep breath and it was as if some big momentous decision had been made.

"You, Beth. I needed you. To see you. Be with you." His voice lowered. "Touch you."

"And now that you're here? Now that you have me in your arms?" She stroked the back of his neck and if she wasn't mistaken, she felt shivers go through him.

He cupped her cheek and tilted her chin up with his thumb. "I want you. You know that." He pressed his lower half against her. "Hell, it's not like it's a big secret. Lady, you've got me so twisted up inside, I can think of nothing and no one but you."

"Not even Carina Dempsey?" Okay, she shouldn't have tossed the actress's name in there. Bryan wasn't asking her to marry him. Hell, she wasn't quite sure what he was asking her, but Carina or any other woman didn't factor into this.

"Who?" Bryan gave her that cocky half smile he was known for and it did to her what it did to millions of other women.

But millions of other women aren't in his arms, so why in the world are you jabbering on about some actress when the man just told you he wants you?

"Never mind." She brushed his gorgeous hair back from his face and let her fingers trace gently over his ear.

"Beth . . ." His voice was low. Almost a growl.

"Yes?"

"If you keep doing that . . ."

"This?" She traced the outer shell of his ear so lightly it was almost as if she wasn't touching him. But she was. She knew it.

And so did he. He shivered again and pressed his lower half against her even more.

His cock swelled against her thigh. "Do you see what that does to me?" he whispered almost in agony. "There's no Carina, no other actress. No other woman. Only you. And me. Here. Now."

And that's all it'll be went unspoken, but Kara's words also ran through her head. *Take this time for you. Enjoy what Bryan's offering just for the simple pleasure of it.* There didn't have to be long-term strings attached. No big, grandiose life plan. Just two people who wanted each other spending time exploring that desire.

"I want you, Bryan." There. She'd said it. Ball was in his court.

He took it and ran with it. Or rather, he ran with *her*. He scooped her up in his arms like Jason had Maggie, but that's where the similarities ended because the look in Bryan's eyes said he most definitely didn't see her as sister material.

"Your room okay?" he asked, striding to the front steps.

"Well, certainly not any of the kids'."

He stopped at the base of the stairs and his smile faded as he searched her eyes yet again. "I just meant, since it was your and your husband's room . . ."

If she didn't already have feelings for him, that would have done it. She reached up to caress his cheek. "It's okay, Bryan. Mike would be happy for me."

"Then he's a better man than I am, but I'm not going to be so noble as to turn you down." He took the steps by twos and strode down the hallway, past each of the kids' rooms, until at last, he reached her room.

Moonlight sifted through the French doors to the balcony and glittered across the bed. She'd chosen faceted door panels for just this reason; she loved the pattern the moonlight cast upon her bed, like something out of a fairytale.

Sort of like tonight.

Bryan set her on the bed, then sat beside her, the backs of his fingers stroking her cheek almost reverently. "You're sure, Beth. I can't make you many promises, but I *can* promise that I want you. That there's no one else I'd rather be here with."

"Shh, Bryan." She ran her fingers over his lips, getting chills when he kissed them. "I'm not asking for the fairy tale. I'm just so glad you decided to come back. For however long you want to be here."

His eyes roamed her face again and Beth was almost afraid to breathe, wondering if she'd scare him off. She wanted him so much, wanted *this* so much, it almost scared *her* off. She hadn't planned on this. Hadn't wanted it. Hadn't even really been thinking about it. All she'd wanted to do was help her kids get beyond the aftermath of Mike's accident and move on with their lives. She hadn't really thought about getting that same chance herself.

Bryan slid his hand into her hair and tugged her closer for another kiss. No words, no preamble, just a God's-honest-truth, raw hunger sort of kiss.

Beth was so with him.

She lay back as he pressed against her, wanting—no *needing*—to feel him on top of her, and somehow managed to work her T-shirt up to just below her breasts. Her aching breasts that were just begging for his touch and his kiss and, *ohdeargod*, his tongue and his lips.

She'd settle for his hands so that when he drew them down her sides, Beth arched into him, wanting that sensation all over the rest of her.

"God, Beth, you're so responsive."

"That's what you do to me, Bryan." She gasped when his fingertips danced across her belly, the sensation making a bee-line straight to her core, and Beth couldn't help the tingles that suffused her and the goose bumps that broke out across her skin, making her shiver.

"Are you cold?" Bryan asked, stilling his fingers.

"I will be if you stop doing that." She wiggled from side to side to make her point and, smart man that he was, he started stroking her again while his lips sought hers.

She could so get used to kissing Bryan Manley.

H E *was kissing Beth.*
Beth Hamilton.
Widowed mother of five.
The one he'd sworn he'd stay away from.
The press would have a field day with this if they got wind of it.
Mac would have a field day if she got wind of it.
She wasn't going to. *No one* was going to. This was only about him and Beth and this incredible chemistry between them.
He inched her T-shirt up the smooth skin of her belly. Five kids and the woman didn't look as if she'd carried one.
She gasped into his mouth when his thumb found her nipple and, holy hell, what that sound did to him. His cock went so hard so fast he was ready to be inside her now. This instant. Wanted to feel her around him, enveloping him, taking him into that most private part of her.
God, he wanted her.
Slow down, Manley. Enjoy it already. It's gonna have to last you a lot of years because this shit ain't happening on a daily—or weekly or even monthly—basis. You got plans, buddy. Big plans. And they don't include six tag-alongs.
He shut the voice down. Way to kill the moment. He wasn't asking Beth to spend the rest of her life with him—and she wasn't asking him to ask her that—so why go down that path?
Because you do want to spend the rest of your life with her, you're just too pig-headed to admit it.
Not pig-headed, *smart.* Driven. Focused. He had a plan. After living in near-poverty during his childhood and adolescence, Bryan would *never* do that again, and this job was the means to securing his future and his peace of mind. A couple mil in the bank and he'd finally be able to rest easier.
Beth shifted under him and Bryan pulled his head out of the future and back into the here and now. He had Beth Hamilton

writhing on the bed beneath him. Her legs felt so good against his, and every flutter of her abdomen when she gasped stroked his cock in a way nothing else could.

He'd done this to her. *He'd* made her a gasping, panting, writhing woman who looked so utterly beautiful on the blue bedspread—he'd been right, blue was a good color on her.

He raised himself enough to take his lips from her and enjoy the sight of her opening her eyes to see why he'd stopped.

"What?"

He kissed the tip of her nose. "I wanted to look at you."

She blushed. Amazing that after five kids and a healthy marriage, Beth still blushed. "Why?"

"Because you're so beautiful, and I've fantasized about this so much that I can't really believe I'm here. That this is going to happen."

She reached up to cup his cheek again. God, he loved when she did that, her eyes all dark and intent—and intense—gazing into his. "Please don't tell me you're having second thoughts." Her thighs clenched on his. "I don't think I could survive it if you do."

If she clenched his hips that hard when he was inside her, *he* wouldn't survive. Already his cock was so hard it was painful, and his fingers were itching to close over her breast.

So he let them. And was rewarded with the sexiest back-arching twisting move he'd never seen before. And Beth moaning, too. Well, a long aching moan interspersed by several gasping breaths as he ran his thumb over her nipple. "Like that?"

She bit her bottom lip and her eyes fluttered open. "Uh-huh."

He flicked it again.

She whimpered and arched into his caress.

"I'm taking that as a yes."

She looked at him then, the look in her eyes nailing him in place. "Oh God, Bryan, don't stop."

"This?" He flicked her nipple again.

"That, kissing me, touching me . . . anything else you want to do to me."

He wanted to do so much more.

"Okay, Beth, don't say I didn't warn you. Now slide down to the bottom of this bed and let me show you how it's done."

Chapter Thirty-four

❧❧❧

HOLY moly, did Bryan show her how it was done.
The man could make a songbird weep.

He made parts of her weep. One very tingly, very aching part in particular.

"Oh my God, Bryan." She gasped moans of sheer pleasure when Bryan lowered his mouth to her thighs. He wasn't even at her center and already she was on fire. "Touch me. Please."

"I will, baby. Don't be so impatient."

She managed a laugh. Two years. Let's see *him* after two years of forced celibacy.

She managed yet another chuckle. She highly doubted Bryan had ever had even two *minutes* of forced celibacy.

He hooked his fingers in the waistband of her panties and Beth felt moisture seep into them. She didn't know how much foreplay she could take because she wanted Bryan too badly, but asking for a quick wham-bam-thank-you-ma'am was just so out of place on this, their first time together.

Next time, however . . .

"What are you smiling at?" he whispered with a sexy-as-all-get-out growl.

"You. There."

He rocked back on his heels a bit and looked at her. *All* of her. "And look at you. There." He tugged her panties down. "*Now* look at you."

He slid them off her legs, then ran his palms up her thighs, over her hipbones, to the curve of her waist, lighting a fire beneath her skin that she hadn't felt in two very long years.

"God, Beth, you're even more beautiful than I imagined."

"You imagined this?"

"This? No. I couldn't come up with *this*. What I imagined doesn't do you justice and if I'd known, *really* known, how beautiful you are, I would never have left."

"But I asked you to."

"And I should have tried to talk you out of it."

She smiled. "But you didn't because you left for the same reason I asked you to go."

"A reason that hasn't changed." He took his hands from her. "Should I leave?"

She grabbed his hands and placed them on her breasts. "Stop talking, Bryan. You're here and the kids aren't and we have tonight. And tomorrow if you want."

"Tomorrow night?" He arched an eyebrow above that sideways grin.

Beth laughed. It felt so good to laugh. "Sure. Tomorrow night. If you think you're up for it."

They both looked at his groin. Oh yeah, he was up for it.

"That's not an issue."

"I can see that." Beth sat up. "But not exactly the way I'd like to." She undid the button on his shorts.

His abs contracted, giving her enough space to brush her fingers beneath the waistband.

"God, Beth, that's amazing."

"That's nothing compared to what I plan to do to you."

"I should never have left."

She slid the zipper down. "Ssshhh. What's done is done. We're here now. Let's enjoy it."

He helped her shove his shorts down his hips. "I intend to."

He kicked them off, then crawled up the bed, straddling her legs and grabbing her T-shirt with his teeth.

His five o'clock shadow scraped her belly, making her wiggle. "Bryan! That tickles!"

He stopped with the T-shirt between her breasts. "That's one I haven't heard before." He waggled his eyebrows. And went right back to scraping her skin with his chin, back and forth over her breasts. And then her nipples.

Ohmygod, the sensation . . . Beth stopped wiggling. Instead she grabbed the sheets and held on for dear life because if he kept that up, she just might fly off the bed.

His lips replaced his chin.

Oh. My. God. Beth clenched her legs because the throbbing there was just insane.

He tugged on her nipple, then released it. "Like that?"

She opened her mouth but nothing came out. He'd taken her breath and her voice.

"Ah, I'll take that as a yes, too." Then he moved to the other one.

By the time he was ready to move on to her collarbone and her neck and her jaw and a whole host of other delicious spots, Beth could barely keep a grip on her sanity, never mind the sheets. Somehow, her fingers had migrated to his hair and she wasn't letting go. Especially when he maddeningly refused to kiss her.

"Bryan." She tugged his hair.

"Mmmmm." He mouthed it against her throat, his lips and tongue and hot breath not driving her wild nearly as much as that vibration against her pulse.

"Bryan, kiss me."

"I am." He sucked on her neck.

"Hey!" She twisted. "No hickies!"

He rested on his elbows and looked at her. "Why not? Hickies are fun."

"Except that everyone will know where I got mine. Or they'll wonder and that's almost as bad as them knowing."

"Ah." More waggling eyebrows. "You're ashamed of me."

"Don't tease me, Bryan. I'm serious."

His face lost that teasing look. "I'm sorry. You're right. I was just having some fun. I wasn't going to give you a hickey."

"Oh. Okay, then."

"Well, at least not there." He lowered his lips to the underside of her breast. "Not where everyone can see. But here . . ." He sucked her skin into his mouth . . . and kept sucking.

Oh God, the tug she felt low in her belly . . .

Desire flooded through her and she cradled his head against her. God, yes, she wanted him to mark her. Only they would know, and she'd have a physical reminder of tonight, if only for a little while.

He slid his thigh between hers and she clenched it. "Oh, Bryan . . ." She couldn't keep from moaning his name. He just felt so damn good on top of her. Between her legs, kissing her, holding her.

"Say my name again, Beth. I love the way you say it." He kissed her nipple again and worked his way back up to her neck, every skin-shivering inch he traveled making her gasp out his name.

He kissed the hollow below her ear, then drew his tongue along the rim and Beth re-clenched her thighs.

"Want me?" he whispered in her ear.

She made some sort of response, half moan, half mew, and she felt his smile against her cheek.

"Hold that thought," he whispered before he pulled away. *Completely* away. As in, climbed-off-her-body-and-the-bed sort of way.

"Where are you going?" Dear God, he wasn't going to leave her like this, was he?

"Right here, baby." He picked up his shorts and pulled something out of the pocket that he tossed on the bed beside her.

Condoms.

"That many?" Either he had a very high opinion of himself or he had an amazing idea about *her*.

"Don't you worry, Beth, we're going to use every single one."

"Bryan, there's at least a dozen there."

"Uh-huh." He crawled back up the bed, straddled her again, his cock jutting out right over the very spot that wanted it so badly inside, and ripped a condom package with his teeth. "Want to do the honors?" He held it out to her.

Beth's hands trembled as she rolled it on—awkwardly. *Figured.* She couldn't be smooth in the moment, but she and Mike hadn't used those in over a decade. It wasn't as if she had tons of practice.

"You don't have to be shy with me, Beth." He covered her hands with his and worked it on the rest of the way. "I like that you're not used to doing this. I like knowing I'm the only man other than your husband who's been in this bed with you."

"I thought you said you weren't as generous as he was? You're willing to share the so-called honors?"

"Baby, just being with you is an honor. Anything else is a gift and I'm so humbled by you allowing me to be here like this with you. For wanting me enough to welcome me in. I know you aren't the casual kind of woman and I'm so touched by this gift."

He kept talking about gifts and generosity as if she were making some sort of sacrifice, but the reality was, she wanted Bryan with a passion she'd thought she'd lost.

"Make love to me, Bryan." She opened her legs and her arms. And her heart.

Because Bryan was right; she wasn't the casual sort and for her to do this, to be so open and so welcoming and accepting, and not feel self-conscious or shy or nervous, that meant that she cared for him. More than just his public persona, more than a man who could take her to physical satisfaction, she *knew* Bryan and she liked *that* man. Wanted *that* man.

Loved that man.

The admission crept over her as he slid inside her and to Beth it was the most natural thing in the world, both to be with Bryan so intimately and to acknowledge her feelings for him. There was no panic, no worry, no indecision. The act of loving him emotionally was as natural to her as loving him physically, so the two became one.

Now where had she heard those words before?

BRYAN'S breath caught in his throat as he slid inside Beth. God, how he wished he didn't have to wear the damn condom. She was the one woman he wanted to be skin-to-skin with. But that was a whole other level of trust and emotion and he was just thankful she was open enough for this.

She clenched around him as he started to move and Bryan had to squeeze his eyes, the pleasure was so intense, the emotion so powerful that he was afraid it was bringing tears to his eyes.

He slid his hands into her curls, those soft, silky curls that'd been teasing him for so long. He couldn't have imagined just how perfect they were. Not like this. Not without touching them and inhaling the scent of her shampoo and feeling the fine strands caress his face. He kissed her jaw line, then along her hairline, wanting to kiss every inch of her face, but being drawn so strongly to her lips that he had to forcibly restrain himself or he might scare her with the passion he wanted to claim them with.

"Kiss me, Bryan," she whispered as her hands gripped his lats and slid down over his ass, clenching him as her inner muscles clenched him. She wrapped her legs around his thighs and he felt her lock her ankles, her thighs widening, allowing him to sink deeper inside her, and the symbolism wasn't lost on Bryan.

And he not only didn't care, but he welcomed it. He wanted to be so close to Beth, so caught up in her, that he couldn't tell where one ended and the other began. It truly was a gift, her allowing him to be like this with her.

It was also hot as hell. Especially when she pretty much forced his lips to hers—not that he was unwilling, but he'd wanted to kiss his way there from her earlobe again and she wasn't having any of that.

So Bryan let her have him.

Beth kissed him with a passion he'd dreamed of and then some, because he hadn't wanted to *let* himself imagine it being like this. But Beth was everything he wanted her to be. Sexy and giving and willing and wanting and taking everything he had to give.

He thrust inside her, wanting to be as close as two people could be physically, wanting to feel her around him, taking him in, wanting him, needing this contact between them, and when she called out his name, her neck arching as her fingernails scored his back, her thighs clenching him with each thrust, meeting him motion for motion, sweat slicking their skin as they glided against each other, Bryan felt a rush of emotion roll over him as if it were a wave on the shore, and he couldn't contain the shudders that raked through him or the pounding he had to do inside her, to feel her, to bring her the same pleasure she brought to him, and it was all he could do to keep from coming until he felt her start to shiver, her breaths coming in short, quick gasps, his name lost among them. Bryan pushed them both a little further, a little higher, until at last, he couldn't stop it. Couldn't halt the ride that was better than any of the roller coasters they'd ridden. The sensations overwhelmed him, and for a few seconds there—for a brief moment unlike he'd ever had before—Bryan thought he could see his future stretched out before him, as if heaven was giving him a glimpse of what could be.

And then he came. That stomach-twisting moment when it rushed upon him and Bryan couldn't see anything but the insides of his eyelids as he had to pound into her to feed this unbelievably, amazingly intense ache that he never wanted to end.

It doesn't have to . . .

He wasn't sure if she whispered it or he'd thought it, but the idea stayed with Bryan as he felt the tremors shudder through her, heard her call out his name in a way that was guaranteed to prolong his orgasm—which it did—then wrapped his arms around her so tightly to stop them both from coming apart at the seams in the aftermath, until he spooned himself around her, kissing her cheek, her ear, her shoulder, his fingers intertwined with hers against her breasts, his foot rubbing her smooth legs as he curled his leg over them. For a moment, just a tiny one but it was there, Bryan almost said the three words he hadn't thought he'd ever say.

Almost.

But he didn't.

Idiot.

Chapter Thirty-five

✥

*S*HE *was in bed with Bryan Manley.*
    The man she loved.

Beth let the smile curve over her lips in the early morning sunlight. He was asleep at her back, his face buried in her hair, the soft puffs of his breath tickling the curve of her shoulder, but Beth wasn't about to move. She was in love with Bryan Manley. And not *the* Bryan Manley, the heartthrob millions of women thought they were in love with, but the Bryan Manley who cleaned toilets and rescued her dog and taught her son to build a clothesline. Who colored with her daughter and didn't mind putting on a tiara or having a tea party to make a child— *her* child—happy. *That* was the man she was in love with.

Unfortunately, *that* man was also the same person as the heartthrob, and the heartthrob had dreams that didn't include kids and dogs and tea parties.

This weekend was a gift. A moment in time. She was going to enjoy it while she had it and treasure it when he was gone. And she'd let him go back to that life with no pressure from her.

"I can hear you thinking." His breath tickled her ear now.

She scrunched up her shoulder. "You can't hear thoughts."

"Sure you can. Your breathing picked up and your fingers are twitching."

"That's not hearing; that's feeling."

He spread his palm over her breast. "Feeling has a lot to recommend it."

She put her hand on his and pressed it against her. He might think she was pressing it into her breast for sexual reasons, but she was really pressing it against her heart because that's where he'd always be.

"Ah . . . It's true what they say."

"Oh?"

"Great minds *do* think alike." He gently squeezed her breast.

Okay, so it wasn't just because he was in her heart that she wanted him to touch her there.

She wiggled back into him. Yup, another part of him was just as awake as she was.

"God, Beth, don't do that. I don't know if there are any more condoms left."

"We did not go through a dozen of them."

"Close."

"Bryan, you're exaggerating. You're not Superman."

"But I could play him on the screen."

She wiggled again, one time. Hard. "Tease."

"In a good way, I hope."

She wiggled again. "Appears so."

"I meant for you. If you're too sore, Beth, or too tired, or sick of me . . ."

She flipped around so fast she could tell he hadn't been expecting it. She cupped his face. "Bryan Matthew Manley, don't you *dare* say such a thing. I chose *you* to be the first man in my bed since my husband's death; that's not a decision I took lightly. I'm very glad you're here and you're welcome to stay for as long as you like."

That was the problem; he wanted to stay forever. But he didn't *do* forever. Not here and not at this point in his career. *People's* Sexiest Man Alive was just around the corner, according to his agent, once this movie released; he didn't want to do anything to jeopardize that. A wife and five kids would take him out of the running—

Whoa whoa whoa! A wife and kids? So you're thinking along those lines, are you?

He didn't know what the hell he was doing; he just knew he couldn't do it here in this town. He was here for the weekend; that was it. Then it'd be back to the hot lights, er, bright lights of Tinseltown, and on his way up the ladder of his career.

Oh crud, he'd meant to get her ladder out of her shed and move it to the garage. The gutters were going to need to be cleaned before fall.

"Okay, what are *you* thinking now? Your face just got a funny look on it."

"Gutters."

"*Gutters?* I mean, I know I was a little uninhibited last night, but I don't think anything we did could be classified as in the gutter, do you?" Beth nibbled her bottom lip.

That move was sexy. Everything she did was sexy. Kissing him, moaning his name, undoing his shorts . . . Even picking up Sherman's toys and hanging laundry were sexy when Beth did them.

Speaking of Sherman, there was some scuffling going on in the kitchen. "The dog's up."

"So is Mrs. Beecham. Which is why Sherman's up. She likes to poke him in the morning."

Bryan arched his back. "I'm not averse to poking in the morning, either."

Beth rolled her eyes with a smile. "I have to let Sherman out or his 'Hallelujah Chorus' is going to start any second." She kissed him quickly—too quickly—and got out of bed.

She picked up her T-shirt.

"Don't."

She looked at him with the shirt over her arms, just ready to stick her head through. "Don't?"

"Don't put that on. Can't you let him out like that?"

"Naked?"

He didn't know if she was more appalled at the idea or the fact that she actually was naked in front of him. "Yes, naked. I want to think of you walking around like that and I'm the only one who can see you."

"Uh, hate to burst your bubble, Bryan, but the curtains are all open downstairs. The entire neighborhood could get a good view if I went down like this." She pulled the shirt over her head. "But I'll keep the panties off if that'll make you feel better."

The little imp was out the door with a shit-eating grin while he was still trying to absorb that mental and visual blow.

She was walking around her house without her panties on. The ones he'd peeled off her.

Bryan groaned while he smiled. God, this was fun. And amazing. And absolutely perfect. Beth was absolutely perfect. And maybe if she didn't have a ready-made family, they could give this a go.

Seriously? You're going to toss the kids out?

He sat up and raked his hands through his hair. No, of course he wasn't. Beth and the kids were a package deal and, honestly, he liked her kids. Really liked them. Jason, and his wanting to be a man but needing someone to show him how. Kelsey, with her approaching womanhood and needing the guidance of how not to behave around horny teenage boys. The twins, with their energy and just wanting to be seen as individuals while still being a team . . . He and his brothers were so close in age that he could give them pointers. And then there was Maggie. Sweet, loving Maggie, who just wanted a daddy to hug her.

Give it up, Bryan. You want them. This isn't just a fling for you. You want Beth and the kids and you're going to have to figure out a way you can have them because you are not going to be able to walk away from them. Not if you want to be the man you say you are.

He stood up and arched his back, a couple of kinks needing to be worked out from some of the positions they'd done last night . . .

God. Last night. It'd never been more perfect. More real. More natural. Beth felt something for him. He knew that as well as he knew she'd never say it. She respected his decision to have his career, and she loved her kids enough to not drag them through the circus it could become.

But could he honestly say he wanted *this* to be their relationship? This weekend and maybe one or two more over the next couple of years until the kids were older and on their own? Hell, that was thirteen more years for Maggie.

No. He couldn't let this be all there was. He wanted Beth in his bed every night and every morning. He wanted her in his home all the time, taking care of the little things that she did so much better than he did. He wanted her kids running around during the day and plopping on the sofa at night with a bowl of popcorn to watch some silly sitcom and talk about their day. He even wanted Sherman and Mrs. Beecham, though he would try to get them to like each other instead of chasing each other all over the place.

He wanted Beth and her family . . . to be his family.

He leaned an arm against the doorframe and rested his forehead against it, looking out over the backyard. There was the clothesline he and Jason had built. The fence he and the twins had fixed when Sherman had gotten out. The yard where he'd posed for pictures for the kids' friends.

The deck where he'd kissed Beth.

What the hell was he going to do now?

Chapter Thirty-six

❧❧❧

BRYAN couldn't remember a more perfect day, and it'd started so mundanely, so "suburbia." Well, after he'd made love to Beth again. Twice.

Okay, so that hadn't been so mundane, but after . . . Well, okay, *after* the shower they took together, and *after* the oral he'd given her in that shower . . . *then* it'd gotten mundane. He'd let Sherman out again, fed the dog and the cat, even stuck a couple of carrots in the hamsters' cage, grabbed the newspaper from the front porch and read it aloud to Beth while she'd made them omelets for breakfast, er, brunch.

Of course, he'd made sure that she'd sat on his lap while they ate, but still . . . suburbia all the way.

He was kind of liking suburbia . . .

Then they'd gone on a bike ride and decided to take a tour of a local winery. Well, half toured it. The other half of the time, they'd made out among the vines and in the cellars when they could slip away from everyone.

Bryan smiled as he poured the Cabernet they'd bought into the new glasses they'd found in the gift shop—new relationship, new wine, new glasses. That's what the owner had said, and he and Beth had just smiled and gone along with it.

But Bryan had put a lot of thought into that word. Relationship. It rolled off his tongue so easily—well, his mental tongue because he wasn't ready to say the word out loud yet. Hell, he didn't even know if he *could* say the word because a relationship needed two people to work, and he wasn't sure what Beth wanted to call this thing between them. He didn't even know if there *was* a thing between them or merely a one-weekend event.

How weird was that? He was used to having to fend women off, yet here he was with a woman he wanted to do the complete opposite, and he had no clue what she'd think of the idea of being in a relationship with him.

"I don't know if this is warm enough." Beth carried plates of the Italian take-out they'd picked up on the way home—

Back. The way *back.* To Beth's house. This wasn't home. *But it could be . . .*

"That's okay. If they're still as good as I remember when I worked there in high school, it won't matter that they're not piping hot."

"I think something's up with my oven. It seems to be acting up. The other day I had to throw out a whole tray of brownies because the outside was hard as a rock but the inside was still all battery."

"Battery?" He took the plates of chicken Marsala, Beth's favorite. He hadn't known that, but now that he did, he'd never forget. "I don't think you mean that the way you think you do."

"Batter-*ee.* As in, like batter, not *a* battery." She sat down. "Well I'm hungry enough to eat a horse, so I don't care how hot it is or isn't."

"I can vouch for the fact that there is no horse in here, so no need to worry about that."

She grimaced as she speared a piece of the chicken. "If I weren't so hungry, that might have killed my appetite."

"Sweetheart, after this morning, I don't think *anything* is going to kill your appetite."

God, he loved when she blushed. He pulled her chair around so she was beside him.

"What are you doing?" she shrieked as she clung to the armrests.

"I want you beside me." He wrapped his arm around her

shoulders and pulled her as close to him as the chairs would allow.

It wasn't enough.

"Oh." Her look of surprise melted into a big grin.

He loved to see her smile even more than he loved to see her blush.

Love. He was tossing that word around a lot.

"The sunset is beautiful." She swirled her wine glass as she looked at it.

He looked at her. "You're more beautiful."

There she went with the blush again.

"God, Beth, do you know what that does to me?"

"What *what* does to you?"

"That little secret smile you get and the way you nibble the inside of your lip and the blush you can't hide."

"You've been looking very closely." There she went with the lip-nibbling.

"I can't *not* look at you, Beth. I can't help myself. I'm with you and all I want to do is watch you."

"*All* you want to do?"

"Okay, not *all*, but yes, I like looking at you. Not because you're physically beautiful, though you are, but because I like seeing *you*. Beth Hamilton the woman. I can't get enough of you." He kissed her forehead, lingering as her scent filled him, that lilac shampoo she used and the rose-scented soap and the very essence of her.

"I want you, Bryan."

His eyes opened and he looked into Beth's dark eyes where the setting sun was reflected like a fire within her.

"I didn't come back just to make love to you, you know," he said.

"I know. But that doesn't mean we can't, does it?"

"Oh, so who's teasing whom now?"

"I hope I can always tease you." She turned in the chair and grabbed his face with both hands. "Let's go upstairs, Bryan. I've wanted to be naked with you all day."

"That would have shocked the other people on the wine tour."

"Hence the reason I didn't strip you down in front of them. But there's no one here now and our weekend is almost half

over. I want you. I want to be close to you. As close as two
people can get." She kissed him and it was all Bryan could do
to recover enough to get them inside because he'd had half a
mind to take her right there on the deck.

Beth couldn't wait to get him upstairs and naked. Like,
literally couldn't wait, and for the first time in her life, she had
sex on her front hallway stairs.

"You carried condoms in your pocket all day?" she said
when they half sat, half slumped on the stairs after one of the
most inventive lovemaking sessions she'd ever had. It was a
good thing she'd had double padding installed under the carpet.

"You're complaining?" He grabbed her chin and gave it a
playful little shake. "This couldn't have happened if I hadn't.
Then where would we be?"

"Upstairs?"

"Except *someone* couldn't wait that long now, could she?"
Bryan leaned over and kissed her again, another heart-stopping
kiss she felt all the way down to her toes.

She'd almost told him that she loved him. Almost said those
three words, and it was only the one iota of sanity that she'd
retained as he'd driven her out of her mind with pleasure that
had kept her from shouting it as she'd come. Instead, she'd
shouted his name. Groaned it. Moaned it. Panted it. Gasped it.
But she hadn't told him she loved him. She didn't want to ruin
the moment and she wasn't going to let herself think about why
giving someone one of the greatest gifts—her heart and her
trust—would ruin a moment of such pleasure. *Enjoy the weekend*; Kara's words had become her mantra.

"Come on, Ms. Impatient. I want you naked on that bed."
He stood up and held out his hand.

"Naked on the stairs doesn't cut it for you?" Beth took her
sweet time standing. The padding wasn't as thick some places
as it was in others.

"Oh it was great, don't get me wrong."

As if she could. He'd growled her name for his entire
orgasm. She hadn't been aware that *Beth* could have so many
syllables.

"But . . . ?"

"But I want to lie beside you. Feel you against every inch
of me. I want to be able to wrap my arms around you and pull

you against me and tangle my hands in your hair and caress your body and wrap my legs around you in a way that stairs aren't conducive to. And maybe there are a few new things I want to try with you."

Beth shivered in anticipation. "Oh? Such as?"

He tugged her hand and picked up the pace. "You'll see, Beth. You'll see."

He was right, she *was* Ms. Impatient. Beth ran to her room in all her naked glory and threw herself onto her bed.

"Make love to me, Bryan."

He fully intended to.

And just as he covered her, just as he fell into that first wild and incredibly sexy kiss, it came to him. He *was* making love to Beth. They weren't having sex or fooling around or hooking up or whatever other people wanted to call it when they were relieving an ache and making each other feel good, but he was *making love* to Beth Hamilton. Giving her his heart and wanting to cherish hers. Wanting to cherish *her*. For the rest of their lives.

"Bryan? Arc you okay?" she asked when he stopped moving. When he stopped kissing her and caressing her and . . . breathing.

He wanted Beth forever. And the idea no longer scared him. He wanted her in his life, and the prospect of not having her in it was worse than never getting another script again, because he could live without being in the movies but he couldn't live without Beth.

"Bryan? Did I do something wrong?"

"No, sweetheart, you didn't." She'd done everything right. "I . . ." He couldn't say it. Not yet. He had to figure out what it meant for him first. What it meant for them. And then there were the kids to consider.

"You what?"

He looked at her worried face. At that dear, gorgeous, sexy, wonderful, passionate face, and he smiled. "I lost my breath for a moment. Just looking at you . . . You take my breath away, Beth."

Tears sprung to her eyes.

"Aw, shit. I didn't mean to make you cry."

She shook her head and smiled. "No, they're good tears. This is a good thing."

"If you say so." He brushed the hair off her face and looked into those sparkling brown eyes he wanted to stare at for the rest of his life.

He ought to tell her. She had to know it, right? Had to see it written all over his face? He loved her. He loved Beth Hamilton.

And it didn't scare him.

No, it energized him. It gave him hope and a purpose and a sense of belonging that, until now, he hadn't realized he was missing. He'd thought his brothers and his sister and his grandmother were all the family he needed. All the connection and ties he wanted in his life, but, God, how wrong he'd been.

"You're starting to scare me, Manley." Beth bit her top lip.

That was new. And he didn't want to be the cause of any worry. "I'm just looking at you. Being amazed that I'm here. That you're here."

"Why? This can't be a surprise or you never would have come back."

How wrong she was. Nothing could have kept him away; he saw that now. He was drawn to Beth as if his life depended on it.

And maybe . . . just maybe . . . it did.

"That's where you're wrong Beth. I had to come back. This is too strong between us. I had to find out what was here."

"And . . . ?"

He felt her catch her breath, felt her hold it, as if his answer was important to her.

She loved him. He knew it then. As sure as he knew he loved her, he knew that Beth loved him.

He bent down and kissed her. Not the passion-filled, couldn't-get-enough-of-her kiss his body would demand in a few moments, but a pledging sort of kiss. One that said he cherished her and valued her and would honor her all the days of their lives if she'd let him.

Holy hell. How was he going to pull this off? There was still the circus of his life to contend with. He wasn't naïve enough to think that a declaration of love would make all the problems disappear, but there had to be a way.

Her husband had figured it out. The guy had had to travel a lot as a pilot; he'd left Beth alone with the kids to raise them by herself. To handle all the problems and issues and whatever else came along while he'd been gone, and she'd still loved him enough to be mourning his death two years later. Beth knew how to love that way; it was something Bryan was going to have to learn if he wanted a future with her. Question was, would she want one with him?

"You're thinking again."

"Ah, so now *you* can hear *my* thoughts?" He worked that cocky grin onto his face, needing its cover to shield her from the thoughts filling his mind. Why *would* she want a future with him? She'd already said she couldn't go through a media circus again, and even if he retired today, the press would be after him, wondering *why* he'd retired, what he was going to do next, and was Beth the reason? Then there'd be the stories about her history, and the kids would be dragged through the whole thing all over again. Of *course* she wouldn't want that. Maybe this weekend was all she could handle. Maybe it was all she wanted. A memory-making time together that would have to last the rest of their lives, because getting involved on a permanent basis was too much work.

"Bryan? Are you okay? Do you not want to do this?" Her hands stilled in the small of his back, and Bryan had to pull himself back to the moment.

Stop borrowing trouble. Gran had always said that. Told him he was too introspective at times.

"Of course I want to do this, Beth." He pulled that cocky grin back out, his shield from the world, the one that covered what he was feeling inside and let everyone think he was okay.

And no one had ever figured it out. Not even Gran.

"I don't buy it. You can smile like that at the rest of the world and have them forget what they asked you, but not me. What's going on, Bryan?"

Okay, so Beth was the exception to that rule. Seemed to be a theme where she was concerned.

"Nothing's going on, sweetheart. I just want to kiss you so badly, I'm almost afraid I'll mess it up."

"Mess it up?" Beth shook her head. "How much wine did you have to drink tonight? You couldn't mess this up if you tried."

He was pretty sure he could, which was why he didn't say a thing and let his actions speak for him, cradling her head in his hands and kissing her. A deep, here-I-am sort of kiss that he poured every ounce of emotion he felt into.

He had to smile when she looked at him with glazed eyes and gasping breath and her fingers trembling against his cheek.

"Oh. My. God," she said when she finally caught her breath.

At least one of them was able to speak. Him . . . What he felt for her, the possibilities it held for him . . . He was incapable of speech.

"I guess this means dinner is going to get cold?" She cocked her head to the side and nibbled her bottom lip—on purpose.

"It does, but don't worry. I'll buy you chicken Marsala again tomorrow night."

"What if I want something else instead?" The teasing light in her eyes was just what he needed.

God, he loved her. "I'm counting on it, woman."

Chapter Thirty-seven

❧

SUNDAY afternoon came much too fast.

Bryan sat back against the tree with Beth in his arms as the sights and sounds of the park bustled around them, the remnants of their picnic scattered on the blanket. The half-finished bottle of champagne in the ice bucket he'd brought, the strawberries and chocolate, cheese and grapes . . . All the trappings of a romantic date with one final part burning a hole in his pocket.

Gran's ring.

He'd left Beth's place to pick up breakfast for them while she'd slept this morning—the only reason he'd been able to leave her was because he'd gone home for that ring—and it'd been talking to him all day.

He wanted to marry her. The decision had come to him in his sleep, and when he'd woken up, he'd known it was the right thing to do. They loved each other; he'd seen it in her eyes when they'd made love last night, felt it in every caress. He knew why she hadn't said it, knew that she wouldn't because of his career, and her selflessness made him love her all the more. He *had* to marry her. Had to keep her in his life forever. That was what was important; everything else was just logistics they could work out.

Now he just had to come up with the logistics of asking her to marry him. Something romantic but not cliché.

He had to laugh at himself as he sat on the gingham blanket with a wicker picnic basket, the biggest cliché there was. But it couldn't be helped; he didn't have time to plan some elaborate proposal. He wasn't leaving here to go back on location without knowing Beth was going to be his for the rest of his life. Then he'd head back, work his ass off, and come back to her and the kids as quickly as possible.

"You're thinking again." She ran her palm up his calf.

He threaded his fingers through her hair. "If my thoughts are that loud, maybe you ought to tell me what they are."

She sighed and leaned back against his shoulder. "I don't want to think about what you're thinking. I don't want to think at all because if I do, I'm going to realize that this is almost over. That my kids will be back soon and you'll have to go back to your movie and all of this will be just a memory."

Her words were like a stake to his heart. He didn't want it to be a memory—unless it was one they'd share with their grandchildren.

"Beth."

She twisted around and put her fingers on his lips. "Don't, Bryan. Let's enjoy the fantasy a little longer."

He kissed her fingers. "Actually, that's exactly what I'm trying to do."

She pulled her fingers away. "Oh?"

He moved around on the blanket, trying to keep her close, get the ring, and not give the whole thing away before he could ask her.

"Bryan, what are you doing?"

"This." He pulled out the ring and held it up. "Beth, I love you and I want you in my life forever." He swallowed a ball of emotion. "As my wife."

"Oh my God." Beth touched the ring with trembling fingers.

But she didn't take it.

"I love you, Beth." His voice was as shaky as her fingers. "Will you marry me?"

She looked at him, tears welling in her eyes. "Oh, Bryan."

She still hadn't taken the ring. And she still hadn't answered him.

"Mommy!"

It took Bryan a second longer than it took Beth to recognize Maggie's voice and he barely got the ring into his pocket before Maggie leapt onto her mother.

"Mommy! I missed you!" Maggie's little face was all scrunched up as she hugged Beth with everything in her.

Bryan could so relate.

"Bryan!"

"Hey, Bryan's back!"

Tommy and Mark launched themselves onto him and all of a sudden the picnic blanket was covered with Hamiltons.

And their mother still hadn't answered him.

"What are you doing here, Bryan?"

"Are you back for good?"

"Did you miss me?"

"Was Sherman surprised to see you?"

"Did you clean Mrs. Beecham's hair out of my dollhouse? I think she's making a nest in there."

"Cats don't make nests, stupid."

"Don't call me stupid."

"Well you are if you think cats make nests."

"Mommy, Mark called me stupid."

"Well she is!"

"Guys! Maggie!" Bryan got to his feet. "No one's stupid just because they don't know something. It's an opportunity to learn something, and an opportunity for you guys to be big brothers and teach your sister something new."

He reached down to help Beth stand, ironically holding her left hand. The one where he wanted to put his ring.

She still hadn't answered him.

And she didn't for the next three and a half hours until they got the kids in bed, the grandparents gone, and an awkward silence waltzed into the family room when Beth came down from her last hug from Maggie.

"She said she was scared I wasn't going to be here when she got home." Beth grabbed a throw pillow from the sofa and wrapped her arms around it as she sat cross-legged in the corner of it.

"Separation anxiety?"

"Yeah. They all have it, but Maggie's the most vocal. The

twins actually climbed into the same bed when I was reading the nightly comic book. That started right after Mike died and had let up, I thought, about four months ago."

"And now they're doing it again."

"Well, at least for tonight."

And what if she married him and the media frenzy did this to them as well? She didn't have to say it, but it was floating between them like a big giant blob of ain't-gonna-happen-Manley.

"You haven't answered my question." Just call him a glutton for punishment. But if this was the end of his dream, he wanted it spelled out for him.

"I know."

"And?" The fact that he had to prod her like this didn't bode well.

Neither did the big breath she took nor the way she turned to face him with the pillow clutched to her abdomen. Protective. Alone.

"I want to say yes, Bryan, but I can't."

There was a buzzing in his head; he hadn't really believed she'd say no. He'd known there would be issues, but he'd expected a compromise of some sort. Maybe even talk about him getting out of the industry. But he'd never really believed that the only woman he'd ever wanted to marry would turn him down.

". . . just me, I'd take the chance, but the kids, Bryan."

"*Chance*? Take the *chance*?" Bryan leaned forward. "I didn't ask you to take a *chance* on me, Beth. I asked you to *marry* me. I'm not taking a chance on you; I want to spend my life with you. I want to be part of your family. I'm not taking a chance like . . . like . . . some poker game. I'm dead serious about this and yeah, you're right. If you're seeing it as taking a chance, then maybe this isn't a good idea."

She put her hand on his knee and he wanted to yank it off because it was too painful to have her touch him and know that he wouldn't have the right to do this when he left here.

"You weren't listening to me. "

"I heard you."

"No, you heard part of what I said." She put the pillow aside. "I want to say yes, Bryan. I do. And if it were just me, I'd do it in a heartbeat. Because I love you."

"I know you do. You wouldn't have made love with me last night if you didn't. So why are you saying no? You do realize you're the only woman I've ever asked this?"

Adding insult to injury, she put her palm on his cheek. And he let her.

"I know. And I love that you did, but your life, Bryan . . . We've talked about this. I can't subject the kids to it. They've lived in the spotlight and they didn't handle it well. Maggie still has nightmares."

Bryan closed his eyes for a second, willing himself to calm down. He had to think of the kids. As a parent, even a stepparent, he had to think of the kids' well-being. "You haven't mentioned any since I've been here."

"Bryan, it's only been a few weeks."

"That she hasn't had any. Since I've been here, right?"

"Well, no, but—"

"No buts, Beth. Maybe she's stopped having them because she wants me in her life."

"Oh she wants you. They all want you. They love you. But they don't really realize what your lifestyle entails. I, however, do. I've been down that road. Every move scrutinized. Every word commented on and analyzed and perhaps twisted in a completely different meaning because it makes good copy. I can't tell you how many times I had to turn off the television when a news report would come in or a sighting of my kids would happen and they'd be plastered all over the screen. You might have thought Mike had robbed Ft. Knox or had downed a keg before getting on that plane with all the coverage of the accident. Everywhere we turned, there were cameras. And your life *invites* cameras. The kids don't understand that, but as their parent, I have to."

"But maybe it'll be different now that I'm in the picture."

"You being in *our* picture isn't the problem. It's the *other* picture you're in that will be the issue."

"So I'll quit." And damn if he didn't mean it. Beth and the kids were more important to him than any movie.

"That'll only make the situation worse. The media will jump all over it."

"Okay, so I'll finish this picture and then that'll be it. I'll retire."

She cocked her head and where he used to find it cute, now he didn't. Now he wanted her to go along with him and see his reasoning, not argue with him.

"Bryan, they're not going to let you go. You retiring will be big news. And the reason you retired will be *bigger* news. We aren't going to be able to avoid the spotlight if I say yes to you."

She was right and this wasn't an argument he hadn't thought of himself, but dammit, why did it have to be one or the other? Why couldn't they compromise and work something out? She loved him, he loved her, the kids liked him, and God knew he loved them . . . This couldn't be the end.

"The constant limelight isn't fair to the kids, Bryan. It's bad enough navigating adolescence with Twitter and Facebook, and heaven forbid if they do something careless online and the press gets wind of it. Things we did as kids that weren't recorded for posterity on YouTube. I can't risk it, Bryan. I've finally gotten them to this place; being engaged to you could send us right back to square one."

She was right; he knew it. The constant spotlight could be hard to deal with—and *he'd* sought it out. The kids, on the other hand . . . Beth was an amazing mother to put her children's needs ahead of hers—and that only made him love her more.

It also made him do the same thing because he loved them, too. "Maybe when they're older—"

"You're going to wait until Maggie turns eighteen? That's thirteen years from now, Bryan. I'm not going to let you do that. You deserve to have a family. Kids. A wife who can give you all of that without all the baggage I carry. I can't be that woman for you."

Her voice broke, the first sign that she wasn't as resolute in her decision as she was trying to make it seem.

This was as hard for her as it was for him. There ought to be some comfort in that . . . but there wasn't. There wasn't anything comforting about this entire situation.

Bryan pulled her into his arms. "I'm not going to apologize for asking you, Beth."

"I don't want you to. I love you, Bryan. But I can't marry you, and you'll never know just how sorry I am to have to say that."

"Oh, I think I have a fairly good idea." He kissed her temple and rested his chin on her head. "This isn't a one-and-done offer, you know."

She stiffened. "Please, Bryan, don't get your hopes up. It's just not feasible. My kids have been through enough. As much as they like you, the fishbowl will get to them. We've already lived it; we know."

"I hate that you do."

"I know."

"I hate that my career is going to be the thing that comes between us."

"Me, too."

"But there's no way around it, is there?"

"I can't think of one."

"I love you, Beth."

She squeezed him tight. "I love you, too. Thank you for this weekend. For the memories. For making me *feel* again. For loving me."

"Always, Beth. Always." Three words. That was all he was capable of because tears were threatening to choke him.

Dammit. Life had been just fine when he'd thought he'd had everything he wanted. Now that he knew he didn't—and that he *couldn't*—he was going to have to adjust. Make some changes. Find something to fill the void. Not *someone* because no one could take Beth's place in his heart. He just hoped that someday there'd be room in it for someone else. And five different kids . . .

"Mommy? Where are you?" Maggie hopped down the front stairs. The stairs he and Beth had . . .

He pulled away from Beth. It'd be okay for Maggie to see them like that if they were going to move forward as a couple, but since they weren't . . .

"I can't sleep." Maggie appeared in the doorway in her nightgown, her curls all fuzzy around her head, and her thumb half in her mouth. "Bryan!" The thumb came out. "You're still here!"

"Hi, Mags." He held open his arms. One last hug. That's all he wanted from her.

She flew into his arms and clung to him fiercely. "I thought you left."

One hug wasn't going to cut it. Bryan cleared his throat. "No, sweetheart. I'm still here."

"What are we going to do tomorrow?"

He looked at Beth over Maggie's head. *Help me out here*, he mouthed because he honestly didn't have a clue what to say to the little girl.

Beth took her daughter from his arms and, honestly, it felt as if she ripped his heart right along with it.

How the hell was he supposed to walk away?

"Bryan has other plans tomorrow." Beth settled Maggie on her lap.

Maggie's head whipped around fast. "You do? What?"

"Um, well, I'm going to help my brother find something in the house where he's working."

"Find what?"

"I'm not quite sure. We have to follow a bunch of clues."

"Like a scavenger hunt?"

"Um, yeah. Something like that." At least that's what Sean had said it was. Among a good three dozen curse words he'd thrown in for good measure. He and Liam had volunteered to help if only to stop their ears from burning. Sean had gotten pretty inventive with the curses.

"I'm really good at scavenger hunts. So are Mark and Tommy." Her big brown eyes—so like her mother's—blinked at him in such innocence. Too bad he'd seen her in action and knew exactly what she was up to.

The thing was he didn't mind that she was trying to play him. He *wanted* to take her and the boys along. He liked being with them. And, hell, the more eyes the merrier at the mansion if what Sean had said was true. They were going to need all the help they could get.

"Sweetheart, Bryan has to work quickly so he can get back to his movie. He can't be watching you and the boys."

"But Mommy," Maggie huffed with all the self-righteousness a five-year-old could muster, "that's why we *hafta* go. We can help and Bryan can go back to his movie really quick." She looked at Bryan and put her hand on his knee. "Please can we come with you, Bryan? We're good helpers. Just like with the clothesline. We can help you."

How was he supposed to say no to that? He couldn't. "I'm okay with it if your mom is, Maggie."

Probably not fair to turn it back onto Beth, but he just couldn't tell Maggie no. He just couldn't.

The look Beth sent him over Maggie's head said she couldn't either and had been hoping he would've.

"Okay, Maggie. Fine." Beth exhaled. "You three can go. But only for a little while. The Martinson mansion is a very big place and I don't want you running around unsupervised."

"What's unsuperwized?" Maggie's thumb went back in her mouth as if she'd gotten what she'd come to do and anything else was just marking time until she got back to her room.

"It means without someone watching out for you."

"But Bryan always watches out for us. Don't you, Bryan?"

Seriously, the little girl was better than a surgeon when it came to eviscerating him.

"That's right, Maggie. I'm always watching out for you guys."

"See, Mommy? Bryan's gonna take care of us. You don't have to worry."

Out of the mouths of babes . . .

Chapter Thirty-eight

❧❦❧

BETH worried the entire next day. She worried she'd break out into tears, or that she'd tell Jason and Kelsey all about Bryan's proposal, or worse, she'd tell *Kara* all about Bryan's proposal and then it'd be all over the neighborhood in no time and once that happened, the media wouldn't be far behind.

So she kept her mouth shut, the tears at bay—barely—and went about her normal day as if her heart weren't breaking because a great man would soon be flying out of her life. Again.

He saved her the heartache of saying good-bye. She wouldn't have been able to fake her way through that, so she was thankful that he'd let the younger three off in the driveway from their scavenger hunt day, waved briefly, and backed out as if he'd be back tomorrow.

They'd both known better.

So here it was, Day One of The Rest Of Her Life Without Bryan, and Kara just couldn't let the man go in peace.

"I honestly can't believe he just left. I thought *for sure* there was something happening between you two."

Beth made a pretense of sniffing the perfume at the department store counter. She had zero interest in shopping today, but there was a petting zoo at the mall and the younger three had been begging to go. She was paying Jason and Kelsey to watch them, so she could have some peace and quiet *she'd thought*. But then she'd run into Kara and once *she'd* realized Beth didn't have the kids with her, well, that was permission to open the floodgates with questions about Bryan.

"He has a career, Kara. I told you that. You can't commute to Hollywood from here."

"Bull. Movie stars do it all the time. They buy private planes and fly in for a day of filming. He could do it if he wanted."

The thing was, he would do it if Beth had said yes. She knew that as surely as she knew Kara would blab to everyone if she told her about the proposal. So she said nothing on both counts and tried to let the matter rest, because, really, she needed it to. She'd been second-guessing her answer for the past forty-some hours and she wasn't any closer to a resolution than she'd been when she'd answered him.

"And you guys could go on location with him. I mean, it *is* summer. The kids don't have school or jobs and you're a teacher, so you're free . . . I just didn't think he was that fickle. I thought he had some substance to him. That he wasn't all Hollywood. God, you don't think he was laughing at us, do you? Using us for research for his next role?"

"Bryan's not like that. He liked everyone." Loved a few of them, actually. "But it's his career. Can't argue with success."

Kara shrugged. "I just don't get it. I mean, you're hot, the kids are great, and it's not as if you're after his money. Mike left you guys in good shape."

If one could call being widowed and fatherless good shape.

Beth bit back the sarcasm. Kara meant well. All her friends did, but they all figured that two years was long enough and time to move on. And while Beth was ready to move on—her time with Bryan proving that—she wasn't just going to forget Mike. She wasn't going to say, "oh well, onward and upward." She'd loved him and she would always miss him. He was her friend and her husband and her lover and the father of her children. She ached that he'd never see them grow up, never know their grandchildren. That her kids would never know Mike as a man when they became adults. Death sucked and there wasn't a damn thing Beth could do about it.

But you could do something about Bryan . . .

"So do you think you might be ready to date someone else?"

"Someone else? I wasn't dating Bryan, Kar."

"I know, but I mean, you know. You kind of got back in the saddle again, as it were, if only looking. And he was nice to look at, you have to admit."

"Yes, he is." He'd been great in the saddle, too, but she wasn't going to admit that.

"So if another good-looking guy came along, you wouldn't be opposed to going out with him."

"Kara, you've already set me up on a few blind dates. They haven't worked out so well. That last one didn't, either. Why don't we just leave it to fate and see what happens?"

"That's all fine and good, but I don't see you making plans to go barhopping with fate any time soon."

Barhopping. Beth shuddered. She was not going barhopping with anyone. "I don't want to date that badly, thankyouvery-much."

"Well where else are you going to meet someone?"

"Why do I have to? I'm doing just fine as I am."

"Bull. You've been alone too long and I saw how you looked at Bryan. You're coming out of your shell, Beth. You need to strike while the iron is hot before you get too comfortable inside it."

Beth gave up trying to hide her shudders. She was so not ready to do the singles' scene. Doubted she ever would be.

Luckily, there was a commotion outside the store as a bunch of security guards went running by, shouting, batons waving, and Beth didn't have to respond to Kara. Then a mall-wide alarm went off and Beth wasn't so thankful anymore. Her kids were out there.

She ran out of the store and hung a right for the petting zoo—which was the direction the guards were running.

It was also where the guards were stopped. And where they had a guy facedown on the floor, arms behind his back, a couple of knees holding him in place and two of them talking to . . . her kids.

Oh God.

Beth pushed her way through the crowd of people gathered around. "Jason! Kelsey! Tommy! Mark! Maggie!" They were all there, looking solemn while they answered the guards' questions.

"Hello. I'm the children's mother. What happened?" She had to touch each one, herding them around her like a mother duck pulling them under her wings and she didn't care. She had to make sure her babies were safe.

"Your kids did a great thing, ma'am," said one of the guards. Hinkle it said on his name plate. "They saw this guy with a hammer—"

"He was gonna smash the jewelry case, Mommy!" Maggie hopped up and down. "Tommy saw it and told Jason and Kelsey. Kelsey ran to the formation boof, and Jason stuck his foot out so the guy tripped. He's a hero!"

"I saw it, too!" said Mark, unhappy at not playing a part in Maggie's narration.

"Did not!" said Tommy. Of course.

"Yuh-huh. That's why I poked you so you could see it, too."

"Did not!"

"Did too!"

"Boys, that's not important right now," said the guard, herding them away from the guy on the floor. "We need you to stand back so we can get him to his feet."

Yes, it *was* important and their faces fell when the guard dismissed them so out of hand. Right now, it was the most important thing in their world and for him to push it aside like that . . . Bryan wouldn't have done that.

Bryan. God, she couldn't stop thinking about him.

"Ma'am," said another guard, "if you and the kids could step over to the teddy bear shop, we'd like to ask you a few questions."

"But Mommy doesn't know anything. She didn't see. Me and Tommy saw."

"And Jason," piped in Maggie. "Don't forget Jason. He's the real hero."

Beth shuffled the kids to the store, running her hands over everyone's shoulders. "Jason, are you okay?" She wanted to yell at him that he could've been hurt and he should have stayed out of the way and let someone else handle it—the same words she'd said to Mike the morning he'd picked up that damn flight at the last minute—but she didn't because of the look of pride on his face. Jason was actually smiling at people and feeling really good about himself and Beth wasn't going to ruin that for him for a second. Still, dear God . . . he could have been hurt.

"Yeah, Mom, I'm fine. Guy shoulda looked where he was going."

"He was," said Tommy. "He was looking at the watches."

"Nuh-uh. It was the diamond rings. Those are easier to carry and they cost a lot more."

"You think you know everything."

"I know a lot more than you do, Tommy."

"Do not."

"Do too."

"Boys." She mimicked Bryan's action and put her hands on their heads and turned them to look at her. "Let's stop the bickering. Just tell the guards the truth and we can go home."

"But I don't want to go home." Maggie tugged on Beth's shirt. "I want to play with the baby goats."

"They're called kids," said Tommy.

"Hey, they are. You did know that." Mark was looking surprised. Beth didn't know why; they'd been in the same classes since kindergarten.

"They are? That's a silly name." Maggie slid her hand into Tommy's. "Thanks for teaching me that. Just like Bryan said."

"We should call him." This from Kelsey. Why was Beth not surprised that that was the first part of this whole episode Kelsey would comment on? "Tell him what we did."

"You mean, what *Jason* did," said Maggie, now moving her hand and her allegiance to her eldest brother.

"I helped. I ran to call the security guards."

Maggie scrunched her face and tapped her lip. "You're right. You did. That was important, too." She reached for Kelsey's hand. "I have the bravest brothers and sister in the whole world."

Of course that would be when the guard started asking Beth questions. She could barely concentrate on what he was asking her as she tried not to cry at all her emotions: fear, pride, love, and a melting heart to see her children banding together.

And then a reporter showed up, sticking the microphone

over top of the guard's head. Beth was pretty sure that violated all sorts of rules and might even have an impact on any trial—

Oh hell. A trial. As witnesses, her kids would have to testify. And Jason had tripped the guy—he'd be star witness number one.

Oh God. The press was going to be all over this.

There was a loud ringing in her ears as all of the ramifications registered. What was about to descend upon them. All over again. The invasive questions. The never-ending interest. Camera crews and news vans staking out her home.

Beth wanted to cry. She'd said no to Bryan's fishbowl and ended up with one of her own.

It took an hour and a half and giving out her cell phone to six different people before she could get the kids out of there. It took another forty-five minutes for them to talk it out of their systems enough so that she could get a word in edgewise. Just two, but they had the effect she wanted. "Ice cream?"

The conversation changed to flavors and Beth could finally take a breath. She was going to have to talk to Jason and Kelsey. Warn them about the press. The twins, too. Only Maggie hadn't been part of the thwarted robbery attempt, but with the way Maggie was championing each one of her siblings, Beth had a feeling she needed to warn her, too. She wasn't looking forward to it.

S HE shouldn't have worried.
      And that worried her.

They no sooner sat down at the ice cream parlor booth when the topic came up all over again. By now, Beth had the sequence of events memorized, so she wasn't surprised when the kids veered slightly off topic.

"So do you think they're going to want to interview us again?" Kelsey was the one to broach the subject Beth had been dreading.

"Well, they might, honey, but you don't have to tell them anything else. You guys are all minors, so, technically, they need to go through me. I'll keep them as far away as I can."

"But I want to talk to them. We're going to be famous."

"We are?" asked the twins. "Cool!" They high-fived each other.

They were talking in unison again.

"I bet they give you a medal, Jason," said Maggie, her brother's biggest fan.

"Nah, no one gets medals anymore." But Jason didn't look like he'd hate the idea.

"Maybe even your own TV show!" Maggie was bouncing in her seat. "Like a kid detective who stops robbers before they can steal anything. Wouldn't that be cool?"

"And Bryan can play your boss or something," said Mark.

"Yeah, then we could see him again," added Tommy.

"Mommy, when is Bryan coming back? I want to tell him all about my brothers and sister. They're heroes." Maggie turned that earnest face Beth's way and the other four followed.

"I . . . I don't know, Mags."

Liar! Tell your kids the truth. That you turned him down to keep them from being in the spotlight and look at them now! Anxious to be on TV. Thrilled to be heroes. You might want to re-think your decision, Elizabeth.

"Can we call him?" Kelsey pulled out her phone. "Oh. Right. He didn't give me his number." She looked at Beth. "Did he give you his number, Mom? Or should I call the maid company and ask them?"

Five expectant, hopeful faces stared at her. Five kids who wanted to see the man Beth had sent away. The man who said he loved her and wanted to marry her. Who wanted to have a family with her. *This* family.

"Um, guys. I have a better idea. How'd you like to go *see* Bryan?"

Chapter Thirty-nine

❧❧❧

"CUT!" PJ blew out a big, frustrated breath.

Number four hundred and seventy-two if Bryan's count was right.

It was close if not right on. This scene was going to hell with every line. Carina just didn't want to follow the script. If she weren't such a big name actress, she would've been out on the street at five after eight this morning, after the fifth take.

"Carina." PJ's fabled "cool" had disappeared. "I'm not changing the dialogue, so you can do it my way or we're here 'til midnight; I don't care at this point. I *will* bring this film in on schedule, so get off your high horse and do the scene as it's written."

"It makes my character sound like a wimp."

"No, it doesn't. It makes her willing to compromise." Something Carina obviously knew nothing about. "And that's who the audience is going to root for, so if you want an adoring public, you'll do it the way it's written. And if you want to work again, you'll do what I say."

Ouch. Not good. Bryan braced himself for the impact.

It wasn't long in coming.

"I don't need you, PJ Cartwright." Carina tossed the knife

she'd been holding into the kitchen sink with a reverberating *clang*. PJ should count his lucky stars she hadn't flung it at him. Even if it was a prop knife, that tip was pointed. "You think *you're* the one people are coming to see when they go to the movies? Most people have no clue who the director is. They know who the stars are, and I'm the star of this movie."

Bryan refrained from raising his hand and reminding her he was here, but only because he felt bad for PJ. The guy had enough of a headache with Carina on a good day; Bryan didn't want to add to the problem. But, oh, what he wouldn't give to take Carina down a peg or two and remind her that *he* was getting a ton of hype for being the love interest of this film. That this script was his vehicle to stardom and everyone knew it. He had as much name recognition as she did when it came to this movie, so she'd better get her act together because there was another name here and losing her might not be what it would have been on her other films.

Nah, he'd keep that little tidbit to himself. No need to poke the sleeping lion.

Who was now roaring.

"I will *not* stand for this." She held out her hand to her assistant. "I'm calling my agent."

The poor kid who'd probably thought she'd hit the lottery when she'd been hired as Carina Dempsey's assistant had to run after her to hand her the phone.

Silence descended on the set, everyone looking at PJ.

"Fine. Great. Whatever." He adjusted his baseball cap. "Everyone take a break. Be back in two hours. We finish this tonight."

Bryan rubbed the back of his neck as he got off the damn bar stool he'd been perched on for the last fifteen takes. His ass hurt, but he'd rub it in private. He didn't need anyone tweeting *that* picture.

He nodded to Josh. "I'll be in my trailer if things move any faster."

"Sounds good. Oh, and you've got some visitors. I was gonna tell you when we wrapped the scene."

Visitors? Who would be visiting him on set?

For a second, his heart—and his imagination—leapt, thinking, praying, and hoping that it was Beth, but he tucked that away quickly. Probably Liam. It'd better not be Sean. He had a scavenger hunt to win if they had a prayer of recouping their investment in that property he was working.

Maybe it was his agent. Or his publicist. Or maybe both. They didn't have a meeting planned, but who knew? Maybe there was some big news about his career that Don wanted to tell him in person.

He grabbed a water bottle on his way off the set and downed it. The lights were hot, and he had a couple of long monologues in this scene. Of course Carina wasn't happy with that, either. He thought line counting disappeared when you started making millions, but apparently not in Carina's case.

Bryan shrugged and twisted the cap back onto the empty bottle and tossed it into the trashcan as he walked by.

"Two points, Manley!" one of the boom operators hollered.

He smiled and gave the guy—Rick—a thumb's up. Too bad Carina didn't get that camaraderie was good on a set.

No, she was still working on getting him into bed. Bryan had had to call it an early night since arriving back here just to avoid having to turn her down again. He didn't want to have to tell her that she just didn't do it for him.

He shook his head as he walked up to his trailer. He had a feeling that no woman would do it for him again for a long time. If ever.

He reached for the door knob. Not after—

Beth.

She was standing there. In his trailer. At the top of the steps. Bryan did a double take. Twice.

"Hi, Bryan."

It was definitely Beth.

"Hi, Bryan!"

And the kids.

"Woof!"

And Sherman.

Bryan grabbed the railing to stay upright while he tried to process the fact that the six people he most wanted to see in the world were in his trailer. And he wasn't even upset at seeing the dog.

"Uh, hi, guys."

"I'm not a guy, silly!" Maggie poked her curly-topped head

up over the stairwell, her impish smile and sparkling eyes making him laugh.

"No, Mags, you're definitely not a guy." He ruffled her curls and managed to get himself up the rest of the steps on wobbly legs. "What are you doing here?" He was looking at all of them, but that question was directed solely at Beth.

The five kids all started talking at once. Something about the mall and the zoo and a hammer and jewelry and . . . guards?

He looked at Beth. "What are they talking about?"

In a calm voice that he *knew* was put on for the kids' benefit, because he could see just how much the story she told him upset her, Beth told him about the attempted robbery and the kids' heroics.

"And we wanted to come tell you all about it because you're working and can't come home to hear it," said Maggie, climbing onto his lap when he sat at the table.

Home. He doubted she or any of the kids heard that slip up, but he had. And so had Beth.

He wanted to ask Beth what this was about. Why she was here. Why she'd prolong the agony. A clean break; that's what they needed.

But maybe she hadn't told the kids about his proposal—which would make sense—and she'd come here for the kids' sake. They were certainly excited to tell him all about it, and he made as much of a fuss as was warranted, pleased to see Jason's pride in himself, and Kelsey beaming when her part was told, and the twins saying how they'd worked together to alert Jason and Kelsey, and Maggie's pride in her siblings.

Sherman nudged his way under Bryan's arm and crawled onto his lap with Maggie.

"Do you think they're gonna give Jason a medal?" asked Maggie. "I want them to give him a TV show. And you could act in it, too."

"If they don't give him a medal, they should." Bryan nodded at Jason. "That was a really brave thing you did. Not many people would get involved like that. I'm proud of you." Yeah, his eyes got misty as he said it. He had no right to be proud of the kid, but he was.

And if Jason's widening smile was anything to go by, he was glad that he was.

"So can we go celebrate?" Mark crawled around the curved bench seat on his knees and put his hand on Bryan's shoulder? "Mom said our catching the bad guy was cause for a celebration."

"We already had ice cream," said Tommy.

"Yeah, but that's not a *real* celebration. Real celebrations have fireworks and salutes and parades and stuff."

"There's no parade around here. We should have stayed home if they were going to give us a parade."

"I'd like to be in a parade. Like Miss America. I could wear a crown and a sash and wave to everybody." Maggie practiced blowing kisses right there in his trailer, cracking all of them up.

"Well I don't know about any parades or fireworks, but we could go out to dinner and see what kind of a special dessert they might have for heroes. What do you say?" This time he avoided looking at Beth. She'd brought the kids here; he was going to spend as much time with them as possible. As much time with *Beth* as possible.

"Yay! I like celebrations!" Maggie jumped off his lap, Sherman following. "But what are we going to do about Sherman? He can't go to a restaurant."

"No worries. I know someone who'll be happy to keep Sherman company." He sent Josh a text, smiling when he got the high-sign. Best couple hundred bucks he'd ever spent.

He texted PJ next. Hell, if Carina could blow the schedule to hell, he wasn't going to sit around waiting for her to show up. He told PJ to text him when Carina was in working form and he'd be back. They couldn't go far, but then, the couple thousand he was about to spend at the first restaurant he came across for a sparkler-infested, chocolate lava mountain dessert, slathered in whipped cream and ice cream, would make whatever they ate the perfect celebration.

BETH was having a hard time keeping it together. She'd been wrong. So wrong. This was what her kids needed. Bryan was what they needed. The sense of family. The shock of Mike's death had been what'd spun them all out of control, not necessarily the press coverage. Sure, that hadn't helped, but when she'd seen the way they reacted to the positive attention after the robbery . . .

"We need to talk." Bryan whispered it in her ear as a giant plate of sparklers arrived at their table.

"Lava cake!" screamed the twins.

"Ice cream!" No surprise that came from Maggie.

Jason and Kelsey were trying to look cool instead of impressed at the monstrous dessert, and Bryan was looking awfully proud of himself.

Or maybe he was just deliriously happy. She hoped that was the case.

She nodded but had no clue when they'd talk. With five kids around—in his trailer—privacy was going to be difficult.

Intimacy, impossible . . .

Beth couldn't stop the blush. Yes, she'd been thinking of her kids when deciding to bring them here, but she hadn't been able to stop that sliver of awareness when she'd realized that if this worked between her and Bryan, if he was willing to take them all on after she'd turned him down, she would be able to make love with him for the rest of her life.

God, please let him say yes.

The cake was—no surprise—a big hit, and the kids debated the best part of it on the walk back to the car.

That was about the only chance for privacy they were going to have, so Beth tugged on Bryan's arm and they hung back from the kids.

"Um, Bryan?"

He put his hand over hers. "Yes?"

"I hope you don't mind us showing up."

"You know I don't. I love seeing the kids. But I am wondering why. I thought everything was decided when I left."

She bit her lip. He loved seeing the kids, but he didn't say anything about seeing her. That didn't sound like he'd want her to change her mind.

"What about Sherman?"

"What about him?"

"Do you mind that we brought him?"

"No."

"I couldn't find anyone to take him on such short notice and the vet was closed for the night."

"It's not a problem, Beth. Sherman's just as welcome as the rest of you."

Okay, that sounded a little more positive.

Up ahead, Maggie squealed and wiggled off Jason's hip. Thankfully, Kelsey grabbed her hand before she went running into the parking lot.

Beth didn't have a lot of time.

"So, um . . ." She tucked her hair behind her ears and took a deep breath. Bryan was looking at her expectantly. "That question you asked me the other night?"

"Yeah?"

"What if . . ." She took another deep breath. God, was this what it'd felt like for him to ask her to marry him? And she'd turned him down? She was an idiot. "What if I want to change my answer? Can I?"

"Change your answer?"

She couldn't tell if he was mocking her or trying to understand what she was asking.

She was going with the latter only because the former was too painful to contemplate. "Yes. What if I wanted to say yes?"

Oh, no. He hadn't been confused. He'd known exactly what she'd been asking.

"Is that what you *want* to do, Beth?"

God, yes, it was. "I do."

Bryan stopped walking. He took her hand off his arm—she hadn't even realized it was still there—and brought it to his lips. He kissed it. "Those are the two sweetest words in the English language, Beth."

Her breath caught. He wasn't telling her to get lost.

"Want to know what the *three* sweetest ones are?"

She nodded—because she couldn't speak—but she already knew. She just wanted to hear him say them. Again.

Bryan kissed the third finger on her left hand. "I love you."

Her breath hitched and she managed to say the same thing back to him. "I love you, Bryan."

"And I love Bryan, too," said Maggie who'd somehow managed to sneak up on them. "Does this mean you're gonna get married, Mommy?"

Jason came running over, shooting a look at Bryan. A very grown-up, manly look as he scooped up his baby sister again.

"Of course it does, runt. That's what people do when they love each other."

"Good, then I'm gonna marry Bryan, 'cause I love him, too."

"Silly girl," said Mark, shaking his head.

"Yeah, you can't marry him if he's gonna marry Mom."

"I can, too."

"Cannot."

"Can too."

"Cannot."

For the first time, Bryan didn't step in and shut down the argument. No, this time, he stepped in and kissed her. Right there, in front of her kids and everyone in the parking lot and whatever cameras people had on them. This would be all over the internet in seconds.

But Beth didn't care. This was what she wanted.

And it was what they all needed.

Epilogue

❧✦❧

"THREE fours beat two aces, Maggie."

"They do not."

"Do too."

"Do not."

"Do too."

"I'm going to go ask Daddy." Maggie huffed herself to her feet and stomped off in the direction of the backyard where Bryan was reinforcing the fencing yet again. Sherman was turning into quite the little tunnel digger, and Bryan was seriously considering having a cement wall put in, three feet into the ground.

Beth wasn't sure that'd be deep enough for Sherman. Especially since the Chihuahua had moved in next door.

"Mom, Maggie's wrong, right?" asked Tommy. "Bryan said fours beat aces if you have more of them."

"And when was Bryan teaching you to play poker?" Hmmm . . . Bryan was an awesome stepdad, but she was going to have to go over some of the finer points of parenting. Like no gambling under the age of twenty-one.

"He didn't teach us. We were watching when he played with Uncle Sean and Uncle Liam. Maggie listened in."

Ah, yes, the monthly poker game. She was going to have to rethink bringing the kids if all they were doing was spying on the guys. But it was nice getting together with her sisters-in-law and Gran.

Beth smiled and patted her belly. She couldn't wait to share her news with all of them. Especially Bryan. Seven months from now, he'd finally have his own child to love.

Not that he'd love hers any less. And, really, they weren't just hers any longer. They were Manleys even if they didn't have that name.

Though Bryan had said something the other night . . .

She looked at Mike's picture on the mantel and felt that familiar pain wash over her that he wasn't here to see his kids grow up.

She walked over to his picture and pressed a kiss to her fingers that she then pressed to his lips. She still missed him but was moving forward. It's what he would have wanted. She just couldn't believe she'd been blessed twice in one lifetime to love and be loved by two such wonderful men.

The sliding door opened in the kitchen. Beth spun around. Bryan wouldn't mind seeing her at Mike's picture—after all, he'd insisted that the mantel stay just as it was for the kids' sake. "I don't want them to forget their father. If it were me, I'd be devastated. I'm fine having him there. The kids should know their dad."

She'd loved him more for saying that and she had a feeling that'd been the night this little one had been conceived.

She hurried back into the kitchen.

Bryan put his hands in the air. "I swear. I didn't teach them to play poker. I know better."

"I know you do, honey." She wrapped her arms around him, not caring that he was all hot and sweaty. "They were spying on you and your brothers."

Bryan chuckled and linked his arms low on her back. "Of course they were. I'd expect nothing less of Mark and Tommy."

"Actually, it was Maggie. She taught *them*."

Now he went to full-on laughing. "God, that kid's a riot. It's a good thing there's only one of her. I don't know what we'd do if there were more."

"Um . . ." Beth nibbled her bottom lip and looked up at him.

"Um, what?" His gorgeous green eyes narrowed.

"Um, this." She took his hand and slid it to her belly.

Those gorgeous green eyes got very wide. "Beth . . . Are you saying . . . Do you mean . . . ?"

She nodded, feeling the tears fill her eyes. She'd always been an emotional hormonal wreck with the other pregnancies. "I do."

"Oh God, baby. I love you."

The sweetest two- and three-word phrases in the world.

TURN THE PAGE FOR A SNEAK PEEK AT
THE NEXT MANLEY MAIDS NOVEL

What a Woman Gets

*COMING IN NOVEMBER 2014 FROM
BERKLEY SENSATION*

Guys' Night . . . Plus One

❦

BELIEVE, dear brothers, you all need to be fitted for Manley Maids uniforms."

Liam Manley bit his tongue at his sister Mac's announcement as she laid her winning hand on the green felt poker table. She'd played him—him *and* his brothers, and she'd played them good.

She'd played *poker* good. Who knew she even *played* poker?

And that bet . . . Four weeks' worth of free cleaning service for her company against their vacation homes and expensive sports cars. Why did Liam feel like a sucker?

"I am *not* wearing an apron." Bryan, the youngest Manley brother, sounded so offended it made Liam bite his tongue even harder—this time so he wouldn't laugh. You'd think Mac had asked them to wear . . . well . . . an apron.

Sean, his middle brother and fellow loser, kept stacking the poker chips, avoiding Mac's jack-high straight flush like the plague while keeping his mouth shut.

Bryan's mouth was hanging open. His movie-star brother was gaping like a fish. Where was a camera when he needed one? Bry would pay anything to keep *that* unflattering picture out of the press, and Liam could use a new hot tub for the house he was renovating—make that, had just *finished* renovating, which meant he had some time on his hands.

No time like the present to get started paying off the ridiculous bet. "When do you want us to start, Mac?"

"I have extra uniforms, so whenever you have the time."

Extra uniforms? Since when did she have extra anything when it came to the business?

Something was going on.

He never would have thought Mary-Alice Catherine would resort to dirty tricks to get her older brothers to do what she wanted. Hell, when they'd gone to live with Gran after their parents had been killed in a car accident, they'd practically tripped over each other to take care of their baby sister. Now he was going to be tripping over brooms and mops and vacuum cleaners. Ugh.

"Hey, can I do my own house?" That was Bryan, working whatever angle he could to come out on top.

"You'd put Monica out of a job to weasel out of the bet? Really?" It was Mac's turn for mouth-gaping.

"I'm not weaseling out of anything." But Bry didn't look happy. "You can count on me for Monday, too. I've got a month between projects and was looking for something to do anyhow."

Liam highly doubted Bryan's choice would be to play maid. It wasn't Liam's, either. Still, he'd made the bet . . .

And so had she.

He finished off his beer then gathered the cards, dragging Mac's winning hand across the felt last. Bryan's gaze was on those cards the entire way. Sean kept his on the chips. They were probably the most anal-retentively stacked chips in the history of the game.

"I didn't know you had guys working for you, Mac." Liam kept his voice even. Controlled. And if there was the slightest hint of something else in it, well, he'd be fine with Mac assuming it was anger at losing. But why would Mac A) want to play poker so badly with them when she couldn't afford the cash if she lost, and B) make that bet *and* win? Something was rotten in the state of Manley.

"Wha . . . what?"

Yeah, that startled look in her eyes confirmed exactly what he'd thought. There *were* no guys employed by Manley Maids, so those uniforms weren't "extra." She'd had them made in advance. For them.

Mac had planned this. Her winning was no fluke. He'd call her on it if he had any proof other than his gut, but he didn't. And God knew, he couldn't always trust his gut. It'd let him down before.

"Never mind." He shuffled the offending cards in with the other forty-seven, then tapped the long edge of the deck on the table. "I'll be there Monday."

And he'd use the mindless monotony of cleaning to come up with some way to pay his sister back.

In spades.

Chapter One

❧

I F there was one thing Cassidy Davenport hated, it was to be kept waiting. And if there was one thing her father did best, it was keep her waiting.

"But Deborah, I just spoke to him." God, she had to go through her father's executive secretary for every little scrap, but that's the way Dad's empire worked. No one got to him without going through Deborah. The woman seriously ought to demand the title of CEO because Cassidy doubted her father ever made a business decision he didn't run through Deborah Capshaw first. The woman had been with him for nearly thirty years and kept the business running while Dad *went* running.

Running around, that is.

"I'm sorry, Cassidy, but he's in a meeting he can't be pulled out of. I'm sure you understand."

Oh Cassidy understood all right. She wondered how old this one was. Probably blonde—most of her father's "meetings" were—and probably with an impressive degree. That was the weird thing. Somehow Dad always managed to snag the Harvards and Yales of the world. You'd think those women would know better, but there was something about Mitchell Davenport that made women lose their minds.

Cassidy was about to join their ranks.

She ran a hand over her Maltese Titania's soft fur. "All right, Deborah. I understand." They both knew what that meant—actually, no, Cassidy *didn't* understand. "Have him call me when he's free." *And showered*, she wanted to add, but Deborah didn't deserve crass. Poor thing had to deal with it on a daily basis.

Or hourly.

Cassidy ended the call then stroked her cheek over the little dog's soft head. When was she going to accept the fact that her father only came through for her when it garnered him something? And the "meeting" in his office was garnering him a lot more than she ever would.

Lunch and, more importantly, the conversation she wanted to have with him were obviously out.

She set Titania down on the floor and picked her iPad off the table in front of the glass wall that looked out over the mirror-like lake twelve stories below her condo, the riot of wildflowers reflecting off all surfaces.

She'd love to spend the day painting, trying to capture this scene. Oils would bring out just the right shimmer of the flowers' reflection on the gray-blue water. Her fingers itched to get to her brushes.

Cassidy tapped the calendar app to make sure she had enough time today. There was nothing worse than getting herself all psyched up to lose herself in her art only to find out she had other commitments.

Which she did. MANLEY MAIDS was written in for ten a.m.

Ah, yes. Today was the day Sharon, her housekeeper, was supposed to train the new girl the service was sending over, but Sharon had gone on maternity leave early over the weekend.

Cassidy checked the time. Nine fifty-five.

She tapped the calendar and set the iPad back on the table. Nothing like having to introduce someone to the Davenport world she inhabited. At first they were awestruck—Dad did like to do *showy* in grand style, with a side helping of *decadent* just to make himself look good, and he'd had the designer outdo herself with this place.

It usually took less than a week for a newcomer to see beneath the veneer and start with the pitying looks—the ones she had to pretend she didn't see because it made no sense for anyone to pity someone who lived a life as fabulous as hers.

Wasn't that what Dad always said?

Actually, Cassidy didn't know what Dad said anymore. If it weren't for email, she'd rarely hear from him.

Right at ten, the doorbell rang. Cassidy shooed Titania into her enclosure, brushed her waves of chestnut hair over her shoulder, straightened the lapels on her beige silk blouse, then smoothed the braided belt at the waistline of her matching linen pants. She'd test the one-week theory with this one.

She opened the door to the condo's vestibule. It took the hunk in the Manley Maids uniform less than one *second* to start with the looks.

Only his weren't the pitying kind. They also weren't leering, which was another reaction she'd come to expect.

No, if she had to guess, she'd call his look angry.

CASSIDY Davenport stood before him in the flesh. Flesh-colored pants, flesh-colored top, and enough buttons unbuttoned to reveal a lot more flesh.

Liam worked hard to keep from groaning. Mac had assured him she wouldn't be here. Not on Mondays. It'd been his stipulation. Yet here she was.

Cassidy Davenport. Pampered socialite whose daily clothing bill was probably more than a blue-collar worker earned in a week—and he doubted she'd know a blue-collar worker if he came up and bit off her ridiculously priced manicure. The woman was frivolous with a capital *F*.

He was done with frivolous. Been there, done that, spent a fortune on designer clothes and rhinestone-studded T-shirts for Rachel that matched the diamond studs she'd insisted on having.

He was really going to have to work for this job. And *not* to keep it.

"*You're* the maid?"

Liam winced. Surely there had to be a better term, but *domestic goddess* didn't exactly fit, while *housekeeper* brought up an image of the Brady Bunch.

He gripped the vacuum cleaner and straightened his

shoulders. His pecs flexed—purely involuntarily of course. "Um, yeah. I am."

He didn't have to be a college graduate—though he was—to read what she was thinking when her gaze ran over him from head to toe. Mac didn't run *that* kind of a business.

"They didn't tell me they were sending a guy."

"Is that a problem?" God, let her say "Yes" so he could get the hell out of here, because he felt a sudden need to clean something—himself. Women like her got under his skin and not in a good way.

Or they used to.

What was the saying about repeating history's mistakes? Liam had zero intention of doing that.

"Well, no. I guess it's not a problem." She tapped one of those ridiculously priced nails on her surprisingly non-collagen-enhanced lips. "Won't you come in?"

"Uh, yeah. Sure." Mac would kill him if he said no. This had been his baby sister's first account. That's why she'd selected it for him, she'd said; she knew he wouldn't lose it for her.

He was going to lose something. His breakfast for starters. Then maybe his cool. Definitely his mind.

Thank God the bet had only been for four weeks. Any longer and he wouldn't be the brother Mac thought he was.

Cassidy stepped back to let him in, and Liam stumbled up the step into the foyer. Damn. Where'd that come from?

He caught himself before he fell on top of her. She was much smaller when they were on the same level.

Then he got a look around the place. No way would they ever be on the same level.

Rich dripped from the chandelier with the pear-sized crystals. It wove through the gold-threaded rug, vined through the marble floor, and scented the air with the hint of millions.

Liam had money, but this . . . Even the frou-frou little dog had a gilded cage. This was on the level of the Donald Trumps and Conrad Hiltons of the world.

And Mitchell Davenports. It was important to remember that none of this was Cassidy's. She lived off *Daddy's* money.

"Sorry," she said, her voice huskier than he'd expected. "I should have warned you about that first step. It's a doozy."

Literally and figuratively.

Liam checked his grip on the vacuum and made sure none of the cleaning products had fallen out of the bucket—so *not* his M.O. around beautiful women. But then, Cassidy Davenport was more Bryan's type than his these days, especially because Liam had known her kind before—when they'd looked down their noses at him . . . unless they wanted something from him.

He glanced at Cassidy's nose. Perfectly pert in that rhino-plastic way of the rich, but she'd never get the chance to look down it at him. He'd learned his lesson, and women like her, while not a dime a dozen—they upped the ante to about a hundred thou a dozen—were so far below women who knew how to make their own way in the world that all he felt for her kind was anger at such uselessness.

But he wasn't here to judge; he was here to clean. For four frickin' weeks.

He should have folded that last hand. Taken his losses and lived with them. But Manleys didn't go down without a fight. It was how he'd made his own fortune, inconsequential though it was when compared to this place. The one he was supposed to be cleaning.

He gripped the vacuum wand and planted it in front of him. "Where would you like me to start?"

Cassidy took a step back. Probably so he wouldn't land on her; Liam was sure she was used to men falling at her feet, but he wasn't the kind to do that.

Well, not again.

"I guess you can start in the bedroom."

Seriously? Did she really think he'd fall for that? Was she slumming today? Pissed off at the boyfriend or something? Wanting a little spice?

"Sharon always started in the bedroom, then worked her way out. She said it kept what she'd already cleaned from getting messed up again before she finished. Makes sense to me, but if you've got another routine, I'm okay with that. Whatever you want to do is fine."

Sharon. The maid. The one he was here to replace.

Liam glanced at the bucket of cleaning supplies and vacuum cleaner as if he'd never seen them before.

That's right. He was here to clean house; not *play* house.

Liam bit back a chuckle. As if she'd be interested in him

that way. He'd forgotten he was in the green golf shirt and
cotton pants that constituted a Manley Maid uniform. He didn't
feel very manly in it, and with the vibe he *wasn't* getting from
Cassidy Davenport, he probably didn't look it, either.

He should be glad. He could get through this nightmare
without having to fight off a society babe who thought she'd
have some fun with *the help*. Been there, done that, ripped off
her *diamond*-studded T-shirts. He wished he could have shredded them, but he'd been the one shredded.

He adjusted his grip on the bucket, took a deep breath, and
headed into Cassidy Davenport's bedroom. If he wasn't
involved with a woman, going into her bedroom should be no
big deal. And if he couldn't even stand to be in the same room
with that woman, her bedroom was just another room.

Then he saw the silky baby-blue robe tossed over a padded
chair. A piece of black lace peeking out from the top of a
dresser drawer. Something peach and frothy lying in a puddle
beneath the flowered bench at the end of her rumpled bed. It
had landed near a pair of shoes.

Black shoes.

With really high heels.

And ankle straps.

Black lace. Peach nightie. High heels. The spiked kind.

Cassidy bumped into him from behind.

He'd called this *just another room*? He seriously needed to
have his head examined and his sense of smell shut off because
the scent of her—still of millions but this time with a good
dose of *woman* threaded through—wrapped around him the
way that silk robe had embraced her curves.

And those curves, the ones her unbuttoned shirt hinted at,
were every bit as lush and soft as he'd expect—except that he
hadn't expected them to be lush and soft. Most women in her
income bracket underwent the knife as if it were a day out with
the girls, but the few nanoseconds she was plastered against
him were enough for Liam to learn that she hadn't subscribed
to that particular social custom.

She jumped back. "Why'd you stop?"

Because the image of her in those heels and that nightie, all
wrapped up in silk, had nailed him to the floor.

"You don't make your bed?" Anger was always good for

dispelling tension, sexual or otherwise, and right now, Liam knew which one he needed to focus on. Not focus on. Whatever.

"I forgot you were coming."

Did she have to use that particular word? 'Cause Liam thought he just might.

God. What was *wrong* with him? He didn't even *like* the woman.

"Are you going to hover over me while I do this?" He wouldn't mind her hovering over him, but he wasn't talking about cleaning.

This was going to be a really long, hard four weeks.

He so wished he hadn't used *those* words.

And when he saw the look on her face—fleeting though it was—he wished he hadn't used that tone. It wasn't her fault that he'd reacted this way to her.

"Um . . . well, no." She backed up, her green eyes wide and—shit—teary.

God, he would have thought he'd learned his lesson when it came to women's tears.

"I guess I'll leave you to it." She spun around on her sexy-as-hell stilettos and strode out of the room, her ass-hugging pants leaving nothing to his imagination. Which sent it into overdrive.

Liam cursed beneath his breath and turned around—

To stare at the rumpled, unmade bed with sheets that had been wrapped around that curvy ass, those long-as-sin legs, and her perfectly natural breasts, and Liam didn't know if he was going to make it four *hours* in this place let alone four weeks.

He'll help unleash the woman in her...

FROM *NEW YORK TIMES* BESTSELLING AUTHOR
JILL SHALVIS

Rumor
HAS IT

An Animal Magnetism Novel

Back in Sunshine, Idaho, soldier Griffin Reid finds comfort
in the last person he'd expect—small-town schoolteacher
Kate Evans. But can their passionate connection turn into
something lasting?

"Jill Shalvis will make you laugh and fall in love."
—Rachel Gibson, *New York Times* bestselling author

"Jill Shalvis writes with humor, heart,
and sizzling heat. A must-read!"
—Susan Mallery, *New York Times* bestselling author

jillshalvis.com
facebook.com/LoveAlwaysBooks
penguin.com

M1395T1013